# OUR TIME ON ROUTE 66

NATALIE BRIGHT    CAIT COLLINS    NANDY EKLE

RORY C. KEEL    JOE R. NICHOLS

Print ISBN: 978-0-9836691-5-9

Ebook ISBN: 978-0-9836691-6-6

Cover design: Rory C. Keel

Cover car photo: Copyright © 2018 Courtesy of the Oklahoma Historical Society (1930_Rt.66_DustBowl.jpg)

# CONTENTS

# PART I

# MAGGIE'S BETRAYAL

NATALIE BRIGHT

# FOREWORD

*Separating Real Life from Fiction*

From the first time I heard about my husband's great-grandmother who married a man 31 years older, she has been on my mind. We do know that she lived in Fort Worth and was forced into a marriage, and most of the family agreed as to the reason her father had arranged the union.

During her first marriage Maggie lost one baby and gave birth to another girl before leaving her husband for his nephew. She did in fact meet the son of her husband's sister, a young Alex, at a family event so the story goes. I can only imagine the courage it took to run away with child in tow. She must have been terrified. Some believe that Maggie actually requested and acquired divorce papers from Washington D.C. before she married the second time, but we can't find any documents to prove that story.

The events and the route they may have taken when they fled Fort Worth are forever lost to history, so that is where my imagination took over. I altered the true dates of their life and fictionalized their story to fit with this Route 66 Anthology.

When researching Fort Worth in the early 1900's, the Highway to Hell dominates the period. It made sense to me that a man who would accept a young girl in trade, must have been involved in the vices of the day. Perhaps he owned businesses that involved gambling or liquor, and most likely frequented the casinos on Texas Highway 199. Maggie's life with a man who laid claim to her must have been unbearable.

It is a well-known fact that both sides of the family strongly objected to Alex and Maggie's union, and the young couple were told that they would be killed if any of the relatives on either side ever found them. It is true that the couple settled on twenty-two acres south of Forth Worth next to Kickapoo Creek. Tucked away and hidden from the main road, they built a one-room cabin that nestled under towering pecan trees where they lived out their days. Maggie and Alex never associated with any family members ever again. They had three more children, one of which was my husband's grandfather. His grandfather and his mother were both born in the same small cabin that is still stands on the property. My husband never knew any other family members from either side.

In another interesting twist about Maggie and Alex, a much older Maggie recalled the time a nice, handsome looking young couple stopped by their place to buy moonshine. She remembers them as being very friendly and they even stayed the night. The couple had come to mind many years later when Maggie had seen their pictures in an old newspaper article and she realized who they were. She remembered the name of the nice young man, Clyde Barrow. Bonnie and Clyde had visited Alex and Maggie on more than one occasion, so the story goes, and always left with a sizable purchase of Alex's moonshine, the recipe of which is long forgotten.

The courage of women like Maggie has left a mark on this area, and that attitude continues to be observed in today's generation of spirited women who inhabit the state of Texas. I'm blessed to know many of them. You'll never meet a more hardy group of people with can-do attitudes, big plans and dreams, and willing to face adversity without complaint. They believe that work is the way to achieve your dreams.

It is my hope that this fictional story accurately represents the strength of character of the people who lived along Route 66 and the colorful period of Texas in the early 1900s.

*~Natalie Cline Bright*

# 1

---

*Fort Worth, Texas, January 1936*

MAMA HAD CRIED, but not in front of me. I could see the tracks of tears on her cheeks under red-rimmed eyes.

Pa told me it was time to leave. "Put on your best dress, Maggie," he said. The deal was final. There would be no argument.

Mama followed me into the room I shared with my younger sisters to help me pack. If you could say my measly belongings were worth taking anywhere. Several blouses, undergarments, a thin nightgown, one pair of pants, and my loafers. They barely filled up half of a cloth flour sack. I left the brush and mirror for my sisters. Stuffing my feet into the black strap shoes that I had worn every Sunday since a neighbor had left them on our front porch, I pointed to a faded blue dress. Mama slipped the favorite of the only two I owned over my head and then she stuffed the beige one into the sack.

My feelings that day are difficult to describe. Hopeless. Angry. Heartbroken. The thought that my own father would do such a thing is something my mind could not, would not, comprehend. I felt numb. Too mad and shocked to cry. Betrayal is a horrible thing to face at nineteen.

Pa had told Mama over breakfast that a deal had been made. I did not realize it involved me until later that morning when Mama told me. "It's really for the best, Maggie. Your father thinks you're too old to be living at home anyway. You need to get away from here and find your own life."

My protests went unheard. With a weary voice my mother repeated the same answer she has for me anytime I express an opinion. "Just do as you're told, Maggie."

It was the best decision for all involved, except for me. How could this be the best thing for me?

We drove to the Tarrant County courthouse in silence. Mama sat in the middle of the pickup truck seat with clenched jaw and pursed lips. I refused to think about what waited for me. Instead I gazed out of the window and watched grey clouds roll over a January sky. It was going to rain later in the evening. I wondered if anyone would remember to put food in the shed for the cats, and to close the chicken coop tonight before the storm. It was almost time to turn the beds and pull weeds for the summer garden. I already had seedlings started for potatoes and sugar beets. Someone better remember to refill the dog's water bowl.

Judge Phillips looked as depressed as I felt. Pa took a seat on the bench that extended the length of one wall just inside the room. Mama and I slid in beside him. The judge's wife peered at us from behind a piano that filled one corner. She suddenly disappeared into the next room and returned with a bouquet of dusty, plastic flowers which she placed in my hands.

A gentleman arrived and my father rushed to close the distance to greet him at the door. They shook hands. "Mr. Brown," Pa said as he extended his hand.

"Mr. Harrod."

"This covers everything then. Are we agreed?" my father asked, and Mr. Brown nodded his head in agreement.

"All is cleared," Mr. Brown said with a nod of his head. He didn't offer a greeting to Mama, but he walked over to me and took my hand. "Maggie, it's a pleasure to see you again, my dear. Do you remember meeting me? You have grown into a beautiful young lady." He towered over me. His hand was fat and clammy, and the smile on his face did not reach his cold eyes.

I did remember seeing him once at our house several years ago. I had been pulling weeds in the front flower bed. A fancy car came to a stop in what little front yard we had, and a man had gotten out and asked my name. Pa had come out of the house before I could answer. They had both gotten in the car and drove away.

Pa gripped my arm and guided me to a spot facing the judge at Mr. Brown's side. "Judge Phillips, let's get on with it," Mr. Brown said. Mama remained on the bench in stony silence, pale-faced, with hands clenched in her lap.

The judge's wife began to play the traditional bridal notes, and stopped when my almost-husband demanded she cease that "head splitting nonsense." I couldn't even begin to recall what was said after that. When Mr. Brown elbowed me in the ribs, none too gently, I mumbled, "I do."

My heart beat inside my chest and I dared not look at the man's face. This stranger was now my husband. At that very moment I hated my mother for not having a backbone to say something, anything, on my behalf. I hated my father even more. There was no one on my side. No one that could see the madness in what was taking place.

This emotion was new to me. I'd never felt hatred towards my family.

The judge pronounced us Mr. and Mrs.

Mama did manage an emotionless peck on my cheek, without looking me in the eyes. My father never looked in my direction. When he turned to leave, I stared daggers into his back. My new husband walked behind my parents and I followed. Just before I passed through the doorway into my new life, I turned to see the judge wipe his cheek and his wife dab a tissue to her eyes.

It was official. I became Mrs. Clarence T. Brown and my father's gambling debt was paid in full.

**2**

———————

I knew the ways of married folk and the thought of what this man might do to me was more than I could comprehend. I choked down the hysteria as I stepped into the sunshine and followed my new husband out of the courthouse. He walked to a Cadillac convertible and yanked a kerchief from his pocket to rub an invisible smudge. "This is my brand-new baby. Ain't she a beaut?"

The black car gleamed like a dark pool of water. He got in without waiting or holding the door open for me. I eased into the passenger seat clutching my sack of clothes tightly to my chest, as if it was the only thing of my old life that could protect me. If I had not been so scared, I might have taken the time to admire the fancy automobile.

Mama and Pa drove past in our green Ford pickup, leaving a swirl of dust that sifted over the roadster. My new husband frowned. I stared at the faces of my parents, shaded from the glare of the sun by the dirty pickup window. They never glanced in my direction. We pulled onto the road behind them and I watched that old truck for as long as I could before it disappeared over the horizon.

Mr. Brown traveled out of Fort Worth. My hair swirled and

whipped around my head as we sped toward my unknown future. We turned on a tree lined road, and as the three-story house came into view, Mr. Brown puffed out his chest with pride.

The air smelled crisp and cool. Spacious lawns dotted with oak trees stretched on either side of the drive. A glimmer of hope crossed my mind that I might be able to grow a garden and put in several flower beds.

"I bought this jewel from a Fort Worth doctor," he said. A wide porch stretched across the front shaded by a sizable portico, held up with large white columns. "I don't eat breakfast. Lunch is to be served exactly at noon, and I want hearty evening meals. Enough for me and my guests."

As impressive as the outside of the mansion was, the inside was not so. It looked forgotten, cold, and lonely. The furniture was threadbare, what little there was of it. It smelled of cigars and human sweat.

"Cook me something. I'm hungry," he said as he loosened his bow tie and walked up a grand staircase that filled the entry hall.

I placed my flour sack of belongings on a bench inside the entry hall and wandered along a narrow hall until I came to a kitchen located at the back of the house. The wood burning stove was charcoal black and beautiful. The cabinets were well-stocked with glasses and china. The pantry was bare except for a few cans of beans. A teal colored icebox with double doors held a ham. Mama would have given anything to have an icebox like this one.

Finding two potatoes in the bottom of a cabinet and a tin bucket of lard, I filled an iron skillet with ham and potatoes. The stove fired up nicely. Grabbing a dish towel to lift the skillet, the dining room had to be somewhere close.

Gold tinted glass set in a dark mahogany wood chandelier hung over a sizable dining room table. The long table, in desperate need of polish, could easily sit twenty, but it only had four chairs. Mr. Brown was already sitting at the far end with a napkin tucked under his chin and holding a fork. My new husband dug into the food as soon as I set it on the table near him. He didn't bother to use a plate, and he didn't bother to offer any to me.

"I'll need some groceries if you want meals cooked," I said, keeping my eyes cast downward. I refused to look at him.

"Leave me a list on the front hallway desk. I'll have one of my men buy you whatever you need."

He dug into the fried ham and potatoes. My stomach growled, but I refused to eat next to this man who was a stranger but now my husband.

"Drink," he said and pointed to the sideboard.

A bright blue decanter and shot glasses were at one end. I opened the stopper and poured. Whiskey. The smell reminded me of my father.

Mr. Brown downed the golden liquid in one gulp.

"Do you remember me, Maggie?" he asked. "I remember you. That day I saw you in your front yard, and as a matter of fact, I've thought of you often." He chewed the last bite of potato and held up his empty glass, which I refilled. "Now you are mine."

I returned the decanter to its spot and leaned against the sideboard for support. My knees went weak, my hands clammy as beads of sweat and fear broke out on my forehead. I swallowed the lump in my throat.

"I've got to check on some things. You be waiting in my bedroom when I get back." He pushed back his chair and left.

I cleared the table refusing to think what came next for a new bride on her wedding night, concentrating instead on the task at hand. I explored every cabinet and drawer in the kitchen, pantry, and dining room, mentally planning a menu. There wasn't a scrap of paper in the kitchen that I could find, so I carefully wrote my list on a fancy paper napkin.

Grabbing my belongings from the entry hall bench, I began exploring. The only room with furnishings that fit the house appeared to be a study. A dark mahogany wooden desk piled high with papers and books stood center stage, with plush chairs facing a fireplace. The room smelled rich and manly. Cigar smoke and fine whiskey, with a slight musty scent from the old texts that filled the bookcases.

I walked slowly up the grand staircase, my heart pounding with every step. By the time I reached the top I could hardly catch my breath. I could not take one more step forward. I felt faint. I stood at the top of the stairs for a long time, thinking about flinging myself backwards, praying that my fear might cause me to just faint dead away.

I imagined my body hitting the floor hard and toppling down the stairs, maybe breaking a rib or two, or better yet, knocking me cold as I tumbled and rolled to the bottom. Would I survive the fall?

The hallway stretched in front of me, dark and long and I did not know where to go. What choice did I have, but to put one foot in front of the other? I moved along the upstairs hallway and began opening closed doors. Several doors led into a wide ballroom with gold gilded ceiling tiles and dusty chandeliers.

The sound of a door slamming echoed up the grand stairs, startling the silence.


I woke the next morning sore and bruised, and with a newfound hatred for my parents. I never imagined I could despise anyone this much, and I knew deep down, to the core of my very soul that I would never forgive my father for what he had done. Mr. Brown may see me as nothing more than a cook and a house cleaner, and he might use my body as he commands, but he would never own the core of who I am.

Deep inside, I had to hang on. I willed myself to stay calm and figure a way out of this life that had been forced upon me.

**3**

———

Clarence T. Brown was a formidable man in size and personality, and at least thirty years older than I. That was my guess, because I didn't know for sure. His wife had died of a lung ailment, and there were no children. I figured she either died from work, or to get away from him. As I cleaned his house, there wasn't much proof of her existence.

Mr. Brown looked upon me as his personal slave who could cook his meals, wash his clothes, and was good for an emotionless tussle in his bed every so often. I would never be a wife or loving partner.

Most of his time was spent making moonshine, a profession he took great pride in. He had perfected the recipe and was quite popular around these parts. He was also a successful businessman of considerable wealth, but all the money didn't make him a decent human being. He ruled over the men who worked for him with a cruel, iron will. Sometimes they trembled when he talked directly to them, and it seemed the faces and names of his crew changed on a regular basis. They appeared to respect his position but behind his back they despised him. There was no doubt though that if anyone crossed him, the consequences would be severe.

As the sun made its last appearance over the horizon during my first week of marriage, I began to weep with terror every time he climbed into our bed next to me. On several occasions, he would grab my arm and drag me upstairs in the middle of the day. He never called me by my name, and I couldn't stop crying during the ordeal.

I tried to stay busy. The house was a disgusting mess, and I cleaned with a newfound vigor as I had no choice but to accept my place in Mr. Brown's world. One day, while burning trash, I threw my favorite blue dress, now my wedding dress, into the flames and watched it turn to ashes with heat. That is what had happened to the only life I had ever known. Gone, turned into a pile of worthless ash.

It appears that the love I had experienced in my childhood home had been false, a lie. The thought that any parent could do to their child what mine had done to me was unforgivable. If I were lucky enough to have children someday, I'd never abandon them like my parents did to me.

The dream of having kids of my own one day became overshadowed by another worry. Besides the fear of nightfall and my place in this horrible man's bed, my next greatest fear was that I'd have his child. I prayed that God wouldn't see fit to test me any further. My heart and soul couldn't take any more. I often wondered how long I would be able to survive this life.

Mr. Brown had as many women friends and as he did men friends. His house was a regular revolving door of a loud, fun-loving group who expected me to serve their every whim, especially on the weekends.

"Cook us up some fried chicken, girl."

"Hey, you. Bring more glasses."

"Looking good Clarence, your house has never been so clean. That girl of yours was a great bargain for sure. Where can I get me one of those?"

Unfortunately, I was cursed with a lack of backbone just like my mother. My name wasn't *"girl"* or *"hey you"*; it was Margaret, Maggie for short. I just didn't have the nerve to tell anyone. And they didn't ask.

One good consolation was that I was banished to the room next to the kitchen because my new husband's bed was again occupied by his many girlfriends.

One evening he had slapped my face. "Stop that incessant whimpering, girl," he shouted. "The deal is done. Nothing can change that. You are here to serve me." That was the first time I'd experienced a slap across the face, and it wouldn't be the last.

He tired of my hysterical sobbing every time he came near me, so I was sent to the kitchen and replaced with more fun-loving companions. There was one in particular, a raven-haired, green-eyed beauty named Lillian who fawned on his every whim and laughed outrageously loud at everything he said. She hated me with a passion.

My days were endless and dull, full of nothing but work. I made every effort to stay invisible, which was extremely difficult because of the houseful of people every night. Mr. Brown would not let me leave, and since we lived so far from town there was no use in trying to run. He was well known. Everybody knew me, my family, and why I was there.

The one thing Mama had done right by me was to teach me how to cook. It could have been a blessing, but in my situation became a curse. One of the hired men kept me supplied with groceries and our visitors always left with full bellies. Days were filled with baking breads, pies, and cakes, and then putting together a meal in time for supper which was consumed by any number of people. I never knew how to plan. Late evenings were spent washing dishes, only to wake up the next morning and start all over again. Mondays were reserved for laundry. I missed going to church on Sundays most of all because I spent that day cleaning house after the Friday and Saturday night parties.

I missed home. I missed the quiet peace of watching our

chickens peck around in my little garden, and I even missed the bustling city of Fort Worth. On the days my father had been in a rare good mood, he gave us kids each a quarter and we walked to the Isis Theatre.

As the oldest daughter of five kids, I remembered our home had been full of laughter and activity. Apparently, I had been mistaken about being a part of a loving family. I guess sometimes life isn't as perfect as you think. My father does have a gambling problem, but it never dawned on me the effect his lack of character would have on my life.

The words left unsaid rambled in my mind, and I promised that if I ever laid eyes upon the man who had sold me, I'd clear my conscience and give him a piece of my mind. That was my plan and I rehearsed that speech over and over in my mind. In reality, I never expected my father to have the nerve to walk into my life again and I never imagined the feelings I would experience when he did.

**4**

———

My father walked into Mr. Brown's big house one Saturday evening about six months into our marriage. I sensed he was there before I looked. I was stacking hot rolls on platters and, turned to hurry back to the kitchen for a cobbler that was ready to come out of the oven. I glanced over my shoulder and saw him. His familiar presence filled the entry hall.

The house was lit up like a fireworks show, and every room was full of a laughing, good-time crowd that didn't give a whit about the God-loving, downtrodden folks of this world.

Mr. Haygood was in the middle of a fiddle solo and all eyes were locked on Lillian. She held her skirt above her knees and twirled around the middle of the living room flashing glimpses of milky white thighs. She entertained with a shuffle, tap routine which only served to expose even more of her cleavage with every low-dipping twirl. Pa never glanced my way. His eyes were on Miss High-kicker as he squeezed through the crowd to get a better view. Someone placed a jar of 'shine in his hand, which he downed in a few long pulls. I don't know how his gut survived that assault without heaving. Years of practice I guess.

The poker game had just begun in the main dining room and

that's where he headed. Obviously Papa had been here before otherwise, how would a man like Mr. Brown know about a plain-Jane nobody girl like me?

My heart ached that very moment for my little sisters. Right up until that moment I had been sinking in self-pity, cursing my lot in life, and hating my parents for even bringing me into this world. The moment I saw Pa's face I remembered the other people in my life that I missed terribly. I'd have given anything to be back in that crowded bedroom with my younger sisters. I wouldn't be scolding them to quit talking and go to sleep. We would talk all night, if they wanted to, and I would let them crawl in bed with me again instead of making them hush and leave me alone.

What if our father tossed them aside, too? The thought was like a punch to the gut. Tears filled my eyes and my throat closed as I hurried into the kitchen. What kind of man barters his own flesh and blood?

I wanted to face him, to look my father in the eye and tell him what a miserable, sorry human being he was to make me leave my family and subject me to an abusive life I did not choose. A cooking, cleaning, piece of human flesh, slave to a man who now claimed me as his property. In fact, I was several pegs lower than his 1936 Cadillac convertible coupe that sat out front.

I kept busy carrying food to the buffet as was my sole responsibility in this household on party nights. Sometimes a wife would lend a hand, but not very often. Most of the women here were party girls and having a good time was their main goal.

My father sat at the poker table. Somebody, not me, kept his jar full. He pulled wads of cash from his pockets to cover his bets. In a show of disgust, he finally slammed his cards on the table and pushed back his chair. His money stayed. The smiling gentleman across the table raked the winnings from the middle and began counting the bills. With glassy eyes and stumbling steps, Pa worked his way through the revellers stopping to watch Lillian.

She had added a raven haired, blue-eyed beauty to the routine. All eyes were transfixed.

I walked closer and stood behind my father. His familiar smell assaulted my nose, despite the overwhelming odor of tobacco and hard liquor. I wanted to reach out and touch his shoulders. It wouldn't take much, just a stretch of my arm. His shoulder was at my fingertips. Just there.

I wanted him to turn and sweep me up in a hug like he used to do when I was little. My father's arms were the safest place in the world. He would kiss my head and tell me, "Sweet, Maggie. You'll be all right."

I wanted to hear his voice now more than anything, to have him tell me the words I wanted to hear like he had done when I was little. *You'll be all right. This has all been a big misunderstanding.* I once believed his words. I wanted to trust those words again.

I couldn't lift my arm to tap him on the shoulder. All strength left me. My limbs wouldn't move. I stood frozen, staring at the back of his head with a longing for my family that near like crushed me.

Mr. Brown yelled from the dining room, "Where's the apple pie? Bring me a piece."

I scurried through the crowd and slipped into the kitchen from the back way, emerging into the dining room with the pie, quickly slicing a piece, and placing the plate into Mr. Brown's outstretched hand.

From the corner of my eye I kept a watch on my father, and when he started edging his way to the door I slipped out the kitchen door and walked around the side of the house. Staying just in the shadows so a light from a window would not reveal my hiding place, I watched my father climb into our pickup truck. That was the last time I saw him.

As he drove away, I realized that was a part of me I'd never get back. The old me, my brothers and sisters, my Mama, the feeling of being loved, belonging to a group of people who together were greater than being alone.

My own flesh and blood had cast me aside like kitchen scraps. To my own father my life was the price of his debt, and nothing more. He had brought me into this world and always reminded me that my life was not my own.

A piece of my heart drove off in that car. The piece that trusted. The very core of all that I believed about those in whom I had the utmost trust in my whole life was a lie, a sham. My father determined my worth and my own mother had turned her back. There was no one left who believed I was worth fighting for.

Mama used to tell me that putting up with a husband and his unpleasant habits were just part of being married. "Someday you'll understand. You'll just have to bear it."

I understood all right. I am worthless, but for the price lost in a poker hand. My prayers that night were for strength and endurance.

I did not pray for my hardened heart to forgive.

**5**

———————

One July afternoon Mr. Brown handed me a brown package along with a small paper bag filled with makeup. I gasped when I saw the shoes. Soft suede in two shades of blue. Dark blue on the heels and toes, and a light blue midsection with a strap and buckle. There were two new dresses perfect for Sundays (except I wasn't allowed to leave the house), three soft blouses, and a bright red apron. My pathetic wardrobe had long since been sent to the rag box, forgotten reminders of a life and a family I'd never be a part of again.

"Wear a nice dress tomorrow and paint your face," he said. "We're going to a picnic. Be ready early."

That next morning, one day after the July 4th holiday, happened to be my birthday. I tried not to think about turning twenty. The thought of spending the day away from my family made me sad, but I still hated my parents. There had been no presents because we never had the money, but Mama always cooked us kids whatever we wanted. I always asked for carrot spice cake. One candle, that was used over and over for everybody, burned for a few seconds while everyone sang "Happy Birthday." It had been one of the few times Mama smiled and laughed. Her kids seemed to bring her the most joy.

Since my last birthday, it felt like I had grown taller. I could almost look Mr. Brown in the eye. From the way my clothes had started to fit, I probably lost about fifteen pounds too. My hands stayed raw and red from scrubbing dishes and jars. Even though I was surrounded by nice things and fancy duds, you couldn't disguise who I was or why I was living in this house.

Mr. Brown woke up earlier than usual to load the back of his roadster with 'shine. He would definitely be the most popular guy there, wherever we were going. I chose one of the new dresses, a bright yellow dotted with tiny blue flowers. The hem swirled and floated in the breeze around my legs. My new shoes felt extra fine. I wasn't sure about how to use the makeup, so I skipped the blue eyeshadow, dabbed red rouge on my lips, and blackened my eye lashes. I didn't know what to do with my hair, so I brushed the heck out of it and called it good.

I chose a silky yellow scarf from a box of things I'd found in an upstairs closet. There had been a brush and comb, face powder, bottle of perfume, gloves and scarves. I didn't think the previous Mrs. Brown would have minded. I'd never owned such things.

Mr. Brown stared at me as I skipped down the front porch steps carrying a basket of fried chicken and yeast rolls which I had cooked the evening before.

This time I enjoyed the ride in his fancy car. The tree lined driveway seemed like distant land. I remembered the dust and dirt from the last time I had sat in the passenger seat of his car, so I wrapped my hair in a headscarf. We traveled about an hour in silence, finally approaching a two-story Victorian style home next to a lake. Towering elm trees shaded a wide porch that stretched across the front of the house. It seemed as though we were some of the last to arrive as people were everywhere. Mr. Brown drove across the grass and stopped between two oaks, their branches forming a canopy over his Cadillac.

Mr. Brown hopped out and ran around to open the car door for me, in an unusual display of kindness. He introduced me as "his little wife," probably because he had forgotten my name. It was then I realized that most of the people there were his relatives. We were at a picnic with his family.

The menfolk gathered under the trees to sample Mr. Brown's pride and joy. Long tables stretched around the covered porch where women worked covering tables with food. I had never seen that many covered dishes in my life.

From the array of brightly colored dresses and floppy hats, this family certainly enjoyed an abundance of wealth and seemed to want for nothing. For once I was grateful for the new dress. There were smiles on every face and outbursts of laughter. I watched the women gather in small clusters and cast curious glances my way. Mr. Brown left me on my own.

"Hello, child," a lady said. "I'm Clarence's younger sister, Bertie. Glad to meet you."

"I'm Maggie," I said as we shook hands.

"Welcome to our home," she said, as she wrapped an arm around my waist. "Has Clarence told you about my violets? Come on. I'll show you." She tugged me towards the front door.

I followed her into that glorious house and was taken aback by the sitting room where an oversized picture window cast light on a swirling, living table of deep purple, lavender, and pale pink. The sight made me smile. "Pretty, aren't they? They've won several ribbons at the state fair," she said.

One plant stand held only plants with snow white petals. I wanted to reach out and touch them. The velvety leaves and perky blossoms lent a cheery touch to the room.

She continued to explain her secrets about plant food, soil, and the watering schedule. I was fascinated.

A young man with laughing hazel eyes bounded down the stairs and spilled into the room with the energy of a whirlwind.

"Alex, come meet your Uncle Clarence's new bride," Bertie said. "Maggie, this is my son."

I managed a smile and a how do you do.

"I need to get back to the kitchen. You just make yourself at home, dear. It was lovely to meet you." She gave my shoulders a squeeze. "Alex, you can show Maggie around, after you're done with carrying more chairs outside. Don't forget those two tables from the basement."

Alex frowned, rolled his eyes, and opened a squeaking door in the hall. His footsteps echoed as he disappeared down a narrow flight of stars.

I wandered back outside to a bench shaded by a huge lilac bush. The smell relaxed me and made me think of home. I always wanted to plant a lilac bush under my window, but never got around to it. From my vantage point, I watched the girls take turns on a tire swing, and a group of rowdy boys play a game of tag. I must have been daydreaming, or maybe I had dozed off; I just remember a shade falling over my face. I opened my eyes to find Alex blocking my sun.

"Did I wake you?" he said.

"Hi," was all that I could manage as I tried to come out of my stupor.

"Welcome to the family," he said. "This is for you." From behind his back appeared a perfect deep purple violet.

I gasped and looked at him in shock.

He laughed. "My mother loves these things more than me. I'll catch hell for it, but it'll be worth it to see your smile. Here. Take it." He pushed the petals closer to my face. "Did you know that the colors have different meanings?"

I couldn't help myself. I did smile. His mischievous eyes sparkled with delight. "I was right. That smile is worth it. Are you hungry? Come on. Let's fill our plates. Mother did say to show you around."

His hand demanded my response. I hesitated because of my

rough, reddened skin. I should have added hand cream to the grocery list. I wished my nails were trimmed and painted red like the party girls.

I took the velvety blossoms from his hand.

The idea of enjoying food that I had not prepared was the best birthday present ever. I hoped there might be a huge piece of cake, even though it would be a celebration that would only take place inside my head.

Everyone there probably knew of my father and why I was the new Mrs. Brown, but I pushed that thought from my mind. I decided the risk of drawing Mr. Brown's anger would be worth a few minutes of feeling normal. I could imagine myself as a fancy lady in a beautiful dress. It was my birthday, after all.

I cautiously placed my fingers into his outstretched hand.

**6**
_______

Alex steered me to the wide stairs that led from the green lawn to the covered porch of the sprawling house. He waited and gently placed his hand at the small of my back as I climbed the stairs to the porch. His touch was electric. I cringed with worry, afraid that Mr. Brown might see us.

Curious eyes looked me over from head to toe, but there was no malice in their faces. A mild curiosity mixed with smiles, and some introduced themselves. Others said, "Welcome to the family." Apparently, Mr. Brown was well-liked by all of his kin.

My basket of fried chicken was already empty, but there were plenty of other dishes to choose from. Without the critical eyes of my husband watching my every move, I soon relaxed and realized I was hungry.

One gentleman bounded up the stairs and stopped at my basket. He frowned. "Who ate all of the fried chicken? Is there any more?"

Bertie answered, "It's all gone. Who brought that anyway? It was so tasty."

"I did," I answered, from behind her.

She spun around. "That explains why Clarence looks different. We were just commenting how he's got a little more meat on his bones. Now we know. His new wife can cook." The crowd on the porch laughed.

"You must tell us your secret," one lady said.

I could feel my cheeks burn. I nodded yes.

"Fill up your plate, dear," Bertie said. "Try some of my creamed cabbage and leave room for a slice of peach cake. I'll give you the recipe before you leave."

Alex led me over to an empty quilt under the tall elms at the back side of the house. I could hear the hoots and laughs of the group that stood around Mr. Brown. He kept everyone entertained, and with an audience to keep him busy he never paid me a bit of notice. I felt at ease for the first time in many months.

"Tell me about yourself," Alex said. He bit into a soft yeast roll. "Yum, these are heaven."

"I made them," I said. I hated drawing attention to myself, and I usually didn't take to braggin'. Mama always said it was a sin, but I wanted this nice young man with the hazel eyes to know something good about me. Despite the circumstances, I was a decent person.

"No! Really?" he looked at me with disbelief.

"Woven basket with a red cloth, sitting next to the fried chicken?" He nodded. "Those are my rolls," I said.

"How'd you learn to cook like that?" he asked.

"My grandmother and my mother. After Mama taught me how to prepare a meal, she eventually turned the kitchen over to me. I fed my brothers and sisters for as long as I can remember. Cooking is easy for me. I enjoy it."

"How do you like living in Uncle Clarence's big house on Jacksboro highway?" Alex asked. "I've been there several times, but my mother doesn't like me going."

"It's all right, I guess. Why can't you visit your uncle?"

"The Jacksboro highway - you know. The highway to hell." Alex filled his mouth with mashed potatoes. "It's three and one-half miles of every debauchery you could imagine and then some.

You live out past the gambling clubs and dance halls, but it's the same road."

"Why would a highway be called that?" I couldn't help but wonder how much time my father had spent on the road, while Mama had been at home trying to scrape together a meal for us.

My attention turned to the plate full of food. We talked about pleasant things, how much he liked working in the yard. The grass and flower beds and blooming bushes were mostly Alex's doing, with strict direction from his mother of course. He gained a love of growing things from her.

I couldn't help but think about my life before. Remembering made my heart ache. I told him about taking my brothers and sisters to the picture show in Fort Worth. We lived out near the stockyards, and I told him how we'd walk the endless alleys and look at the pigs, lambs, horses, and cows. One time, in the coliseum we watched a horse show.

The best part about living in the city was the state fair. We had saved our nickels and pennies all year so we could ride the Ferris wheel. I talked and Alex listened. I hadn't talked that much to anybody in a long time, at least somebody who was interested in what I was saying.

"Tell me a secret, Maggie. Tell me something about you that nobody else knows."

I looked at his smiling eyes for a moment and considered the private details of my life. I can't say I had that many from my past, but now I had dark, horrible secrets that had become a part of me. Things I could never say out loud. Things I will forever keep buried and hidden within myself.

"Today is my birthday," I said.

Bertie suddenly appeared carrying two bowls of cake and homemade vanilla ice cream. "If this isn't the best cake you've ever tasted, I'll eat my apron."

I stuffed a big hunk in my mouth and closed my eyes at the flavor. Light and fluffy and peachy, the taste of a summer day.

Bertie laughed. "I can tell by the look on your face, you're gonna want that recipe."

Alex laughed too. "Today is Maggie's birthday," he said.

I smiled and took another big bite. This had turned into the best birthday ever, and one of the best days of my life.

Mr. Brown's sister begged us to spend the night, but he would have none of it. He gave Bertie a bear hug as a crowd of family surrounded him on the wide porch. He had already loaded his empty jars, shook a few hands, hugged many necks, and announced it was time to go. "Get in the car, Maggie." The sound of my name coming from his lips sounded strange.

Someone handed me my empty baskets. Mr. Brown took my arm in a tight grip and guided me down the porch steps. From the back of the crowd, leaning against a post, I caught a glimpse of hazel eyes watching us. The smile was gone from his face, and the look in Alex's eyes was almost sympathetic, with a tinge of anger.

I didn't need anybody feeling sorry for me. I couldn't change my fate, but I could still hold on to what little pride I had.

The air was muggy and the stars bright during our drive home. Mr. Brown didn't speak to me. He disappeared into his office, slamming the door behind him. I collapsed on my cot thankful for another night without his unwanted paws all over me. That night I went to sleep with a contented smile on my face.

**7**

---

If Mr. Brown had noticed the time I spent with Alex at the family picnic, he never mentioned it in the weeks that followed. It seemed that easy summer day had been a part of somebody else's life, a fuzzy scene from an almost forgotten dream.

We returned to our same routine. Me cooking for a houseful of grifters and so-called friends who showed up for free hooch. There was the group of regulars that showed up on Friday and Saturday nights who laughed at everything he said and reminded him what a great man he was. Mr. Brown loved every minute of their fake attention. I never became too familiar with any of them. I was the cook and housekeeper, just a part of the furnishings. Not anyone worth their time. Until that next Saturday night when everything changed.

I WAS CARRYING food back and forth to the dining room. At one end of the table, I placed my first attempt at little sister Bertie's peach cake. I had to say, it looked delicious. The smell reminded me of that simple summer day and I couldn't help but smile.

A few people gathered around and piled their plates with roast beef, mashed potatoes, and corn, but for the others it was too early in the evening. The alcohol would begin to wear off, they'd sober up a bit, or not, and eat before heading home. I turned to the sideboard to fill the percolator with coffee.

"Who's the tomato?"

I turned to see a man wearing a double-breasted navy blue jacket that looked like it cost more than most people made in their lifetime. His face was prettier than it should have been. He stared at me with cold, dark brown eyes. The other women in the room took notice, too. I'd never seen him at the house before. He must be somebody important because Mr. Brown seemed nervous in his attention.

"Come over here and meet Mr. Russo. Joey, this is my wife."

I extended my hand even though my husband never called my name, but instead of shaking hands the man grabbed my arm and pulled me close. "You are one lucky son-of-a-bitch, Clarence." His breath smelled like stale cigars. "What do you see in this old buzzard, Doll?"

Mr. Brown laughed and slapped him on the shoulder. "Come this way to my office and let's talk business. I've got a brand new bottle of Gordon's. Shall we open it?"

"Lead the way, my friend," Joey Russo turned me loose and brought my rough, chapped hand up to his lips. "Such a shame to waste such beauty on scrubbing pots and pans." He winked. "Maybe you could go home with me."

A chill etched my spine and my stomach churned with warning. This man was trouble, no doubt about it. I wondered if that was even his real name.

"I need to try a jar of your rot gut, Clarence, before we make a deal, and I'll take a piece of that cake," he said.

"Certainly. Right this way." Mr. Brown glanced my way. "Bring us cake and make it quick."

I sliced two pieces and carried plates and forks into the study. Russo twirled a liquid in his glass as his brown eyes followed me. I tried not to look, but I caught him study me from head to toe. The look in his eyes told me what he had in mind. I made my exit as quick as I could without saying a word.

The rest of the night I stayed hidden in the kitchen, which wasn't unusual. No one ventured into my space at the back of the house. This was the place for the servants, and I was glad to be left alone. It had become my safe haven. I had brightened up the drab space somewhat by painting the backsplash pink. I kept fresh cut stems of honeysuckle and lilac branches on the windowsill.

Surprisingly, the kitchen had been full of nice china and serving pieces. His late wife had spent his money wisely, and she had expensive taste. I wasn't sure how long Mr. Brown's wife had been dead, or if she even cooked. No one ever mentioned her name or talked of his life before me.

Sometime close to midnight, the usual party noise seemed to go silent and it appeared that everyone made a rush outside. I slipped out the back door and eased my way around the corner of the house, being careful to stay in the shadows. I backed into the lilac bush at the corner of the porch.

The yard was full of people and the tension in the air was so thick you could have sliced it with a knife. It was just a matter of time before the rot gut and tempers clashed, and it looked like that time had come.

## 8

The front yard of Mr. Brown's mansion bulged with men. The women stood in a wide-eyed huddle on the porch. I gasped when I saw the shotguns and pistols that seemed to be in every man's hand. In the middle of the group Mr. Russo held a Tommy gun. Standing directly in front of him was Mr. Brown with outstretched arms and a big smile on his face.

"Jo-o-o-e-e-ey. My friend. You don't want to do that. We can work this out," he said.

"You promised fifteen cases, and my man tells me you shorted us. I'd say that's not good business practice, if you want to live."

Mr. Brown's smile widened. "I have a batch ready for bottling. You just gotta give me a few hours. I'll deliver it special." His charm and personality might not get him out of this mess.

Russo raised his gun higher and pointed it at Mr. Brown's face. "Tell you what. I'll take that little wife of yours, and we'll call it square."

My heart stopped and my legs felt like jelly. I was afraid to breathe or blink. The worst part of it was Mr. Brown hesitated without giving an answer. Was he considering passing me off to someone else? I felt tears stream down my cheeks but I did not dare move to wipe my face.

Mr. Brown glanced over his shoulder and said, "Tell my wife to get out here now." One of his underlings dashed up the stairs into the house.

The tension hung in the air as one of the fellas disappeared inside. All was silent as Russo's men and Mr. Brown's men stood at the ready, holding their guns pointing at the other.

"We can't find her, boss. She ain't in the kitchen," one of the men reported.

"So sorry, Mac, that bank's closed, but this one isn't." Dianna stepped into the porch light, a red scarf around her shoulders and a slit in her skirt to the top of her thigh. She smiled and had everyone's attention. "Stop all of this nonsense, Joey. You know Clarence is good as his word, and you know you're getting a quality product. Now get on in here and dance with me while they fill the rest of your order." She licked her lips and shifted her weight causing more of her thigh to show.

"Boys, get the rest of Mr. Russo's order and make it quick," Mr. Brown said. "I assure you that heads will roll over this mistake. Now come back inside, Joey. Food, drink, whatever you want - name it." Mr. Brown raised both arms over his head. "Whatever is mine is yours."

I tried to keep what little food I had in my stomach. As everyone made their way across the yard and back into the house, I collapsed farther back into the lilac bush and buried my face in my lap. Sobs racked my body and I tried to keep silent.

A warm hand squeezed my shoulder. "It's going to be all right, Maggie. I'm here now." I couldn't see the face in the dark but I knew the voice immediately.

Alex.

I sobbed even harder. He sat on the ground next to me and wrapped his arms around me. He almost squeezed the breath out of me, he held on so tight. I didn't care. I felt comfortable and safe in those warm arms. I finally cried myself out, wiped my dripping nose on the hem of my apron, and was able to find my voice.

"What are you doing here?" I whispered.

"I couldn't stop thinking about you," he said. "I just wanted to see how you're doing. Not too well from the looks of it."

"He...he...he almost traded me to that man. Who would even do such a thing?" The terror struck me all over again and yet I knew who would do such a thing, my own father. Tears bubbled from my eyes. I couldn't turn them off.

"It's all right, Maggie. I'm here now and I would never let him do that to you." Alex kissed my head and squeezed me tight.

"You have to leave," I said as I pushed his arms away. "We shouldn't be here like this."

"We haven't done anything wrong, and besides I'm family. Blood is thicker than water you know."

We sat together in the darkness. The music and laughter started again inside and sounded miles away, as cicadas and bullfrogs almost drowned out the partiers. We watched the lightning bugs dance and blink under the leafy oak trees. The backyard seemed like a fairy tale land frozen in time.

"Are you going to stay out here all night?" he asked.

I wanted to. "I don't know," I said. "Maybe." I pulled blades of grass and tossed them out into the yard. I broke off a branch of lilac blossoms and inhaled deeply.

"Come on. Let's go in. You'll be okay. I'll be there to watch over you," Alex said.

We stood. He pointed me in the direction of the back of the house, and he walked in the opposite direction towards the front. I made my way silently to the back door and slipped inside, standing at the sink wondering what to do next.

"Where have you been?" Mr. Brown demanded.

I jumped clean out of my skin and dropped the lilac bush

branch. My tongue refused to answer. My brain refused to form any words.

"Outside I see, picking more damn flowers. We are out of coffee." Before he could say anything more Alex appeared in the doorway. My heart skipped a beat.

"Uncle Clarence," Alex said.

Mr. Brown turned.

"Now this is a surprise. It's always nice to have family visit me," he said. Alex gave Mr. Brown a big bear hug, which seemed to please the old bastard. "How is your mother? Can I get you a drink?"

"Mother is doing well, and I would love a drink." Alex slung his arm around Mr. Brown's shoulder.

"I've also got a brand new box of Cuban cigars."

"Thanks, sir. That would be great." They disappeared.

My hands were shaking so bad I couldn't stop them. I collapsed into a kitchen chair and tried to hold my emotions in check. The coffee pot was empty. That's what I had to do. Focus on the task at hand.

"Let's dance, Doll." Russo appeared from nowhere and squeezed me from behind as I stood at the sideboard in the dining room. "You can call me Joey."

The percolator lid clattered to the floor. He swung me around and pulled me in close. I could hardly breathe. His hand slide down and rested on my bottom. He buried his face in my neck and I thought I'd vomit with fear. With an arrogance and surefootedness, he suddenly twirled me to the stairs and yanked my arm to follow him to the second-floor ballroom. We glided around the polished floor several times. He never let go, not even enough for me to catch my wind. The last spin had made me dizzy.

The small band lit into a boogie-woogie, a lively piano number that my parents would have never allowed me to listen to. Dianna squeezed in between Russo and me. "Let's show them how it's done, Joey."

Relief flooded over me. Mr. Brown stood at the end of the room and caught my eye with a glint of rage on his face. I hurried down the stairs to finish the coffee, and then I'd have to face the mountain of dirty dishes. I'd be up long past midnight when the party died down, and hopefully Dianna would keep Russo occupied.

**9**

———

After I cleared the lunch table on Thursday, Mr. Brown handed me a brown paper bag wrapped in twine. Inside, I discovered a dress made from the softest, grey silk I had ever held in my hands. Delicate fabric covered buttons started at the bottom of the low back and ran down the middle to the top of gathered folds. The front was sleek and plain, with two straps over the shoulders dotted with sparkling sequins and dark blue beads. It sure was a fancy nightgown. When I saw it, I remembered the words of Russo. My heart turned cold with fear, but I refused to cry. I had to stop being so weak and accept my fate.

Later that afternoon, Mr. Brown came into the house and went straight to his bathroom upstairs. I heard the water running, which was unusual so early in the day.

I busied myself with punching a mound of dough for rolls, an easy task to help take out my frustrations. A light cloud of flour drifted in the sunlight that streamed through the window. Sometimes I get lost in my head when I'm cooking, and it's almost as if I'm a normal wife and happy in this life.

Dianna appeared in the doorway wearing a silver dress, sleek and shiny, which fit like a glove around her full hips and ample bosom. She had never ventured into my space before, leastways she might get her nails messed up. "Get ready. Clarence is taking us out," she said.

I made quick work of the dough, using a mason jar to cut off small biscuits. Filling two pans with the round pieces, I covered each with a dish towel and left them to rise. In the bathroom just off of the kitchen, I brushed my hair, washed my face, and hung my apron on a hook behind the door.

Dianna startled me, standing at the doorway.

"Wear the Milgrim," she said, holding the dress I had just unwrapped.

"That nightgown?" I asked, in shock that she should even suggest it.

"It's a dress by a very famous designer. Sally Milgrim. It didn't fit me, so you can wear it. We're going to the Four Deuces for dinner. I promised Clarence that I'd try to bring out your fun side, so he's taking us both. It's you and me with one of the wealthiest and most successful barrel house owners in this town. Can you try to relax and have a good time?"

"This dress has no back."

"It's to be worn without undergarments. You'll ruin the line of the fabric if you wear a brassier." She pushed the dress at me again.

I had never heard of such a thing. Going out in public without undergarments. I was heading straight for hell, and it was my father's fault for putting me on this path.

My silk boxers stayed on, and I covered my shoulders with a velvet shawl. I had to admit the dress made me feel very grown up and fancy. The fabric was the softest thing I'd ever felt, and it fit perfectly, snug around my hips and tucked close at my waist. I added lipstick and darkened my eyelashes. It wasn't the Maggie I knew who stared back from the mirror. I was some other girl who looked older and wiser for her years, and so much more worse from the wear of life. The innocent Maggie was gone.

Dianna looked me up and down with a hateful glare. "You are one little piece of trouble," she said. I wondered if that was a compliment or based on jealousy that I had invaded their world. I followed her to the front entry.

Mr. Brown waited at the front door and watched me walk towards him. The look in his eyes made me dread the evening even more. He barely glanced at Dianna when she passed.

"Are you ready to tear up the night, ladies?" He followed us outside with a bellowing laugh. "Let's show them how it's done, shall we?"

Dianna shot me another hateful glare, but gave Mr. Brown her sauciest smile before planting a kiss on his cheek. "Let's tear this town up, sweetie."

I rode in the back seat, and Dianna was up front. Mr. Brown's car sped through the night. From what Alex had told me, Mr. Brown's house was on the Jacksboro Highway, a road that ran from Fort Worth to the northeast towards Lake Worth. Just outside of the city, the highway was known for its clump of saloons and gambling halls. Whatever your vice, you could find it on the Jacksboro Highway.

We pulled in to a lot of Cadillacs and parked in front of a sprawling Spanish style complex of buildings. As I stepped out of the car, Mr. Brown jerked the shawl off my shoulders and tossed it back into the car. I tried to cover my front with folded arms, but he placed my hand in the crook of his arm, and Dianna grabbed his other. With a big smile on his face, he strutted through the front door of a place called the Four Deuces.

"Mr. Brown!" An overly enthusiastic waiter gushed with excitement. "So delighted you could join us this evening. Right this way, Sir. We have your usual table ready. Ladies, you are looking lovely tonight."

"Anybody who is anybody eats here," Dianna hissed in my ear as Mr. Brown took his seat. The waiter held our chairs out for us.

Before I could read the menu that was placed in my hands, Mr.

Brown ordered steaks all around. A napkin was placed in my lap. Our table became a flurry of waiters with silverware, clinking china, and then someone poured a golden, sparkling liquid into the most beautiful glass I'd ever seen.

"Taste it," Dianna said. "It's champagne." She held the slender fluted glass between her thumb and two fingers at the stem, so I did the same, bringing the liquid slowly to my lips. It tickled my nose as it slid down my throat. Before my glass was half empty, the waiter filled it again, and I kept sipping, getting more and more depressed by the minute.

The room dripped with elegance. Ladies with kohl black eyelashes and wearing shimmering dresses balanced slender cigarette holders between two fingers as they stared intently at men in fancy suits. Lively notes from a band floated around the room. Dianna oohed and awed at the dresses, and dropped names of politicians and celebrities who were of no importance to me. The Four Deuces on the Jacksboro Highway seemed to be the place to be seen.

Smiles widened, glasses were filled, and waiters hustled back and forth. The steaks arrived, served with much flourish and cooked to perfection. The evening was magical and I hated every minute. This was a world where I did not belong.

Mr. Brown kept his attention on the room instead of us, waving and nodding, while some stopped by our table to exchange pleasantries. I kept my head down as if my meal held my attention and prayed for it all to be over soon. I sipped champagne until my head got swimmy. Until I didn't care that my breasts were out for all the world to see. Until I stopped cringing when Mr. Brown's fingers touched my bare back.

Joey Russo suddenly appeared at our table while we dined on steak and fried potatoes, holding the attention of every woman in the room. Dressed impeccably, his wicked smile and arrogant bearing caused a girl to forget about anything else. Mr. Brown greeted him like a long-lost brother, with a wide grin and stood to give him a bear hug. It was hard to believe they had just had a standoff in our front yard only a few nights before.

Greetings were exchanged. Dianna made sure he noticed her cleavage, and when she had his attention, sent an air kiss followed by, "Hey there, handsome."

Russo looked my way as well, and I nodded because it seemed rude to not, but I did not offer a smile.

"I'm here to extend an invitation for you and your party to join my table at the Casino Ballroom," Russo said.

"Wonderful idea," Mr. Brown smiled. "Who's up for some dancing?"

"Oh, me, me," replied Dianna, with what seemed to me too much enthusiasm. She stood, drained the last bit of bubbly from her glass, and announced, "I'm ready."

"Maggie," Russo said, as he stepped closer and offered his hand. "You'll be joining us, I hope."

My heart actually fluttered, but not with desire so much as the intense attention from this devilishly handsome man. Warning signals made my stomach lurch. I had no money, no car, and no way of escape. I trailed behind the group as we made our way outside to the parking lot.

The night had only just begun.

**10**

———

Sleep.

That is all I wanted. Just to rest my head and close my eyes for a few minutes. I pulled my wrap closer around me and lay back while Mr. Brown's Cadillac sped through the night, or was it almost morning? I had to hold my hair in one hand and scrunch down in the seat to find shelter from the warm evening breeze that swirled into the open windows.

My tummy was full from dinner and champagne. Way too much champagne. My body felt noodle limp and my head buzzed. I pulled my wrap around my shoulders and thought about my cot in the little room off the kitchen. I had played dress up long enough. This wasn't my world. These people were not my friends, nor would they ever be. I wanted no part of their fake flattery and momentary pleasures. I wanted my simple life back.

As we sped through the night, I had never felt so helpless and out of place. Russo scared me, but Mr. Brown frightened me even more. The powerful and arrogant Mr. Brown took great pride in the things he had accumulated, and he surrounded himself with an overabundance of treasures. His car, a massive mansion with doors wide open every weekend for all to admire, his thriving business, and a wife 30 years his junior. I had become one of his possessions, his property. If someone desired something of his, I had no idea what his reaction might be or how violent he could become.

The stare down between Mr. Brown and Russo in the front yard had surprised me. Mr. Brown had not blinked or showed fear, even when facing Russo who had leveled a gun straight at his face. Neither one of them had given ground. These men were extremely ambitious, powerful, possessive, and cruel.

We pulled into a parking lot located in front of a stucco building next to the shores of Lake Worth. Mr. Brown and Dianna emerged from the car with a newfound burst of energy. Giggling with heads together, they made their way towards the entrance. Mr. Brown cast a glance over his shoulder to make sure I followed. Hopefully the crowd would be overwhelming, and I could hide away in a far corner. This time I kept my shawl around my shoulders.

We approached a massive Mediterranean style stucco building. "They have a dress code here," Dianna said. "Suits and ties required."

Inside, the dance floor, made from strips of stained oak, stretched forever. At the far end of the room the bandstand bulged with more musicians that I had ever seen in my life, and the sound was perfection. Couples glided over the polished floor under rotating crystal balls. One couldn't help but feel the cares of life slipping away. Large arched windows provided a view of Lake Worth and a lighted boardwalk that stretched along the shores.

"It's like a carnival, isn't it?" Breathless, with sparkling eyes, Dianna pointed out the window. "That's where the food vendors and rides are. They even have a roller coaster."

Mr. Brown shook many hands and greeted everyone like a long-lost friend as we made our way to an empty table. Dianna drew attention, which is what she wanted. A few gentlemen fell in line behind her with lustful glances. She eased into the dance floor crowd in the arms of a silver-haired gentleman. I wormed my way through the crowd and sat with my back against a wall. I was happy to watch from the sidelines.

I gasped when I saw him. Watching the crowd intently, my eyes must be deceiving me, but I wasn't wrong.

Alex danced by again with a long-haired blonde in a bright red gown. The flutter of jealousy that radiated through me took me by surprise.

"My beautiful Maggie, let's dance." Joey Russo appeared before me with outstretched hand blocking my view. I cringed inside but forced myself to place my hand in his. The truth was I was worried about causing a scene and drawing attention to myself.

He led me to the dance floor and we merged into the crowd. Suddenly he pulled me close with a death grip around my waist. His arms were solid and strong, his eyes seemed to bore into my soul. I couldn't look away from his handsome face. Time seemed to stand still as the noise of the crowd faded away. My feet seemed to float as if I was in a dream.

"Why such sad eyes, Maggie Brown? Let me save you from this life," he said as he kissed my ear. A shiver ran from my neck down to my toes. "We can travel the world. We can go anywhere you'd like. Name the place. We will leave right now." His lips were a breath away from mine.

Empty promises and empty words. I saw no emotion in his eyes.

The song ended and he led me over to a table where Mr. Brown sat with an arm slung around Dianna's shoulders. Smoke curled from a fat stogy between his teeth. Russo pulled out a chair for me. My insides trembled. I was intimidated about having to look at Mr. Brown although I didn't have anything to feel guilty about.

Suddenly, Alex appeared at our table.

Mr. Brown stood and draped an arm around Alex's shoulder. "Look who's joining us, my nephew. Good to see you again, boy.

How is your mother?" Mr. Brown was one to never hide his enthusiasm for kin. "You remember Alex, don't you?"

"Hey there." Dianna smooched the air as she waved one hand. "Don't you clean up nice?" The smoldering look she gave him made me want to yank her hair out.

"Are you having a good time, son?" asked Mr. Brown.

"Great time, sir." Alex grinned. "This is a fantastic ballroom. Fun crowd."

"Joey Russo. Nice to meet you." They shook hands.

"Bring your date over. I'd love to meet her," said Mr. Brown.

"I'll do that." Alex sent an impersonal nod in my direction, then turned and walked back to the table where the lady in red waited.

Alex's lack of words hurt me more than just a little, but why should it bother me? I was a married woman, which was a fact I needed to remind Mr. Russo.

"Let's dance, handsome," said Dianna, as she grabbed Russo's arm. They disappeared into the crowd while Mr. Brown raised his arm. A waiter suddenly appeared with bottles of champagne and fluted glasses. He carefully poured me a glass and sat it in front of me. I was thirsty, but my brain fog had cleared and I didn't want a swimmy head again. I wanted to stay focused and aware. I was afraid of losing control and I was panic-stricken at the thought of Russo coming anywhere near me.

Mr. Brown stared at me for a few minutes and then turned his attention to a gentleman sitting at the next table. They shook hands and bent their heads together in conversation.

I caught Alex glancing my way, but he didn't walk over to speak to me. He turned his head quickly when I caught his eye, grabbed the hand of the bimbo in red, and gave her a wide smile as they walked onto the dance floor. They glided by and I downed half the glass of champagne in one gulp. Alex was a very good dancer, which surprised me for some reason, and he looked very handsome. I couldn't take my eyes off him and found myself shifting in my chair to find him in the throng again.

The night seemed endless. I sipped champagne, found the ladies' room several times, discovered a snack table, and enjoyed the big band sound. Then Russo directed his attention towards me again. Mr. Brown gave us a glance when Russo pulled me to my feet, before turning his attention back to a tall, thin woman dripping in jewelry.

We stayed on the dance floor during the next four songs as Russo held me closer than was appropriate. He didn't speak of what he had in mind, but there was no doubt he was drawn to me. I couldn't begin to guess why. I was simple, uneducated Maggie and he could have any one of the sophisticated women in the dance hall. Maybe it was a silent revenge against Mr. Brown? Perhaps they hadn't resolved their differences from the other night in our front yard after all.

This competition by two bone-headed criminals couldn't end well, and I was the pawn in their game.

**11**

———————

I searched the sea of faces at the Casino Ballroom for the one hundredth time hoping for a glimpse of the familiar brown hair, hoping for a friendly flash of hazel eyes. Alex had disappeared.

Russo returned with a bottle of champagne in one hand and in the other clasped the hand of a pert-nosed, petite girl in a shockingly short skirt that barely covered her knees. Her hair was cut in the latest short bob, which framed her stunning features. Bright, cornflower blue eyes full of laughter and life and plump, bright red lips made for a perfect picture. The Flapper grinned and two dimples popped out on her cheeks.

"This is Cherry," Russo said.

I returned her smile and liked her immediately. Mr. Brown swallowed her in a giant bear hug. Dianna swirled to a stop and her dance partner brought her hand to his lips and left. She turned to eye the beautiful Cherry. They shook hands.

Russo pulled out a chair for Cherry, and then he popped the top of the bottle. He filled our glasses to the rims and signaled a waiter to bring more. He never looked my way, but I felt his presence and knew that he was aware of me. I couldn't resist partaking of the bubbly. I loved the sweet, refreshing taste and how it tickled my nose. I sipped and watched the couples as they twirled past. Russo soon disappeared into the crowd again. I searched the dancing couples for Alex. I felt guilty being a married woman and searching the crowd for another man, but my hope was to at least talk to him, even if for a moment.

The long night continued. It was a fog of glasses of bubbly, big band music, and spinning crystal balls. I couldn't seem to wake up from it. I wanted to clear the haze in my head, but despite my best efforts I just kept drinking every time they filled my glass.

Mr. Brown stood up with one arm around Dianna and the other around Cherry, announcing that it was time to leave. I felt such relief. I stood on wobbly legs and waited for the room to stop spinning before I dared take a step.

"Let me help you," Russo dropped my shawl around my shoulders and put a steadying arm around my waist. We followed the others towards the door.

I had no idea what time it was. Didn't anyone wear a watch in these places? Some couples were still going strong on the dance floor, while others rested weary heads on the tables.

The darkness enveloped us as we made our way around the cars. I could hear Dianna and Cherry giggling. Before I knew what was happening, Russo spun me around and backed me up against the fender of a car. He surrounded me with the warmth of his arms and kissed me. Gently at first, with champagne sweet, soft lips. I couldn't help but sigh. My body gave in and my swimmy head betrayed me.

His kiss became more possessive and demanding. He shoved his tongue into my mouth. Fear stung my mind. I needed air. I placed my hands on his chest and pushed, but it was like pushing a solid granite wall. My resistance made him grow bolder. His hand trailed shivers down my bare back, and then he slipped his fingers into the side of my dress.

"Let her go." The words came deep and demanding. A hand clamped on Russo's shoulder and he suddenly spun around leaving an empty breeze between us to replace the heat. A solid fist landed square on his jaw which knocked him back several steps. I blinked and looked into the eyes of Alex. His face only inches from mine, he said, "Go to the car now."

Anger flashed in Russo's eyes as he stepped closer. "I will kill you, boy," he said, followed by a right to Alex's gut. In the breath that whooshed out, Alex said, "Run, Maggie."

Tears stung my eyes. I didn't know which way to go, and then I heard Dianna's laugh to my right so I hurried in that direction.

"There she comes," Dianna said. "You don't look so well. Are you okay?"

"Do not get sick in this car," demanded Mr. Brown.

I climbed into the backseat with Cherry, wiped my cheeks, and tried to calm my heart. Alex was all right. Alex had to be all right, but I dared not turn around to look. With eyes closed, I willed my heart to slow down and keep the champagne from coming back up. I prayed for Alex's life and that Russo would spare him.

I must have dozed off because when I woke we were parked in the yard right next to the front porch steps.

"Just leave her. She'll be all right," Dianna said. "It's not like she'll freeze or anything." She was on one side of Mr. Brown and Cherry was on the other, as they stumbled and swayed, trying to guide each other into the house. I could hear their giggles as they made their way up the grand staircase.

As I followed them inside, to say I was shocked would be an understatement, but I also felt overwhelming relief. Cherry and Dianna would keep Mr. Brown occupied and hopefully they'd sleep past noon. My only problem was Russo because his obsession held a sense of urgency. I did not know what the man was capable of.

I collapsed on my bed and closed my eyes. Alex's face filled my head. My stomach lurched and I hurried to the bathroom. All the champagne came back and then some in between heaves and sobs.

My sobbing turned to fear as the idea suddenly hit me that Joey Russo may have followed us home. I made a pallet on the floor of the pantry and locked the door behind me. Mr. Brown had taken the lock off the small servant's bedroom where I had slept several months ago. Surrounded by canned goods and linens, the storage closet was the only place I could think of where I might feel safe and secure. With my back against a flour sack and my knees drawn up to my chin, I closed my eyes again. I was exhausted.

The best solution for my situation would have been for a very drunk Mr. Brown to crash his car that night. How simple it would be if I could die in a fiery crash never to be heard from again, but the easy way out was not in my stars. I had no life. No future. No hope.

There had to be a way of escape, even if it meant the end of me.

## 12

---

Cherry left around mid-morning with one of Mr. Brown's men. I enjoyed a quiet morning working in the kitchen. Alex never left my thoughts, which was strange. I had only met him once and we had enjoyed a pleasant afternoon, yet I felt drawn to him. It seemed as if we had known each other my entire life. I pushed the idea that he might be dead from my mind. If I only had a way of getting in touch with him. I hesitated to ask one of Mr. Brown's men for help because of the interest Joey Russo had taken in me. I did not need any more trouble or unwanted attention, and I didn't want anyone to squeal on me.

Mr. Brown and Dianna came downstairs later that afternoon dressed to the nines. "We're going out for dinner," she said.

That gave me about four hours to make several desserts and figure out something for the night's meal. Before their dining out would be over, Mr. Brown would manage to invite everyone in the restaurant back with him to continue the party. It was going to be a full house tonight and no doubt there'd be many bottles of 'shine consumed and sold before the evening was done. Mr. Brown was his own best walking billboard.

I rolled out several pie crusts and sliced apples. The can of peaches I opened smelled so good, reminding me of that summer afternoon I spent talking to Alex.

The party guests began to arrive around nine o'clock. While the coffee perked, I loaded the sideboard with banana cake and at the other end placed pecan, apple, and peach pies. In between I stacked plates and forks. That would keep the fools busy for a while. I planned to stay hid out in the kitchen. My work was interrupted by a voice that made my heart leap. "I'd sure like a piece of that cake."

I turned and when I saw Alex's face, I ran to his side not caring who might be watching. "You're alive!"

His left eye was swollen shut and his chin was covered in a bloody scrape. He opened his arms and I did not hesitate. He winced when I hugged him.

"Bruised ribs," he explained.

"We can't talk here. Meet me out back, but you go out the front door." I darted back through the kitchen and slipped outside. When Alex appeared from around the corner of the house, I put one finger to my lips and led him past the trash pile and behind a lilac bush that stood in a far corner of the property.

"You can't be here. Mr. Brown will be back any minute and if Russo shows up tonight, I don't know what he'll do."

"I know exactly what he'll do," said Alex. "He's going to kill me."

"Are you going to be all right, Alex?"

He shook his head, yes. Thankful tears filled my eyes.

"I've been in worse scrapes, but Russo will kill me if he gets the chance," he said. "I have to leave, and I want you to come with me."

I was stunned. My heart leaped with joy, but my head couldn't imagine the solution could be that simple. Just leave? Is that possible? I crossed my arms and turned my back to him. Things were much more complicated. "I took an oath before a judge. I'm a married woman," I said. "I can't leave with you."

"We will go to the judge and ask him what to do. We can tell him it was a huge mistake. You can't live like this. I don't think I'm wrong in saying that you have feelings for me."

I blinked away tears and focused on what he was saying. "You didn't even speak to me at the Four Deuces or the dance hall. How can it be you suddenly want to sweep me away from this madness? I don't even know you. How do I know what you offer would be any better?"

"I didn't trust myself last night. You were so unbelievably beautiful. I wanted to take you in my arms and if I had, I would have never let you go. I respect the fact that you are a married woman, and that's why we need to speak to the judge. When he hears what your life has become, he will know this is wrong. You are nothing but a common slave in your own home sold and bought over the price of a deck of cards."

I couldn't stop the tears. All my days of heartache were now flowing out of me.

"I want you to be my wife, Maggie. I will protect you. I promise." Alex wiped the tears from my cheek and hugged me tight. I was so frightened it made my stomach ache, and I was overcome with joy at the same time. The feelings I had for him were wrong. My father had set me on this path and there was nothing I could do about it.

"Maggie, please." Alex's eyes were so soft and pleading, but I turned my back to him.

"I can't go with you. I have to get back inside."

"You don't know me, but when I look into your eyes, I'm sure you feel the same way about me. I know it." He grabbed my shoulders. "I want to protect you, Maggie. I will be back for you on Sunday night," he called to my back as I hurried towards the house.

The crowd was rowdy and full of steam that night, which kept me busy. I collapsed in my bed right after the musicians called it quits, too tired to care about a man named Russo. The dream of running away with Alex brought me peace and some wishful thinking, but I had to stay away from him. The reality of my life was the thing of nightmares. And I was stuck in them.

**13**

———

Joey Russo made an appearance the next night on Saturday. He cornered me in the kitchen just as I was rinsing dishes. With both hands on either side, he pinned me against the cabinet. Gently moving my hair to one side, he kissed the back of my neck which sent chills down my spine.

"Know this," he said. "You and I will happen. I am a patient man. But I can't wait forever."

Mr. Brown interrupted us with a clearing of his throat and his usual booming voice, "Russo. There you are."

Russo turned and offered a hand. They shook.

Mr. Brown looked at me. "What's going on here?"

"Just getting reacquainted with your wife," Russo pulled a slim cigarette from the inside pocket of his jacket. He leaned against the counter, looking more handsome than sin and smiling at Mr. Brown. He always seemed to appear calm with no emotion on his face, looking like he just stepped out of a Hollywood movie set.

"I won't have this, whatever it is," said Mr. Brown. "That's overstepping your privileges around here, Joey."

Russo crossed one leg in front of the other. He casually pulled a match box from a vest pocket and struck a match, sticking the flame to one end of a slender, brown cigar. Smoke curled in a lazy S over his head. After he had inhaled for several times, he looked at Mr. Brown. "How do you like Cherry?"

Mr. Brown's face lost all color as he turned a sheepish glance in my direction. Russo grinned and placed an arm around my waist, pulling me close. "I recall you saying that 'what's yours is mine'." He turned his handsome face towards me with a brilliant smile that did not reach his eyes and ran a finger down the side of my face. What I saw in his gaze scared me to the core. No emotion, but a cruel, impersonal glare. Mr. Brown's face turned to a deep purple rage.

Russo laughed and turned me loose. "Where's that nephew of yours?"

"You mean, Alex? What do you want with him?"

"Just a little job is all," said Russo. "We have some mutual friends."

"I'll tell him you're looking for him, but back off Joey. He's a good boy and I promised my sister that I'd keep him out of trouble."

Russo laughed again. "I'm not all bad, Clarence."

"Got a new box of Cuban cigars," said Mr. Brown.

Russo nodded his head. "Well, lead the way then."

Mr. Brown spun on his heel and left the kitchen.

Russo turned at the doorway to look at me. "I'm still curious as to why that young man defended your honor so fiercely in the Casino Ballroom parking lot. Know this. If you don't do as I want, I will tell Brown all about what you're doing behind his back with his nephew." He sneered.

I grabbed the back of a kitchen chair to keep from collapsing. The laughter, the clinking of glasses, and the fiddle player warming up his instrument seemed like a hazy dream. My face flushed hot and my stomach lurched, except on this night it wasn't from alcohol. I ran through the back door and threw up in the flower bed. Right or wrong, I had to find Alex and warn him.

## 14

It was Sunday night and I was exhausted the moment I woke. The crowd had partied full steam the night before, so I woke early to clean. Sometimes they returned to pick up where they'd left off on Saturday and sometimes they slept in. I never knew if we'd have a full house again. Mr. Brown's 'shine kept them coming back.

That morning, as I pinned my hair in a tight bun, the girl that looked back at me was unrecognizable. I looked at least fifteen years older beyond my age. My eyes had dark circles from lack of sleep and my forehead had new worry lines. I put on the ugliest calico dress I could find and covered that with an old, worn apron I had found in a kitchen drawer. It must have been several decades old. Two sizes too big with circles of stains, it hung from my body like a faded flour sack.

Let Alex get an eyeful of me now. One look and he'd forget all about this running away business. What an idiot he was. I wasn't no prize, that's for sure. I said a silent prayer that Alex would not show up here. If he lost his life because of me, I didn't know how I would survive living with that reality.

The morning began as all the others – laundry, dirty dishes and empty jars scattered about, and preparations for the evening's free-loaders. They were a filthy, nasty bunch.

"I want to make one thing perfectly clear." Mr. Brown's voice startled me. I looked up from the pile of potatoes I had just dumped on the table. His presence and size filled the doorway. "You belong to me. I will decide who you may associate with, and if I so choose, there will be business conducted in return for your privileges. Is that clear? No wife of mine is to sleep in the servant's quarters next to the kitchen. People are talking. Move your things to my bedroom today."

All of the pent-up anger I had suppressed for these many months came to the surface as I stared into the ugly face of that awful man. The fact was I didn't belong to any man. Not my father, who had tossed me aside without a word, and certainly not this hateful excuse for a human being. And now he had the nerve to look me in my face and remind me that he had the power to trade me out to any man willing to pay the right price. They could all rot in hell.

I turned to face him and looked him square in the eyes. "No. Your bedroom is a little too crowded for me."

I don't know where that came from, but the moment the words escaped my lips I regretted them. His response was two long strides into the room and a back hand to the side of my face which made my head snap and my ears ring. It knocked me into the counter.

"You stay away from Joey Russo," he said, his face only a few inches from mine. His cruel eyes and whiskey breath etched chills into my back. I didn't dare give him the satisfaction of seeing even one tear.

THE REST of the day was weary work mixed with hopelessness. The same as every other day, but at the back of my mind I prayed that Alex wouldn't keep his word. The crowd started trickling in around nine o'clock, but the party wouldn't get started until midnight. It was going to be a long evening. Russo likes to make an entrance into a packed room and command everyone's attention. Maybe Alex would show up earlier and I'd convince him to leave me alone and never come back.

My prayers went unanswered. Alex appeared at the back door just before midnight. "I waited until the house was crowded so you could slip away unnoticed," he said.

"I'm not going, Alex." I said this standing at the stove. I couldn't look him in the eyes because I might lose my resolve. "Please. Don't come here anymore."

He placed a gentle hand on my shoulder and turned me around. The love in his eyes turned to rage in a flash. "Who did this to you?" He pulled me into the pantry and traced a finger along my bruised cheek. "Maggie. You can't live like this. Come away with me."

I felt so weary and worn from this reality, this prison I was in. There was no use in trying to change things. My life would never be my own.

"Joey Russo. Don't you look like the cat's meow tonight?" Dianna's voice broke the silence coming from the kitchen. Alex put a finger to his lips. I held my breath.

"Come dance with me," Dianna said.

"Sure thing, Doll Face."

I couldn't move or speak. I felt certain they could hear my heart beating. Alex pulled me into a hug. If anyone found us, Mr. Brown would most likely kill Alex before Russo could find him, but at that moment I didn't care. I couldn't force myself to pull away from the warmth of his arms.

"Leave with me, Maggie. Now," he whispered.

The pantry door creaked slowly open and it was Dianna's face that came into view. "Leave with him, Maggie. Joey is on the prowl for you both. It's too dangerous to stay. Wait here. I'll grab some of your things from your room."

I was too stunned to answer. Alex grinned and kissed me on the nose.

Dianna was back and handed me a paper bag. "Don't ever look back."

"Why are you doing this for me?" Tears stung my eyes. This woman had shown only contempt for me since I'd known her.

"You'd be surprised at the things you'll do for the man you love." She touched my bruised cheek and her eyes brimmed with unshed tears. The swirling skirt and flawless face were gone.

"Joey. Darling. Why are you in the kitchen? The bar is this way." Dianna's voice faded before I could hear Russo's answer. Now was the time to leave.

"I can't leave with you," I said.

Alex did not answer. He stared at my face and tucked a tendril of hair behind my ear. His stare was so intent and pleading. Those sad eyes made my knees weak and almost pushed through my resolve. He leaned close and gently kissed my lips. I avoided those eyes, looking down at the floor, my insides in turmoil.

There, in the back corner, rolled up under the bottom shelf, was the blanket I had used a few nights ago. If I remained here, would I sleep in the pantry the rest of my life? Is this all there was to my existence? Held prisoner to do as I'm told without argument, wear what he wants, and pleasure men who are necessary to close a business deal? I swallowed my pride and my fear, grabbed Alex's arm, and pushed him out of the pantry. We dashed for the back door. This time, I didn't hesitate, and I held tight to his hand. I tossed the sack of clothes that Dianna had gathered for me on the counter and stepped into the blackness of a new future.

# 15

Alex's blue Ford sport coupe had a trunk strapped to the back, but we didn't slow down for me to put anything in it since I had left everything I owned behind me. I didn't want any reminders of that life. He drove like a maniac towards Fort Worth.

Fear and my imagination got the better of me as we drove through the night. My heart thundered in my chest, my ears roared with a building headache, making me think that I'd be sick at any moment. I kept glancing over my shoulder to make sure we weren't being followed. It was just a question of who would find us first, Mr. Brown or Russo. Either way, we'd be dead. I was certain of it.

Dianna had surprised me. I doubted that she could be trusted though. She probably went straight to Mr. Brown right after we left and told him about finding us in the pantry. Proof enough for him that I had betrayed our marriage with his own nephew. Her revelation would certainly earn her favor in her lover's eyes. He used her just like he used me, and in a way I felt sorry for her because she really did love him.

My breathing didn't calm until we had parked in front of a simple, white-frame house. "Where are we?"

"The judge's house. Come on. Let's see if he can help us. I'm not marrying you until you can divorce Uncle Clarence."

"Marriage? You want to marry me?" Had we even talked about marriage before? He really wanted me to be his wife? The last few weeks seemed like a blur of emotion and tears and terror. I couldn't remember what he'd said.

"Of course, Maggie. I love you. You'll be the mother of my children someday, and we have to get married."

Apparently my soon-to-be husband was very practical and level-headed. A good man. He took my hand and pulled me up the front steps. With both fists, he banged on the door. "Judge Phillips. We need to talk to you. Please, open up, sir."

The door swung open and the judge, in a worn plaid robe, stared at us. His tousled grey hair stuck straight up in all directions. His wife stood behind him clutching her faded dressing gown, which looked as old as my apron.

"What is it? What do you want?" His gruff voice made me want to get back in the car. If he called Mr. Brown, I doubted that I would get by with a quick slap to the face this time. I pushed the thought out of my mind of what my fate would be if I had to go back to Mr. Brown.

"It's Alex Henderson, sir, and we want to get married."

"At this hour? You kids run along and come back tomorrow during office hours. My office is in the Tarrant County courthouse."

"Dear," said the judge's wife as she stepped into view and laid a hand on his arm. "It's that young lady again."

Judge Phillips opened the door wider and stepped outside. Alex pulled me into the light. The judge frowned when he saw my face. "You best come in then," he said.

"Can you grant Maggie an annulment of her first marriage? She can't continue living there. We are hoping you can help us."

The judge's brow creased into a deeper frown as he stepped

closer and looked intently at my face. "Did Clarence Brown do this to you?"

I nodded.

He took my trembling hands in his. "Are you sure this is what you want?"

"Yes sir, this is what I want."

He turned and stepped back inside his house, walking into a room next to the front door. He lifted the rolltop of a mahogany desk which seemed too big for the space it occupied. "Ahh, here it is," he said, a beaming smile on his face as he held up a piece of paper. "I never signed your first marriage certificate. I just couldn't force myself to do it. I hoped that you might find a way to escape that unfortunate circumstance."

"She's not married?" Alex squeezed my hand. "You can marry us then?"

"Yes, my boy. I can marry you right now."

Alex gave a whoop of excitement and hugged the judge. His wife laughed when he gave her a big bear hug, too. I couldn't help but giggle, and then the pain in my cheek reminded me of where I'd been only moments before. My future husband suddenly turned serious, cleared his throat, and stood soldier straight next to me. "We're ready then."

Judge Phillips cleared his throat. "Dear, can you be our witness?" Mrs. Phillips pulled her robe closer and smoothed her hair, and then walked over to stand next to me. With a broad smile on her face she linked her arm into mine and patted my hand.

The judge made quick work of the vows. I said 'I do' for the second time in my life, but this time was different. I felt it was right all the way to the core of my bones.

"I don't have a ring." Alex looked at me with total shock and sadness. His eyes brightened as he patted his coat pocket. "Wait. I have this."

He pulled out a long Cuban cigar from his inside jacket pocket, removed the band, and slipped it on my ring finger.

"You may kiss your bride," Judge Phillips said. Alex hugged me first and then gently kissed on the corner of my mouth opposite the bruises.

The judge gave us a ten spot. "Breakfast is on us. Now you'd best be off, and have a happy life." Alex handed him the cigar. "I need to pay you something, Sir. How much for your services?"

"You owe me nothing. Leave. Love each other and have a happy life," he said.

"Oh, wait. I forgot. I brought you this." From his jacket pocket, Alex pulled a bunch of snow white violet blossoms on crimped stems tied together with a tiny white ribbon.

"Those are for me?" asked the judge. We all laughed.

Alex faced me. "From the very first day I met you Mrs. Maggie Henderson, I loved you and I gave you a blue violet which means, *I'll always be true*. Today, you've made me the happiest man alive. I give you these white violets which mean, *take a chance on happiness*. Thank you, Maggie, for taking a chance on me."

As I watched the judge and his wife wave from their front porch I prayed that Alex and I would be together until we are old and grey.


WE DROVE all night straight north out of Fort Worth on Highway 77 towards Oklahoma. Alex kept his foot on the pedal. I didn't know how fast his tin can could go, but I felt sure he had hopped it up a bit. We sped through the dark, devouring miles like that bunch of idiots who gulped down Mr. Brown's 'shine. The lights of the city soon faded, taking me farther and farther away from my nightmare of existence. I never wanted to see Mr. Brown or that house or those people ever again, even if it meant we had to keep running for the rest of our born days.

We talked that night for hours. It's like we'd been saving up all of the words we ever wanted to say just waiting on the right person to say them to. We made plans, a lifetime worth of plans. Finding work at a diner would be easy for me, and Alex was a handyman of sorts. He could fix anything, plus he knew about growing things, not just violets. He had worked at the feed store since high school. A job he really enjoyed and he felt bad about leaving them in a lurch, but he did it for me.

We reached the Oklahoma state line just as the sun greeted us with the promise of new beginnings and stopped at the first diner that was open early for breakfast. I slipped into the restroom and splashed water on my face, removed the pins from my hair, and shoved that old apron into the trash bin.

As we ate, we overheard the waitresses talking about a new road they were building. Route 66 it was called. Some of it was paved, and some was still dirt. Most folks packed food and water and slept in their cars if they had a long distance to cover, but when it's finished there'd be motels and diners in every little town along the way. Route 66 would link Chicago all the way to the beaches of Santa Monica, California. I'd never been anywhere outside of Fort Worth.

A grand adventure waited for me.

**16**

———

Alex drove to downtown Oklahoma City where we looked for the corner of 1st Street and Broadway. It was easy to find because the three towers of the Skirvin Hotel rose tall and proud.

"This is the swankiest place in town, and since it's our wedding night I thought you might like to stay some place nice," he said. "We need to shop for some clothes for you, too, since you didn't pack anything."

"I didn't want my things. I'm leaving that life in the past."

"All the same, I wish you had at least grabbed that dress you wore to the Casino Ballroom." He wiggled his eyebrows at me and mouthed the word *"Wow."*

I laughed. That dress was the fanciest thing I'd ever worn in my life but it felt like wearing a nightgown. I had no idea that flimsy fabric had made such an impression.

I stuck my head out of the car window and looked up to admire the hotel, majestically rising towards a cloudless sky. "How did you know about this place?"

"Me and my parents come here all the time. The legend goes that it's haunted."

It was mid-morning by the time Alex pulled into a parking spot over two blocks away. We hopped out and walked towards the front entrance.

The Skirvin Hotel was unlike anything I'd ever seen. The lobby was at least two-stories high with dark wood pillars, velvety wallpaper, and plush furniture. Sounds of voices and laughter drifted through the lobby.

The clerk at the check-in counter provided a few facts. Built in 1904 it had 525 guest rooms that rose fourteen stories above downtown. He called attention to the chandeliers which were from Austria. I giggled at the thought of seeing a ghost and realized life with Alex would never be dull.

"It gets a little crazy around here. When the band gets going, it's a regular cat's meow party that goes on all night," the clerk said. "I'm guessing by the way you two keep looking at each other that you're newlyweds. Yes?"

When Alex mentioned we had indeed just gotten married, the grinning clerk checked us into one of the suites in a quieter part of the tower but gave us the regular room rate.

As I headed towards the stairs, Alex stopped at a pair of ornately etched gold metal doors. He had to explain to me what an elevator was. "Do you want some food or sleep?" Alex asked.

To be honest I couldn't hold my eyes open any longer. It had been a long and stressful day before and a night spent driving. I didn't know whether to break down in a fit of sobs or laugh with pure joy. A hot bath and soft bed were waiting. I looked into the eyes of my new husband and he knew my answer.

I don't understand how a person knows that they've found the one true person who would make their life complete, but I knew. I was tired of denying my feelings, and I couldn't explain why we were drawn to each other. I had hardened my heart and promised myself that I would never trust anyone again after what my own father had done, and it would take me a long time to get over the hatred I felt for Mr. Brown. But after my wedding night with Alex, I knew I had found the one person I could trust, the man I was meant to be with, and I knew without a doubt that we would never be apart again. That night together was unlike anything I'd ever experienced before.

They say it only takes one kiss and you know. Alex had become the deepest desire of my heart.

**17**

———

The next morning, we agreed to telephone our families.

We checked out of the Skirvin after a leisurely breakfast and walk through downtown Oklahoma City where I found a few undergarments and splurged on two nice dresses. Alex insisted. A wedding present, he had said. I looked longingly at wedding rings in the window of a fancy jewelry store, but we couldn't spend on such frivolous things. The cigar band would do for now.

With hands tightly intertwined and leaning on each other for strength, we found our way back to the Skirvin Hotel lobby to inquire about a phone we might use. The clerk kindly directed us to a pay phone.

"Hello, Mama?" The silence at the other end only made the crackling line seem louder. I wasn't sure if anyone had answered. "Hello. Is anyone there?"

"I'm here," came the terse reply.

"Mama, it's me, Maggie."

"I know who it is," she said. I could barely hear her. "Where are you, Margaret? Men have been here asking about you."

"I'm sorry. Is everyone all right? I know I've let you down, but I just had to leave. I couldn't live there any longer."

"You did wrong. You've brought shame to this family. Your father is a great man, a man of his word, and you've destroyed that. While you may not agree with the decisions he makes, it was the best thing for all of us. You should be grateful to your father."

I gulped back tears. A man of his word who gambled and drank away everything we had? What about me? What about the thing he did to me? No one would ever understand the horrors I had endured because of my father's decision and because of a mother who refused to choose her own child over a drunken husband.

"Tell the children hello for me, will you?" I felt suddenly nauseous. I could hear sobbing sounds and then realized it was me.

"Don't ever call here again," she said.

"I love you, Mama." I hung up before she could reply. It didn't matter what the truth might be, she would always see the world through my father's eyes. She would never cross him, not even for her own daughter. I said a silent prayer that the same betrayal wouldn't happen to my sisters and brothers. There was nothing I could do for them now. I was in the middle of saving myself.

Alex placed both hands on my shoulders. "Are you all right?" I couldn't move, frozen in shock. I had cried enough for one lifetime and I hated the dampness on my cheeks. I wiped my face with the hanky he took from his pocket.

"Nothing has changed," I told him. "Now it's your turn."

Alex slowly dialed the number and waited a few minutes until someone picked up.

"Hello. Mother?" His face brightened into a big smile. Alex and his mother were very close.

"What have you done?" Her shouts reached me from where I stood. I leaned in and Alex turned the phone towards my ear so that we could both hear. "How could you do that to my own brother? Your uncle? You have brought such disgrace to this family. What is wrong with you? If you turn your back on us and run off with that hussy, don't ever call here again. You were not raised to act this way. You're just dizzy over that dame. She means nothing."

"I love her, Mother." Alex's shoulders slumped, and he hung his head. His knuckles turned almost white as his grip on the phone tightened.

Her voice changed. Gentle and pleading, she tried to reason with her son. "Where are you, Alex? I need to know. Clarence wants to talk to you and sort this out. And there's been another man looking for you, too. He has a job for you. A Mr. Romo, or something like that. His first name was Joey. Oh, I remember, Russo. That was it. You drop that gold-digging Jane at the next corner and you come home right this instant. Do you hear me, Alexander?"

"I love you and father very much. Goodbye." Alex gently returned the phone to its cradle. His mother's angry voice screeched over the line until the final click. One tear escaped from his eye and left a trail on his cheek. He quickly swiped it away with a shirt sleeve.

"So much for calling our families. We can't rely on them for protection. My uncle and Joey Russo will bump us both off, if they find us. You know that, right?" I could see the muscles of his jaw flex as he clenched his teeth.

I shook my head in agreement. These were dangerous men. They would never forgive and forget. The ability to recognize the notion that two people are in love is something they would never comprehend. Giving us their blessing would be the last thing they'd ever do. "I understand. Let's see where this Route 66 that everybody is talking about will take us."

We returned to the front desk where Alex specifically asked for the way to Route 66 going north.

"You kids heading to Chicago?" the hotel clerk asked. "Here's something from us, on the house." He handed me a colorful metal tin. "Cookies and chocolate fudge for the road. Enjoy. You both have a wonderful trip and all the best in your new life together."

I smiled and mumbled a thank you. Alex didn't answer the clerk's question and let him assume our destination. After clarification of directions, he seemed to be in a rush to get to the car. I hurried to catch him.

"We may very well have to stay on the run. Are you willing to live like that, Maggie? Are you certain this is the kind of life that you want? I have nothing else to offer. This is it."

"We'll be too busy driving forward to look back." I smiled at him over the back of the car.

He walked around the vehicle and grabbed me in a tight, warm bear hug. We stood there for a few minutes, and then he opened the trunk for me. I packed my new things and shut the lid. His Ford coupe puttered to life.

It was just the two of us against the world.

**18**

---

Alex steered his Model A through the bustle of Oklahoma City and before long we pulled into a station. Ten cents a gallon later and a little more money gone from our stash, we found the right road. I felt at that moment that our new life together had officially begun.

On the edge of town we stopped at a little mom and pop market and bought fruit, a jar of water, hard cheese, and a loaf of yeast bread, fresh from the oven. We decided to stay to ourselves for most of the journey, avoiding people and trying not to attract attention. With provisions and a good wool blanket, we would sleep most nights in the car.

It was late afternoon and I had been Mrs. Alex Henderson for almost an entire day. We found the road sign for Route 66 that would take us from Oklahoma City to the coast. What an adventure, despite the potential danger of being found. A worry about traveling into Texas stayed in the back of my mind, but maybe they'd think we'd never be stupid enough to go back into the same state. Mr. Brown and Russo had unlimited resources and countless connections and manpower. They'd send men after us. Men who would ask questions. It wouldn't be hard to track us once they discovered the general direction.

Alex had brought his entire savings and we'd find work along the way. Despite the danger to our lives and the constant fear of being found, I couldn't help but smile as I looked up ahead at the open road. The future looked bright because we had each other. I grabbed Alex's hand.

This new Route 66 highway that would take us all the way to the California coast was narrow and just wide enough for one car. When we happened to meet another vehicle, Alex dropped off into the grassy shoulder. Everybody waved as they passed.

The part of Oklahoma we drove through was heavy with trees and underbrush. Small plots of plowed ground dotted the land-scape, interrupted by grassy patches of grazing cattle. We crept over narrow bridges that stretched across trickling streams. Alex slowed when he came to curves as the trees sometimes blocked the view of oncoming traffic.

We puttered through El Reno. With an extra can of gasoline, we didn't want to take the risk that somebody might notice us and remember.

The beautiful landscape and peaceful morning drive was inter-rupted by a prevailing sadness over the haunting conversations with our families. I couldn't get my mother's hateful voice out of my head. Alex didn't say a word for a long time. He stared straight ahead gripping the steering wheel until his knuckles turned white, his jaw clenched. Several times he would pull into the grass and glance over his shoulder, watching the road for several long minutes before continuing.

What should have been a loving, joyful drive was stressful and tense. I didn't want to die even though only a few days before I had prayed for death. An end to my existence was the only way I could think of to escape. Now I had someone who loved me. A future. Hope. I had to keep remembering that.

We stopped at a service station in the tiny town of Foss, Okla-homa for fuel.

At several points along the way the pavement ended and we

drove on gravel. The skies had turned overcast and a slight chill swept through the car. I pulled my sweater closer around my middle.

"Let's stop and eat a bite before it rains," he said.

Thankfully, he pulled off of the road and stopped near a large clump of trees. I appreciated the break and the privacy. Alex laughed when I jumped out of the car before it had even stopped rolling and ran behind a scraggly bush.

In between bites of fudge, I enjoyed even sweeter, gentle kisses. The heat of his presence took the chill and worry away. We sat as close as we could get on one end of the blanket, with the other end pulled up over our shoulders. Alex leaned in for one long, deep kiss and as we leaned back on the grass, I sighed.

Suddenly, Alex sat bolt upright. "We can't finish this. We have to keep moving."

He was right.

Reminders of the stock market crash in 1929 and the hardships that followed were visible all along the route. Curious children, running barefoot in baggy overalls, glanced in our direction as we drove past. Others seemed not to notice, refusing to interrupt their game of kickball. Groups of men rested in dusty suits in front of closed businesses, staring at us with haunted eyes and deep frowns. What dutiful housewives called laundry, looked more like a collection of rags flapping from their clotheslines. It seemed such a contrast to the people of wealth and self-importance who danced the night away in the opulent Casino ballroom. Only a few days ago, I had worn a fancy dress and tasted champagne for the first time. Alex had not been mine then.

Not all was destitute along the route. Billboards presented a colorful choice of thriving businesses. At every stop we discovered brochures and picture postcards advertising roadside attractions, food specials, modern cabins, and auto courts. I became fascinated with the thought of this winding and narrow Route 66 becoming a part of our life.

By evening, we reached Elk City, an old frontier town, or so Alex told me. He loved history, and after the break he was in a better mood and began talking about the area. Elk City was a famous stop on the cattle trail that went from Texas to Dodge City, Kansas.

Alex wasn't driving in such a frenzy as he had the night of our escape out of Fort Worth. I enjoyed the sights of the towns we drove through. When we headed out of Elk City, we faced the last light of a burning horizon. The sun flashed colors of bright orange, with the lower parts of the clouds burning a pale pink and the tops a dark grey. After living in the city all my life, I had never seen anything like that sky. It took my breath away, stretching on forever, giving me a sense of well-being. I said a prayer of thanks. As we got closer and closer to the Texas border, the sun disappeared, and the sky turned to a pale golden light.

The clouds directly overhead were overcast and when the last rays of light snuffed out, it turned suddenly dark. The car lights burned a dim pathway on the lonely road.

Blending in with the hustle and bustle of the city had been easy, but out here in the open Alex tensed again. We seemed more vulnerable. He kept glancing over his shoulder. If the beam of lights from another car cast shadows, he would suddenly swerve a hard right or left into the nearest clump of cover, kill the motor, and wait for the other vehicle to pass.

His high level of stress caused me worry. What if we were caught? What would they do to us? I didn't dare voice my concerns out loud, but the tension was there, hanging in the back of my mind.

I rested my hand on his thigh, and even with that comforting gesture, he never turned to look at me. His eyes stayed fixed on the road ahead.

"Keep a look out behind us," he said. "Let me know if you see any car lights."

I turned in my seat and rested my arm on the back until Alex suggested we stop for the night. I gratefully agreed, looking forward to some rest.

He pulled a tin lantern from the trunk. We snacked on the bread and cookies, shared a tin cup of water, and then snuggled under the wool blanket. Alex put a tightly wound wad of his clothes behind his back on the passenger side and stretched his legs across the edge of the seat. He had to open the driver's side door to make room for his feet. I leaned against his chest with my legs resting on top of his, and closed my eyes, perfectly content to feel his warmth and the steady beat of his heart against my cheek.

"Are you comfortable?" I asked.

"I won't sleep much anyway," he said. "Close your eyes. I'll keep watch." He planted a soft kiss on the top of my head.

The heart wants what the heart wants, and sometimes there's no convincing it otherwise. I couldn't change fate or the circumstances that had set us on this path. I couldn't undo meeting Alex, change the fact that he was Mr. Brown's nephew, or ignore the way I felt about him. In a way, I guess I should be thankful to my father. Without his betrayal, I would have never found this love and a new life.

**19**

———————

It had been a long day and I slept like a rock in the car even though I had spent the night sitting upright in the front seat of Alex's Model A. My legs and back were stiff and one arm was numb and tingly.

I woke to the loud chirping of birds and a whispered "shush" from my new husband. I looked in the direction of his finger which pointed towards the trees. Raising up in the seat to look out the open door, a skunk moseyed along in our direction. He paused to nose something on the ground, a bug perhaps. He walked out of sight to the right, and then appeared in my line of vision before walking to the left. I breathed a sigh of relief, thinking he'd gone on his merry way.

Suddenly, the top of his head appeared on the car's running board and curious eyes came into view as he looked in the car. I gasped, and Alex clamped a hand over my mouth before I could let out the scream that was caught in my throat.

I sat motionless, trying not to breathe. The skunk's little nose wiggled as he sniffed the air. After several seconds, his face disappeared from sight. We glanced out the window behind us where the skunk had walked under the car coming out the other side, seeming to be more interested in the bushes beyond.

When our curious visitor was well out of sight, we doubled over in laughter.

THE CLOUDS BROKE and the sun shone brightly as we pulled onto the narrow gravel roadway called Route 66. As we left Oklahoma for Texas, the road became more dirt or gravel and less patches of pavement. We had to stop several times and open and close gates, as the road took us through ranch land dotted with cattle. The landscape changed from wooded areas and trickling streams to rolling hills of grass. The colors became muted shades of browns and tans as the last green of summer had faded into fall. Route 66 stretched like a crooked ribbon before us, disappearing into shallow valleys only to reappear in the distance trailing over the next hill.

It hadnt rained where we had been stopped for the night, but very soon the road turned to mud. Puddles dotted the road in places. Alex steered onto the shoulder and around the muddy pools. He continuously looked at the road behind us. I could tell he was on edge. I began to relax and to enjoy the leisurely drive. It seemed as though we were the only two people in the world.

The scent of rain hung heavy in the air. I never realized how noisy the peaceful countryside could be. In between the car's puttering, I could hear birds chirping from all directions. Alex told me they were meadowlarks. A hawk circled overhead with wings outstretched, riding the wind as he searched for breakfast. On occasion our motor stirred a covey of quail from a clump of sage and yucca. Their short legs moved in a blur as they scurried to find new cover.

Before we topped the next hill, shouts drifted clear on the morning air. "Get on up now!"

Our car rolled over the crest. At the base of the small hill, the road was blocked by a mule team pulling a flatbed wagon. Hooked to that was a pickup truck overloaded with a family and their possessions. The pickup was leaning to one side, wheels hanging off the road, stuck all the way up to the middle of the hubs in a thick, soupy, mud hole.

"Maude. Mable. Let's go!" the farmer shouted again. He stood in the center of the wagon bed holding the driving lines. Next to the roadway, a mother and five children stood in a clump. The woman held a baby on one hip and the children stared in wide-eyed excitement. Three men pushed the truck from behind. Just as we pulled to a stop, the pickup popped out of brown muck and rolled onto the hard packed dirt. The farmer shouted, "Whoa!"

The kids came alive with cheers and claps and we couldn't help but join them. When they asked our names, we didn't answer. We smiled and replied with, "Hello. Safe journey to you and your family."

We watched the kids climb to the top of their loaded vehicle, and we all waved at each other as they rumbled up and out of sight over the next hill. The farmer steered his team in the same direction.

"I don't like being in the open like this," said Alex. His face was covered with whiskers and his eyes were strained and haggard from lack of sleep.

"Let's just keep going until the next town. Maybe we can blend in with the crowd and you can get some rest," I said.

We pulled into the bustling little town of Shamrock and noticed the tower of a Conoco station. After we had filled the tank, Alex pulled out and turned down a side street parking several blocks away.

"Let's go back to the U-Drop Inn and eat at their diner," he said.

The waitress told us the café was new, just opening last year on April 1. Picture windows faced the street side giving us a clear view of the cars and people beyond. Sitting close together in a booth with our backs to the wall, we whispered about the miles ahead over the daily special—fried chicken, mashed potatoes with extra gravy, green beans, and coffee. I wiped a few tears from my cheek. My mother had cooked the best fried chicken and with every bite I grew more and more homesick. The echoes of her cruel words were still fresh on my heart.

"You two save any room for dessert?" the waitress asked cheerily. Without a response from us, she recited the dessert menu.

"Two peach cobblers, please," Alex answered. "And more coffee when you get a chance."

"Sure thing," She said. "Are you two newly married? It's none of my business, but you both have that starry-eyed look and you've held hands during the entire meal."

I felt my cheeks grow warm with embarrassment. Were we that obvious? So much for blending in and passing through town unnoticed.

A kindly gentleman who sat facing us in the next booth nodded, and then asked, "Where you two kids headed?"

Alex had warned me to be careful about saying too much to anyone. If Mr. Brown was on our trail, he'd certainly question the waitresses. Any specifics we might say could be overheard and repeated.

"Visiting family." Alex smiled broadly and squeezed my hand under the table.

"You two are newlyweds, aren't you?" the man said with a chuckle.

Alex's smile froze as I looked down at my plate. "Yes sir, we are," he said.

"Congratulations!" the waitress called out. She brought over the coffee pot for refills and set down two bowls of steaming cobbler. "Whipped cream is on the house."

I whispered a prayer under my breath, "Please God, don't let them talk to us. No questions. Just let us eat and get out of here." My prayers went unheeded.

"Say, you kids wouldn't be looking for a new place, would

you? My uncle has twenty-two acres for sale down south of Fort Worth. I know it's a long ways from here, but it would make a hell of a new home for some young couple. Oh, excuse my language, ma'am," he said touching an imaginary hat with his fingers as he looked in my direction. "Kickapoo Creek runs right through the land, and it's got tall pecan trees. Loads of squirrel if you have a mind to fry'em up. They're great with gravy and toast. Now it's kind of off the beaten path. I'd have to give you directions, because otherwise you'd never be able to find it."

"Sounds lovely," I said.

"We're heading on to Oklahoma City." Alex pointed south.

The old man laughed. "No, son. That's the wrong direction. You need to go back east if you're headed to Oklahoma. Just follow Route 66. You can't miss it."

Smiling, I scooped a hefty bite of crust and peaches. The aroma was heavenly. As I brought the spoon to my mouth I glanced over the head of the friendly man and looked out the window to the street beyond.

Suddenly, every part of me turned cold and still as I watched a familiar Cadillac ease past the windows.

**20**

———————

I couldn't move. I stared, transfixed at a car that looked just like Mr. Brown's Cadillac. It came to a stop on the street in front of the U-Drop Inn. The words of warning hung in my dry throat like a wad of cotton. Surely there must be hundreds of Cadillacs like that one. What are the odds it's his?

Alex was digging in to his cobbler, making fast work of emptying the bowl. He scraped the last bit of dessert, his spoon clinking on the sides. He smacked his lips and glanced in my direction. "If you're not going to eat that, can I have it?" he asked. "What's wrong? You sure are pale. Do you feel all right?"

"Are you okay, ma'am? You look like you've seen a ghost." The old man in the next booth watched us with a curious gaze.

Alex followed my stare to the street. "Leave," he said. "Out the back."

"What about you?" I asked.

"Go," was his answer. His eyes had turned hard and his jaw clenched. He stood and dropped a few bills on the table. "How much do I owe you, ma'am?"

With a trembling hand I laid my spoon and uneaten bite of

cobbler on top of the bowl and scooted out of the booth. I was not going back with Mr. Brown.

"Something wrong with your cobbler, honey? Are you feeling all right? You didn't eat a bite," the waitress asked as she took the bills from Alex. "I'll be right back with your change."

"No," he said. His reply came short and terse. "Just keep it."

I walked around the counter and went straight through the swinging door into the kitchen. The heat and smells of grease met me, but I quickly scanned the room and focused on the back entrance.

In a blind horror I ran. Heading straight out the back of the café, I ran through the streets of the town, turning one way and then another at the next intersection. My breath grew hard and labored in my chest. Even with aching sides, I kept running.

I crossed through backyards, hurrying across the next street to go in between houses. Housewives sitting on their porches, and kids playing in their yards stared as I ran past, but I didn't care. I ran until the orderly streets turned to land stretching flat and empty before me.

Slowing to a stumbling walk and drawing sharp gasps of air into my lungs, I glanced around for cover. There had to be some place to hide. I would never return to the life I had before.

Across a flat piece of plowed ground, a small shed stood only a few yards away. Without giving it a second thought, I ran towards the shelter. The ground was uneven, and I tripped several times falling to my knees on the dry, clodded dirt.

The inside of the shed was dark, musty, and smelled of moldy hay and engine grease. Hoes, wrenches, saws, and a variety of other tools hung from nails along the wall. Against the back were sacks of chicken feed. I dropped on the dirt-packed floor, leaving the door open just a crack for a clear view of town.

A sob escaped my lips when I thought of Alex. Was he alive? I felt sure that he was, otherwise I was certain that my heart would stop at the moment his did. Maybe that had been a car that just looked like Mr. Brown's. Maybe it wasn't Mr. Brown after all. Maybe I had a moment of hysteria for no reason and Alex had misjudged the situation.

I pulled my knees against my chest and wrapped my arms tightly around my legs. Concentrating on taking slow, even breaths to calm my racing heart, the ache in my side soon went away. I remained in the silent darkness for what seemed like forever, too scared to leave my hiding place.

The sound of footsteps crunching on plowed ground made my heart skip, then nearly stop. I clamped my hand over my trembling mouth to stifle the scream that almost exploded out of me.

Slowly the shed door squeaked open and the voice of a child broke the silence. "Pa! Pa, come quick. There's a girl in our shed."

The curious eyes of a young boy with tousled blonde hair and stained overalls that came to the middle of his shins gave me the once over. He stood motionless on dirty bare feet that seemed too large to fit the size of the rest of him.

I squinted at the light when an older man opened the door wider. "Are you hurt, ma'am?" he asked. He leaned down and with a firm grasp of my arm, helped me to my feet. I wasn't sure what to say or how to explain.

"I'm not going back." The words came out before I could stop them. I glanced around him, half expecting to see the familiar Cadillac parked on the edge of town. The dirt streets beyond the barbed wire fence was empty.

"Not going back to where? Are you lost?" he looked at me with concern in his eyes while his son peeped around his father's leg with wide-eyed curiosity.

"My husband," I said.

"Did your husband hurt you? Let's get you to my house. My wife will get you cleaned up and then you can tell us how we can help you." He put his hand on my arm again, but I jerked away. "It's okay. I'm not going to hurt you," he said tenderly.

I couldn't stay in his shed forever. There wasn't anything else to do but follow him back across his field towards a small house surrounded by trees. He pointed to a chair on the wide front porch and disappeared inside. The little boy perched on the railing directly in front of me, his eyes non-blinking and curious.

"Why is your dress dirty?" he asked.

"I fell several times."

"Why did you fall?"

"The ground is uneven, and I was running."

"Why were you running?"

"I was scared I guess."

"Why were you scared?"

"I'm hiding from someone."

"Is he a bad person? Is that why you're hidin'?"

"Yes, he is bad. Very bad." Despite my fear, I had to smile at my young friend. He grinned back. Even if Mr. Brown found me and took me back, I'd just run away again as soon as I got the opportunity.

"Josiah Lee Bennett. Stop bothering the nice lady." The screen door slammed behind a woman wearing a bright pink apron and holding a mason jar of water. "Let's have a look at you, Miss. I brought you a drink in case you're thirsty."

I downed the cool liquid in several long gulps. I was thirsty and hadn't realized it. "Thank you kindly, ma'am."

"Call me Suzanne. Now how long have you been hiding in my husband's shed?"

The nice farmer stepped onto the porch and stood behind his wife. I had no idea what to say or how to explain. They stared at me with concern and I blankly stared back.

The Bennett family stood around me in a protective circle of concern. They didn't ask questions and I didn't offer any information. I had to do something. I couldn't sit on their front porch forever.

Mrs. Bennett finally broke the silence. "Are you hungry? Come inside and let's get some of that dirt and mud cleaned off of you." She placed a hand on my shoulder. "I have a dress you can borrow. I'm sure it will fit. It was my Sunday best before I had Josiah. I used to be as big around as a pencil then." She giggled.

I stood, trying to decide what to do when the familiar *chug-chug, putt-putt* of a Model A broke the silence.

"That's my husband!" I leaped off their porch and ran into the street waving my arms. Alex pulled to a stop in front of me. He jumped from the car and we stood in the middle of the street hugging, like we'd not seen each other in a month of Sundays.

Alex kissed my face. "I am so stupid. Will you ever forgive me?"

"Forgive you for what? What happened? Was that Mr. Brown's car?" I bombarded him with questions.

"It was Mr. Brown. Of course my mother knew I'd take you to

the Skirvin for our wedding night. She knows how much I love that place. That's how they found us." He hugged me tighter. "Can you ever forgive me?"

"Of course, I forgive you. How did you get away?"

Alex took a deep, shaky breath. "I recognized one of his goons as he stepped into the U-Drop Inn. He was packing heat, and he wasn't trying to hide it either. I didn't have time to follow you out the back, so I joined that nice gentleman. From the pole at the end of the booth, I grabbed his jacket and pulled his hat low over my face. I focused on eating your cobbler and kept my head down."

My heart raced at how close we came to being discovered.

"Brown's man asked our waitress if there'd been any young folks in, looking like newlyweds. Any young couple mentioning Oklahoma City or the Skirvin Hotel. He was arrogant. Rude. And then he ordered her to wrap him four pieces of pie, and 'Make it quick, Doll,' he says. She wasn't impressed, and she didn't give us up. I could see Mr. Brown waiting in the car, but his man never recognized me when he cased the joint. I stayed in that booth until he left, then I hurried out the back to find you. I am so thankful you're all right."

We hugged again. "I am so thankful you're all right, Alex. I've never been more frightened in all my life."

"I've been driving around for several hours. I know you were scared. I'll never forget that look on your face. How can I put you through this again?"

"What are you talking about?"

"We're not running anymore. I know now that this is the only kind of life we'll have. Always running. Always looking over our shoulders. I can't expect you to do that for me and it's no way to raise our children. I should have never asked you to come with me."

"You didn't kidnap me." I placed my hands on his cheeks. "I made that decision on my own, Alex."

"I have a plan. We have to find a place to hide out. Disappear for a while."

Mr. Bennett cleared his throat. "Is this the man that you're runnin' from?"

I glanced over to see the family standing in the road next to us. "No sir. This man hasn't hurt me. This is my husband."

As Alex's words echoed in my head a rage built up inside of me so great I can't explain where it came from. I faced Alex and poked his chest as hard as I could.

"You have a plan? Just what is this big plan of yours that includes me? You are not going to decide for me. I took a chance on you. We are in this together, whatever this life brings us."

My sides heaved. The worst part was the ache in my heart. My insides were torn apart and my soul was broken into a million pieces. Once again, the decision had been made for me. Why can't someone ask me what I want?

"There'll be no argument about this, Maggie. I've made my mind up." Alex glared at me, his jaw clenched and his fists balled tight at his sides. "Running across the country for the rest of our born days is not the kind of life I want for you. You deserve better."

"I don't want better, you idiot! I want you."

We stood in the street glaring at each other. I spun around and got into his car, slamming the door behind me.

With tears streaming down my face I shook my head, my voice calm and low. He's not the only one who had made up their mind. "We are in this together. You are certainly welcome to tell me your plan, and then I will let you know if I approve."

"Sounds like she's made her mind up," said Mr. Bennett.

Alex cut him a stern glare before opening the car door. He tugged on my arm.

"How about some coffee and cake? I just took a spice cake from the oven. Let's help your wife get that mud off her, and then we can all calm down. Doesn't that sound nice?" Mrs. Bennett wrung her hands and stepped closer to Alex.

"It sounds lovely, Mrs. Bennett. Thank you." I stood the car door open and shoved Alex out of my way. "My name is Maggie by the way."

I followed her into the house and there was nothing else for the men to do but follow us inside.

**22**

Feeling refreshed and wearing a clean dress, I joined Alex and Mr. Bennett at the kitchen table. A hefty piece of cake covered most of the dainty china. The plate was bordered with dark orange and pale coral colored scroll work. Clumps of brightly colored flowers circled the rim. I closed my eyes and focused on every moist and delicious bite. One day I'd be in my own kitchen serving cake and coffee on my very own china to our guests.

I drained the last bit of my coffee and stood. "My husband and I really appreciate your hospitality and thank you for the dress. You are a precious family. I have to go now." I gave Mrs. Bennett a hug.

Alex looked at me with surprise. He'd never seen the take charge side of me, and neither had I. It felt good. He stuttered a thank you, shook hands with Mr. Bennett, looked confused but followed me out to the car.

"Where are you going?" he asked.

"Away from you," I said.

From the road, I turned to wave at the Bennett family who stood on their front porch. Walking around the car, I kept my eyes on the street that stretched out in front of me. I didn't need anybody and I wasn't going back to Mr. Brown. I'd find work somewhere, and then I'd make my own life's decisions.

"Get in the car, Maggie." The car rolled slowly next to me.

"No." I kept walking at a fast pace, staring straight ahead. I'd walk this whole darned Route 66 before anybody would make me bend to their will again.

"You can't run off on your own like this." He goosed the car and stopped a few feet ahead, leaning out of the window to look back at me.

"You stop making decisions for me." The gravel crunched under my shoes. My mother's words, which I'd heard all my life, echoed in my head with each step. *Do as you're told, Maggie. Don't argue with your father. Do. As. You're. Told.*

"Will you get in the car and we'll talk about it."

I stopped in the middle of the road and spun around to look at him. "By talking about it, do you mean you talk and I agree? Not interested."

"Get in the car!" Alex yelled. I looked at his red face and white knuckles clenching the steering wheel.

"Don't you ever use that tone with me. I have a father already. I don't need another."

Alex jumped from the car and blocked my way. "Maggie, please. I can't go on without you. Please forgive me. Please get in the car."

He did use please three times, and he wasn't yelling anymore, but it was those eyes that finally did me in. So full of love and anguish and guilt.

I twirled around, hopped into the car, and turned in my seat to face him. "I chose you, Alex. I'll run wherever you say, even if it's for the rest of our lives. Even if it's all the way to the Pacific Ocean on this highway as long as we decide together."

Alex leaned closer and kissed my nose. "Did you know that you can be mean? I never imagined that my sweet, soft-spoken Maggie had such a stubborn streak."

I giggled.

"I know when I've been defeated," Alex said. "You win. We decide together. I love you more than life itself, Maggie Henderson."

"I love you too, Alex Henderson. Are we going to sit here all day? Get this tin can moving and tell me your plan."

"There is something I want to talk to you about. While I sat in the booth with the nice man, Addison was his name, he told me more about that place his uncle has for sale. It sounds perfect for us. I'll circle around past it once I'm certain we're not being followed."

I cleared my throat and glared at my husband.

"Uhmmm, that is if you agree and would like to see it, sweetheart. We could have a looksee at that place. It sits on Kickapoo Creek in central Texas."

While Alex chattered on, I smiled and stared at the houses lined up on this quiet street. One day I'd have a house like that, I thought. So it wouldn't be our life right away, but I felt strong, empowered. We couldn't stay on the run forever. But we had each other. And that's all that mattered.

**1**

———————

The fumes from the Yellow Coach Greyhound parked in front of the Tower Station and U-drop Inn cafe swirled around the vehicle. The odor of diesel fuel was familiar to him on the farm but it never lingered very long in the swift West Texas wind.

Standing on the sidewalk between the cafe and the open door of the bus, Brennon O'Neill held his new bride Patricia as if it would be the last time. Pulling her close, he inhaled deeply, drawing in the sweet aroma of cinnamon, apples, and the hint of rose perfume that always hid in Patricia's thick auburn hair. He knew the one thing that the stiff breeze could never blow away was the scent of her.

"I'll be home soon," Brennon said.

"But what if..." Patricia started when he softly placed his fingers on her lips to stop her from speaking the words that neither of them wanted to consider.

"Don't say it. You'll curse the luck of the Irish. I'll be okay, honey," he assured as they slowly swayed to the silent music of their hearts in one last dance.

The Japanese had bombed Pearl Harbor on December 7th of `41, and three days later Germany and Italy had also made a declaration of war against America. The United States had been drawn into the conflict along with its allies to fight against the Axis nations. The Texas Panhandle had hardly thawed from winter's deep freeze in the early spring of '42 when the emotion of the nation had grown both red hot with excitement, and ice cold with fear. Excitement, because the American spirit roared, "we're going to make them pay!" And fear, because every mother's son and every young bride's husband was drafted into the military to go fight the enemy.

Brennon had been called up by the local draft board and sent to train in the Thirty-sixth infantry, *Arrowhead* Division of the Army. After basic training, he had spent many long hard months training in maneuvers in the Carolina's and then Camp Edwards where his division staged in Massachusetts. While on the East coast, the army practiced their invasions of foreign countries on the beaches of Martha's Vineyard, as they prepared for service in the Mediterranean Theater of Operations.

Brennon took a few days leave to come home and marry his childhood sweetheart; if he didn't now, he might not ever get the chance. The reality that he was going overseas to the front lines steadily filled his mind making it hard to think about leaving.

"I promise. Nothing can keep me away from you." Brennon said pulling Patricia closer.

Brennon O'Neill was one of three brothers, and each of them was as protective of their two younger sisters as the others. From his earliest memory, his father had raised him to work hard plowing the fields, planting cotton, and hoeing weeds out of the rows to keep them from taking over the crop. Of all the chores he did while working for his father, he dreaded picking the locks of cotton the most when the harvest was ready. Before he could get to the end of the first row, it never failed that the dried burrs always cut his fingers and made them bleed.

His father, William, owned a section of land west of Shamrock and had recently deeded a piece of the back forty to Brennon and his new bride as a wedding gift, a place for them to build a house together and call it their own.

"As soon as we whip the Axis, I'm coming home to build you the finest house in the county," Brennon said, "and it will have everything exactly like you want it,"

Patricia Arrington, now the new Mrs. O'Neill, was eighteen and the oldest of four girls. Her mother, Mary, was the schoolteacher at the rural school. After her father Walter died, Patricia was forced to grow up quickly to help raise her sisters Linda, Carol, and Sandra.

At the tender age of ten, Patricia had been the first to find her father lying dead in the corral when had not come home for supper. The Wheeler County sheriff had determined that the horse spooked at something, most likely a rattle snake according to the trail it left behind, and bucked him off into the rail of the fence.

Losing her father so young had made her strong and independent, but Brennon knew it would kill her if he went to war only to die on the battlefield. But he had to go. It was his duty.

Brennon looked down into Patricia's eyes flooded with tears. She returned the glance but couldn't hold them back as they ran down her cheeks. "I don't want to be a widow after only being married two weeks. Promise me you'll come home," she sobbed.

"I promise," Brennon said kissing her forehead tenderly.

As he cuddled her against his chest and closed his eyes, his mind erupted into chaos. Anger washed over his thoughts. He was angry that another nation had attacked America his homeland, and in turn threatened his way of life. He was mad that he had to leave his farm and couldn't plant his crops or build his house. He was irate that today, he had to leave his wife, the love of his life.

A surge of fear suddenly washed over the anger. Brennon had heard the stories from the old-timer's who fought in the first Great War in Europe, the war that was supposed to end all wars. They would often gather at the U-Drop Inn for coffee and talk about watching their buddies die in front of them. Some told of the hand-to-hand combat in the forest of Argonne, where over twenty-six thousand American men died fighting the Germans. They wrinkled their nose as they recalled the stench of warfare, and how they fought, lived, and slept in the same trench for days on end, praying that it wouldn't be their final resting place. And many of the men shed tears every time they spoke of the mountainous piles of bodies of the men, women, and children out in the country villages.

*If I do what I've been trained to do in Basic and all the other training they've put me through, I'll make it out alive. I'm a fighting machine. I can fight, and I can shoot. I've hunted everything in this part of the country, from prairie dogs to deer. I'll be ok.*

In the back of his mind, what Brennon feared the most, was dying and never seeing Patricia again.

*Lord, please let me come home.*

Frustration divided his thoughts and invaded his mind. He could deal with his anger and choke down his fear, but he didn't know how to comfort Patricia. Usually, he could think things through, make a plan, and then place them in some logical order to find a solution, but today he was lost for the answer.

"All aboard, Let's load up!" the bus driver yelled.

Brennon felt Patricia's arms tighten, not wanting to let him leave. "I don't want you to go." She sobbed.

"I know. And there's no place I'd rather be than right here with you, but I have to go." He said taking his red paisley bandana and dabbing her tears.

A loud, high-pitched whistle pierced the air, "FWEEEEET!" and sounded again with two more short bursts before stopping. "Now that I have your attention lovebirds, it's time to load up!" the driver yelled a final time.

He could feel his chest tighten as if his heart would burst through his ribs. His stomach twisted in knots. His throat closed making it hard to breathe. He swallowed trying to clear the lump and speak, "I've got to go. I love you."

He pulled from her reluctant grasp and picked up his suitcase. Turning back to look at her, he saw the anguish on her face and the tears streaming down her cheeks. He kissed her.

He kissed her like he did the first time, and he kissed her again as if it would be his last.

Brennon climbed into the bus and found a seat. Pressing the latches of the window, he let down the glass and stuck his head out. "I love you, and I'll hurry home. I Promise."

The sunlight glinted from the tears in Patricia's eyes, "I love you more, and I'll be waiting right here when you get back."

**2**

————————

Patricia stayed with her mother while Brennon was off serving the country. As she continued with her daily chores, she often thought how her wedding day and the honeymoon had felt like a dream. You lay your head on the pillow and fall asleep, and in the middle of the night your mind travels to far away places, you see magical worlds fulfilling your every wish, and when you wake up, everything's the same. She still lived in the same house where she grew up and slept in the same bed. She loved her mother and sisters dearly, but she was a married woman now and wanted her own house, her own home, and her own family.

Several weeks had passed when a letter arrived addressed to Mrs. Brennon O'Neill. In the upper left-hand corner of the envelope, it listed the sender as PFC, B. O'Neill, Rabat, Africa.

She paused at the abbreviation PFC, where it usually listed PVT, but when she scanned over the rest of the sender's name, she instantly knew who had sent the post. With her letter opener in hand, she carefully knifed open the seal and unfolded the letter. As she began to read, the world around her faded away.

APRIL 27, 1943

*Dearest Patricia, I miss you terribly. I hope you are doing okay and everyone is well back home. As you may have noticed on the envelope, I ranked to Private First Class, it's only a small increase in pay, but any raise is better than none at all. Right?*

*I would have written sooner but we started training as soon as we arrived in Africa, and it's been none stop until now. I think we've invaded every empty beach available. I thought West Texas had a lot of sand, Ha!*

*The Thirty-sixth was ordered to train several small cadres of troops to send to different divisions in other places, and some of them have already shipped out and are seeing combat in the Pacific.*

*We did finally receive our new orders, and we are scheduled to ship out on our first real mission soon. We are training to make a landing somewhere. I don't know where yet, they're keeping it secret until we get there. They said any information is "classified until further notice."*

*In some ways I'm glad, we finally get to do something other than train all the time. With the Thirty-sixth in the fight, I'm sure this war will be over a lot sooner. Some of the guys are starting to believe that the 'T' on our arrowhead patch stands for "Trainer" instead of "Texas."*

*All joking aside, there's a part of me that's scared. I know I've been well trained for combat, and I've taught other men to fight, but It's like there's a bad omen hovering over my head.*

*The one thing I honestly wish for is that I could see you one more time before we go. I have your picture, and I carry it in my shirt pocket all the time. I'm sure it will protect my heart from any stray German bullets.*

*This war will be over soon, and I'll be home with you.*
*All my love,*
*Brennon*

. . .

PATRICIA READ the letter four times before slowly folding it, careful not to make any new creases and slid it back into the envelope. Walking into her bedroom, she picked up a colorful cigar box that sat on her bureau. All traces of the White Owl perched on a ten-cent cigar hid under glue and scrap pieces of red, white and blue plaid percale from a dress that she had sewn to wear on the fourth of July. Pulling on the small bow attached to the lid, that she had made from a small piece of red ribbon she opened the box.

Lifting the large bundle of letters from Brennon she kept cradled inside, she shuffled through each envelope looking at them one-by-one and smiled when they addressed her as Mrs. Brennon O'Neill. They taunted her to reread each one of them. She held them close to her nose inhaling the odor of ink and paper, trying desperately to capture Brennon's scent. When she exhaled, she placed the letters back into the box and added the newest to the top of the stack before closing the lid.

And she waited.

3

After three weeks of grueling war games in the hot North African desert, Brennon was dog-tired. In fact, the whole division was exhausted. Thinking back over the last year, he had been training since the first day the draft board shipped him out of Shamrock, Texas.

For what now seemed like an eternity, he had learned the army way of doing things. The everyday things such as making his bunk, wearing the uniform, when to eat and how long to sleep, became the new way of life.

He loved to go hunting back home, so the rifle training with the M1 Garand came naturally to him, and he especially enjoyed the marksmanship competitions. From the very beginning of his training, the Army taught the soldiers hand-to-hand combat techniques; they studied the enemy's battle strategies, and every day since his trip home to marry Patricia the Thirty-sixth infantry division had worked even harder.

Logically he understood the reason why, and it made sense. A well-trained soldier was less likely to die on the battlefield or make a mistake that would get his brother fighting beside him killed. Mentally, he was anxious about dodging real bullets, and how it would feel to cause another human die. He wondered if it would be like watching a deer or a hog die? But physically, Brennon was mostly tired.

His desire to go home grew stronger every day. He gave every bit of his strength to the mission in front of him and pushed forward through the stress knowing it was the only way he could go home. He endured the constant running, the overbearing heat of the desert, the sand getting in places where grit shouldn't be, and eating the same bland military rations every day. Every evening he dug a fresh foxhole to cradle him while he slept. And every night when he closed his eyes, he dreamed the same dream. In his nightmare, he would dig his own shallow grave in a foreign land and settle into the cool sand to sleep. And one-by-one, the other men would shovel the sand over his body while he slept and forget where they buried him. And he would be alone forever.

As the sun began to set, the Sergeant shouted "Mail call."

Brennon prayed that he would get a Victory Mail from Patricia, she always did write more letters than he wrote to her. Listening, he heard his name "O'Neill!"

Holding the red, white and blue-bordered envelope with a typed address, he glanced at the top left corner and saw the name he longed for, Patricia O'Neill. Sliding his finger through the seal, he ripped the envelope open and began to read.

<hr>

*MAY 15, 1943*

*My dearest Brennon,*

*I pray you are doing well, considering all the heat and sand. It has been sweltering here at home too. However, this weekend we were blessed with two and eight-tenths inches of rain, and all of that in the last three days. That makes a total of three and four-tenths inches of rain this year, finally breaking our terrible drought. I'm afraid it may get hot again and bring another dry spell.*

*Mr. J.O Stibling, the Wheeler County salvage committee chairman, and mayor Walker made an appeal to the whole community on Monday. They asked everyone to bring in all the empty tin cans and scraps they could find to the designated a collection site at the edge of town. They announced that the latest information from the War Production Board was that the copper and tin situation in the United States has become very critical. So Mother, Carol and I, gathered up as much as we could find and took it all to town on Saturday.*

*We decided to do our shopping while we were there and bought sugar, flour, lard and some cheese. With all the canning we have in the cellar, we should have plenty to last a while. The coffee though, the Government dropped the ration to only one pound, and they expect us to make it last five weeks, unbelievable! If we get in a tight, we can add some Chicory or make watered down "Roosevelt coffee," to stretch it out. Well, I guess we do need to make some sacrifices to keep our fighting men awake.*

*We saved half of our stamps; we can use them, as we need them. Some families are spending them all at once; I hope they get through the month. The Office of Price Administration should send our next red and blue food coupons on the first of the month.*

*The Shamrock Texan Newspaper reported that the Slaughter's son is "Somewhere in Africa" and Mrs. Elnora Pitcock's son, A.T. Pitcock, ranked to Private First Class in North Africa. I know there are a lot of men there with your division, but maybe if you run across one of them, it might feel like a connection to home.*

*Enough rambling, I've saved the best news for last, so sit down. You're going to be a Father! Yes, it's true. How I wish you were here so I could tell you in person. Now all I need is for this war to be over, and you to come home to your family.*

*Love you with all of my heart, waiting.*
*Patricia*

.   .   .

*"YEEE HAWW!"* Brennon shouted as he jumped to his feet and danced a jig of excitement. All the men standing around at mail call stared at Brennon as if a scorpion or a snake had bitten him. Holding the letter from Patricia at arm's length and showing it to all the soldiers he shouted, "Look, I'm going to be a DAD!"

"Congrats." The sergeant shouted. Another G.I. chuckled and blew the smoke he had inhaled from the cigarette perched between lips into the air. "I knew you had it in ya."

"Sarge," Brennon shouted, "we need to get this war over with, so I can go home and see my kid."

The Sergeant looked at Brennon and shook his head, "It'll be a while before you can see the kid, the bun's gotta' cook in the oven a little longer."

The men laughed, and each one turned to reading their own V-mail as Brennon walk back to his foxhole, but the smile on his face grew wider with each step as he stared at Patricia's words, *"You're going to be a Father."*

**4**

———

The porch swing, swayed gently in the evening breeze as Patricia saw the sun lay low in the west. She watched the blades of the windmill spin in the wind, silhouetted against the dusky deep blue sky. Clouds hovering above the horizon were washed in violet, red and glowing orange colors trying to cover the yellow sun before it sank behind the horizon.

"Patricia, Patricia!" yelled Sandra, "Look, a letter from Brennon," she gasped. Patricia's youngest sister ran from the mailbox near the road, across the yard and toward the porch waving an envelope in the air. Sandra made it her duty to check the mail every day to see if Brennon had written Patricia, she believed that writing "love letters" was "so romantic."

The V-mail letters were easy to spot. They all looked the same. A white envelope bordered by red, white and blue stripes with the addresses in the same typewritten font, and they were different from all the other mail they received.

The military had developed a new victory mail system to deliver the millions of letters by airmail to different points on the war front. Rather than flying tons of paper mail, they photographed every letter going overseas or coming back and saved them to rolls of microfilm and flew them to distribution points abroad. This process allowed the Government to transport more correspondence on fewer planes hauling less weight. When they arrived at their destination, the slides would be enlarged from the microfilm and copied to card stock. Before placing the letters into an envelope, each letter would be read and censored. Any sensitive information that could give an advantage to the enemy or demoralize the American troops was blacked out.

Patricia sliced through the edge of the seal and opened the letter as Sandra turned on the porch light.

---

*June 22, 1943*

*To the sweetest gal, there is.*

*How are you doing? I hope you're over all that morning sickness. Are you eating better? I have to say; I can't stop thinking about being a father. If we have a boy, I think we should name him Clifford Allen. I've been writing down the names I see on all the guy's uniforms and saying them out loud to find the name that sounds the best. And I think Clifford Allen has a ring to it. As for a girl's name, I'll have to think about it some more. There's not a lot of gal's in the desert, and really, the only girl's name I can think about right now is Patricia. I sure do miss ya!*

*We've picked up a few more troops recently, and they're not shipping them out like all the others we've trained. I think the Army's making plans to hit the Germans hard to get this war over with quick. At least I pray that's the way things happen. I sure do want to get home, I know it's wishful thinking to hope that I could be there when the baby's born.*

*I'm sorry I haven't replied to all of your letters, we've been on maneuvers, and we're out in the desert for days on end, and sometimes it feels like weeks. It sure helps me to appreciate what I have back home and how comfortable our new house will be when we get it built. Don't stop writing, your letters really help me through the hard times, and they keep me attached to home.*

*I love you more than ever,*
*Brennon*

As the sun cast itself below the horizon, moths gathered, circling the porch light like a flock of vultures waiting to land and feast on a carcass. Their fluttering shadows caused the light to flicker as she reread every line several times and imagined that she could see Brennon's face speaking the words directly to her.

Patricia entered the house and went to her bedroom where she slid the envelope into the cigar box. The room began to spin and the sweat beaded on her forehead. Before she could lie down, she felt her stomach flutter sending her supper back up and she wretched into the bucket her mother had placed at the foot of her bed. She wiped her face with a cool, moist rag and sat on the edge of the bed holding her belly.

And waited.

**5**

Brennon had sailed out of the New York Port of Embarkation on April 2, 1943. He had prepared his mind and had accepted the fact that they were going into battle immediately. At least that's how he coped with the fact that he was leaving behind everyone and everything that he had ever known and loved. He was leaving the country of his birth and traveling to a strange land to fight an enemy he had never seen.

After crossing the Atlantic Ocean the Thirty-sixth Division hit the beach of Arzew, on the French North African coast on April thirteenth, to start their training on foreign soil. From there, they moved east to continue their military maneuvers making amphibious assaults on the beaches of Rabat, Africa. After months of grueling training day in and day out, the men in the Thirty-sixth were the best-trained division in the Army and ready to go to war.

Rumors had circulated among the men that new orders had come down from the war department, that they would take part in the invasion of Sicily, codenamed Operation Husky. Like well-trained racehorses they wanted to run, anxious, on edge and ready for the starting gate to open.

The mental state of a soldier going into battle fluctuates

rapidly. He goes from thinking about the past, back to the present, and then to the future all within a few seconds, fighting within his mind to convince himself that the cause is a just one, and that it is one worthy of giving his life.

Brennon's mind flooded with questions like, *What if someone in the family dies back home while I'm gone? I won't get to see them again. What if I get captured and tortured? Will I give in? What if I get shot, will it be painful, will I lay rotting on the battlefield cold and alone? What if I die?*

His thoughts spun like a West Texas tornado thinking about all the lessons his father had taught him while hunting rabbits and deer. He never imagined that he would use them to kill another human. He remembered the many days he spent as a bushy-haired kid exploring the back forty, and always found his way home. He convinced himself that he could do the same in a strange foreign land.

His stomach growled, and he thought about his mother. He could see her face blanketed with a look of resolute determination as she stood in the kitchen wearing her apron. Oddly, the red and white checkered, bib-apron gave Brennon a feeling of comfort, not that it was soft or pretty, but to him, it was a symbol of strength like a General's uniform.

When his mother put on that apron, she always seemed strong, in charge. She commanded the entire house, even his father saluted her as she inspected for mud on his boots. Dressed in her apron, she controlled a pack of rowdy children, gathered food from the garden, cooked hot meals and kept the house in order. Every morning she put on the apron tying it around her waist, and she wore it until the end of every day when all the work was done. Brennon was thankful for his mother's example on how to persevere through a never-ending job. He didn't know when his fight would end, but he would honor her by wearing his uniform until his work was done.

He wanted to be home. His mind drifted to his wife. In reality, his most challenging battle was Patricia. His heart desired to see her face, to hold her close and smell the hint of roses from the perfume in her hair. But as a soldier, his mind called him to fight, and fulfill his duty to free the world of the evil enemy.

*If we don't fight, the enemy will continue to slaughter innocent people. And they won't stop until they consume every other nation. But what if I don't make it? What good will I have accomplished? It's not fair for me to die saving someone else so they can be together with their wife, and I never get to see Patricia again.*

As soon as he closed the door on his emotions once more, and set his mind back on going to war, he heard someone yell "ATTEN…TION!"

Brennon snapped to attention as an Army green Willis Jeep pulled in front of the formation and stopped. The Company Captain stepped out, saluted and began to speak. "Men, I have come to deliver some good news. East of our current position, many of your brothers, have fought and died in Tunisia. However, they have prevailed over the enemy and the campaign there has been successful. The Nazis have surrendered, and we have moved into cleanup operations."

"As a result of this, they assigned us to Major General Ernest J. Dawley's VI Corps, of the fifth Army supply services. We have the privilege of guarding twenty-five thousand German and Italian prisoners of war."

The Captain folded his order papers and saluted before leaving.

"What about Sicily? Operation Husky?" Brennon said under his breath.

Romalo Aapel Taavetti, known by the guys as RAT, slapped Brennon on the shoulder and spoke in his Bronx accent, "Hey O'Neill, I heard Patton didn't want to use the Thirty-sixth because we didn't have enough 'combat experience.' So now we're just gonna' be babysitters for these Nazis."

In a way, Brennon felt some relief they were not going to battle. However, he had trained to fight for almost a year. He had put his life on pause and psyched his mind over and over again into facing death in battle. It was a slap in the face to tell him, "you're only good enough to babysit." It twisted his mind toward anger.

As Brennon lay on his cot at camp that night, he pulled the latest letter from Patricia from his duffel bag.

---

*JULY 1943*

*My sweet Brennon,*

*I pray you are safe and well. I'm am feeling much better, and I haven't had morning sickness for a few days now. The summer heat doesn't help though. It causes me to swell. Speaking of swelling, I'm starting to show pretty well. I had to let the seams out in a couple of my dresses.*

*I don't know how it is where you are, but the temperature here hit one hundred four on Wednesday. They're predicting it will stay in the high nineties for a week or so with no rain in sight. Everything is drying up. Roger O'Gorman lost over a hundred acres of grass just three miles north of Shamrock in a fire last week.*

*At least we do get some relief when the sun goes down. I usually sit on the porch swing and stare at the moon thinking of you and how wonderful things will be when you get home. The last few nights the moon seems to shine brighter than usual. I wish you were here to see it. It's so big and beautiful. I know that sounds silly because it shines where you are too. If you see the moon shining where you are, stare at it and think of me. It will be a connection, both of us reflecting our love to each other by the moon.*

*How I long for you to be home with me—with us, the baby and me. We're waiting*

*I truly love you.*

*Yours always,*

*Patricia*

. . .

BRENNON PULLED the flap on his tent and saw the glow of the moon through the heat rising from the desert sand. The vapors created a veil through which the moon appeared to wave back and forth at him from the night sky.

Brennon waved back at the moon. "I love you too, Patricia."

**6**

---

"No! Please God, No!" She screamed.

Sitting on the porch swing, Patricia stared at the notice. Tears welled in her eyes blurring her vision. She blinked feverishly trying to finish reading the words. Her mind went blank. She felt frozen in time, unable to move. Fear, anger, and despair for the future all merged at the same time, and her whole body shook uncontrollably. She had never felt this way before.

She remembered finding her father dead in the corral when she was ten years old. His face had haunted her dreams at night, and she had cried for months, but she never felt afraid of the future. It felt like every emotion she had known combined and filled her mind as she reread the notice.

*Why is this happening now?*

Patricia wanted to see Brennon, to hold him and hear his voice, but she couldn't. "I hate this war!" She screamed.

She looked down and rubbed her belly and felt the baby move, "We're only six months along, and I don't even know if you're a girl or boy," she sobbed as teardrops spotted the paper and spread through the ink. "And he doesn't either."

She sobbed as she tried to reconcile her feelings with what she had heard the preacher at service on Sunday say when he explained that death is a part of living. The fear of someone you love dying didn't feel like living.

"Patricia? Patricia dear? What's wrong?" Mary said as she opened the screen door, wiping her hands on her apron. She stood behind Patricia and the porch swing and glared at the newspaper she held open.

"Mom, the children in Wheeler County, are dying from infantile paralysis disease," Patricia moaned. "We need to keep Carol and Sandra home for a while."

"Calm down," Mary said softly patting Patricia's shoulders.

"Mr. And Mrs. Keys six-year-old son, Duwayne, died, and they know of two more cases.

Mr. Morrow, the school Superintendent, said that the other pupils were not exposed as far as he knew, but they're closing the schools for at least two weeks."

"Maybe it's just a coincidence they have the same thing," Mary said,

"It's more than a coincidence," Patricia said and began to read the full-page public notice.

---

*HEALTH WARNING TO THE PUBLIC*
*(On the recommendation of the County Physicians)*
*...Three Cases of Infantile Paralysis, Including One Death,*
*Reported from Mobeetie.*
*HELP PREVENT*
*Spread of Disease*

*YOUR COUNTY COMMISSIONERS COURT acting on the advice of county physicians feels it should advise the public of the existence of Infantile Paralysis in our county, and to caution you to exercise all possible care in preventing the spread of this dread disease.*

*Three cases were reported at Mobeetie this week, and one death has already resulted. So far no other cases have been reported.*

*Clean up your premises. Remove all possible breeding places of flies, which are the carriers of this disease. Stay away from crowds, and this applies to adults as well as children as Infantile Paralysis is not confined to youngsters. Stay out of swimming pools. Watch your drinking water and food.*

*Dispose of Trash and Rubbish*

*The most important preventative against the spread of disease is SANITATION. Clean up chicken pens and stock pens. Burn all rubbish. Place containers for disposal of scraps from the kitchen table and burn or remove frequently.*

*COOPERATE WITH YOUR NEIGHBORS IN THIS HEALTH CAMPAIGN.*
*WE M-U-S-T prevent the spread of this fatal disease.*
*COUNTY OF WHEELER*

---

PATRICIA PAUSED as she wiped the tears from her eyes. "I don't want my baby to die from this polio."

"Oh honey," Mary said as she bent down and hugged Patricia. "We'll do our part and clean up around here with a little bleach. It's going to be okay."

Patricia hoped that she could be as good a mother to her baby as Mary was to her. She always had the right words to say and a hug that never hurt.

"Speaking of doing our part," Mary pulled an envelope from her apron pocket. "A letter came in the mail today while you were napping. It should take your mind off things for a while." Mary handed the post to Patricia.

"A letter from Brennon? Why didn't you tell me sooner?"

Patricia grabbed the envelope and carefully opened the seal. She always felt connected to him when she read his letters.

*August 1943*

*My dearest Patricia,*

*I sure do miss you. As the old--timers say, "absence makes the heart grow fonder." but my heart's grown so fond it's about to bust. I hope you're feeling okay, is everything going well?*

*Anyway, nothing's changed over here. We're still babysitting these Nazi's. We're guarding the famous Rommel's crack Africa Corps. They're not as tough as people say. I thought they would resist a little more than they have, but it's been easier than I thought. Most of the Germans seem to be relieved to be in a P.O.W. camp. They get to sleep in nice tents, hot food, and heck, we're loading some of them up on ships and sending them to P.O.W. camps back in the states—Lucky them!*

*With perks like that, maybe all the German's will just give up and end the war.*

*Sending ya all my love.*

*Brennon*

PATRICIA FELT CALMER after reading Brennon's letter and watched the sun go down as she waited.

**7**

———

Field Marshall Erwin Rommel, otherwise known as the Desert Fox, had used up his German Wehrmacht in the rugged North African desert. The extreme fluctuation of the cold nights and daytime heat, combined with the endless grinding sand and lack of water took a toll on the men and their morale. The equipment fared no better with the lack of supplies and parts. Rommel returned to Germany, on orders of Hitler, leaving his men under the command of the Italian Generals. On May 13, 1943, the Italian General Messe surrendered the African front to the Allies.

The prisoners of war captured in North Africa consisted of both German and Italian soldiers. Benito Mussolini had declared himself the Dictator of Italy in 1925. Mussolini, having visions of grandeur and hoping to bring back the greatness of the Roman Empire to the world, invaded Ethiopia and quickly captured the Capital of Addis Ababa. The people of Ethiopia were no match for Italy's modern planes and tanks, and within weeks they were claimed as part of the New Italian Empire.

Impressed with Mussolini's military success, Adolph Hitler began talks with Mussolini and joined in a military alliance called the Pact of Steel in 1939. These two dictators, both filled with pride and lust to rule the world, determined to use the other to get what they wanted.

With Mussolini's Ethiopia as a base and Hitler's Africa corps, they felt like Africa was theirs for the taking. However, just as the Roman Empire had stretched itself to the point of collapse centuries earlier, the two dictators had pushed their resources to the breaking point and failed.

Brennon's unit stood guard watching the prisoners in the sweltering Tunisian heat. He was amazed at how most of them were thankful to be captured by Americans and not placed in a Russian camp. Rumor had it that the Russian's were a little less merciful in their treatment of German prisoners of war. The American's treated the prisoners of war almost as good as the soldiers who guarded them. They had hot food, tents and blankets. And after clean up detail around the camp, they had time to exercise or for personal use.

There were still a few obstinate Nazi's dedicated to the Furher's cause. Some would test the American soldiers by refusing to obey orders. Others challenged the guards by taunting them with German words that sounded like cursing even though most of the Americans couldn't understand the meaning. When they could understand, they harassed them by calling them weaklings because they had not fought them on the battlefield and spewed propaganda with the intent of weakening the American soldier's morale. Going into long tirades, they spelled out how the Americans were simply puppets of Europe and servants to the Jews. And both were using the U.S. soldier to do their dirty work for them.

Brennon listened as one of the German officers who spoke in broken English, "You American soldiers were forced to leave your family behind and die for the Jews on the battlefield. And after you die, and your blood is pouring into the ground, the Jews will go back to America, to your home and comfort your wife and children for you."

Some of the prisoners plotted an escape and convinced some of the others to start a riot to cause a distraction. However, most of the prisoners were content not to be in the desert starving. And even though they were still looking down the barrels of rifles, they seemed relieved that no one was shooting at them.

While Brennon stood at his post, a young sandy-haired German soldier came to the fence and stared directly at him. With his left hand, the boy pointed to his right, which held a small wad of paper. Drawing closer to the wires, the soldier flicked the crumbled bundle through the fence toward Brennon and walked away. The rolled lump bounced toward Brennon and stopped two feet from where he stood. He picked it up. Not knowing what was in it, he slowly opened it and saw several words written in German.

"Sergeant Carter" Brennon shouted to get his attention.

"What do you need, O'Neill?"

"Sir, I need you to take a look at this," Brennon replied.

"What is it?"

Brennon held the paper out to the Sergeant as he approached. "Sir, one of the prisoners, came to the fence and tossed it through the barbed wire. He signaled for me to read it and then walked away. I can't translate German, Sir."

"Do you remember which prisoner it was?"

"Yes sir," Brennon said, "It was P.O.W. number 17601, Sir."

The Sergeant stared at the note and mumbled in German. "It says, 'Tonight at midnight, a planned break out.' If this is true, we may have an ally among the Nazi's."

The words of prisoner of war number 17601, Wilhelm Reinhold Johannes Kunze, turned out to be true. The Sergeant stationed extra troops around the camp, and at midnight four Germans were caught tunneling under the fence behind their tent.

Fate has an interesting way of connecting events that eventually circle back to touch another person's life. And this chance meeting with a particular German soldier was no different. Johannes Kunze was scheduled to sail out to the United States and be interned in a prisoner of war camp in Tonkawa, Oklahoma.

Brennon envied prisoner 17601, who would soon be living only 200 miles from his home in Shamrock, Texas, and Patricia.

---

THE NEXT DAY, Brennon pulled out the latest letter he had received from Patricia.

*DEAR BRENNON,*

*I can't stop crying. It seems like I cry over the smallest things. I'm having a hard time sleeping because the baby wants to play kickball with my bladder all night, and then I'm so tired during the day. All I want to do is to sleep and cry!*

*I'm swollen and look so big. My dresses don't fit right, and it's getting hard to move around. I can't take care of the chores I need to do around the house. The heat here doesn't help either. It's staying around 100 this week and still no rain.*

*We had a scare of infantile paralysis outbreak here in Wheeler Co. Mr. And Mrs. Key's son Duwayne died, and two other children contracted it before the County Physician declared an emergency. Everyone is taking sanitary precautions, and so far no one else has come down with it.*

*Mother, Carol, and Sandra are a big help to me; they try to pamper me in between all the chores. I believe they're as excited about the baby as I am. The girls think it will be a boy, but mother says I'm carrying the baby wide and not out front, so she says it's a girl. I think Brenna Marie O'Neill sounds like a good name for a girl, what do you think?*

*Please be careful and come home, I couldn't live without you.*
*Always waiting,*
*Patricia*

A NEW MISSION codenamed Operation Avalanche was ordered to insert the allied forces into European Theater of Operation from the south. With the British in the north and Russians fighting on the eastern front, a push from the south would squeeze the Axis.

Lieutenant General Mark W. Clark knew the Thirty-sixth division well. Before his promotion, he served as Chief of Staff to Lieutenant General Lesley J. McNair, the commander of Army Ground Forces. For months he had watched the Thirty-sixth prepare for battle and train other troops as well.

Now as Commander of the Fifth Army, the United States Northern Command, he chose the Thirty-sixth Division, rather than the more experienced Thirty-fourth Infantry Division, placing them together with the British Forty-sixth, and Fifty-sixth Infantry Divisions, to spearhead the Allied assault landings at Salerno.

Brennon had received his orders to go into battle. After all the time training and preparing his mind to fight, he started having second thoughts.

*I have a weird feeling, like a bad omen hanging over my head, like I may not ever see her again.*

**8**

———

The Sun peeked over the eastern horizon as if the crowing of the rooster had ordered it. Patricia opened her eyes; her mind already filled with dread and uneasiness, today was not a day she ever wanted to see.

Many times she thought how easy it would be to surrender to the struggle and not get out of bed, but the baby was kicking her bladder, reminding her of why she couldn't.

Today, she fought hard to overcome the urge to stay in bed. It was going to be another hot and miserable day. Even though the Sun wasn't far from the horizon, she could already feel the heat radiating through the windowpane.

Every morning her rituals grew more difficult and felt more like a burden. Today was no different, and she forced herself to sit up and put one foot on the floor followed by the other.

After freshening up, she sat at her small-mirrored vanity brushing the overnight tangles from her hair. She began to cry when the dark circles under her eyes glared back at her. No doubt they were caused by all of the sleepless nights and the puffiness of the tears that she was yet to shed. The smallest things could start the river flowing down her cheeks, things that, months before she would have never considered twice.

Today the tears came easy.

Patricia stood and waddled to the closet pulling out her darkest dress and spoke to the air, "Tradition says to wear black to a funeral."

Images of Brennon flooded her mind. She remembered his smile that spread from ear-to-ear when he looked at her. She could still smell his scent as he held her close before he got on the bus. It had been so long since he had held her, but she could almost feel his lips as they met in a long farewell kiss months ago.

Slowly unzipping the dress from its hanger, Patricia wondered if it would fit. Slipping it on, she tugged at the waistline, twisting and turning it to get the hem to drape evenly in front. Another wave of uncontrollable sobs started as she gazed into the mirror at the wrinkles. After dabbing her eyes with her handkerchief, she cradled her belly and whispered as she gently swayed, "I pray you will know your father one day."

It seemed as though everyone was scraping by to fund the war. Wheeler County had fallen behind in raising funds for the County war chest and increased their campaign to raise the money. Earlier in the year, the United States Government had instituted the rationing of leather shoes. Each man, woman, and child were only allowed to purchase up to three pairs of leather shoes a year, using designated stamps in War Ration Books.

Patricia felt like she had given all she could, her swollen feet ached in her old shoes. And she felt the pain of personal sacrifice when Brennon was shipped out to go and fight.

Mary, Patricia's mother, drove her and her sisters to the funeral. Each step Patricia took from the car to the Church was painful. Her feet cramped, and her legs began to shake as she entered the sanctuary. Just inside the doorway, she stopped letting her eyes adjust to the dim light. At the opposite end of the room directly in front of her, stood a casket with the lid open and the lower half draped with an American flag. Her heart raced faster with each step she took down the aisle toward the soldier dressed in uniform, lying with his arms folded.

Her eyes closed in rebellion refusing to look at the soldiers face. This moment seemed unreal like a nightmare. Afraid she would wake up to see Brennon's face.

Her mother and sisters held her arms offering her strength as she approached. The odor of Carnations, Roses and other floral arrangements around the coffin grew stronger with every breath. The ebb and flow of the mournful sobs and weeping surrounded her from every corner of the room. She could feel her throat tighten, the tears welling in her eyes.

Summoning the courage to look, she opened her eyes and looked. Patricia froze as a sudden loud wail filled the room. Turning toward the shrilling sound, Mrs. Winchester ran to embrace the casket and sob over the flag. Her son, Lewis J. Winchester was only eighteen when he left to go overseas to war.

Patricia sat in the church pew behind the family and cried knowing it could have been her sitting in the front row sobbing over a flag.

When they arrived back home, Linda, her oldest sister, brought Patricia the mail, which included a letter from Brennon.

---

*Dear Patricia,*

*I miss you more than I can say. All I can think about is holding you and our baby.*

*Even though I am helping rid the world of evil oppression, I have grown to despise this war because it has taken me away from you. This letter may be my last for a few weeks, as I have received orders that we will be going to the battlefront. I cannot tell you where we are going in this letter, but I will write again as soon as I can.*

*I hope that our efforts will quickly end this war and we can all come home.*

*The General chose our division because of our extensive training. And he feels confident that we can carry out this particular operation. I am sure that we can make a difference in this fight. We have the best-trained men in the World.*

*Please pray for the day that I can be home with you.*

*All my love always,*

*Brennon*

PATRICIA COULD SENSE apprehension in Brennon's letter. She felt helpless that she could not hold him and assure him. After all the stress of the funeral, the overwhelming feeling of despair filled her mind. Her breathing labored causing her to become lightheaded. She sat the edge of her bed to keep from crumbling in a pile on the floor. Nausea filled her stomach, and the bitter acid taste rose in her throat. A sharp cramp started in the front of her abdomen and squeezed her body, radiating around to her back. Gasping for air, she could feel the pain travel to her sciatic and down into her legs.

Oh, Lord No! She thought.

She felt a sudden silent pop as her water broke and pooled on the floor.

"Mother help!" she screamed, "The baby!"

As Mary ran into the room, Patricia looked at her mother and cried like a small child who was completely lost and couldn't speak for crying.

She held the letter out to her mother, "Brennon's going to battle."

Pausing long enough to suck in another breath of air, she screamed again, "And the baby's coming too early!"

**9**

---

September 9, 1943


BEFORE TODAY, the salty sea air and rolling swells had never bothered Brennon, but pushing through the waves of Salerno Bay at
0300 hours, in a Landing Craft, Vehicle, Personnel carrier, made
his stomach churn. It felt like it would take an eternity to reach the
shore cutting through the water at only eight knots. On the other
hand, no matter how long it took it would be too soon.

The Thirty-sixth infantry division had set sail out of Oran,
North Africa four days earlier traveling on thirteen transport ships
and escorted by two light cruisers, the USS Philadelphia, and the
USS Savannah, surrounded by twelve destroyers. Joined by the
British Forty-fifth and Fifty-sixth infantry Divisions, they would
take part in an invasion called Operation Avalanche at Salerno
Bay.

On the surface, the morale of the men seemed high, excited to
finally get a chance to carry out what they had been trained to do
for over a year. Every man blustered about how they were ready to
fight and whip the Nazi's so they could go home.

The reality of today's amphibious assault flooded Brennon's mind. With every step, he grew more anxious as he climbed down the thick rope ladder that hung from the side of the transport ship. Stepping into the LCVP otherwise known as a "Higgins Boat," his apprehension of facing death and not going home, could be heard in his silence.

Diesel fumes from the droning engine of the landing craft, drifted around inside the thick hull of the barge style boat as it swayed and pitched with the swells of the sea. With a platoon of thirty-six men, each one carrying a rifle and full combat pack, there was no room to move. Breathing wasn't any easier, being packed tight like sardines in a tin can.

When a man wretches, it's usually a sure sign of having a stomach bug or seasickness, but tonight inside this boat, the fear of dying was the disease.

The T-patchers' mission was to make a surprise landing, shrouded in the morning darkness, on a two-mile stretch of beach on the southern end of Salerno Bay near Paestum. After establishing the beachhead, they would move inland. Their next objective would be to take control of the town of Paestum and the railway that supplied it. If they were successful, they would advance ten miles further inland and assemble at the foothills of the mountain ridge that overlooked the bay.

H-Hour for the landing was 0330. The time Brennon dreaded the most; the moment the boat would slide onto the beach, and the exit ramp would hit the ground. Standing in front of the group of men, he would lead the charge. He would be the first man into the water or be a sitting duck with no escape and nowhere to hide from a well-aimed German machine gun.

The assault was planned using Major General Fred Walker's Texans of the Thirty-sixth Infantry Division leading the attack. The 142nd Regimental Combat Team would make their landing further north to the left flank, and 141st would stay to the south on the right. The landing crafts, which carried the troops, were spread across a two-mile area and divided into four lanes heading east toward the beach, code-named Red, Green, Yellow, and Blue. Each of these sectors would be landed in six consecutive waves, separated by intervals of eight minutes. Each group landing would provide fresh troops and artillery to overwhelm the resistance, like a hammer striking the same nail over and over.

The standard plan of attack for a beach landing was to soften the enemy positions defending the shoreline. Massive bombardments from the Naval ships would be used to destroy any machine guns, reinforced anti-aircraft pillboxes, and tank placements, giving the troops coming ashore a chance to take the beach. On the other hand, this kind of attack would be a sure sign of invasion and alert the Nazi reinforcements further inland and call them toward the beach.

In this invasion, the attack would take place in the dark and without the benefit of softening the shoreline. The plan was designed to catch the enemy by surprise.

---

"THREE HUNDRED YARDS!" the coxswain shouted.

Brennon's heart pounded in his chest. In all the months of drills and beach landings that he had practiced, he had never felt so close to dying. He knew how to exit the craft, he knew how to run and fight, but he didn't know how a bullet felt.

Romalo Aapel Taavetti who stood next to Brennon, turned and stared with a glazed far-away look in his eyes, "Is it true?"

"Is what true?" Brennon replied.

"Is it true that your life flashes before your eyes as you're dying?"

Brennon returned the stare, "I hope not, RAT, 'cause I'm seeing mine right now."

He remembered being a young boy running, toward no one and from nothing, just running—free.

He missed the taste of his mother's fried chicken after church on Sunday. And how his little sister claimed the chickens were her baby's hoping to persuade their mother not to use them for dinner.

A smile spread across his face thinking about simple things like the smell of freshly turned dirt. When his father plowed, he had easy pickin's of the worms to use in the fishing pond.

Come harvest time; his brothers would race him picking the locks of cotton from the burr to see who could fill their bag first. He thought about how hot the sun would get and being so dirt-dry thirsty. He remembered how much he hated pickin' and dreamed of the first drop of cool water from the burlap wrapped jug in the shade.

*I wish I were pulling cotton right now.*

"Two hundred yards!"

The Sergeant's shout called Brennon back to the reality of the moment. The rattle of equipment filled the hull of the boat as every man checked his gear. Brennon tried to imagine the layout of the beach according to the maps he had seen and prayed he could find a steep embankment for cover.

If the Germans were expecting them, the beach would most likely be covered with concrete blocks and steel I-beam hedgehogs in the water to impede the landing. *They might damage the boats, but they would at least give me something to hide behind.*

His mind drifted back to summertime when he used to play hide and seek with his brothers by the creek. He would climb down into the draw and crawl under an old log, or sometimes he would dig a hollow in the sandy bank wall under a ledge and hide in it.

"One hundred yards! Get ready men!"

Before the words finished rolling off the pilot's lips, he heard the thunder of artillery and the sky above them turned bright orange and yellow. German flares lit up the beach as if the sun had reached its noon peak.

"It looks like 50 yards from the water to the first line of trees!"

The Sergeant yelled. "When we hit the beach, duck, and run. Find cover and then work to take the tree line."

The sound of Eighty-eight's fired from a Tiger tank from a Nazi Panzer group, screamed across the sky in the darkness. An occasional splash near the landing craft followed some of them. The pop of rifle fire and the chatter of machine guns forbid any quiet space between the tank rounds.

"50 yards!"

Their craft was close enough now they were taking a few hits. The sudden thud and ricochet whine of a bullet hitting the hull of the boat were sounds that Brennon would not soon forget.

"Get ready, men!"

Brennon stared at the inside of the metal ramp that created a wall in front of him. The thick steel was the only thing separating him from a bullet and death. He felt the floor of the boat slide onto the sand and come to a stop. He heard explosions and the agonizing screams of unlucky soldiers being torn apart as they disembarked from another boat down the beach.

*For a soldier to go home, he must go forward. And Patricia's waiting at home.*

Like the flick of a light switch, his fear turned to anger and rage toward the Nazis.

The gate in front of him opened as if it were in slow motion. The sound of metal screeching and moaning filled his ears when it began to move. The cables squealed as they slid through their guides to lower it into the water. Every second it took to fall, was less time he had to escape. He needed out. And the men behind him needed a chance to run for cover.

Brennon was halfway out before the ramp hit the wet sand. Scanning the horizon, he saw orange flashes, like small stars coming from the darkness under the tree row and the tall grass of a giant dune. He crouched low and ran. Within a few yards, he spotted a small ridge in the sand, not very steep, but high enough to dive behind and take cover.

Aiming his M-1, he carefully sighted in on the flashes of German gunfire and returned a volley of rounds at each one. Directly in front of him, near the tree row, he noticed a barbed-wire fence surrounding a machine-gunners nest. Brennon pulled the pin and tossed a grenade into the placement and watched as pieces of two German soldiers flew into the air when it exploded.

"O'Neill! O'Neill!"

Brennon turned to see RAT running toward him. "Over here!" he waved.

Just as Taavetti sunk into the sand beside him, a spray of bullets plowed the ridge in front of them sending a curtain of sand into the air.

"That was close," RAT said.

"That was too close," Brennon replied. "We need to make it to the foot of that dune. That machine gun is behind the hill. We've got to knock it out before the next wave of guys hit the beach."

Dodging sporadic rifle fire was bad enough, but the German MG-42's could throw enough lead to mow men down like cutting hay for baling.

"On the count of three, we run to the dune," Brennon said.

"On the count of three," RAT repeated.

"One—two—three!" Brennon jumped up and scrambled over the ridge and headed toward the sand hill near the tree row. Crouching low, he ran in a zigzag pattern praying to avoid the crosshairs of a German Mauser.

He jumped over the body of a dead American soldier, and he ran faster, not out of fear, but to make the enemy pay for killing his brother. He had to stop the Nazis from killing anyone else.

Brennon reached a large log from a fallen tree and dug down in the sand behind it. He grabbed a grenade from his belt, squeezed the handle, pulled the pin and threw it over the hill. After he heard the explosion, the machine gun stopped.

Pausing long enough to catch his breath, he turned to see RAT running up behind him. When he reached Brennan's position, he fell into the sand a few feet away taking cover behind the log.

Brennon saw a look of terror on Taavetti's face as he hit the ground. The sudden sound of a "CLICK" echoed louder than the constant rattle of machine guns. Time stood still as the explosions of grenades and screams of wounded men faded. The high-pitched whistles of incoming projectiles stopped. Before either of them could move, the world went silent with a deafening blast.

The Germans had sown the beach with anti-tank Teller mines. And RAT had found one.

Brennon blinked, and RAT disappeared. Sand filled the air and darkened the light from the German flares as it rained down. Brennon fell into a giant crater where RAT used to be.

Rolling down into the pit, he cried, "Patricia!"

Then Brennon's world went dark.

**10**

———

*Office of the Chaplin*
*Washington D.C.*


*20 September 1943*


*Dear Mrs. O'Neill,*

*We regret to inform you that Private First Class, Brennon O'Neill has suffered severe wounds in Battle. He is in very critical condition. As of now, we have administered last rights and pray he will survive the next few days.*

*We are sending him to the nearest military hospital where the most exceptional care will be taken to save his life. It is a real possibility that he will not fully recover from his injuries. The doctors have advised that on the chance he does survive, we recommend that you acquire a permanent care facility for him to reside, as he will likely be limited in his usual function, either physically or mentally.*

*We will keep you informed by regular correspondence of any changes in his condition.*

*Please know that Brennon O'Neill fought valiantly, not only for his county, the United States of America but also for all the people of the world that would be oppressed and afflicted by tyrants and enemies such as we are fighting against currently.*

*Most Sincerely, Horace Vanderpool*
*Chaplin (Capt.) USA*

APRIL 10, 1948

IN SHAMROCK, Texas after the war, the smell of spring drifted with the wind. The lilies stood tall in the flowerbeds, and the roses began to bloom. The Elm and Cottonwood trees were budding, and the birds sang as if the world was fresh and new. In reality, most of the people in America had started over.

The soldiers that came home spent weeks and months re-programing their minds after seeing so much death. And the fear of dying in combat forced a man's heart to become calloused to life to allow him to kill another human, rather than being killed himself.

Along with this internal struggle, the time spent separated from family, a wife or girlfriend was not kind to some of them. GI's were transformed to become part of a fighting machine, and it would take time to learn how to relate and live in their home relationships again. In reality–how to start over.

Not only did the men change, but their home also changed, America had changed. The job a man was forced to leave, was now filled by someone else or gone altogether. For months on end, a soldier lived in poverty conditions on a battlefield, or in the rubble of a decimated city or town in a far-away land. But in America, life moved forward.

Coming home was like moving to a new city and trying to learn the names of all the neighbors. Some of the soldiers would tell how that it felt more like being in a coma for years, and then you wake up. They would have to ask a million questions like, "Whatever happened to…? When did they…? Why didn't anyone tell me…?" Trying to get a bearing on where they were.

As for the families at home, the war had changed them too. A son or husband would go off to war one day and never come home. And all the family held on to was a government letter that stated their soldier is Missing in Action—never seen again. Some men went to war full of excitement and determination to save the world and came home in a casket. For these families, it was like blinking. A loved one is there one moment, and the next they're gone—with nothing in between.

------

BETTY STOOD behind the serving counter in her blue poplin waitress uniform. She had moved across the state line from Oklahoma to find work when she stumbled on an opening at the U-Drop Inn. For the last six weeks, she had watched Mrs. O'Neill come into the cafe on a weekly basis, every Monday at ten O'clock, with the same man. But today was different. The man sat outside on the bench in the sun. Tagging along with them was the cutest little-redheaded girl wearing a pink dress printed with blue and red flowers. The young girl climbed onto the bench and kissed the man on the cheek and quickly scrambled down to follow Mrs. O'Neill through the freshly painted café door. They walked up to the display counter filled with cinnamon rolls, apple pies, and other freshly baked desserts.

"I'd like three hot cocoa's please." Mrs. O'Neill said.

"Coming right up. That'll be thirty cents," Betty replied as she turned to the serving line behind her and began pouring cocoa into cups. "That sure is a cute little lady you have with you today." She said placing the steaming cups on the counter. "I've never seen you in here before. What's your name, sweetheart?" Betty asked.

"Brenna, my name is Brenna," she said with a five-and-half-year old smile.

"Would you like a cookie to go with your Cocoa?" Betty asked as she reached into the glass cookie-jar beside the register.

"Yes, please." Brenna said, "Can my daddy have one too?"

"Brenna!" Mrs. O'Neill interrupted "Please excuse her."

"It's no problem; my treat." Betty handed the cookies to Brenna who immediately began gnawing one of them.

"I don't mean to pry, Mrs. O'Neill, but I've noticed that you come here a lot with that man, he doesn't ever say anything?" Betty nodded toward the cafe window where Brennon sat outside on the bench.

"That's my son." Mrs. O'Neill sighed.

"Oh, I didn't know," Betty replied.

"We almost lost him in forty-three during the war. A mine explosion—almost killed him. Damaged him real bad," Mrs. O'Neill continued, pointing to her head with a slight circling motion. I bring him here because this is the last place he saw his wife when he went off to war." She glanced toward Brenna who was halfway through her cookie, "Her Momma. She died the same year."

"What happened to her?" Betty asked.

"Patricia died giving birth to Brenna. And every few weeks Brenna goes to visit her grandma Mary, Patricia's mother."

"I'm, so sorry." Betty sighed.

"It's been hard on us since then, but we've managed." Mrs. O'Neill took a napkin from the counter and wiped the chocolate from Brenna's mouth, "Between us, we've raised them both." She patted Brenna on the head "This one gets smarter and brighter every day," she twisted the small nibs on her change purse and counted out thirty cents. "I've raised my son, twice," She turned and pointed toward Brennon, "but this time he'll always be a child."

"Does he remember anything before the war?" Betty asked.

"The only thing Brennon seems to remember is that Patricia said she'd wait for him here at the U-Drop Inn when he came home from the war."

Both women watched Brennon through the window as he lifted his face toward the sun and smiled.

---

BRENNON SAT on the bench outside the U-drop Inn café feeling the warm sunshine on his face. He closed his eyes and inhaled deeply, and he could smell the sweet aroma of cinnamon, apples and a subtle hint of rose perfume that always hid in Patricia's thick auburn hair. He knew the stiff breeze could never blow away the scent of her.

# PART III

# SUDDEN TURNS

## JOE R. NICHOLS

# 1

Shamrock Texas, September 1944


"THE U-DROP INN," HE SAID ALOUD. "Guess I'll go in here and figure out my next move. Talk to some of the locals."

A sweat-stained silver hat rested tipped up on the back of his head. Using both hands, the hat returned to level and adjusted down tight on his brow. The rusty light blue Ford pickup turned in to a parking space. The door opened, and his long frame slid off the seat. He wiggled his saddle as he walked by, just to make sure it was still cinched down tight on the stock-racks.

The smell of strong coffee and biscuits greeted him as he entered the little café. Feeling the eyes of the wait staff on him, he settled into a booth facing the street.

The taller slender waitress was prompt. "Coffee?" She said with a steaming cup in her hand

"Yes please."

She set the mug down in front of him. "Would you like to see a menu?"

"Well, to tell the truth, Ma'am, I sort of don't have any

money. Well, not sort of. After I pay for this coffee, I guess you'd have to say I'm all the way flat broke. You see, I bet all my money on…"

After a snort and a flip of her head, she informed him, "When you finish your coffee you'll have to make way for paying customers."

"Well, say, Ma'am, I was wondering if there might be some work around here I could do to earn my breakfast. I'm purty handy at fixin' things and I…"

"We don't have any work for you. You'll have to leave so there's room for the customers that have money," She snapped.

"Don't look like you're all that busy. I was hoping to maybe talk to some local ranchers, maybe hustle up some work. You see, I have a friend in Amarillo if I could just get there and…"

"Ranchers of this area eat their breakfast much earlier. And they don't wreak of whiskey either." He watched her spin away to leave his table. "I think she likes me," he said to himself.

"Who is that, Liz?" The other waitress asked.

"A low life drunk and broke cowboy. He wanted to know if we had work for him so he could eat. I told him to move along."

"Gosh dang you, Liz. I don't know about where you're from, but most people in Texas have some good in them. Maybe if you tried to be nice once in a while, you'd find that out. Besides, he's terribly good looking."

"Oh, I'm sure he's a prince," Liz said as she resumed wrapping silverware in napkins.

The short little pleasant-faced waitress grabbed a pot of coffee and headed toward the cowboy's table. "Would you like some more coffee?" she asked with a warm smile.

"Well, that would be alright if your partner wasn't so agin me. I don't think she likes me much."

"Now you don't pay her no mind. She's really not a bad gal. It just takes her a while to warm up to strangers," her smile grew as she talked.

The waitress and the cowboy both caught Liz looking their way, and she instantly ducked her face back to her work.

"What's your name cowboy?"

He quickly scooted out of the booth, stood up, and removed cover. A nearly permanent hat ring circled his long wavy blonde hair. "I'm Buster. It's nice to meet you."

The same warm smile resurfaced on her shiny face. "It's nice to meet you Buster. I'm Katy. You sit back down and I'll see if we've got some leftover breakfast."

"That's mighty kindly of you ma'am. Thank you."

Katy pursed her lips and shook her head at her co-worker as she walked past to the kitchen. "Francisco? Have you anything left over from breakfast?"

"I have three biscuits, one sausage patty, and some bacon pieces. I can scrape up some gravy, but it won't be very warm."

"That would be perfect. Thank you Francisco."

Katy approached her friend. "Honestly, Liz. He seems very nice and polite. He's obviously made a living on a horse. I bet he could help you with your cattle situation."

Returning to the kitchen, Katy carried a plate of food out to the hungry cowboy. She placed it on the table and asked, "What else do you need?"

"Not a thing Ma'am. Thanks for being so nice to me."

She returned to the waitress station and gave Liz a crusty look. Liz folded her arms in front of her as she leaned against the wall, starring at the cowboy. She drew a deep breath, held it for a count, then, exhaled long and slow. At the bottom of her breath, her shoulders fell in a slump.

"His name is Buster," Katy encouraged.

Liz frowned and stepped her way to the cowboy's booth. Uninvited, she sat down, poised with erect posture. "So... Buster. It appears you need work. I might have something for you."

Buster looked up, but didn't stop eating.

"Are you interested?" She asked.

"Don't know. I'm listening."

"Well, I have some land a few miles north and east of here. I need someone to capture all the cattle."

"Capture?"

"You know, gather them into a corral. A round-up."

"Yeah, I get it. Capture doesn't sound to me like one guy could just ride around 'em and drive 'em into a pen, or sook 'em in with a feed sack."

"Well, ever since my husband …. Well never mind about that. Okay, yes, you could say they may have gotten somewhat wild in the last few years.

"Years?"

"Well, yes, but there's never been anyone of your caliber to attempt them."

"So how many times have they been tried?"

"Only four or five times. Unless you count the times my neighbor and his cowhands tried to lasso some of them individually. I could pay you five dollars per head for every one you get penned up."

"What kind of shape are your corrals in?"

"They need a little refurbishing, but I think I have everything you need to repair them to good condition."

Buster finished his breakfast and shoved the slick plate a few inches away. He relaxed against the backrest and asked, "Do you have horses?"

"I have several. Fine, well-bred horses."

"How broke are they?"

"Well, they're not actually trained to ride at this time, but you won't have any trouble with them."

"How old are they?"

"They're five, four, and…." She hesitated, put her hand to her chest and strained to swallow. "They're three, four, and five years of age."

"Do you have a cowboy shack?"

"I do."

What kind of shape is it in?"

"Oh, it's in very good condition. It just needs a good cleaning."

Buster looked her up and down. She wore no makeup, and her dress buttoned all the way to the top. He admired her flaming wavy red hair, but her tiny waist and curvy figure kept most of his attention.

"What's your name?"

"My name is Elizabeth Anderson."

"You know, Elizabeth, you could be about half good looking if you just tried a little bit."

"I guess that's your weak effort at some sort of compliment. The fact of the matter is, it's been a long time since I've been in the company of a man worthy of prettying myself up for. Now are you interested in my proposal or not?"

"So let me see if I've got this straight. You want me to spend weeks rebuilding your corrals, try not to get killed breaking your five-year-old broncs to ride, and then try not to get killed again chasing your crazed, wild, and spoiled cattle. For five bucks a head? No thank-you."

"I thought you were broke and needed money. It would appear you are not in a good position to negotiate."

"I may have lost all my money, but I haven't lost my ability to make money. And I haven't lost my mind either."

"So Mister, Mister, oh, whatever, Buster, do you have a counter offer?"

"How many total cattle are we talking about here?"

"I have no way of knowing for sure, but the original herd was sixty-five."

"And how long since they were gathered?"

"It's been three years."

"Could I have some more coffee please?"

Liz gave the cowboy a disappointed look for a moment, then took his cup. Steam rolled off the fresh coffee when it landed back in front of him. She sat back down, hands folded in her lap in the exact same position she was in before the coffee errand.

"Thank you," he said as he raised the mug to her as if it were a toast. "Here"s what I would do for three meals a day and a bunk. I'll fix your pens, however long it takes, as long as you furnish all the materials. When the horses are broke enough to use gathering wild cattle, I'd have to own half of them. And every critter I "Capture," I'd get half of them too."

"That's preposterous!" She exclaimed.

"Maybe. But your cattle haven't got any closer to market any other way. I can get the job done, but that's the deal." He raised the coffee to his lips with a smile.

"I need some time to think about your terms."

"Don't think too long. If I get a tank of gas before you decide, I'll be Amarillo bound."

Buster stepped out of the U-Drop Inn to what was left of the September morning. He stood facing south, and the sun felt good on his face as he looked over the town. He walked to the corner service station that connected to the restaurant. He leaned up against the wall, out of the way, and watched the attendant at work. "That highway 66 sure brings a lot of activity through here, doesn't it?" he said in a friendly voice.

"Is there something I can help you with?" the skinny kid asked.

"Oh, I was just wondering who the big cow men were in the area. Might need some work."

"You need to talk to Laurence Walker."

"I've heard of him," Buster said.

"He's the biggest operator around here. If he don't need help, he knows who does."

"How would I find him?"

"He eats dinner next door every day bout eleven-thirty. He's a fat man with gray hair; Wears one of them little gentleman rancher hats. Always has a cigar stub in his lips."

"Thanks for the information friend."

"You bet," the kid said with a smile. "Good luck."

Buster noticed a clock on the wall. "Quarter past ten," he said to himself. The hangover, sunshine, and full belly had him craving a nap. He returned to his pickup and laid down in the seat, using his satchel as a pillow. He dozed for about ten minutes, then fell hard asleep.

Slowly coming out of his coma, he suddenly sat up. As he tried to figure out how long he'd slept, he saw a little round man wearing a short-brimmed silverbelly hat with a fat cigar in his mouth walking into the restaurant. He was accompanied by a slender cowboy looking feller about half his age.

"That would have to be him," he said out loud. "Perfect timing." He ran his fingers through his

hair and wiped his face. His hat returned to the indentation on his hair, and he stepped out of his truck.

Lawrence Walker and his foreman were just being seated when Buster approached.

"Mr. Walker? I was hoping to visit with you a moment."

The old man looked up as he settled into the booth. His eyes brightened as he focused in on the good-looking cowboy. "Sure. Sure, sit down young man. What's your name, son?" he said holding out his hand.

"I'm Buster Bonds." He said with a firm grip.

Lawrence hesitated for a moment, then said, "I've heard of you. In fact, I've heard a lot about you. You've done a little bit of cowboying in your time, haven't you."

Buster gave a wide grin, "I guess you could say that."

"Yes, I guess I could say that. I want you to meet my Ranch Manager, Orville Johnson."

"Please to meet you, Orville," Buster said extending his hand.

Orville was slow to reach for Buster's hand and only nodded.

"So what's on your mind, son?" Lawrence asked.

Buster took his seat beside Orville. "Well, sir, I was wondering if you could use any help for a few days."

"If I did son, I hire you in an instant. But we've already

shipped everything early this summer. We're trying to let this grass heal up from last years drought. Are you down on your luck?"

"Oh, it's nobody's fault but mine. I just came from Cheyenne, Oklahoma. I had a little grub stake put together, and I bet it all on that PeeWee horse against Gray Badger."

The gentleman rancher smiled. "Folks in this country know better than to bet against Walter Merrick."

"You can count me as one of them people from now on," Buster said embarrassedly. I was working for some of the fellers that owned that horse up at Pampa. They were real confident. I just thought it might be my chance to break out of this ole hired hand routine. You know, start something on my own."

Liz approached the booth with iced tea for Mr. Walker and Orville. "What would you like today Sir," she asked. "We have chicken fried steak on special."

"That's what I'll have," Lawrence replied.

"Me too," said Orville.

"I'll have it right out," Liz said as she whirled to leave.

"Wait Liz," The old man blurted out. "I'd like to buy this man's dinner as well."

Liz slumped as she turned back. Her face wrinkled. "What would you like?"

"I'll have the same ma'am."

Liz hurried off. Orville offered his opinion. "I bet she's got icicles between her legs."

"Heh, heh," Lawrence chuckled. "You're still peeved cause she wouldn't go out with you."

Orville huffed. "I'm just glad she didn't waste my time."

Buster smiled at Lawrence.

"Well, son. Age will make you think ahead a little bit. But don't worry, you still got plenty of time to make your way."

"Well, I hope so. I have had one offer that does interest me a bit. That waitress, Liz, approached me about gathering her cattle."

Orville covered his mouth and began a howling laugh. "You'd

sooner stuff a wet noodle up a Bob Cat's ass than you'd catch any of those lunatic cattle."

Buster looked over at Orville with a cool stare.

Lawrence spoke up. "She neighbors me to my west. I wish you would get them damn things shipped out of there. They ain't got anything to eat, and they're always getting on my land. We've tried to catch'em, run'em off, fence'em out, I'm sick of 'em."

"What's the story?" asked Buster.

"Well," Mr. Walker began, "Elizabeth and her husband moved here from Minnesota. His family apparently had a lot of money and bought that ranch for him. I think they made their wealth with cranberries. I wanted to buy that place, but I didn't think anyone in their right mind would give the price. John, her husband, died after they were here for only about two years. Guess he had a bad heart. He didn't know much about cattle, but he built a helluva ranch. She knew nothing, always kinda out of place. Well educated, you know. Anyway, his family paid for the land, but he borrowed the money to buy the cows. The bank is coming after her for the note. She's not in bad shape if she could just sell her stock."

Buster listened intently. Lawrence continued. "We don't have the manpower to gather wild cattle, but with time, you could do it. Some of them older cows would come to feed and gentle back down. I understand she has a whole barn full of hay. But there would be some of them old steers and bulls that are damn sure rank."

"What about her horses?" Buster asked.

"Oh, they're a helluva set of horses. They had some kind of Morgan bred mares with them when they came. I guess this John was a polo player. Anyways, they bought a Peter McCue bred stud to cover them mares. They're big stout horses that will watch a cow and cover some ground. Excellent disposition, and tough. I bought some colts from John before he died, and they all turned out real good. I've offered to buy more of them, but Liz is scared she's going to get cheated. "

Liz returned with the plates of food, gracefully setting them down in front of the three men. "I'll bring some more tea. Is there anything else I can get you?"

"I'm fine Liz," Lawrence said.

She spun away and hurried off. Buster raised his hand, "I don't need anything either Ma'am," as if she was still present. Lawrence and even Orville gave a sneaky laugh.

"Sometimes you have to hurry to tell her you don't need anything," Orville allowed with a smile towards Buster.

Buster smiled back, "I think you're right about that."

Lawrence responded. "Oh, that Gal is darn sure all right. She's just alone and a little out of her element."

The conversation died down as the men ate, most of the small talk was about common people they all knew. When Lawrence finished his meal, he immediately returned the cigar to his mouth from the napkin it laid on. "Well, Buster. It was sure nice to meet you, and I wish you the best of luck. If you decide to gather Liz's cattle, I'll help you any way I can."

Buster stood up to say goodbye and to let Orville out of the booth. "Good to meet you Sir, and thank you for dinner."

"Anytime son, anytime."

"It was good to meet you too, Orville."

Orville grinned and reached for Buster's hand. "Yes sir. Glad I got to know you."

Buster sat back down. Liz cleared the table and began wiping it clean. Buster smiled and said, "Elizabeth, when you find time, I'd like to visit some more about your situation. Maybe I'll be a little easier to deal with."

Liz abruptly stopped her wet rag as her and the handsome cowboy's eyes met.

Buster took note of the new soft look that came his way.

**3**

THE NICE SOFT LOOK QUICKLY WENT AWAY, and the guarded attitude returned. "Mr. Walker doesn't need any help?" she asked with raised eyebrows and a twist in her mouth.

"No, he didn't. But more importantly, he came to your defense. Said you weren't near as mean as you act."

So, you think I'm mean?"

"I didn't say that. But I do think you're highly suspicious."

She stood up straight and put her hands on her hips with shoulders back, "You can't blame me for that."

Buster chuckled, "No, I s'pose you're right about that. Anyway, I want to make you a little bit different offer."

Liz sat down in the same erect posture Buster was getting used to.

"Some of your cattle, especially the older cows, probably won't be that hard to retrain. With a little time, they'll coax in with some feed. In fact, I could most likely use the ones that get gentle to lure in a lot of the wilder yearlin's. I'd take the five bucks a head on those type cattle. But those crazed bulls and old smart steers, it would be fifty-fifty. I'm going to have to use my extraordinary skill and cunning to "Capture" them. And as far as your horses, I got a real good report on them. I'll break all of them for my choice for one of each age."

Liz said nothing while a look of deep thought came over her face. Buster waited patiently for his offer to soak in.

Liz began her thought out response, "I can well understand the compensation on the cattle, and I appreciate your candor in that regard. But I'm afraid I am still reluctant to agree on the horse proposal. That seems to me, very extreme."

Buster smiled, "That's the deal I've made breaking horses my whole life. My agreement with you is not going to be any different. If your horses are better bred than most, then that's just all the better for me. I deserve a good deal now and then."


LIZ STARED THE COWBOY DOWN. Her mind became a blur of thoughts. Her childhood, adolescence, and young adulthood raced circles around her head. How did she ever come to this life? She grew up with wealth, prestige, a respected family name, and a formal education. And now, she had to make a home in this desolate, wide open grassland, dealing with heathen men and simple women.

"Well, Elizabeth?" Buster asked.

Her process of thought continued back to present day. Life's desperate situation she now found herself in, had become agonizing. Something had to change.

"I will agree to your terms if you agree to some additional conditions during your time on my ranch."


BUSTER GOT REAL CURIOUS, and a little nauseous, "Like what?"

"There can be no drinking, swearing, or lewd behavior of any kind."

"That sounds completely unreasonable."

"Maybe. But you need a job, and I can hire you. But that's the deal." she smirked with renewed confidence.

Buster hid his smile behind his hand. "Well, I'll be damned. I guess if thems the rules, I will abide."

"You just said a cuss word."

"Now look here, you got to cut me a little slack. I've been cussing my whole damn life."

A feminine finger shook straight at him, "And you just said it again."

Buster wagged his gnarly finger back at her, "We ain't on your ranch."

"Point taken," she acknowledged. "I get off at two-thirty. You can follow me home."

"Very good," Buster said with a nod of agreement.

Liz jumped back into action, cleaning tables and tending to the remaining customers. Buster climbed out of the booth and headed for the door, and Liz paused her activity to watch him walk out. A pleasant smile appeared on her face, until she noticed Katy looking at her. That smile disappeared from Liz, and immediately transposed to Katy's face.

"What ya lookin' at Liz?" Katy asked with a giggle.

Liz got real busy and acted as if she didn't hear the question.

"It's okay, Liz. I was looking too." Katy laughed out loud.

Liz continued to briskly wipe a table without looking up.

## 4

BUSTER EASED AROUND TOWN, visiting with whoever wanted to, and taking a general survey. He especially took note of the merchandise offered at the Mayfield Tire and Supply store. At a little after two O'clock, he returned to the U- Drop Inn to meet Elizabeth.

Liz eyed him as he walked in, "I can't leave for another twenty minutes," she snapped.

Buster threw his hands up as if she were pointing a gun at him. "I'm not here to rush you. I just wanted you to know you don't have to wait on me."

"Oh. Yes, okay, I see." Liz said with a hint of embarrassment. "Would you like a cup of coffee while you wait on me."

"Of course I would."

Buster smiled as she set a hot mug in front of him. They made eye contact, but Liz quickly changed the direction of her attention. When she darted away, he said aloud in a low soft voice, "I wonder how hard her shell is?"

"Are you ready?" she said at exactly two-thirty.

"Yes I am." He said quickly.

"We'll go north on highway Eighty-three, five miles, then turn east on a dirt road for eight miles. Do you have enough gasoline in your truck?"

"Yes, I should be fine."

I drive a red and white Cadillac. I'll come past behind you."

"A Caddy? That's quite an auto. Don't run off and leave my old Ford pickup."

"I would never drive in any such reckless manner." She stated as she aimed herself at the back door.

"I'll bet that's damn shore right," he said aloud to himself.

Buster slid in his truck, turned the key and mashed the start peddle with his toe. At the same time, he applied just the right amount of pressure on the gas with his heel. Baby Blue rolled over one time and fired up. The cowboy then allowed the truck to idle as he waited for Elizabeth to drive by behind him.

He waited. He waited some more. He looked down the street to the north. "Surely I didn't miss her come by." He continued to analyze out loud to himself. "Of course I didn't. She's got to be having some kind of trouble. That high society Cadillac must have a dead battery. I guess I better see what's the matter."

Buster opened the door to his pickup and stepped out. In the exact same moment, Elizabeth came around the corner. Both hands on the steering wheel, same erect posture, her eyes focused straight ahead.

Buster studied intently as she drove past. "My God, she must be approaching ten miles per hour! And what the hell could she have been doing or the last ten minutes?"

The cowboy remounted his truck and puttered down the street in pursuit.

**5**

---

"THIS LOOKS LIKE GOOD COUNTRY. I s'pose a man could run cows or yearlin's just fine. Kinda pretty."

The sound of his own voice, and following an attractive woman to her ranch, made him think he could be lonely. "Ah hell, I ain't that lonely. Sides, a man would sooner melt all the ice in the Yukon before he could warm her up."

It was hard to tell, but it looked like to Buster she was maybe slowing down to turn. "Sure enough, there she goes. I hope she can avoid a sideways skid and don't lose control."

Buster idled along in third gear, trying not to let his pick-up breed the Cadillac. "Shit. I hope we get there 'fore dark."

"Well, I'll be damn. Would you look at that." Buster's mouth fell open as he crested the last hill and the ranch headquarters came into view. A beautiful two-story stone horse barn garnered so much of his attention, it took a while before he realized the house too was made of matching rock. Both nestled in the southeast side of a hill, live water flowed through the back of the horse corral, and then wound its' way to stream into the cattle pens as well. "Well I'll be damn," Buster said again. "This is a Gawdamn showplace."

Crazy thoughts of this ranch being his home detonated in his mind like a bomb. This was a property like he had always dreamed of, although he never considered it possible. "I can't believe this place is real. I can't believe this ole prude owns a real live fantasy like this." He then took notice of the layout of working corrals, gathering pens, and out buildings. "A whole lot of thought went into this place. This is unbelievable."

Liz drove up to the bunkhouse, also made of stone, and parked. Buster eased up beside the Cadillac, turned off the engine, opened the door, stepped out, shut the door, and waited very impatiently for Liz to exit her car. Then, he waited impatiently some more. Eventually, the heavy door of the Cadillac slowly opened, and she placed her feminine feet on the ground. She arose promptly with perfect posture and stepped purposely towards Buster. "Well, what do you think?" she asked with a proud smile.

Buster stared into her pretty eyes, unable to speak.

Her smile vanished, "Is there something wrong?" she asked.

"Oh, no, no, nothing's wrong at all. You have a real nice place here Ma'am. A real nice place for sure."

"Oh, well, thank-you. Let me show you inside."

The door opened stubbornly and shrieked a loud creak. A dust cloud from the threshold hung in the air. Liz hurried to the west wall and opened two windows, also very stubborn. "It's been quite some time since anyone has stayed in here, as you can tell." She opened a closet door just off the sitting room. "Ah yes. Here's a broom." She held it out towards him, and Buster slowly reached for it. "You do know how to operate a broom, do you not?"

Buster smiled. "Just barely."

"Well then. I'll fetch a pail of water and some rags. We shall wait until later to make your bed when all the cleaning is done," she said as she walked past.

Buster listened to the clip-clop of her feet on the wood floor as she left. He rested both hands on the broom handle as he slowly gazed at his surroundings. He had lived in many bunkhouses and cowboy shacks, but nothing compared to this. So well constructed. The walls were covered with shiplath, and all the trim, baseboards, and molding were rough cedar. The doors also were solid cedar, and everything had a natural lacquer finish. A wood-burning stove divided the sitting room from the four iron beds. A maple drop leaf table with matching chairs, and two comfortable looking rocking chairs were the only furniture.

He began to sweep, and there was surprisingly little dust on the floor. Liz returned carrying a bucket of water and an arm full of cleaning rags. He watched as she dunked a cloth and wrung it out. She then placed a chair in front of the cedar cabinets, which she stood on to wipe out the shelves. The broom stopped while he gazed at her figure swaying side to side. "How old are you?" he blurted out.

Liz jerked and grabbed the cupboard to steady herself. "Goodness. You startled me."

"Sorry 'bout that."

Liz continued her task.

"Well? Are you gonna tell me?"

"Don't you know it's not proper to ask a lady her age?"

"Maybe not, but sometimes having poor manners can work to a fellers advantage."

Liz hesitated and looked over her shoulder at Buster. "I am twenty- nine years of age."

"I figured you pretty close, though you don't look much past school age."

"Well now, what is your age?"

"Thirty-four."

Liz dobbed her brow on her sleeve. "I believe you have held up very well, considering your lifestyle."

"Is that your weak attempt at a compliment, or are you snubbing me. I can't tell."

Liz smiled. "You never married, Buster?"

Buster resumed the stroke of the floor with the broom. "My ole pappy used to say, 'Son, it's best to wait till you're thirty-two to get hitched, then wait two more years.'"

"You obviously took him literally."

"Why wouldn't I? Ah hell, truth is most women ain't too interested in marrying a guy like me."

"You just said a cuss word. Maybe that's the reason women are not attracted to you."

"I didn't say a cuss word, and I never said women weren't attracted to me. I said most women wouldn't marry my kind, and hell ain't a cuss word."

Liz stepped down from the chair. "It most certainly is. Especially on this ranch. You agreed to refrain."

Buster leaned on his broom. "I didn't realize you were going to be so unreasonable about it."

Her lips mashed together. "Is it unreasonable to think you would keep your word? I thought you might have a shred of integrity somewhere in your person."

Buster paused while he studied the hate in her eyes. "I told you I would abide by your rules, but I don't believe you have any call to question my integrity over a slight and unintentional slip from my tongue."

Liz waited to respond. "That was actually well said." She hesitated again. "Perhaps I may have overreacted."

"Perhaps?"

"Well, yes, I suppose I did. My apologies."

Buster gave a weak smile and put the broom back to action.

**6**

---

"YOU'RE SOMEWHAT PROFICIENT WITH A BROOM," she stated as she wiped her forehead with one of the remaining clean rags. The cabinets, table and chairs, counter, and stove had all received a thorough cleaning. Buster had finished whisking the floor speckless. "Would you like to sit for a while on the porch?" she asked.

"Yes. I'd like that," He stowed the broom back in the closet. "Just hope I don't have another cussing fit."

Liz rolled her eyes and frowned. Buster stepped out on the little porch and seated himself in one of the metal chairs. He slumped down and crossed one knee over the other and heaved a comfortable sigh. Liz followed, sat prim and proper on the edge of the other chair.

"Do you ever relax?" Buster asked.

"What do mean by that?"

"Well, it appears to me you spend all your time being ladylike."

"Is that such a bad thing?"

"Well, no, but your mannerisms seem kind of extreme."

"Yes, I suppose I don't fit in so well in this area of the country. It is how I was raised up from the time I was a small child."

Buster thought for a moment. "Did your folks expect a lot from you?"

Liz tilted her head slightly. She took a breath and opened her mouth, but no words came. She then exhaled all of her air and leaned back into her chair. "I ended up being a terrible disappointment to my parents."

Buster waited. The silence didn't seem awkward at all. He knew she would explain when she was ready.

"My mother and father despised John. "He's an irresponsible playboy," my mother would say. My father said he was shiftless and untrustworthy. Oh he was a bit of a rounder all right, but I knew his heart, and I knew he loved me. His reputation from his youth and professional polo playing days made for outstanding gossip fodder, but that's not who he was with me. He was good to me. I believe he was misunderstood because he was fascinated with the Western way of life. He wanted to be a cowboy."

Again, Buster remained quiet.

Liz gathered some more thoughts. "He wanted to be like you. In fact, he wanted to be exactly like you."

"Are you sure about that?" Buster inquired.

"Well, I'm sure you have some aspirations that are worthy. John went against his upbringing to pursue his dreams. He was discarded from his family, as was I. His father agreed to purchase this land, mostly to rid himself of his son's embarrassment to the family. They didn't care for me either. I was from the wrong lineage. We were both outcasts. I think that is why we were so close."

"You think you'll ever get over him?"

Liz swallowed as she lowered her head. "I don't even remember the first year without him. Nothing. Just an absent blur in my life. The second year I mourned terribly. I sobbed, I threw violent fits. I even thought of suicide. I considered burning the house to the ground, with me in it. I was pitiful."

Buster squirmed in his chair and leaned forward with his arms on his knees, hands clasped together. "Are you sure you want to be telling me all this?"

Liz breathed deeply and gazed affectionately at the rough cowboy in her presence. "You know? I have just related things to you I've never told anyone." She threw her head back and cackled. "Who in this hell hole could I have had a conversation with anyway?"

"You just said a cuss word."

Liz quickly covered her mouth, and then she boldly pronounced, "According to you, hell is not a swear word."

"So all of a sudden, you're giving me some credibility?"

"Well, this is probably the first time in your life you have been correct."

"It could be," Buster said with a large grin.

Liz giggled heartily. Her laughter caused a chuckle from the cowboy. Buster's amusement progressed the lady's joy to a shrieking hysteria. The high pitched laugh from Liz became contagious, and the cowboy broke down to a booming heehaw. Liz doubled over, not able to get enough air to make a noise. Buster slapped his leg and howled. "You done lost your good sense, woman."

Tears rolled out of Liz's eyes as she tried to straighten up. The two snickered and shook in their attempt to stop the comedy. The silliness lingered for quite some time. Then, Liz abruptly halted her funny attitude.

A solemn and serious look came over her face. Buster's laugh drizzled to an end when he saw the change of mood. He wondered what would come next.

"I don't think I've ever laughed that hard for that long of time. I can't remember the last time I laughed at all."

Buster became truly sober. "You have a wonderful laugh. You should share it more often."

Liz smiled and stared. Her face flushed red, and she stood quickly. "I will begin preparing the evening meal."

"Can I hep ya?"

"That will not be necessary. I'll bring your supper and tend to your bedding."

"I have a soogan, Ma'am."

"Nonsense. You're not making camp on the prairie. I wouldn't feel right unless you have fitted sheets."

"Thanks for being so nice to me, Liz, although I'm not accustomed to it."

She gave a quick smile and stepped towards the Cadillac.

Buster stood in the doorway and watched her drive up to the main house. His stomach growled. "I wonder if she cooks as slows as she drives."

The cowboy walked down to the cattle pens. He rested his arms on the top rail and set his right boot on the bottom board. Four separate corrals in a square with an alley down the middle. Four gates intersected in the middle, one of which lay on the ground, and one laid sagged open. A few planks needed replacing and a few needed to be nailed up, but the cowboy was pleasantly surprised how well built and what good condition they were in. "Hell, one good day and I'll have these ready to hold cattle." He laughed out loud. "Good thing hell idn't a cuss word."

A motion caught his eye on the horizon. Dusk had begun to settle in, and he strained to see. His eyes adjusted, and he could make out a dozen cows or so, most with good sized calves, grazing away from him. Then, a behemoth caught his eye. What looked to be a huge longhorn steer stood facing him. He was a short distance from the cows to the right and appeared to be looking straight at the cowboy. A tingle went through Buster's soul, and his heart sped.

"I'll bet you're a crafty son-of-a-bitch." The steer tossed his head as if he heard, then trotted into the middle of the cows. They soon disappeared over the break. "I'll bet I can't convince her son-of-a-bitch ain't a cuss word."

The cowboy eased back to his truck and uncinched his saddle from the stock racks. He reached in the passenger side and took hold of a Navaho blanket and three headstalls. With the blanket under his arm and the bridles on his shoulder, he pulled the saddle down off the rack and hoisted it on to his hip. He walked in the horse barn with all his tack on his body in the exact position as when he left the pick-up. The tack room door opened with a groan. "Guess I better git the broom after this too." The room was mostly dark, but he could see enough to find a saddle rack and bridle hooks. Other saddles and headgear could be seen in the dim lit room. He became anxious to look it all over in daylight.

Returning to the pick-up, he grabbed his satchel and went inside. He dug around in his belongings and pulled out a book. Turning the lamp to shed light on one of the rocking chairs, he settled down and opened the book. His face became attentive, yet peaceful. In what seemed like a very short time, there came a knock on the door.

"I have your supper."

Buster sprang up from his chair and opened the latch. "Come in, please." He backed away from the door, holding his book behind him.

"I hope you don't mind a cold plate. I usually eat a very light evening meal, and I wasn't prepared for serving a hungry cowboy."

"It'll be fine, Ma'am. I've already ate better today than I'm used to."

"Well, you sit and eat while I make your bed."

Buster returned his text to the suitcase and took a seat at the table. He studied the food. Boiled eggs, cheese, pickled beets, sliced tomatoes, salami and saltine crackers. Everything carefully placed and arranged on the platter in its own space.

"This looks damn near too pretty to eat."

"I beg your pardon?"

"Oh. Uh, I mean, this just looks so nice. You went to more work than you needed to, to just fill my belly."

"And you had to swear to express your feelings?"

"Well, Liz, sometimes it takes explicit language to get your point across."

"Explicit?"

The cowboy looked over at her with a surprise.

"You may have a more sophisticated vocabulary than you let on."

"I doubt that. Maybe you're already rubbing off on me."

"I doubt that for sure. I couldn't change you in a hundred years, much less in an afternoon and evening."

"And yet, you're gonna try?"

"What do you mean?"

"Well, you know, this whole cussing thing. I will do my best to be respectful and considerate of you. I just ask that you would afford me some leeway."

"Respectful, considerate? Afford leeway? I'm growing suspicious of you Buster Bonds."

"I'm just a simple-minded cowboy Ma'am. Nothing more."

Liz looked strangely upon Buster. "I'll leave you to your new quarters. I leave for the café at five-thirty. I will prepare your breakfast and your noon meal for tomorrow and set it on the porch."

"That will be appreciated, Liz. Are the tools and supplies in that outbuilding east of the barn?"

"Yes. There are also poles, posts, and planks behind that shed. I'm sure you will find everything you need."

"Yes, ma'am. I'll be fine. Thank you for supper."

"You are welcome," Liz noted the cowboy's sincerity. "Good-night Buster."

"Goodnight Liz."

The lady closed the door firmly behind her.

Buster washed his slick plate and turned it upside down on a dishtowel. He then retrieved the old book from his personals and returned to the light by the chair. His mind couldn't focus on the words he read. He closed the book and reflected on the days' happenings.

In a matter of thirty hours, he had squandered a nest egg, got drunk, and found a new opportunity.

## 7

---

BUSTER'S EYES OPENED. He widened his view to take in the room. The previous day regenerated in his thoughts. His surroundings, situation, and new task became familiar. Then, the day before became prominent and the shame that came with it. He wasn't hung over now, and his first clear mind allowed the reality of his actions to hit home. The covers flung off, and his feet jammed to the floor. He found the switch for the lamp, yanked his pants on and went to the basin to wash his face from the pan of water left from cleaning. A comb dipped in the same water slicked his hair down. He put his shirt on, but it remained unbuttoned as he pulled his socks and boots on. The sound of a car approaching made him hurry to straighten his shirt as he went to the door. Liz stepped on to the porch carrying a plate covered with a towel, a steaming pot, and a paper sack. "Good morning Liz."

"Good morning to you Buster. I have breakfast and coffee. I also made a sandwich for your lunch. I hope you enjoy it and I hope you have a great day."

The cowboy relieved her of the bounty and set it on the table. "Thank-you, Ma'am. I'm sure I will. You have a great day yourself."

Liz smiled, "Yes. I will see you this afternoon."

"Bye now." Buster returned a smile. With the door closed, he hustled to the cabinet to find a coffee cup. He poured it level, then found a fork in the drawer. The anxious cowboy sat down and removed the towel covering the plate. Steaming scrambled eggs, fried bologna, fried taters, and two heavily buttered biscuits. "Just right," he said, scooping up a load of eggs on the fork.

All the breakfast disappeared in rapid order, and he rinsed off the plate and poured more coffee. When he finished buttoning and tucking in his shirt, he swigged from the cup. He threw on his jean jacket, placed his hat purposely over his blonde hair, then downed the rest of the coffee. The cup was sloshed out and turned upside down on the towel next to this morning's and last night's plates. With gloves in hand, he bulled through the door and walked briskly to the barn.

**8**

———

"COME ON," HE HOLLERED. He figured any noise out of the ordinary would attract the horse's interest. "Come on," he bellered again. This could take several days, even weeks, but one of the most important beginning accomplishments was to get the whole herd of horses coming in every morning. He poured a bucket full of oats out of the burlap bag, and carried it and an empty bucket outside. He slowly poured the oats into the empty bucket from chest high. There was just enough breeze to separate the dust, mouse turds, and trash from the grain. He repeated the procedure again and felt confident the oats were safe to feed.

He carried the bucket out in front of the horse pens and yelled again, "Come on!" He sat down on the bucket and took a pouch of leaf tobacco out of the pocket of his jacket. A small singular leaf nestled in his right cheek, and he carefully rolled up the package and returned it to the right pocket. He gazed out over the creek bottom, looking for any movement. His mouth salivated, soaking up the small piece of tobacco. He spread his legs and spit between them.

When he raised his eyes up, he caught some motion on the opposite side of the creek bed. He flipped the leaf over with his tongue. "Come on." This time his voice had a softer tone. More like a coax.

The movement paused for a short count and then resumed a slow progression. Buster smiled and waited.

In a few minutes, several horses lined up side by side, remaining below the creek bank, but able to see the corrals and the strange new man. Buster stood up and said, "Come on," as if he could care less if they came. He swung the bucket side to side in a very prevalent manner, then walked into the corral and exaggerated pouring the oats in the troughs. He held the bucket up high and shook the grain out a little at a time. He kicked the metal bunks and caused a commotion at the same time. When he finished, he never looked back and returned to the barn.

---

TAKING INVENTORY AS HE WALKED, Buster strolled slowly through the shed and material yard behind. "I believe there really is everything here I need."

He gathered cans of nails, a big hammer, and a pry bar. As he walked to the cattle corrals, he gazed towards the horse pasture. One glance revealed, all the horses stood in the exact same position he last saw them. Totally ignoring them, he went about repairing the pens.

"This is rough fir," he said out loud. "I wonder where this came from?"

By noon, gates were rehung and adjusted as needed. His mind wondered to the sack lunch and sandwich that awaited him. As he walked to the bunkhouse, he looked over his shoulder. No horses were in sight. The cowboy grinned.

Buster made short work of the baloney sandwich and flopped on the bed. His snooze lasted no more than twenty minutes, and he arose abruptly. He hurried to the counter and scooped a cup full of water from the pan. The sleeve of his shirt caught the slobbers as he headed for the door.

All planks were either replaced or nailed back. The work seemed to pass rapidly for the cowboy. His handy work displayed his skill, both in quality of workmanship and the time to accomplish it. By evening, the pens were nearly airtight, for sure would hold cattle.

He let himself begin to feel tired as he walked to the bunkhouse. It had been a productive day, and he felt good about his progress. Without horses to work, he became concerned how he would keep busy. The corrals were in shape in one day, and now he had to figure out how to proceed with no horsepower. He remembered the hay in the barn. That would be his focus.

**9**

———————

BUSTER SAT ON THE PORCH with a cup of water resting on his knee. He gazed across the creek and up to the horizon. He saw the same set of cows from the evening before, grazing from the same direction. Then, the longhorn steer showed himself. He looked down on the homestead as if it were his, proud, defiant, and big. His horns looked to span the length of the cows he followed behind. Buster adjusted himself in his chair.

He thought deeply about the task in front of him. He knew his talent as a fearless cowboy would be tested. The likes of that steer and several like him, would only come to be caught by a fast horse and a long rope.

The sound of an automobile took his attention. The red Cadillac pulled up in front of the cowboy shack. Buster smiled.

"How are you cowboy?" Liz said as she opened the door. She began gathering up sacks and swung her petite frame out of the car.

"Oh I'm good, Liz. You all right?"

"I've got meatloaf and mashed potatoes for you. I assumed I couldn't go wrong with that. How did it go today?" she asked stepping towards the bunkhouse.

"It went very well. The pens are done."

Liz stopped. Her jaw fell open. "Are you serious? The corrals are repaired?"

"Yep. There ready."

Liz smiled as she walked on to the porch. Buster opened the door for her.

"You know how to get things done, eh? I thought it would take you a while."

"Well, I just do what I do."

"I guess you do." She said with a smirk. "May I join you for dinner?"

"I had dinner at noon."

Liz sighed. "Can I join you for the evening meal?"

"Oh. Of course. I'd like that."

"I just prepared a salad with some beef for myself. I hope you like your meal. One of the advantages of working in a café."

"Oh yes Ma'am. This is very thoughtful of you. I'm sure I will."

Liz watched with pleasure as Buster dove into his supper. She picked at her salad as she watched the cowboy. "You like to eat, do you not?"

"I suppose I do. A good meal is a part of a good day. Everyday. If you can't enjoy all your meals, how can you enjoy life in general?

"Well, I guess you have a point."

"I don't just have a point, I'm right as hell."

Liz jerked her body straight.

Buster waited to see what her reaction would be.

She resumed balancing more lettuce on her fork. "Fortunately for you, hell is not a cuss word." She said in all seriousness.

Buster smiled, and waited for her to smile back. He could tell she was trying not to, but it wouldn't be long.

Sure enough, Liz could sense the cowboy staring at her. She giggled as she looked up at him.

The smile on Buster's face evolved into a grin.

"I've seen a group of cows with one big Longhorn steer with them the last two evenings." Buster pointed to the horizon. "They grazed up that hill headed south both times."

"Yes. That seems to be their habit this fall. There is another large steer similar to the one you've seen. He stays with a different group more to the east."

"With your approval, I'd like to start feeding some hay. I'll use my pickup, but I'll need you to bring me some gas from town."

"Oh yes. That's a splendid idea. I will bring you gas tomorrow evening."

"That'll be fine. I've enough petro for tomorrow. I'm gonna see if I can't bait them up a little bit. When I get them horses coming in, I'll go to working with them. But in the meantime, I should be able to gentle some of them cattle down. Probably get several coming in before I even get a horseback."

"Well. It seems as though you have a plan, Mr. Bonds."

Buster grinned. "Looks good on paper anyway."

The next morning, Buster anxiously checked the troughs in the horse pens. They were slick. There were lots of tracks where the herd had come in and stirred around in the corral dirt. He had not put out much grain, in case only a few horses came in, but he was pleased at the activity and knew it would only be a few more sessions before they would all come in every morning.

"Come on." He yelled. Buster walked to the barn and sifted some more oats. He eased out to the troughs. "Come on." He sat down on the bucket and reached for his tobacco. No more had he tucked away a singular leaf to his cheek, he saw the remuda descending the far creek bank. The cowboy stood up and coaxed, "Come on."

He swung the bucket and banged it against the bunks. The horses formed a line, but three head came on up the bank. They proceeded half way to the pens, and stopped. "Come on," he said more softly. A flax main sorrel lowered his head and walked up a few steps. He paused and raised his head up high. Buster shook the oats with a grin. The sorrel came a little closer. "Come on, Buddy." The other two horses turned and went back closer to the herd. The sorrel looked back at his buddies. Buster immediately began pouring some oats in a trough, which regained the horse's attention. The cowboy made a little pile at the end closest to the sorrel, and strung out a light dusting of grain in the remaining bunks. Then, he turned his back to the horses and entered the barn. He stayed hid for a few moments, and then peered through a corner of a window. The two buddies, a little brown and a dark red sorrel, bravely crept closer towards the corral. As they did, the flaxen sorrel went through the gate and straight to the mound of grain. He took as big a mouthful as he could get, then raising his head, made sure he wasn't in a trap. He slobbered oats as he looked up towards the barn. Seeing nothing suspicious, he glommed another big bite. The other two ponies couldn't stand seeing the sorrel enjoying the feed, and also entered the corral. Flashy, as Buster had already named him, pinned his ears at his longtime companions. They both went wide around him to avoid conflict, and found the spattering of grain spread thin along the bunk line. Their lips worked frantically to gather in every single oat. The rest of the Cavvy began milling around, threatening each other with not too serious bites and kicks. It was their way of dealing with the frustration of not being submissive enough to come in and partake of the grain they so badly wanted. Buster was pleased, and cheerfully went about his work.

He fired up his faithful blue pick-up and drove around to the loft side of the barn. Carefully, he backed up close to the sliding door and turned off the engine. The door opened with surprisingly little effort, and he soon had two bales of beautiful alfalfa hay loaded on the truck. He drove off and left the door open.

There was a wire gate a little ways past the cattle pens. Buster threw it open and proceeded down the two-track road that looked like it might get him close to the ridge where he had seen the group of cows and big steer the past two evenings. He had picked out a cedar tree and a rock formation to landmark the spot he wanted to put the hay out. Totally unfamiliar with the lay of the land, he hunted and pecked his way along in low gear until he was as close as he could get. He turned off the motor and stepped out. He relieved himself as he studied the terrain. Hoisting a bale to his shoulder, he started the climb up the hill. His breath began to puff. He trudged onward until his legs turned to mush. Laying the bale on a dirt bank, he rested a moment. He scooped the bale back on to his shoulder and resumed the climb. There was a nice flat place just below his rock and tree, and he dropped the bale down and sat on it to catch his air.

He could now see the ranch dwelling from the same view of the Longhorn steer. "That's the prettiest damn ranch I ever saw." He gazed affectionately at the whole scene for quite some time. He thought of what it would be like if Liz would fall for him and he made this his home. He got off the bale and broke it open.

Separating the alfalfa into the thinnest flakes possible, he strung the hay out in a straight line. He folded the wire from the bale while walking back to the truck. He strained a little more in the second trip, but once again made it without stopping more than once to rest. Again he sat down on the hay bale and heaved deeply. Casting his eyes again to the headquarters, he talked aloud to himself. "This could be a helluva operation, and a beautiful place to live."

The second bale lay spread out in a continuation of the same straight line and evenly placed. "That ought to look mighty inviting to a hungry set of cows. And one ole rangey steer."

The blue truck slowly bounced and half slid back down the steep hill, finally reaching the two-track road. Eventually, he was at the wire gate and closed it behind the pick-up. He parked at the barn door and loaded three bales of hay, and closed the sliding door. Leaving the pick-up there, he anxiously went to the tack room.

With the saddle house door propped open by a bucket half full of used horseshoes, Buster surveyed the contents. Wooden racks held four saddles. Buster pulled the first one out. A heavy made ranch saddle showing little use. The cowboy licked his thumb and wiped the dust off the makers stamp behind the cantle. "Fred Mueller, Denver Colorado. The goods." He slid the saddle back and grabbed the next one. An A-fork rig made by R.T. Frazier. The next saddle garnered his full attention. This was a fully tooled youth or ladies saddle. Wetting his other thumb, he exposed the mark. Olivers Saddle Shop, Amarillo Texas. "That's a nice son-of-bitch."

Seeing the last saddle warmed his heart and grew his affection for Liz. A ladies sidesaddle. He pulled it out and read the stamp. "S.C. Gallup Saddlery Co., Pueblo. Well I'll be damned. She might be more horse savvy than I knew."

He thought of what it would be like riding across this ranch with Liz. Checking their cows, seeing baby calves and newborn foals in the springtime. A slight smile formed on his rugged face.

Searching the shelves, he discovered glycerin soap and some olive oil. He also found a short-bristled brush. He carried the sidesaddle and a rack out to the breezeway, then retrieved two buckets full of water. He thoroughly cleaned all four saddles, then gave his own saddle the same treatment. After his dinner and a short nap, he returned with the broom. He cleaned, swept, and organized everything in the room. After oiling each saddle, he placed them back in line of their original order. When he finished, he admired his work. "Now this is how it should be."

He couldn't wait to show Liz.

**10**

———————

Buster sat on the porch with his water cup. He got somewhat excited when he heard Liz's car coming up the drive, though he did a good job of not showing it.

Liz gathered the supper she brought home and opened the car door. "How was your day, Cowboy?"

"I had a great day," he said, taking part of her load and opening the door.

"Well, you seem to be in a rather chipper mood."

"Let's eat, then I have something to show you."

Liz paused and studied the cowboy. "What are you up to?"

"I'm not up to anything. I just want to share my day with you."

The couple sat and began their meal.

"I learned something about you today," Buster said with pride.

"Oh? Well, that can't be good."

"I think it's very good. You ride."

"Well, yes. It has been a while, but I use to enjoy riding for sure. I was accomplished at horseback equitation before I met my husband. In fact, that's how we met."

"What about that side saddle?"

"John bought that for me when we married. It was made from a design that Charles Goodnight came up with for his wife. What do you think of it?"

"I think it's capital. Very stout and well made."

"Capital?"

Buster ducked his head.

Liz dabbed her mouth with her napkin. "Yes, It's very well made. Molly Goodnight often rode and travelled with her husband. The saddle allowed her to ride cow horses on the range with ease. I love that saddle."

Buster smiled. "I'd like to see you ride it."

"There's a little brown gelding I use to call mine. He wasn't a great ranch horse, but he took care of me."

"I think I saw him this morning. He didn't come in at first, but he wanted to. A good looking flax mane sorrel came in first, then, the little brown and a red sorrel came in after him."

"Bob came in?" Liz said with excitement.

"Bob?"

"Yes. Brown Bob. He's the kindest horse. I haven't had any contact with him for… I haven't seen him in a long time. How did he look?"

"All them horses look pretty good. They darn sure don't have any bloom on them, and they're a little thin, but they're stout."

Liz set her fork down. "I miss riding."

Buster laid his fork down as well. "I'm fixin' to change that."

Liz affectingly gazed at the handsome cowboy. "How do you intend to do that?"

Buster stood and reached for her hand. She cautiously placed her hand in his, and rose up. He opened the door for her, and they walked in silence to the barn. The tack door opened wide, and Liz exclaimed, "Oh my lord. You've done a remarkable job. Thank-you. Thank you so much."

Buster walked to the rack holding her sidesaddle. He pulled it forward slightly and waited for her reaction. The leather glistened and every detail of the tooling jumped out in prominent beauty.

Liz stopped and covered her mouth. "Oh my gosh. It looks so elegant. That is unbelievable. You've made it so beautiful. That saddle has never looked better."

She took both his hands in hers. "Thank-you so much. I didn't expect you to go to all this extra effort."

"It's not extra effort. It just needed to be done." They stood for a moment, eyes locked on each other. She moved close to him and exhaled deeply. Buster took a short breath, but Liz withdrew and turned away. Buster's arms fell limp at his side.

She turned towards the cowboy. "Thank you again. I appreciate what you've done. I'm going to retire now."

"You have to sit a spell with me on the porch."

"Oh I do? Is that an order?"

"No, I, no I didn't mean it like that. I just have something else for you to see." He saw the strange look come across her face. "Would you please sit for a while? It won't take long."

"Okay, Buster," part of her suspicious look remained.

They walked side by side, but no words were spoken. Buster knew there was something developing between them, and he sensed that she knew as well. Upon reaching the porch, they each took their chair. Liz smiled. Buster returned a smile, then looked to the horizon. He quickly scooted to the edge of his seat and pointed. "Look."

Liz cast her attention to the direction the cowboy pointed. "Oh my gosh. What are they doing?"

The cows and Longhorn steer were attacking the alfalfa, and fighting over it. It only took a few moments before they got spread out the full length of the hay line, and settled in to eating.

"They're eating alfalfa hay," Buster said matter of factly.

"How in the world did you get hay all the way up there."

"I just stepped out the barn door and threw it up there."

Liz giggled her feminine laugh which ended with a bit of a snort.

Buster looked surprised. "You don't believe me? It was just two bales."

"Well, I suppose I shouldn't be shocked at anything you do, Mr. Bonds. It looks like your plan is progressing." She stood up to leave, as if she needed to be somewhere else. "Good evening Buster."

"Good night Elizabeth."

He watched with a grin as she drove to the main house. "I believe I'm gonna have this ranch yet."

**11**

———————

Morning came with the sound of Liz's auto driving away. Buster hurried to the door and saw her leaving. Breakfast and a sack lunch were left on the porch. He took his time enjoying the eggs, sausage, biscuits and hot coffee. "Pretty damn good cook. And kinda shiny too."

After a near full bucket of oats was sifted, the cowboy ambled down to the bunk line in the horse corral. He had already seen the ponies line up just below the bank, so he smooched and coaxed "Come on," with an inviting tone. He shook the grain, making as much noise as he could. "Come on you hosses," he cooed.

Flashy, Brown Bob, and the dark red sorrel came right up to the gait. A few of the others came up the bank. Buster poured the grain and kept on walking to the barn. The first three horses came in directly behind them, and about half of the others watched until the cowboy disappeared into the barn. All but four head came in and charged the troughs. Buster watched from the window, and he noted that none of the horses crowded Flashy. "He's the stud duck all right," he said with admiration.

Blue fired right off, and the hay truck ascended to the ridge.

The bales were broken connecting to the previous day's feed ground, but lured the cattle farther down the hill. It was all going to plan, both with the horses and cattle, but there was just no way to hurry the process.

After descending the ridge, Buster headed east with the third bale in search of signs of the other group of cattle. He would much rather be prowling the country a horseback instead of pounding the pickup across the prairie. In time, he would be mounted, but for now he had to make do. Knowing the little brown horse was broke to ride tempted him to catch him up, but he didn't want to risk discouraging any of the horses from coming in.

The cowboy drove aimlessly for the rest of the morning and saw no evidence of the mavericks. "This is bullshit." A new plan came to his mind.

After dinner and a brief snooze, he loaded more hay for the next morning. There was a stiff breeze he wanted to take advantage of. He rolled a barrel into the center of the barn and sifted it full of oats. With a lid secured on top, he wrestled it back into the feed room. Now he had a ready supply of clean oats.

Next, he drug one trough into the smaller pen beside the main feed pen. The gate for the big pen swung to the inside and was chained flush to the fence. He hoisted it off its' hinges, then used a monkey wrench to adjust the hinge bolts. The top one was screwed out a couple of turns, the bottom bolt turned in the same amount. After a good physical straining, he managed to rehang the heavy and awkward wood gate. To test his engineering feat, he laid the gate back against the rails and turned it loose. Slowly, the gate swung away from the fence, gaining sped as it went. With a soft bang, it settled against the latch post. "Perfect," he proudly proclaimed.

The last step was to rig a wire to hold it open with a cord attached that ran along the fence and through a knothole in the barn wall. The trap was set. "COME ON," he hollered.

One can of oats dipped from the barrel covered the bottom of the feed bucket. He walked to the door, "COME ON," he yelled again. He waited. Knowing this would be out of the routine he had tried to establish, he wondered if any horses would show up. Drawing a deep breath to call again, he saw Flashy coming off the far bank. He softened his voice and shook the bucket. The flax mane sorrel came out of the creek bottom and hesitated. Brown Bob and the red came loping through the trees and up the bank. Buster rattled the oats around in the bucket as he walked to the bunks. "Come on boys." Soon as the grain hit the troughs, all three horses came right in. Buster ignored them in his lackadaisical return to the barn. Once inside, he grabbed the cord and gave it a firm yank. The gate swung shut and when it bumped the post, all three horses threw their heads up and ran a lap around the pen. They wadded up in the corner at the gate, and then whirled back out to the middle of the corral. They faced the gate, snorted and blew, trying to figure out how they had been trapped.

"Easy boys, easy." Busters' presence caused more anxiety for the three horses and they milled around the pen nervously. The cowboy slowly walked to the edge of the first bunk and sat down. He continued to speak softly while he relaxed in a non-threatening position. The ponies became less scared and more curious, approaching closer to him. "There you go. You're all right." About the time they acted like they wanted to come near, Buster eased up from his sitting and left the horses standing in place. Their eyes followed him until he disappeared into the barn.

Buster exhaled in relief. He now had horses to work and at least one to ride. This had been accomplished without causing any set back in the rest of the herd. He returned to the three horses with more oats, and they followed him into the small pen. They contently munched as Buster shut the gate on them. He then opened the main corral gate and chained it open.

A few of the outside horses showed up, and the cowboy poured out the remaining grain and called to them. Buster watched from his barn window. They came in, ate, and hung around awhile investigating their buddies' situation. When they left, the penned up horses stirred around and became a little upset. That didn't last long though, and they appeared to settle in.

Buster was pleased with the day and retired to the porch and his drinking water. He anxiously waited for Liz.

## 12

Liz arrived with fried chicken, mashed potatoes, and green beans. It sure tasted good to the cowboy, and the conversation was lite. When they both finished eating, Buster asked, "Is that flax mane sorrel broke to ride at all?"

"I'm not sure. I really don't think so. John may have started breaking him to ride, but he certainly would not be very far along in his training. I do know that he was a favorite of his."

"Well, he definitely had a good eye for horses. I kinda like him myself. Did he have him named?"

"Yes, he called him Flashy."

Buster lunged forward half choking on a swig of water.

Liz stiffened her posture. "Do you have a problem with that name?"

"Nope."

When Buster regained some composer, he continued, "I've got Flashy, Bob and a dark red sorrel caught in the little pen."

"Oh my, you do? Let's go look. I want to see them."

Buster stood up and offered his hand. "Let's go," he said.

He kept hold of her hand as they strolled along, until when nearing the horse pens, Liz dropped his hand and quickened her pace to the wood fence. She folded her arms on the second from the top rail, and leaned in to rest her chin on her wrist. She smiled. "I didn't realize how much I missed riding until just now."

Buster Braced himself on the same board. "Nothing better for the inside of a man than the outside of a horse."

"I assume that applies to a woman also?"

"Not my quote, but I'd say yes."

Liz spoke fondly of Brown Bob and told of several of their experiences together. When he felt the timing was right, Buster asked, "Would you let me ride him until I get some of the other's going?"

"Oh yes, that would be fine. I can't imagine him misbehaving, but I would prefer you ride him a while for me anyway."

You never know how one will act with that much time off without any attention. Buster placed his arm around her waist. "Kinda like me, I guess."

Liz pulled away. "I must go now."

Buster couldn't hide his disappointment. "I'll walk you back to your car."

Liz opened the car door. "Thanks for catching my horse and walking me to the corral."

"Oh you're welcome. I enjoy…" Busters' knees nearly buckled when Liz hugged his arm and kissed his cheek. She quickly jumped in the car and shut the door. She smiled at him through the window as she backed away.

Buster felt the wetness of her kiss with his hand. "Well I'll be damn. I may be closer to this ranch than I thought."

## 13

THE SUN TURNED THE EASTERN SKY orange, yellow and pink. Buster had finished his breakfast and read a chapter in his book. His mood was good, knowing he had horses to work.

More than half of the outside horses were in the pen, and the rest came right in as soon as the grain hit the troughs. He purposely did not feed Flashy, Bob and Red.

The cattle feed line had become much easier to access in that it was farther down off the ridge, and he didn't have to carry the hay bales up the hill anymore. After returning to the barn, he loaded the next days' hay.

The three horses in the small pen watched his every move as he shut the main corral gate. He disappeared into the barn for a moment, and reappeared when the other barn door opened to their pen. The cowboy carried a halter and a bucket of oats. He shuffled the grain in a noisy manner and spoke gently. They finally met halfway in the center, and taking his time, he eventually had them all eating out of his hand. With the halter on his arm, he set the bucket between his boots, and while letting each horse eat from his hand, he required them to allow being petted and stroked with the other hand. Patiently, he spent enough time with each horse until he sensed they didn't care about being caught.

Bob figured to be the easiest of the three to catch, so he slipped his arm over his neck and smoothly grabbed the tail of the lead rope. The brown horse backed up a few steps, but didn't booger and try to get away. He fixed the halter on his head, fed them all some more oats, and led Bob to the barn. After putting Bob in a tie stall, he fed him a generous portion of oats. He repeated the procedure on the other two ponies, First Flashy, then Red. They were both gentle, but Red didn't lead very well. With all three horses eating contently, he began combing and brushing them. When they finished eating, he saddled Brown Bob and took him outside.

He eased the cinches into him and studied his reaction. After leading him up a few steps, he tightened the cinches the rest of the way and jigged him in a circle, making the horse go around on the end of the lead rope. No ill intent could be detected.

Buster asked the horse to take the bit and gently bridled him up. He shortened the reins and filled his hand with mane and grabbed the saddle horn with his right hand. With his foot in the stirrup, he carefully bounced a couple of times before stepping in the stirrup and swinging his leg over him. The cowboy placed his right boot in the stirrup and relaxed in the seat of the saddle. Bob made no moves until Buster asked him to ride off, which he did without incident. He rode him around for a few minutes and two things became apparent. The horse wasn't very well trained, but he was definitely gentle. Buster dismounted and led Bob through the pasture gate. Back in the saddle, he loped off to find the missing cattle.

He rode along keeping the perimeter fence in sight. On the east side, he saw a band of horses

across the fence. They saw him a few moments later, jerking their heads up abruptly. After watching a short time, they high-tailed it towards the mounted horseman. The closer they got, the more they slung their heads, bucked, kicked and generally acted stupid. Brown Bob paid close attention, but didn't get excited. Buster could see a W brand on their left shoulder and remembering Lawrence Walker saying that Liz bordered him on the west, he knew they were his. The cowboy also took note of two big Belgium draft mules. "Those big stout sons-a-guns might could help me out of a bind." Buster continued to the southwest corner. Walkers' bunch of horses eventually lost interest and retreated.

He found a windmill with lots of tracks and fresh manure all around it. The tank had a big cork for a stopper. He tied his pony to the windmill tower and set the brake on the fan. Looking around, he found a piece of wooden sucker rod and used it to knock the plug to the inside of the tank. There was a small dirt pond to catch the overflow, but it wouldn't be long before they'd be out of water. This would force them to drink from the creek and hopefully get the two bunches together.

Buster continued around the fence headed west. He was starting to get the lay of the land, but he hadn't seen any cattle. Topping a long rolling hill, he saw the wild bunch. He pulled up and asked Brown Bob to back up. He slung his head and acted like his feet were stuck in the ground. Buster sawed the bit side to side until he reluctantly took a few steps back. Buster gave him slack and relaxed. The wind was against him and the unsuspecting cattle grazed without concern. He began to count. He tallied one hundred forty-nine. He started again, this time counting only what he thought were cows. Sixty-three. Next he counted calves. Fifty-two. All the bulls, yearlings, and old steers were counted last as one group. He got forty head, six long from his total. Attempting to get an accurate count from so far away wasn't realistic, but he now had a good idea of the job at hand.

He rode just below the crest to get in front of the herd. He walked his horse down the hill to the leaders of the bunch. He got remarkably close and they still hadn't spotted him. He stopped and waited.

A big longhorn steer grazed ahead of the herd. He appeared to be as huge as his mate. Suddenly, the big steer threw his head up. With only a slight hesitation, he wheeled and tore off running right through the cattle. Total panic overcame the herd and they broke and ran for the creek bed.

Buster watched the stampede as they scattered away over the next hill. "My gosh. Them sons-a-bitches are plum wild. Well, most of them will settle in when I get them with that other bunch."

The cowboy urged his pony towards the direction of the last sighting of the spooked cattle.

He only went at a walk. When he reached the trees at the creek bed, he turned toward the ranch headquarters. It wasn't long before the crazed bunch of cattle busted out of the trees and headed east. Buster stayed hid all the way to the barn. "I've got to learn what time my little bunch at the house goes to water," he told Bob. Bob didn't seem to care.

He tied the brown gelding back in his stall and left him saddled. Taking a blanket from the tack room, he eased up beside Flashy and showed it to him. Cocking his head to the side, the horse examined the blanket with several quick short sniffs. When he finished smelling of the blanket, Buster rubbed it on his neck, draped it carefully over his back and rump, slowly dragging it off and putting it back. Flashy wasn't too concerned, so Buster moved to the other side for more of the same. Satisfied with the horses' reaction, he settled the blanket correctly on his back.

Returning with the ranch saddle, buster spoke to his student as he approached. "Whoa son, easy now."

He let him look and smell the saddle until he lost interest, then stood not too close and raised the cack over his head. Flashy took a step sideways, looking a little suspicious of the cowboy. Buster lowered the saddle and lifted it again several times. He then held it where the horse could smell it again, but he declined. The cowboy skillfully set the saddle on his back with one smooth motion. Flashy watched, but did not flinch. Buster spoke to him as he walked around behind, "Easy son, you're good." He took down the stirrup and cinches without letting them flop against the horse's side, and went back to the other side to cinch him up. He did this very slowly making sure he didn't surprise the horse, and stopped when things barely started getting tight. Flashy swelled up a tiny bit but took it well.

"I can't tell if this is your first time or not," he said as he stroked the pony's forehead and rubbed his eyes. He took a little more slack out of the front cinch. "I guess we'll find out in just a bit, won't we?" The horse was led outside and the cinch tightened some more and tied off. Buster removed the halter, turned him loose, and went inside the barn.

The flaxen sorrel didn't untrack right away. His head was up and he acted a little tense. He moved out in a bit of a crow hop that continued to the back of the pen. After a pause in the corner, he half ran and half bucked up to the barn. Buster encouraged him to keep moving, and he loped, trotted, and then walked for a while before he stood still. "Whoa, buddy. Easy son," the cowboy talked to him as he neared. "That a boy," he said rubbing behind his ears and petting him on the neck.

Buster went through the steps to gain the horses confidence and in short time the cowboy sat in the middle of him before Flashy even realized it. Buster was pretty sure what the result would be when the horse took off and he was in no hurry. The longer they set still, the more relaxed the situation might be.

Flashy took a few steps, and then broke in two. He bucked to the other end, whirled and sprinted back. He stuck his head in the corner and froze up. Buster calmly pushed him on his neck and aimed him back to the middle of the corral. Maybe he didn't buck quite so hard, but he made the same tracks. Buster pushed his head out of the corner again. This time he ran to the other end and trotted back. Buster kept him from getting in the corner and he freed up his gait trotting around pen. A while later, he walked slowly and finally stopped. He was rewarded for this and allowed to rest while being rubbed and talked to kindly.

In the next phase, Buster asked him to move ahead by leaning slightly forward and pushing on the base of his neck. A little squeeze finished the cue and Flashy departed in a trot. The horseman waited for him to walk, feeling for the timing. When he could tell the horse had stopping on his mind, Buster scooted deep in the seat of the saddle and shifted his weight back of center. He pushed on his stirrups slightly in front of him. At the same time, he pulled firm and steady on the handful of mane in his hand. He maintained all these cues as the horse continued to move forward. In a few more steps, Flashy slowed and then stopped. Buster released the pull of his mane, dropped his feet and relaxed his legs and slumped to the center of the saddle. Once again, the horse received soft language and physical pleasure.

Twenty minutes later, Flashy was stopping and even backing up with nothing but a mane hold. Buster stepped off, and went in the tack room. Flashy waited patiently and his man returned with a snaffle bit bridle. He led him out the gate, stepped up on him and confidently rode him off.

The cowboy didn't know what time it was or how long he'd been gone, but he sensed he should be getting back to the barn. Flashy walked in a straight line, head down with slack in the reins. Sweat dripped off every part of his body, but no foam or lather. His nostrils flared and his breath was quick, but not in any stress. Buster felt a satisfaction he hadn't experienced in a long time. This horse was special.

Riding to the pens, he noticed Liz's Cadillac at the bunkhouse. Just as he dismounted to get the gate, he saw Liz come out of the Shack and scurry to her car. He had never seen her drive that fast. The car was barely stopped when the door flew open. She briskly hurried towards the barn. Buster had closed the gate and led Flashy along. "Hey Liz," he hollered.

She stopped and searched in the direction of his voice. A huge relief came over her face when she saw the cowboys' wide grin. "I thought you would be on the porch, I got worried."

Buster led the colt up to the fence next to Liz. "You? You were worried about me?"

"Well, why wouldn't I be?" Liz bashfully ducked her head to try to hide her smile.

"I don't know, I'm just not used to anyone caring about where I'm at."

"Do you think you might get used to it?"

"Well, it is kind of a nice feeling."

"I have supper in the bunkhouse."

"I'll be right there. I just need to turn these horses loose."

Liz offered a sweet smile. "I'll wait for you."

Buster nodded. He led Flashy in the barn. "Who'd of thought a pretty woman with a nice ranch would ever be sweet on me."

Brown Bob was turned loose first. He lowered his head, searching for a place to roll. He knelt, dropped, and squirmed several times up on his back until he successfully rolled completely to his other side. After grinding his hide a few more times, he stood, shook, and gave a big sigh.

Red didn't roll but instead went to the water.

Flashy lay on one side and thrashed vigorously. He stood up and lay back down and satisfied the urge on the opposite side. The other two horses yielded to him as he came to water with his ears pinned.

Buster put out some hay and then directed his attention to Liz. "Ready?"

"Yes. Looks like you had a productive day."

Buster pondered briefly, "I would say very productive."

"Are you hungry," she innocently asked.

"What do you think?"

Liz laughed as they got in the car.

Buster never had a meal that tasted better. The conversation was as good as the food. He noticed the affectionate look on Liz's face. "Thanks for a good supper, Liz."

"You're very welcome, Cowboy."

"Oh, don't fix me any dinner tomorrow. I need to go to town and visit with Mr. Walker."

"I see."

Buster could tell she obviously wanted to know why, but she didn't ask. "I seen he's got a couple of draft mules. I want to ask him if I might could borrow them."

"I see."

I may need them if I get something "captured" a ways off from the pens. He'd said he would help me any way he could."

"Oh I'm sure he would be willing to do that. He's a nice man." Liz stood up to leave. "I'll have breakfast for you and then I'll see you at the café."

"Night, Liz."

"Goodnight, Buster.

The cowboy opened the door for her and watched her until she drove out of his sight. "One of these nights, she's either gonna stay or invite me to her quarters. Then I'll have that starchy little thing where I want her. I can wait her out. Her and this little ranch will be well worth it."

## 14

-------

ALL THREE PENNED UP HORSES acted a little suspicious that morning, but Buster was able to catch each one in time. In their tie stalls enjoying a good brushing and chewing oats, they were all saddled as soon as the grain disappeared. He led Red out of the barn and turned him loose.

The outside horses were gathering up, but found the gate shut. He carried a full bucket of feed to the bunks and hollered the now familiar, "Come on." The grain was poured out and Buster opened the gate, but this time he leaned on the fence and made them walk past him. Some came in right away, others hesitated, and several wouldn't come in at all. He waited until almost all the oats were gone before leaving the gate, so the last horses to come in hardly got anything to eat. "You hosses might be in more of a hurry tomorrow, I bet."

Buster spent about an hour with Red. He wasn't near as fiery as Flashy, but didn't have near the smarts or feel either. He returned him to the stall, unsaddled Flashy, let him go, and led Brown Bob through the pasture gate. "Bob, let's go see if we can find some cattle at the creek."

Bob plugged along, totally numb and without care. Riding

through the thickest grove of trees, Buster saw the little herd coming from the creek. He got a good look at them before they scattered, and they looked full. He rode on to the creek bed and saw they had indeed just left. "I figured that alfalfa would have them thirsty pretty early in the morning." He crossed the creek to get familiar with the area. He wanted to be able to recognize this part of the creek from the other side. "Okay Bob, were done. That wasn't so bad, was it?"

When Bob and Flashy were unsaddled and fed hay, he hopped in Baby Blue and headed for town. He drove straight to the U-Drop Inn. He gave Liz a one arm hug, and she actually hugged him back. "Ahh. A public display of affection," he remarked. "I would say that's a good sign."

Liz rolled her eyes with her mouth crooked. "Sit down and shut up. I'll get you some coffee."

"Hello Buster."

The cowboy looked up to see the other waitress. "Oh, yes, Katy. How are you?"

"I'm good. It's so nice to see you again."

"Yes, it's nice…"

"I don't know what's going on out there on that ranch, but whatever you're doing, keep it up. This Elizabeth is a changed woman. Happy, friendly, it's unbelievable."

"Really? Well I doubt I had much to do with that."

"Oh you most certainly did. I guarantee it." She smiled at the cowboy, then smiled bigger at Liz as she brought a steaming coffee cup. "Bye now," she said, giving both of them an obvious wink.

"What was that all about?" Liz asked.

"Don't know. Sit down a minute. Will they let me charge to you at the Mayfield Supply?"

"I think that wouldn't be a problem. John had an account there. They can call me here if they have any questions. The account is under John Anderson. I hope you are not planning to spend too much."

"No, just need some cotton rope."

Liz slid out of the booth. "There's Mr. Walker. I'll tell him you'd like him to join you."

Lawrence Walker's face lit up when Liz pointed to the cowboy, and he came right over. "Well hello young man. How are you?"

"I'm good, sir. And you?" Buster rose up and shook his hand.

"Oh I'm doing well for an old fat man," he said with sparkling eyes. "You having any luck gathering wild cattle?"

"Don't actually have any in captivity, but I'm making progress."

"Well, like I said, if I can help ya, I sure will."

"I was wondering about those mules of yours. Would you consider loaning them out?"

"I don't have to consider it very long. Just come get the sons-a-bitches. I'll have Orville leave them up whenever you want to come get'em."

Buster grinned, "You s'pose you'd furnish harness too? I don't have anything 'cept the idea."

Well, if I loan you the mules, I sure won't have any need for the harness. Just hang it on them when you get'em."

"I sure appreciate it, Sir. I've got a colt started that could use the miles. I'll ride him over and get them Monday morning if that's alright."

"That'll be fine. They're a good gentle team and sure enough broke."

Liz brought Mr. Walker some tea and more coffee for Buster. "What can I get you fellas to eat?"

Lawrence spoke up quickly, "Bring us the special, whatever it is, and I'm a buyin'."

Buster shook his head, "It ain't often you borrow a man's mules and then he buys your dinner too."

"Ah, hell. I know you ain't got any money." Lawrence leaned forward and looked over both shoulders, then lowered his voice.

"Say, has Liz said anything about selling an oil and gas lease on her ranch?"

"No."

"Well, there was a feller came in my office the other day, said his oil company was looking in to reopening some of these lower producing wells, you know, cause of the demand from the war. Liz hadn't said anything?"

"No, she hasn't said a word. What do you suppose is going on?"

Buster realized the concern in Lawrence's eyes. "I don't know, but I think I'll look in to it. Don't say anything to Liz just yet."

"That won't be a problem, Mr. Walker."

"I don't know, from what I hear, you two are getting kinda chummy."

Buster leaned back. "That goes to show, you can hear just about anything."

Liz brought out the dinner plates of roast beef, mashed potatoes, cooked carrots, and hot rolls. "What else do you men need?"

"Not a thing, Liz," said Lawrence.

"Thank you, Liz," Buster said.

Liz smiled with her lips and her eyes. "You're welcome, Cowboy." She gazed at him over her shoulder as she walked away.

"Well, I'll be," Lawrence said. "I've never seen her look at anyone that way."

Buster's mouth hung open. "Me neither."

---

TWENTY FEET of one-inch cotton rope lay in the floorboards of Blue as the cowboy drove back to headquarters. The cowboy smiled at the thought of there being oil on Liz's ranch. "This is just too good to be true."

Buster drove to the barn to spend more time with Red on the ground. He knew the colt needed some confidence in his foundation, and this would make him a better horse. Buster had plenty of time and used all of his patience. Finding a good place to quit, he unsaddled right there in the pen, turned the colt loose, and carried the tack to the barn.

Retired to the porch, with his water, he waited for Liz. The little bunch of cattle came a bit earlier every day, and they had already come and gone when Liz drove up. "You missed the show." Buster hollered as she stepped from the car.

"What show?"

"The cattle eating hay show."

"Oh, I've seen that before. Why don't you find a different way to entertain me?"

"There's a good idea," Buster said opening the door. "I've got something in mind you might like."

Liz tried to hide her red face. "That didn't sound very proper. I didn't mean it that manner."

"You sure about that?"

Liz smiled and ignored the question as she arranged the meal on the table. "How was your visit with Mr. Walker?"

"I really like that feller. He told me to come get those mules."

"Yes, he's such a good man. He was so nice to me when John died. I'm afraid I didn't show very much appreciation at the time."

"Well, you apparently reciprocated good feelings somewhere along the way. He sure cares about you."

"Reciprocated? Okay, Buster, I think it's time you tell me more about yourself. In fact, all about yourself."

Buster heaved a big sigh. They both sat down to eat.

"Well, I was raised in Kansas. Near Abilene. Dad farmed. Mom and Dad both died in 1918 from the Flu pandemic when I was eight. The state sent me to St. Johns Military School in Salina. I think I was the youngest boy there. An older kid named Wyatt befriended me and looked after me. He's still my best buddy today. He's the friend I told you about that lives at Amarillo."

Liz listened intensively. "I remember you mentioning that."

"He had an Uncle in Canadian, Texas with a ranch. All Wyatt talked about was going out there and hiring out as a cowboy. They had a horse program there at St. Johns. If you acted right, you could be involved with those horses. That's all I wanted to be ever since. A cowboy."

Liz acknowledged with a nod and a smile.

"Anyways, Wyatt wrote to his Uncle and asked if he'd come get him. It had been so long without hearing from him; he gave up. Then, Wyatt got notified his Uncle Everett was coming to get him. We had us a plan. When Wyatt got in the car, I hopped in too. He told Everett, "This is my friend Buster. I ain't leaving without him." Ole Everett dropped the car in gear and took off. "Sounds good to me," he said. I was so relieved. I didn't have anybody in the whole world, and I would have been devastated without Wyatt.

"So you went to work for this man?" Liz encouraged.

"For about five years. He was a fine man and an unbelievable horseman. I learned everything worth knowing from him."

"So that explains your way with horses. I'm sure he was like a father to you."

"Exactly. He just died a couple of years ago. The funeral was the last time I've seen Wyatt.

"I thank-you for sharing that, Buster. I was sure you had some formal education somehow."

"Well, now you know everything about me."

"Oh, I doubt that."

The conversation seemed to be over. Neither had anything left to say until Liz broke the pause. "I don't have to work this weekend. Tomorrow, I'll strip your bed and bring you clean sheets. You will have been here a week."

"You think you might be interested in some of that entertainment you talked about?"

Liz stood up slowly and spoke softly. "I think I should go now," though she didn't make any move to leave.

This was the moment Buster had been looking for. He placed

his thumbs and forefingers around her tiny waist. His palms and bottom three fingers hooked over her hips. He pulled her close. She put up a slight resistance, but he could read people as well as horses. He gently yanked her next to him. He studied her face, and her eyes confirmed what he already knew. She threw her arms around his neck.

**15**

———

In the middle of the night, Buster reached across the bed. His arm came up empty. He sat up and looked around to find himself alone. His head flopped back to the pillow. In a few moments, he fell sound asleep.

There came a knock on the door. Buster leaped from the bed and jerked his britches on. Liz opened the door about the same time. "Good morning," she said in a high note.

"Good morning," he said, not knowing what to do or say next.

"Are you ready for breakfast?"

"I'm always ready for breakfast. Especially when you cook it."

Liz smiled as she placed the food on the table.

"Why did you leave last night? I didn't know when you left. Are we okay?"

"Oh yes. I couldn't go to sleep. You know, I was just very emotional. I wasn't comfortable. I hope you aren't offended."

"No. I think I understand." He bear hugged her, and she felt limp in his arms. "I hope you don't regret last night. I sure don't."

"No, I don't at all. I just have some feelings to work through. Please don't expect too much from me all at once."

Buster smiled and hugged her again. This time she hugged him back. "I'll give you all the slack you need."

"Thank-you Buster," she kissed his cheek.

They sat and enjoyed the fried eggs, bacon, hashbrowns, and biscuits. "Good breakfast." Buster allowed.

"You're not hard to please," Liz commented.

"That's not true. You are just so good at pleasing me." He knew he could get that pretty crooked smile from her for saying that, and he was right. "Do you suppose you could help me this evening?"

"Mmmm, I'm not so sure how good of help I'd be."

"Oh, you can do it. I guarantee it. I need you to drive for me while I string out the hay to our little bunch of cows. I want to wait till they come in before I feed them."

"I'll give it a try, who knows, it might be exciting."

"You're exciting. I'll go feed the horses, and then I think I'll give you some more entertainment."

Liz blushed. "I won't go anywhere."

Buster hurried out the door. He didn't take time to do any horse training, getting back to the bunkhouse, for sure the priority. When he entered the door, she was waiting for him. They fell together and indulged. They lay together all morning until Liz got up. She put on his Levi work shirt and lit a fire, putting the coffee on the stove while Buster lay in bed. An old Kings James Bible lay on the stand beside the rocker. She picked it up. It was not only well worn; it was somewhat tattered. On the inside cover it read, Mary Bonds family Bible. She placed it back on the stand and watched the cowboy sleeping. "Lord, be with me," she asked.

The coffee percolated, and she poured a cup. She took a sip to sample it and sat down on the edge of the bed.

Buster felt her weight and smelled the coffee. He stirred around and focused in on her. "I made some coffee," she said, offering it to him. Buster sat up and took the cup.

"Always the right thing at the right time," he said. She snuggled up next to him.

He slurped from the mug and thought about what it would be like to be on this ranch with her permanently. Contentment overtook his face.

Afternoon came, and Buster loaded hay on Blue. He wanted to be in position long before the cattle showed up. He and Liz made the jarring climb to the feed line. Buster turned the pickup around, shut the motor off, put the tailgate down, and cut the wires off all three bales of hay. "When them cattle show up, I'll start the pickup for you. I'll get in the bed, and you slide over. Put it in first gear and ease the clutch out. No gas. Just steer it straight the way it's pointed. Get it?"

"Got it."

"It will be awhile for they come in, but I won't have time to give you instructions then. Soon as they see us, I'll need to be throwing hay out, or I'm afraid they'll leave. If I can get them coming to the pick-up, that would be a huge battle won." Buster slouched down in the seat and looked out over the ranch. "This is the best damn ranch I've ever been on. Big enough to make a living on, yet small enough one man can run it by himself. And the nicest barn, pens, and houses you could want."

Liz sighed. "I have to admit, I haven't enjoyed living out here for some time. It is a beautiful place. It's just been hard to be out here alone."

"I can sure understand that," Buster said.

"I will say. Since you've been here, things sure seem a whole lot brighter. I've done more living this week than the total of the three years previous."

"It has been a good week." Buster returned her smile and reached for her hand. "A real good week."

Buster turned to study the darkness through the trees behind them. "I think I'll start the truck and get in the back. They might be here pretty quick. I'll tell you when to go."

She nodded.

Buster stepped into the bed and sat down on the hay. Liz assumed her position behind the wheel.

"By the way, Buster, you've been using bad language."

"Ah, it ain't that bad." The cowboy strained his eyes into the cedars. He thought he saw movement. He stood up and threw some hay out a way from the pickup. A few cows appeared in the open. Buster tossed some more hay. "Get ready Liz," he said softly. Liz put the truck in gear and waited. The cows in the clearing stepped closer and more cows surface from the trees. Buster grabbed up another flake of hay. "Okay Liz," he instructed.

Liz was nervous. She knew it was time to go, but she was unsure. Her leg trembled from holding in the clutch for so long.

"Go, Liz," Buster said sharply.

She panicked. She dumped the clutch all at once, and Baby Blue violently lurched forward. Buster made a high arcing departure from the pickup, landing squarely on his left ear. He was a good fifteen feet from the truck when the rest of his body settled to the ground. He struggled to stand from his piled up body, as the truck kept leaving him. Trying to hurry back aboard the truck to avoid spooking the cattle, he was timing his leap when Liz hit the brakes. Buster's upper torso folded over the tailgate, and all his remaining air he rushed out of him. He kicked and wiggled the rest of the way in the bed and crawled up on the hay.

"Are you all right?" Liz inquired.

Buster gasped for air. "Gawdamit! Are you trying to kill me?"

"What do I do now?"

"Let the Gawdam clutch out."

Blue shot ahead, almost as far as the last time, but leveled in to a smooth pace. Buster regained his feet and pitched some more hay out. The cattle balked at the goings on, but they hadn't taken off. When all the hay was thrown off, Buster let Liz drive on farther. "That's good. You can stop now." The pickup came to a halt.

Buster waited, crouched down, holding on to the side rails. "Is it out of gear?"

"Yes," came the answer.

The cowboy climbed over the side of the bed, taking an assessment of his aches and pains. He wasn't hurt bad. When most of the cattle lined up on the hay, he got in the cab, shut the door, and looked over to Liz. She had a terrified look on her face. Buster said, "You don't drive so good."

"I'm sorry I made you cuss."

Buster grinned, then chuckled, then broke into his hee-haw laugh. Liz held off her laughter.

"I'm sorry you made me cuss too," he said.

Liz snorted and giggled as Baby Blue half rolled and half skidded down from the ridge.

"Gosh dang, I'll be lucky if I can get out of bed in the morning. I feel like I been run over by a herd of hogs."

"You should be more careful," Liz stated.

Buster looked over at her in surprise. She only peered at him through her peripheral vision. "You do have a sense of humor," he told her.

She cocked her head and sat up straight. "Yes, I do," she proclaimed.

"Maybe that's why I'm in love with you."

Liz jerked her head towards him. She couldn't hide the shock of what he had said. "Oh, Buster. How can you say that? You've barely known me a week."

"I've never been more sure of anything in my life. I love you, Liz."

**16**

———

"Would you like to take a bath?"

Buster looked over at Liz. "Yes. Yes, I would."

"Well, I'll draw you a hot bath while I fix dinner. I'm sorry, supper."

"That sounds really good to me. I'll bring some clean clothes."

"And bring me your dirty clothes," Liz added.

Buster dropped Liz off at her house and drove on to the cowboy shack. He tied knots in the cuffs of a pair of pants, gathered up his laundry and stuffed it all in the legs. With two fingers hooked through a belt loop, he picked up the dirty clothes. A clean shirt and jeans were draped over his other arm. He also carried moccasins, in which he had a razor and comb. The ranch house felt inviting as he walked up the stone path. He knocked on the door. "Come on in." he heard.

Liz hurriedly stirred a pot on her stove before she attended to the cowboy. She took the laundry from him. "Right this way," she motioned. "I have a nice hot bath ready for you."

"It's a beautiful home," Buster told her.

"Thank-you, Cowboy. I believe you will find everything you need on the stand. Enjoy your bath."

Buster skinned off and poked his toe in the water. "My God that's hot. She must think I need to be scoured off pretty bad." He slowly eased into the tub, letting his body get used to the heat as he went. Settling into his eyeballs, he found a relaxing position. "Oh yeah, I think I could live like this."

Clean, fresh, and smooth shaven, he emerged from the bathroom. Liz gave a pleasant smile as she looked him over. "My, you look so very handsome."

He approached and grabbed her hips. She pushed his hands down and returned to her cooking. "Sit down. It will be ready in a bit. Would you like something to drink?"

"What would you be offering?" Buster quickly responded.

Liz faced the cowboy with an ornery grin. "I have some very nice wine if you would like."

Buster perked up. "Really? I can't say I'm a connoisseur of fine wine, but I'd sure try some of whatever you've got."

Liz reached high to a cabinet and pulled out a dusty bottle of red wine. After searching in several drawers, she found a corkscrew and put it to the task. Buster watched as she strained and worked the cork out which came with a prominent, "Pop." She went back to the same cabinet and pulled down two high-end looking wine glasses. A damp dish towel wiped them spotless, and she proudly poured the wine. Offering a glass to her friend and at the same time also offering a toast, she said, "May we always respect our differences, and may we always enjoy each other's company."

"I'll drink to that," Buster said, as he downed the entire serving.

"My goodness!" Liz exclaimed. "Were you able to even taste that glass of Merlot?"

"Merlot? I don't know about that, but it went down mighty smooth, whatever it was."

"This is vintage wine from the very best producers in Iowa. You don't guzzle it like cheap bourbon."

"Oh. I'm sorry. I guess I need retrained in such matters. Please don't be mad."

Liz's eyes softened. "I won't hold it against you," she said in admiration. She poured him another glass. "Try to savor this one a little more."

Buster raised his glass with a sheepish grin, and Liz quickly clinked her glass against his. "Here's to you and me," he proclaimed.

"Yes. Here's to you and me," she repeated.

A well prepared supper soon reached the table, although Buster couldn't recognize most of the food.

"Do you like Norwegian Meatloaf and Red Cabbage?"

"I don't know. I haven't had any of it yet. I'm sure if you're serving it, it's wonderful."

"I hope you like it. It's one of my favorite meals to prepare."

Buster awkwardly attacked his plate, not sure as to how or what to do first. Liz tried to provide some relief to him. "Just eat it like you would anything else, Cowboy."

"This is really good. Tastes really good."

"You like it?"

"Hell yes, I like it."

"Oh, I'm so glad. I love to cook for a hungry man."

"Maybe I'll provide some more of that opportunity for you," Buster smirked.

Liz cleared the table and began the clean-up. Buster watched her at the sink washing dishes, taking note of her nice figure. He approached from behind, hugged her close, and began kissing her neck. She squirmed out of his hold and pushed him away.

"Not here, Buster. Go on back to the bunkhouse. I'll be along shortly."

"Okay, Liz. That sure was a good meal. Thank-you. And thank-you for letting me take a bath."

"You're very welcome."

Buster entered the cowboy shack and sat down next to the

light. He randomly opened up the bible to Galatians and read. "This I say to you then, walk in the spirit, and ye shall not fulfill the lust of the flesh."

**17**

The cowboy awoke with the pretty woman lying next to him. He smiled. "Can it really be this easy? Can it really be this good?"

He took his turn this morning to make the coffee. "You gonna sleep all day?"

Liz sat up, and he shared the cup. "What are your plans for today," she asked.

"You mean after breakfast?"

She smiled. "Well of course."

"I'm gonna do a little riding. Would you like to come with?"

"I'd love to. Go feed and come to the house. I'll have breakfast ready for us."

"Yes, Ma'am."

Brown Bob had a hard time keeping up with Flashy. Buster worked on some turnarounds to give Liz a chance to catch up. "Flashy travels well, doesn't he?" she asked.

"He can cover some ground all right. I really like this horse. You sure ride good, Liz."

"Thank-you, Cowboy. What is the purpose of this outing?"

"We're gonna get to the back side of this pasture and get a little distance between us and ride towards the creek. I'll drop you off where I need you, and then I'll ride on farther south since that plug you're riding can't keep up anyway."

Liz frowned. "He's not a plug. He's perfect for me."

Buster looked up to the sun. "Okay, Liz. Just stay at a walk and ride straight to the creek."

"And then what do I do?"

"Just wait for me on this side."

Buster stepped Flashy off into a nice short lope heading south along the east fence. Before reaching the corner, he put his horse to a walk and headed west. Flashy labored up the long slope, and Buster stopped him just short of the crest. He could see Liz ambling along on the next hill over. "Whoa son," he said as he dismounted. He began to relieve himself. Flashy stretched his stance and started his own stream. "You too, huh buddy?"

When Liz reached the top of her hill, Buster got back on. As she continued downhill, he cued his mount ahead. He again checked the position of the sun. "I think our timing is good," he told Flashy.

Looking to the bottoms, the cattle had already seen Liz and were at a good run headed south. He asked for a trot and began waving his hat in the air. The longhorn steer led the wild bunch, and he boogered straight west when he saw Buster. The cowboy slowed to a walk and returned his hat to his head. He put slack in the reins and pointed Flashy towards Liz.

Liz had a huge smile on her face when he rode up to her. "Did you see those cattle? I think they went that way. I think they crossed the creek. What do we do now?"

"We're done."

"That's it? Why did we just let them go?"

"We should have some more cattle coming to the hay this evening. Hopefully, you won't throw me out of the truck."

"How do you know they'll get with those other cattle?"

"Cause they crossed right where those other cattle come to water. Which would be just a few minutes ago."

Liz thought for a moment. "You did some research didn't you? You knew where both groups of cattle would be, and you used me to spook those wild cattle toward you. I'm impressed, but why didn't you explain your plan to me beforehand?"

"I didn't want to give you too much to think about."

"You don't think I'm capable?"

"I don't think that at all. I just didn't want to make you all nervous."

Flashy had a considerably slower pace, and Liz's excitement improved Bob's speed. They rode along side by side. Liz looked over to Buster. "We make a good team, don't we?"

"Hell yes, we do."

"Damn right we do," she said.

Buster broke into a surprised laugh.

"Damn you, Buster. You've got me drinking, cussing and screwing. You have ruined me!"

"Ah, it ain't all that bad."

------

BLUE CARRIED eight bales up the ridge. Buster turned the pickup around at the end of the last feeding. I want to string out this hay before they get here. Think you can ease that clutch out?"

"You better hang on, just in case."

"Don't worry."

Liz let the pedal up smooth as could be. "How'd you like that?"

"Good job, Darlin'."

Buster climbed back in the truck.

"Darlin'?" she asked.

"Well, yeah, is that okay?"

"I like it, Cowboy." She leaned over and kissed his cheek.

"I feel some entertainment coming on."

Liz giggled and snorted. "You are just horrible."

"Let's crack that wine back out and see how many cattle come get on that hay."

"You're so romantic," she teased.

———

THE PORCH of the main house provided the same view of the ridge as the bunkhouse porch. Buster and Liz sipped wine and visited. "Here they come," Buster said. The Longhorn steer and the cows came at a trot, and with them were a few of the new cattle. Several more came from the cedars and when they smelled the hay, ran to it. They kept coming for a while, but when no more cattle showed themselves, Buster stated, "It ain't like I could get a count, but I don't think that's all the cattle. Some must of went back to the other side."

"What will you do now?"

"I'll keep spooking them back every morning till they figure out it's easier not to be harassed on this side. When they all get on the hay, It won't be long 'fore we have a gathering."

"I won't be able to help you, you realize."

"I know, but I can put them cross the creek now by myself, and the feed line is far enough down the ridge the pick-up can drive itself."

Liz took Buster's wine from him and set both glasses down. She then straddled him and kissed him. "Take me to the bunkhouse."

**18**

——————

LIZ GENTLY SHOOK THE COWBOY'S shoulder. "You're breakfast and lunch are on the table. I'll see you this evening."

Buster grabbed her and pulled her on top of him. She let out a squeal and laughed uncontrollably while he loudly smooched all over her. She finally escaped his grasp. "Bye Cowboy."

"Bye Darlin'"

——————

BUSTER HAD Flashy in a long trot headed west. The horse puffed a little when Buster got to the gate into Mr. Walker's ranch, so he let him walk until he aired back up. Then he short loped him until the headquarters came in sight. He put him to a walk, pitched slack in the reins, and Flashy dropped his head.

Buster could see two men standing beside a car. A little closer and he could tell it was Orville and Lawrence. "That's a pretty nice pony you're riding," hollered Lawrence, as he came in range.

Buster rode on up and stepped off with a grin. "He's a dandy alright. How are you, Lawrence?" They shook hands.

"I'm good, son. Good to see you."

Buster turned to the foreman. "Hi, Orville."

"Hello Buster," he said reaching for his hand. "Well, I'm going to get to it. See you all later."

"I had Orville harness those mules," Lawrence said. "They're ready, but I need to talk to you a minute."

"Sure," Buster said cautiously.

"You remember me telling you about that oil rep coming to my office?"

"Yes, Sir."

"Well, what I didn't tell you was, that feller told me he had bought a new lease on the William Anderson ranch next to mine. I said, "You mean the John Anderson ranch?" He said, "No, that ranch is owned by William Anderson who lives in Deerwood, Minnesota." I was pretty sure that was John's father's name."

Buster looked puzzled but didn't speak.

"Well, since then I've done some checking. Turns out, the ranch was never in John's name. I'm sure Liz doesn't know that. The president of the bank is supposed to be overseeing the property. I asked him why Liz hadn't been told and why she was still living there. He told me Mr. Anderson said she could stay as long as she didn't remarry. He said he didn't know if Liz knew or not, but he didn't want to be in the middle of any controversy. Kind of chicken shit if you ask me."

"Well, I'll be damned. She don't own that ranch?"

"No part of it."

"Is there anything that can be done?"

Lawrence shook his head in disgust. "Not a damn thing. It's sewed up tight."

"Well, I'll be damned. I just can't believe it. Are you going to tell her?"

"Unless you want to."

"No, sir. She thinks highly of you, and trusts you."

"I'll have her come by my office when she gets off work. It'll be tough to tell her, but she's got to know."

. . .

Flashy didn't know what to think about the mules at first, but in a short distance, he decided they were okay. Buster rode along with a lump in his throat and a knot in his stomach. "This is terrible. This screws everything up. Liz is going to be devastated. Hell, I'm devastated."

It was half past noon when he rode up to the barn. He put the mules up and took care of Flashy before heading for his sandwich. The day lost all purpose for the cowboy, and he didn't feel like doing anything. He tried to nap, but couldn't. He hazardly opened the Bible to Proverbs. "Cast but a glance at riches and they are gone, for they will surely sprout wings and fly off to the sky like an eagle." He closed the good book and made himself get up and go put the hay out.

He stayed out in the barn and leaned on the bottom Dutch door to the horse pen. All three horses watched to see what he would do. Not too much time passed until Flashys' curiosity got the better of him. He walked part way to Buster. "Hey buddy," Buster said to him. The horse made his way a little closer. "You're safe. I ain't gonna ride you or ask anything of you. In fact, you and me might be done, my friend." Buster thought of the work he had done, the pens, tack room, saddles. He thought of the progress made with the cattle. Flashy came close enough to smell and nuzzle Buster's arms. "And then there's you my good buddy. I'm not sure what's gonna happen." Flashy let Buster rub his forehead. When he stopped rubbing and folded his arms, the horse rooted his arm with his nose. "Need some more of that, Flashy?"

In one quick moment, it came to him. Buster understood his feelings clear. He knew what he was going to do.

He made his way to the porch to wait for Liz.

**19**

———

LIZ DROVE UP, BUT SHE DIDN'T get out. Buster cautiously approached the car and slowly opened the door. Liz stared straight ahead, tears rolling off her cheeks. Buster knelt down and slid his arm behind her and hugged her shoulder with his left hand. "Lawrence told me this morning," he said.

"How could John do this to me? I don't understand."

"I don't know, Liz. Maybe he didn't figure on dying."

"What am I going to do?" she blubbered.

"I don't know, but we'll figure it out."

"Here's your dinner, I'm going to the house."

———

BUSTER CHOKED DOWN MOST of the cold supper. The sadness overwhelmed him.

He knocked on her door. No reply. He knocked louder and longer.

"Go away!"

"Ah, come on Liz. Open the door."

"I don't want to see you. Go away!"

"I'm not going away; please let me in."

Liz jerked the door open and violently pushed Buster backward. Her red face shot fire from her eyes. "Get away from me! You never cared a damn for me. The only thing you've ever cared about is getting this ranch. Well, I don't have a ranch, so why don't you just leave. There's no reason for you to be here anymore."

"Liz that's not true. I want to …"

"Get out!" she screamed. "Get out!" She hurried through the door and slammed it shut.

Buster stood on the porch in disbelief. "What on earth?" He lumbered down the path back to the bunkhouse, stopping once with his hands on his knees, thinking he was going to puke. The bunkhouse proved to be so lonely, he went to the barn just to be alone somewhere else. He meditated until past dark, no answers or solutions came to him. Only despair.

---

No breakfast or dinner showed up that morning, but Buster continued his routine. He saddled Red and used him to drive the cattle back from the east side. The Longhorn steer and about a three-year-old bull led the pack. "Those crazy sons-of-bitches are gonna keep quittin' the herd and always be taking some with them. I gotta put a stop to that." Buster successfully put the two bunches together and rode to the barn. It was a lot more work to ride Red, but the colt did fairly well.

Buster assumed there would be no supper as well, and he had to eat something. He drove into town to Mr. Walker's office, making sure he got there before noon. The good looking young secretary gave him a glowing smile. "Good morning," she said.

"I was hoping to see Mr. Walker."

"Why, sure handsome. You go right on down the hall; he's on the right."

"Thank-you."

"You're welcome," her smile and voice turned very seductive.

Buster knocked on the open door. "Well, Buster! Come on in son. How's Liz?"

"Not so good."

I was afraid of that," Lawrence said leaning back in his chair. "She held her composer pretty well when I told her, but I could tell she took it hard."

"Yes Sir, she plum lost it last evening. Tried to run me off. Said I was only interested in trying to get her ranch."

"Oh hell, son. She'll come around."

"I'm not so sure. In the meantime, I want to keep my end of our agreement, but that included meals, which was pretty handy, seeing's how I don't have any money."

I'll spot you some cash until you get some income from catching those cattle. How much you need? Would thirty dollars keep you from starving?

"Oh yes, Sir. I don't need much to survive, but the thing is, I don't feel right with the arrangement I made with Liz. I mean it was based on her owning that place. I just want to square her up and give her a chance to start over. I want her to have the money and horses. If I could get out of there with that flax main gelding, I'd be tickled to death. So I don't know how I can pay you back, short of working for you."

"I ain't worried about it son. We'll work something out. Maybe I can buy some of those horses, and you can get them riding around for me."

"I sure appreciated Sir."

Lawrence laid forty dollars on the table. "Now let's go to the café, and I'll buy dinner."

"I'm pretty sure that's not a good idea. I don't want to stir things up. One more thing, Sir. When I get these cattle caught, who around here would buy them."

Let me know when you've got eight or ten to ship. I'll contact

Chick Crisp at Sayre. He owns the sale barn there and can send a bobtail truck to get them."

"Very good," Buster said as he stood.

Lawrence pushed the money closer to him. "Be careful son."

---

BUSTER SHOPPED at the Piggly Wiggly for pickled foods, dried beef, cheese, and crackers. "Hope she don't come take her coffee back."

He never saw or spoke to Liz for three days. In that time, he had all the horses coming in and had settled them twice before turning them back out. Several cattle kept company with the Hereford bull and Longhorn steer, but everything else stayed together and came into hay, although several wouldn't eat until he drove off. Flashy and Red made good progress as well, and he decided to put the mules to work.

Tying and extra rope to his saddle before mid-morning, Buster rode Flashy around the west side of the creek and stayed upwind headed north. He hid in a thick grove of trees and got off to pee and tighten his cinches. Flashy stood still as if he knew they were hiding. They waited. Buster stood next to his horse, arms folded over the saddle, studying the landscape. "Here they come, buddy." He lost sight of them as they walked into the creek bottom, but he waited until he was sure they had time to tank up on water. This would limit their speed and distance they could run. He swung into the saddle and eased Flashy forward. The cattle saw him shortly after Buster saw them. They broke away to the east, just as the cowboy had hoped. He hurried across the creek in pursuit but hung back. He didn't want to get close enough they could circle back around to the creek. With some more good luck, the bull peeled off in a separate direction. Knowing he would run out of air before the steer, the bull became his target. He urged Flashy for more speed. They gained ground. Buster patiently helped his horse track the bull. He felt Flashy lock on, and at the same time noticed the bull weakening his pace. Now was the time. Continuing to follow farther would increase the chance of the bull getting hot and on the fight. He encouraged more run from Flashy, and he had plenty left. Buster raised up with his rope swinging, timing his throw. His loop settled cleanly around both horns, and he jerked his slack straight to the horn and dallied. The bull ducked off to the right and Flashy tried to negotiate the same turn. Buster actually asked God to help the horse keep his feet. He had drug a log on him, but this was going to be a big surprise when everything came tight.

The big bulls head and neck gave enough to the rope; Flashy got himself gathered up. Buster sat deep and asked for a stop. It became a process, but eventually the horse and bull stood facing each other. The cowboy took a deep breath, and so did Flashy. Buster waited. Everybody got some air back, and the bull tried to take off. When he lined up with the creek, Buster quickly cued Flashy to go with him, putting slack in the rope. This made the critter think he could get away, and he ran for the creek. Buster kept his dallys and controlled the speed. With only a few stops, they made it to the edge of the creek bed. When the bovine made his next move, the horse and rider tracked behind. As they reached the first few trees, Buster purposely rode on the opposite side of a tree from the bull. They passed each other as the bull wrapped himself around the tree, and the cowboy rode on to the next closest tree and tied the rope off. "There you go Wooley Bully. You could have been having your fill of alfalfa hay this evening, but no, you're tied to a tree instead. Take that you Hereford prick. Hope your head is nice and sore when I come back to get you tomorrow."

Flashy lowered his head on a loose rein as he headed for the barn. Buster leaned forward and stroked his neck. "Good job, my friend. That was a lot to ask of you, but apparently, you're okay with it."

Flashy ignored his rider as if to make a point. "What did you expect?"

Upon returning to the barn, the first priority was to get the hay put out. Then, he prepared for tomorrows project.

Buster retrieved the cotton rope from the tack room and pulled up a bucket next to the harness hanging on the wall. He tied figure eights on each side of the tugs, and bowlines in the center. He cut and tied another piece about six foot long with a bowline in the center. This would tie the two draftees together after they were harnessed. "I sure hope they're as gentle and broke as Mr. Walker thinks they are."

He missed his time with Liz, and was sad their last time together was so bitter. He wanted so badly to tell her how he felt, and that everything would be alright. He had gone about his business without any contact from her, and he hated it.

Next morning, he saddled Brown Bob to give Flashy the day off. He didn't need talent, only compliancy. He harnessed up the mules, gathered up all his extra ropes, and ventured off to where the bull was tied.

When Buster came in view of the brute, he saw him standing with slack in the rope. The cowboy smiled, knowing his prisoner was ready. He backed the team up to the tree on the opposite side from the bull. Each set of tugs were tied together with the prepared piece of cotton rope. Hooking a lariat over the horns of the bull and then tying it off to the horses, he remounted. He picked up the lead rope to the mules and eased up behind them to cut the rope anchoring the bull to the tree. Before the bull knew he was free from the tree and before the mules knew they were tied to the bull, Buster got out of the way. He purposely had a long lead for this reason. He could simply let the bull and the mules figure out where they needed to be, and afterward, he would lead them all home.

It worked out perfectly.

———

EMBOLDENED by his success and the performance of his steed, Buster didn't see any need in letting the Longhorn steer run loose anymore. The whole project would be much easier if the last bad actor was subdued.

Two more fresh ropes gently slapped the sides of the saddle as Flashy marched to his next objective.

"This deal is gonna test you, my friend. I hate to ask it of you, but I think you can handle it."

Flashy acted as if he heard, but could care less.

They hid in the same grove of trees and waited a long time. Buster nearly gave up, but at last the Longhorn and the cattle with him topped the hill. Their behavior was quite different. They only came a little at a time. Restless, suspicious, and leery.

It appeared that the small group led by the big steer didn't want to come in. Buster's patience grew thin, as his confidence rose. "What the hell?" he stated. "I'm mounted. Let's show that outlaw how it's going to be."

He guided Flashy across the creek and walked in a straight line towards the renegade steer. When the ole tough Longhorn snapped his head up, the cowboy asked his horse for all had. Flashy responded, but the maverick was fast. He disappeared over the hill, and when the cowboy and his horse topped out, the crafty steer had ducked back towards the cover of the creek bottom. It was now an all-out race. The steer had no evasive maneuvers in mind. He ran in a straight line for the trees. Buster knew this was his best and only chance of hooking on to this animal. He communicated to his mount the desperation of this situation. If they got beat to the creek bed, it was only going to be more difficult the next time. Flashy seemed to understand. He flattened out and exhibited his amazing speed. The ground rapidly disappeared between them and the creek, and the distance between horse and animal evaporated. Buster timed his throw, offering a "Blocker loop."

The rope went over the right horn and the nose of the steer. Buster dallied, thinking everything would come in to control. The rope came tight with the horse lined up straight behind the Longhorn. This put the horse at a huge disadvantage. He tried to slow his opponent down, as he was asked, but the speed and the strength of the big steer proved to be more than the young horse could negotiate. The trio of man, horse, and steer, crashed into the trees.

The Longhorn went left of a tree, laying the lariat across Flashys' chest and front legs. Hide and hair from the horse attached to the rope as it burned past his skin. An abrupt change of direction occurred when both ends of the rope came tight. The steer kept his feet, but Flashys' legs were jerked out from under him, and he was slapped to the ground. The cowboy's head made contact with the earth with the same velocity.

The raps around the saddle horn, the horse's weight on the rope, and the turn around the tree was enough to hold the steer as Buster lay stunned. He wasn't totally unconscious, just dazed. Flashy laid still, as he had not been told to do anything else. In a few moments, Buster regained part of his senses. He half hitched the tail of his rope over the horn and crawled out from under his horse. His right leg burned and stung.

Putting some slack in the reins, he smooched to Flashy to get up. He undid the rope off the saddle horn and tied it off to another tree, then led Flashy away from the danger of the steer. "You all right, buddy? I think we both lost a little hide in that deal." Buster felt the side of his face and checked his bloody hand. His limp quickly developed to hop, and he knew he better get mounted before he became too stiff to get on. He rode to the barn, relieved that his horse showed no sign of being lame.

**20**

---

"Well, hello there cowboy. Do you need to see Mr. Walker?"

"Yes, please."

"You can go on back," the secretary said.

Buster enjoyed her sexy smile and gave her a little wink.

"Come on in here, son." Lawrence reached across his desk for Buster's hand. "How are you getting along? Looks like you've been scuffed up."

"A little. Got underneath my horse for just a minute."

Lawrence smiled and nodded.

"I've got thirty-some cattle to ship for Liz. Several calves. I'll keep some of the gentler cows to help lure in more cattle, so whatever they can haul will be fine."

"I'll let Chick know. He may have a bigger truck that can load most of what you've got gathered."

"Would you let Liz know, Sir?" Buster asked politely.

"I sure will."

"And could you mail this for me?"

Lawrence took the envelope which read: Wyatt Davis, LX Ranch, Amarillo Texas.

The secretary gave him a cute wave as he left.

Lawrence waddled into the U Drop Inn a little earlier than normal to catch Liz before the cafe got busy. Sit down, Liz. I need to talk to you. "How's Buster?"

"I have no idea. I haven't talked to him."

"I know you haven't. You're not holdin' up your end of the deal. I had to loan him some money so he could eat. Liz, I know this is a terrible situation for you, but that young man has his heart in the right place. He cares about you to the point he's not only going to finish the job; he's not planning to take any payment. He's hoping to get that flax mane horse, and that's all."

Liz hung her head.

"I told him to let me know when he had some cattle to ship, and he's called for a truck. I think you need to rethink this a little. Oh yeah, he's also missing some skin and has a horrible limp."

She raised her head and looked at Lawrence. "Is he okay?"

"Oh I don't think you could kill him with an ax, but he's been in some kind of wreck."

Liz stood up and untied her apron. "Thank-you, Mr. Walker." She hurried to the waitress station. "I have to go, Katy."

"Is everything all right?" Katy asked.

"No, but I'm going to make it right."

Liz came through the bunkhouse door without a knock. Buster sat at the table slicing some cheese and chewing on a piece of jerky. Liz folded her arms. "Did you go on a diet?"

"I guess you could say that."

She approached and examined his scrapes and bruises, stroking his hair. "Are you all right?"

"I'll be fine. I'm on the mend."

"Buster, I'm sorry. I was hurt and took it out on you. I was afraid you wouldn't want me anymore without this ranch, but I had no reason to accuse you the way I did."

"Hell, Liz. Truth is, I did feel a strong attraction to this ranch." He scooted his chair back to stand up. "I would've loved to have lived here and been a part of this place. But my feelings for you have always been sincere. When I first found out about the deal, I had to think things out a while. It didn't take long, though, to realize how important you are to me. I'm so sorry you lost your ranch, but I'll take you any way I can get you."

Liz covered her mouth as tears streamed to the floor. "I love you, Buster."

He hugged her tight and held her. She shook as she cried in his strong arms.

"It'll be all right," he said. "Everything's gonna work out fine."

**21**

———

Liz got busy cooking up an extra special supper and opened another bottle of wine. When Buster came in, she stopped long enough to give him a wet kiss. He swallowed her up in his arms. "I missed you, Darlin'."

"I'm sure you did," she teased. "But I'm here for good now."

"Yes, you are. You ain't getting' away from me again."

Liz poured him a glass of wine. "Sit and visit with me while I finish cooking."

Buster took a seat at the table facing her. He smiled when he watched her slender body twisting and swaying as she tended the stove.

She turned her head slightly to speak over her shoulder. "How many cattle do you have going to ship?"

"Thirty-some. Tomorrow I'll bring in that no good renegade steer with them mules. That will make everything else work a lot easier."

"Buster, I want you to know, our agreement needs to stay the same. I want to honor the original deal we made."

"No Liz. Our agreement was made when we both thought you owned this ranch. That's not fair to you, and we're going to make it right. I have to tell you; I'm in love with that Flashy. He's by far the best damn horse I've ever throwed a leg over. I'll gladly forgo all of our arrangements if I could own that horse."

Liz left the stove, bent over to the cowboy and kissed him. "He's your horse," she whispered.

A solemn look came over Buster's face. "Thank-you, Darlin'."

After Buster became enlightened with more Norwegian cuisine, Liz began the clean-up. Buster helped in his awkward way, and Liz paused, holding his hands. "You're spending the night here with me." She said.

**22**

———————

THE MULES HAD THE LONGHORN in tow, and Buster planned on getting him on the first truck. Eight head of tame cows were already turned back out to mix with the herd. He hoped to drag several more cattle in the pens that evening. "It's all gonna happen a lot easier after today."

A truck and floor trailer came over the hill and turned up the drive. Buster had just finished putting up the mules. "Here comes your ride," he told the big steer. Thirty head even fit nicely on the semi-trailer, including the Hereford bull and the Longhorn. He told the driver he would have another load by morning and he agreed to come get them.

Only the cattle that followed the pickup into the lower corral received hay. Those that were used to eating alfalfa in the pasture were missing out, and they didn't like it. He lured in over fifty head of new cattle that evening, enough for two more loads. The truck doubled back the next day, and Buster assured the driver he would have at least another load in the morning. The process continued each day until the gentlest eight cows, two crazy old cows, nine three-year-old steers, and six long yearling bulls and heifers, were all that remained. None of which would follow the lead cows into the corral. He thought about having Liz drive the pick-up, and he would come in behind them horseback. But if he spilled any, they would all most certainly have to be roped. He opted for taking a little more time to train the cattle to come in. By allowing the cattle to come in to the hay after he left, it wouldn't take but a few days to get them trapped. The truck driver knew to wait for word to come back for the final load.

LIZ SAT at the kitchen table with Buster. Supper needed a few more minutes. Buster had a piece of paper filled with figures, and his pencil wasn't slowing down. "What's all the arithmetic about," she asked.

"How much is your note at the bank?"

"I'm not sure. If I remember correctly, John paid one hundred and twenty-five dollars per head when he bought those cows. They were bred, and there were sixty-five of them, but I'm pretty sure he borrowed seven thousand. He only paid the interest and a small principle payment the first year. He reduced the principle substantially the next year. I don't know what the balance is. I haven't paid anything since John died. Not even interest."

Buster laid his pencil down. "Well, Lawrence said feeder steers at Kansas City Stockyards are bringing ten to eleven cents a pound. I'm just guessing at a lot of this, but if they would bring eight cents here, I figured five cents up on the stockers and five cents back on the cows, of course, I'm estimating the weight, and not considering that some of the cows might be worth more as replacements, I'm gonna say the whole mess, after freight and commission, could be somewhere close to," he picked his pencil up.

"My lands, Buster! I don't understand any of that. Just tell me how much money they'll bring."

"Nine thousand."

"Oh, my. Really? Well, I should have a good portion left over, don't you think?"

"Yes. And you still have the horses to sell."

"That's right. Do you think Mr. Walker would be interested?"

"I know he'll want some of them. Don't know if he'd buy 'em all. Either way, we'll get 'em all sold."

"I want you to handle that for me, Buster."

"Yes, Darlin. You're gonna have a nice little stash."

"That money is for both of us, Cowboy."

**23**

———

"MR. WALKER?"

"Come on back, son."

Buster was somewhat disappointed and somewhat relieved the cute little secretary wasn't at her desk.

"How are you, Sir?"

"Good, good. What are you up to today?" Lawrence said. "I've got some mail for you," He handed it over to Buster.

"Well, Sir, Liz wants to know if you would be interested in her horse herd. All except the little brown horse and the flaxen sorrel."

Lawrence smiled. "Tell me what there is."

"Eight broodmares. Six five-year-old geldings and three fillies. Four four-year-old geldings and four fillies. Four three-year-old geldings and three fillies."

"Any of them geldings broke?" Lawrence asked.

"I got a red gelding pretty well started. He's a bit common but will make a nice horse. I was hoping you'd bid him like he wasn't broke, to wash out that forty dollars you loaned me."

"Fair enough," Lawrence said. He leaned back, chewing on his cigar stub. "How 'bout I buy all them horses at a hundred a piece?"

"Would you throw in that two-horse trailer I saw you at your place?"

"That won't be a problem."

"Then I'm sure that will be fine. I'll tell Liz."

"You going to work at the LX?"

Buster opened the letter. "Let's find out." Buster read a ways, then folded the note back to the envelope. "I guess I am," He said smiling.

"Liz going with you?"

"I sure hope so. She doesn't know anything about it yet."

Lawrence raised up and offered his hand. "Good luck to you, son. I'm glad I got to know you."

It's been a pleasure knowing you, Sir. And thank-you for all your help."

---

THE COWBOY WRAPPED HIS arm around Liz's waist as she cried. "Are you ready?" Buster asked.

She took one final look, nodded, and got in the pick-up.

Baby Blue squatted down under its' load of household goods, Brown Bob and Flashy stood side by side in the horse trailer. Two ranch saddles and a sidesaddle were strapped to the stock-racks.

The ole rusty truck rattled down the dirt road, turned right on Route 66, and headed west.

# PART IV

# SHOWDOWN AT U-DROP INN

CAIT COLLINS

**1**

---

Chicago, Illinois
March

Moira O'Hara stood on the corner of Jackson Boulevard and Michigan Avenue. This was it. From 1926 to 1933 this corner marked the eastern beginning of the Mother Road, Route 66. Even the damp and gloom of a Chicago spring day could not destroy her excitement.

She'd been planning this trip since the day she'd met a happy Japanese immigrant on this very corner. He and his wife were celebrating his sixty-sixth birthday by traveling the Mother Road from Chicago to Los Angeles. His grin was infectious. And for the first time in months, Moira had a hope of coming out of the pain and funk she'd been experiencing.

Brushing a heavy chestnut lock of hair from her cheek, she raised the hood of her fleece lined rain coat. The over-sized hood protected her cameras from the misting rain. Lifting her 35mm Minolta she snapped a photo of the Jackson Blvd sign. For good measure, she switched to a newer digital camera and took three more pictures. A quick check let her know at least the last three photographs would work.

A distinguished gentleman stood to the side watching her work. His reddish brown hair had a touch of silver at the temples and his green eyes were wrinkled at the corners. "Are you sure this is what you want to do, Moira? I mean just you and Baron. What if something happens?" His brow furrowed and his eyes glistened.

She knew letting go of her after the last eighteen months would be difficult for him.

She pushed the hood back. Rising to her full height of five feet and six inches she faced off against her father. "Dad, we've talked about this. I'm taking my life back. I won't continue to lean on you and Dr. Williams. The two of you need a break from doctoring and nursing. And I want freedom from the bubble wrap."

"Mutt, come," she called to the service dog. The registered German Shepherd trotted to her side.

"Why do you insist on calling Baron Mutt?" Colin O'Hara's disapproving frown was evident.

"This is an old argument. I told you a registered dog was not necessary, but I've fallen in love with this wonderful animal. But he's not royalty. He's my friend and companion; a mutt at heart."

She scratched behind the dog's ears. "You don't need to worry. We've been training together. Mutt knows the signs. He'll keep me grounded." She stepped back and placed her hands on her hips. "And if I get anxious, he knows how to calm me."

Moira eyed her father. He'd aged over the last months. "I have to make this trip, Dad. I need to find out if I can handle the rigors of being on my own. I know I can't go back to the Middle East, but I can use my talents in other ways. Trust me. If it gets to be too much, I'll turn in the rental and fly home."

His eyes misted. "I nearly lost you, Moiri. Forgive me if I hover. You may be nearing thirty, but you're still my baby girl."

She bit her lip. Blinking away the tears she whispered, "And you're my best friend. You always will be." Throwing her arms around her father's neck she held on for a couple of minutes. "Wish me well. I'll check in every evening and send you pictures." With one last hug, she stepped back. "I love you, Daddy. But I have to find myself."

"I'm trying to deal with that. You'll understand better when you have kids."

Moira smiled. "Dream on, Dad. For kids I'd need a husband and there are no prospects."

"You can change all that when you get home."

She toyed with the key fob. "Are you staying in Chicago for a while?"

"I fly out in the morning. I'll be waiting for you in Amarillo."

"If the weather cooperates, I'll see you in a couple of weeks. Please, wish me well, Daddy."

Wiping her eyes, she turned to her dog. "Mutt, shake."

The dog sat up and offered a paw.

"Say goodbye."

"*Woof, Woof.*"

Colin O'Hara shook the paw. "Take care of my baby, Mutt."


MOIRA SETTLED Mutt into his space in the passenger's seat. The back of the seat was reclined to give the dog more wiggle room. He could stretch out a bit or curl up. He could even find space for a nap.

Climbing into the driver's seat of the new SUV, she reached for the seat belt and buckled herself in. Mutt had his own seat belt. It gave him some protection, but also allowed him the ability to reach her. She reached across the console and ruffled the dog's fur. "Ready to go, Mutt?"

She started to merge into the traffic, but a vintage Mustang painted bumble bee yellow with black racing stripes cut her off and raced up to tailgate a deep blue Jeep Cherokee. Moira took a deep breath. "So this is driving in Chicago," she muttered to Mutt. "I hope it's better when we get on the Mother Road."

Once on the road, she checked the rear view mirror and saw her father standing on the corner watching down the road. He waved.

"Poor, Daddy. He doesn't really get it, does he? When he got to Germany, I was in really bad shape and they didn't think I would live. And if I did survive, I would be paralyzed. He never left my side, Mutt. As soon as I was stable enough, he brought me back to the states and found the best doctors and surgeons available." The corners of her mouth lifted in a misty smile.

"It changed me. I refused to let IT take me. I fought back, but I changed in the process. So did my father. I think he felt every pain, and every frustration I experienced.

"The pain medication wasn't working and my blood pressure kept going up. A volunteer suggested a pet might help. But instead of going to a shelter and getting a rescue dog, he found you."

Mutt laid a paw on her leg.

"The head surgeon nearly had a heart attack when Dad brought you into my room. But he finally gave in when I started getting better. I would have sworn you were an empath. When the pain was unbearable, you'd put your paw on my leg and the pain drained away. I wouldn't have made it without you and Daddy."

The remainder of the nineteen mile drive to her first stop, Cicero, passed in silence except for the panting from her road trip companion. She pulled up in front of the Castle Car Wash.

The old stone building sported a notched castle turret with double car wash bays. The business was once a hideout for Al Capone, the notorious Prohibition Era gangster responsible for the St. Valentine's Day Massacre. She moved gingerly around the lot. The red and black lettering was faded and peeling, but it made an interesting series of photographs.

She stopped to view the ruins of the old highway along the forty-six mile trip to Joliet. The photos she took were forlorn and haunting. Miles of the original highway were buckled and broken. Weeds grew between the cracks.

Quarrying occurred within fifteen feet of the old road and a tunnel was excavated under the roadbed. It could be the road was destabilized and the section of Route 66 was too unstable to be reopened to the public. The few feet of the old road were discarded and deteriorating.

*Is this the way some people feel? Like I felt when my network producer took one look at my battered face and then told me the network was planning to buy out my contract and give me a nice bonus. They found a man to take my place. Used and abandoned. Is this part of the true Route 66 story? No, the road would survive in legend and in song. And in the hearts of a generation who remembered the glory days and would pass the magic onto future generations.*

## 2

---

Joliet, Illinois

Arriving in Joliet, she found a place to park and allow Mutt to answer the call of nature, to sniff around trees, and track unseen creatures through the brush. Moira watched him be just a dog for a while. But when she called him to heel, he bounded to her side displaying a happy doggy grin.

A yellow and black Mustang parked behind her SUV. A man emerged from the vehicle. Pale and gaunt, he limped across the grass to a bench. He dropped his head into his hands and began massaging his temples with his thumbs.

She thought the car was the same one that had cut her off back in Chicago, but that would be impossible. Maybe she should leave before he got back into his car and headed out. She wanted distance between the careless driver and herself.

The views of the Jackson Street and Ruby Street drawbridges that spanned the Des Plaines River were worth the forty-six mile drive from Cicero. The bright green girders and the easy motion of the rising and lowering of the bridges made her smile.

But her real stop was Ruben's Rialto Square Theater. Unfortunately, the tour was not scheduled until tomorrow, so she decided to call it a day. The Olde Keg Bar and Grill offered a good meal along with a fabulous wine selection. Besides no one said she had to drive the 1,271 miles from Chicago to Amarillo in one day.

WHEN MOIRA and Mutt entered the Rialto Square Theater the next day they were greeted by a panicked tour group. Twenty-three senior citizens were in limbo because two of their members had come down with colds and didn't feel like taking the tour. The minimum for a guided tour was twenty-five persons.

"We'll pay for two more tickets," one white-haired lady offered. "Please don't cancel our tour."

Moira walked over to the tour coordinator. "Maybe my dog and I could make up the number. If it's okay with the group."

Nods and smiles responded. She reached into her camera bag for her wallet and counted out the cost of the tickets. "It's official, Mutt. You are a member of the tour group." She attached a ticket stub to his vest."

The lady who begged for the tour to go on approached Moira and Mutt. "Thank you, my dear. The theater was on our Must See list. It was so kind of you to help us out."

*"Woof."*

"And thank you, handsome fellow." The senior citizen grinned at the dog who now sat at attention, head high, and looking every bit as royal as his registered name suggested.

"Mutt, shake."

Mrs. Green, Moira read the name on the group's lanyard, accepted the paw. "It's a pleasure to make your acquaintance, Mr. Mutt."

The guide began gathering the ticket holders. She explained the tour would take about an hour and questions were welcomed. A young man ran up. "Am I too late?"

"Of course not," Mrs. Green stated. "Nice looking gentlemen are always welcome."

Aiden Thornton's smile faded when he saw the chestnut haired younger woman in the group. She was joking with a couple of the older men. When she laughed, his heart almost stopped.

*It couldn't be. Moira O'Hara was alive? The doctors had said her survival was impossible as a military transport lifted off with the broken young woman aboard. She was being transported to a military medical facility in Germany, but no one expected her to survive the journey. She'd been buried under rubble for three days and her injuries were severe.*

"Young man, are you alright?" Mrs. Green's brow furrowed and her faded blue eyes studied him.

He smiled at the older lady. "I'm quite well, thank you. I thought I recognized a ghost from my past." He offered his arm to her and escorted her to the rest of their group.

The guide led them through the lobby with its eighteen white marble Corinthian style columns and twenty-foot crystal chandelier. Moira wanted to stop and capture the beauty of the fixture. But picture taking could wait. They were entering the theater. Plush red seats filled the auditorium. Ornate carvings decorated the front around the stage.

She dropped Mutt's harness. "Sit, she ordered," and began taking pictures. There was so much beauty. A white and gold trimmed pipe organ sat on the stage. She photographed the instrument from every angle. The signature wall was fascinating. Famous artists that had performed at the Rialto left their marks on the wall. She ran her fingers over Lee Greenwood's signature and notation of his final road tour. Then stepped back and captured the image.

The hour ended too quickly, but she flashed her press credentials and was allowed to go back and continue taking her pictures.

Returning to the lobby, she changed her lens and added a filter. She caught the light dances of the crystals and the colors reflected on the white columns.

"Beautiful, isn't it?" The slight Irish accent jerked Moira from her creative pursuits.

She gasped, and moved closer to Mutt. "Yes, it is." The man looked familiar but she couldn't place him. The voice haunted her. Mutt rubbed against her leg alerting her to a change in her mood.

Moira clutched the dog's harness. "We've met before?"

Aiden Thornton smiled. "A long time ago and under much different circumstances. I doubt you would remember our brief meeting."

Mutt's low growl warned the stranger to step back. "Settle, boy. I'm okay." The Shepherd sat next to his mistress at his alert stance…full height, ears pricked and eyes focused on the stranger.

"I'm Aiden Thornton, Miss O'Hara. I didn't intend to startle you. But it seems that is my life's calling. I continually make you uncomfortable.

"What do you mean?"

"The last time I saw you, I was helping the medic carry your litter to a waiting evac."

"I knew you in Afghanistan?"

"You were in pain and every movement was agony for you. I wished I could have taken the hurt away, but all I could do was help get you on that airplane. I never saw you again and I never heard whether or not you made it. Someone hushed any reports of your rescue."

"My memories are spotty. Besides I don't talk about IT. I'm sorry you were left to worry." Tightening her hold on the harness he stepped around the stranger. "Mutt, come."

Aiden watched the woman and dog exit the theater. She had a slight limp and needed a service dog, but she was alive. He couldn't believe her face. Her left cheek bone had been broken and her nose was also off kilter, but the cuts and scrapes had left her face bruised and bleeding. Eighteen months ago, he would not have expected her to live, much less recover movement and mobility. Or regain her beauty. Yet here she was out doing what she loved best…taking pictures.

THE NEXT DAY, Moira stopped at the Route 66 Raceway and Chicagoland Speedway. The facility hosted National Hot Rod Association (NHRA) drag races on the drag strip and NASCAR stock car races. While she was not an auto racing fan, her dad was. The tour was for her father.

"Want to go racing, Mutt? How about a quarter mile down a drag strip?" Her companion whined. "What's the matter, pal? Is it too noisy for you?" She stroked his head. "Okay, Big Guy, let's find some place less loud."

THEY STOPPED at the Polk-a-Dot drive in Braidwood. Moira fell in love with the classic 50's décor. She could see Richie and Fonzie sipping soft drinks in a booth. *Perhaps I belonged in this time. I long for simpler times. The days before computers, tablets, and cell phones took over our lives; the days before 24-hour news and the demand for footage. If not for my network assignment, I wouldn't have been in that village when the 8.2 earthquake shook it into dust.*

Moira shook her head. Don't think about it. Don't remember the dark and the cold. Don't listen to the cries and death rattles of the dying.

She clenched her fists and released them.

Clench. Release.

Clench. Release. Her breathing came in short staccato bursts.

*"Woof."*

Mutt's soft bark brought her back. Moira's eyes opened. She blinked as if trying to clear a fog. Placing her hand on the dog's head she began stroking the soft fur as her breathing returned to normal.

Moira reached for a bottle of water from the cooler in the back seat. "Thanks, Pal." She sipped the cold liquid as she scratched behind his ears. "Give me a minute and I'll pour you some water."

Her hands shook. "I went back there, Mutt. It was dark and cold. I don't want to remember it."

Soft whimpers spoke sympathy and concern.

"Why am I sitting here feeling sorry for myself? I survived. I'm alive and I'm not wasting another moment." Moira poured the rest of the water into Mutt's bowl.

Going to back of her car she grabbed her tripod and favorite camera. She needed to take pictures.

The Polk-a-Dot hosted life size characters…Elvis, James Dean, Marilyn Monroe, Betty Boop, and the Blues Brothers. Moira set up the tripod and camera and set the timer. She posed with her head on James Dean's shoulder. Then she tried to mimic Elvis' "all shook up" pose.

Mutt was enchanted with the ladies. She snapped pictures of the Shepherd his head cocked and looking up at Marilyn who was attempting to control her billowing skirt. Her favorite was her dog's innocent expression as he placed a paw on Betty Boop's hip. "Oh, Mutt," she laughed, "you are such a guy."

Stowing her camera equipment she grabbed Mutt's harness and headed inside to order lunch. The crowd had thinned out and there was space for both of them in one of the smaller booths. She ordered a burger and fries for herself and two grilled hamburger patties for Mutt. Table food was a treat and he deserved the treat.

Just as they were finishing lunch, Aiden Thornton walked in to the drive in. Spotting her, he strolled over to the booth. "Good afternoon, Miss O'Hara."

"Are you stalking me, Mr. Thornton?"

He grinned displaying deep dimples on either side of his

mouth. "I'm not stalking you. I'm taking the scenic route to my new home. It just happens to be the same road you are traveling."

"Where's your home going to be?"

"Amarillo, Texas. I'm the new curator for a large gallery in the city."

"AMARILLO?"

"Don't sound so shocked. Yes, I'm moving to Amarillo. It's going to be a big change from New York, Washington D.C., and Philadelphia, but I'm excited about the opportunity. May I join you?"

She dipped her head.

Aiden slipped into the booth across from Moira. "I've spent most of my adult life traveling from one place to another recovering the most exquisite artifacts and art treasures and then returning them to collectors who keep them hidden in vaults. No one has a chance to appreciate the beauty."

"But why Amarillo?"

"I have a friend who inherited a small ranch near the city. He paints instead of herding cattle. Are you familiar with Ryan Sutton's work?"

"Yes. I own one of his smaller pieces, but I didn't know he lived in my town."

Aiden grinned. "I didn't know you owned the city."

She ducked her head. "That did sound a little pretentious. I'm a native, but went East to study photography and journalism. But I always spend my down time at my home in the city of my birth."

"I've visited a couple of times," Aiden stated. "I find it peaceful."

"The land can enchant you if you allow your heart to open to its beauty."

Mutt brushed his head against Moira's legs. He stood and headed toward the door. "And that's my cue to take my furry friend outside." Pushing open the door she turned and smiled. "Thank you, Mr. Thornton. Maybe we'll see each other when we get home.

"Can you believe it, Mutt? I actually had a conversation with a man that didn't include an assessment of my physical attributes, how much money I made as a photojournalist, or would I like to go to his room and have a drink. There weren't many women on the front lines and the men; well some of them thought any female was fair game."

"Thornton seems like a decent guy. I really don't remember him, but I'm not afraid of him. And at least he looked me in the eyes instead of staring at my chest."

Mutt cocked his head as if he understood every word. Or maybe his was trying to determine her mood.

"I wish we'd had time to learn more about this new art gallery. If Ryan Sutton is involved with this project it must be spectacular. Just imagine the artists he can draw to Amarillo. It will be interesting."


THE AFTERNOON WANED as she entered Lexington, Illinois. In its heyday, Route 66 promised economic opportunities for small towns along the route. Lexington proudly announced its location with a simple neon sign LEXINGTON with an arrow pointing downward. The iconic sign now served as a photo op for travelers along the old road.

Moira pulled off the main drag and on to a dirt parking lot. She opened the passenger door and allowed her companion freedom to do his business and explore. Taking her 35mm Minolta from its case she snapped images of the sign from different angles. Though simple in design, the sign had an odd beauty. It was a sharp contrast against the bright reds, oranges, and pinks of the sunset. She took a few more shots before returning the camera to its place in her kit.

Mutt trotted to her side. He bent his head and nosed her hand.

"Poor baby, you must be hungry." He jumped into the passenger seat. She added water to his dish and presented him with a couple of doggy treats. "Our motel is a couple of miles down the road. As soon as we check in I'll fill your bowl with your favorite chicken meal."

The Shepherd licked her hand as if approving her choice for dinner.

"I haven't been very good to you the last few days. I've been so busy thinking about what I want to do, I forgot what you needed. You've been cooped up in this car for hours. It couldn't have been much fun for you." Rubbing behind his ear, Moira continued. "Tomorrow is your day off. While I'm hiking, you can hunt squirrels, pee on a tree, and chase rabbits. You can do anything you want as long as you have fun."

The dog laid his head in her lap and sighed.

The small motel was reminiscent of the motels on Amarillo Boulevard. The three-sided structure allowed visitors to park in front of the room's door. A restaurant offering good home cooking sat on the corner opposite the lobby. It reminded Moria of some of the pictures she'd seen of old motels that had sprung up along the Mother Road. Sadly she'd seen too many of the iconic structures had been abandoned and left to rot.

Opening the heavy door to their room she allowed Mutt to enter first and do his walk-around while she brought in her cameras, luggage, and his necessities. "Ready for dinner?"

Mutt sat next to his dishes watching as Moira filled them. His eyes moved from watching her hand dip a cup into the bag to his empty bowl. He leaned over as Moira poured the contents of the cup into his dish. He poked his nose into the bag as if to say, "Better be chicken."

"You get started on your dinner and I'll go across the parking lot and get mine." Mutt stopped munching his food and eyed her. "It's just a few steps. I'll be fine." He assumed his guard stance, but Moira would not allow him to follow her. He was still standing watch when she returned carrying a plastic bag that smelled like a kitchen.

Exhausted, Moira crawled into the queen size bed. The mattress was perfect; not too hard and not too soft. The bedding was crisp and smelled of sunshine. "Mutt, bed." He responded by going to the oversized cushion that served as his sleeping place.

MOIRA OPENED her eyes to bright sunlight. But the chill in the room made her wish she'd turned up the heat before going to bed. Mutt huddled at the foot of the bed seeking warmth. Grabbing her robe she jumped up and rushed to the heating unit. Ramping up the thermostat, she turned to the dog. "Come closer to the heat." He came and sat by her as she warmed her hands. "You should have crawled under the blanket. I'll get you one of your own. Maybe we can find one that has Route 66 on it. It'll be your travel blanket. Maybe we shouldn't rush that trip to Memory Lane. You want to stay inside today and keep warm?"

He yipped and danced around her feet.

"I guess this means you approve." Turning she rushed back to the bed and snuggled under the covers. "Come on, big guy, get up here and get warm."

**3**

Memory Lane
Lexington, Illinois

The cold front that had stalled her trip moved through during the night. While still chilly, it wasn't so cold that she couldn't make that walk down Memory Lane.

Commissioned in 1926 as part of the original four-lane highway, Memory Lane was now reduced to one mile of two paved lanes preserved as a bike and hiking path.

It is said that Memory Lane was a doorway to the past. Moira wondered what would happen when she stepped on to the road. Would she find the missing memories and then go forward? Or would the pain and guilt keep her lost in shadows. Bending she released Mutt's leash. "Go on, big guy, run. Chase the will 'o the wisp."

He cocked his head as if reading her mood, and then made a run for the trees that lined the road.

Moira strolled along the way allowing her mind to roam; not

focusing on any one thing in particular. Slowly the trees dimmed and disappeared. In their place was a dusty street in a war-torn village. A hot wind blew. Closing her eyes, Moria allowed the scene to come into focus. A child's face appeared. He grinned, held up a battered baseball to a young soldier. "Play, please."

The troops had called him Hal mainly because none of them could wrap their tongues around his Arabic name. She took a picture of his angelic face. The boy tossed the ball to the soldier who threw it back to the kid. The game continued until the town's only teacher rang a cowbell calling the children to school.

A smile curved her lips but a sudden sense of vertigo made her wobble. She looked across the compound. The buildings swayed. Vertigo was not her problem. The ground shook. Cracks appeared in the sun-hardened ground.

Moira watched herself run toward the hut that housed the school. She entered the two storied mud building hoping to get the children out, but fate had different ideas. The walls crumbled and the roof caved in crushing the occupants beneath the load of rubble.

One by one the cries were silenced and she was left alone to die in the cold darkness. Until he lifted a boulder aside. Gentle hands laid a handkerchief across her eyes.

"It's bright out there, Miss O'Hara. You don't want the full force of the sunlight in your eyes."

She tried to move. "Be still, Miss. We don't know how bad you're hurt." A warm hand held her in place. "Be patient. We've a ton of rock to move before we get you out. I'm not leaving you, Moira O'Hara. Stay with me."

And then she remembered Aiden Thornton; the man who had saved her life in Afghanistan.

MOIRA SHOOK her head clearing the fog and returning her to the present. She staggered to a tree along the road side. Dropping her tote to the ground she removed a solar blanket and spread it on the brown grass. She wrapped a fleece blanket around her shivering body. She closed her eyes allowing the memories to return.

His touch had been gentle and his voice calm, reassuring. She recalled the pain as each layer of mud and rock was moved from her broken body.

"The others," she had asked.

"I'm sorry, they're gone." With soft words he confirmed what she already knew. "We got here too late to do much. There are survivors in other parts of the village, but not here."

Blackness returned and her next memory was of the doctors in Germany trying to stitch her back together. They would send her back to the States for further surgery as soon as she was stable.


"Miss O'Hara. Moira?"

She raised her head and met his eyes. "Aiden Thornton?"

"Are you okay, Moira?"

"Yes. I mean no... The earthquake. All those people died and I lived. I don't understand why I survived."

Without an invitation he joined her on the blanket. "Maybe we don't need to understand everything. Some things may always be a mystery. "


Mutt darted out of the trees, paused a moment his eyes on the man and then bounded across the paved path to the tree where She sat. Pushing his head beneath her arm he licked her chin and whined. She did not laugh.

Mutt sat watching as his mistress closed her eyes. A tear slipped down her cheek. He wriggled until she scratched behind his ears.

"It's your day off, big guy. Why aren't you playing?"

The Shepherd whined and burrowed under her blanket. "I can't believe you're cold." Moira turned to Aiden. "It's a big blanket. Do you want to share?"

"I thought you'd never make the offer. It wasn't too bad when I was walking around. But just sitting here it's a bit cold." He accepted a share of the deep purple blanket. Mutt moved between them. His fur added a layer of warmth to the group.

"So what have you discovered along the Mother Road?"

"I remembered you. You kept me alive while the rescuers dug me out. I also remembered how you used to sit in a corner of the officers' club and pretended the rest of us didn't exist."

"I didn't have many choices. Because we were after antiquities smugglers, I couldn't talk about the job, so I tried to keep a distance. I have to say I enjoyed listening to the various ways you fought off amorous advances."

A light blush crept up her neck and face. "Maybe I crossed a couple of lines with my put downs."

"You were creative, Moira. You tried to keep everything friendly. Until the man crossed a line, and then you came up swinging."

The conversation stalled.

"I hated my job, but the money was good. Have you ever felt like you accepted a job just for the money? I don't know why that was so important. I have money. I never had to work. Maybe I wanted something my family name couldn't buy. I needed to be someone other than Colin O'Hara's daughter. And I was, am, a great photographer."

"But?"

"I won't go back to war zones. I'm not enamored of the adrenaline rush. I'm afraid something worse will happen."

Aidan searched her eyes looking for a hint of the old spark that always lit up her face. He found nothing.

"What happened to the girl I used to watch from behind my newspaper. Where did she go?"

"She died. Died before she ever lived."

"I think you sell yourself short, Moira.

"My journey of discovery is not going as well as I anticipated. I've only been on the road a couple of days and I've seen some interesting places and enjoyed taking pictures again. But I keep thinking I will find that woman, but so far nothing resonates."

"But…"

"She's not on this road, Aiden. I'm learning that. The woman you knew is gone. Maybe she's gone for good. I don't know if I can ever be her again.

"It's time to go home and pick up the pieces. I don't know who I am any more, but I intend to find me. I may cut the trip short. I have a couple of places on my bucket list. Mutt and I will go to Funk's Grove tomorrow. I may stay there a couple of days. They make maple sirup and my daddy loves the stuff. Maybe I can watch the process or tap a tree.

"I must tour Meramec Caverns. I need to conquer my fear of the dark and closed places. And there's the Trail of Tears monument. Then Mutt and I will go home. We'll surprise Daddy by getting to Amarillo sooner than he expected. I think I'm ready to be home."

Aiden nodded. "I'm taking a risk here, but I can't let you go just yet. That night before the earthquake, I watched you take that young officer apart. I thought you just might be a woman I could enjoy having as a friend or maybe even…"

She placed a finger on his lips. "Don't. I'm not ready to consider relationships or what could be. But with both of us in Amarillo, we can meet and see if we have something."

Mutt nudged her shoulder.

"I know, buddy. Go ahead and find the white rabbit.

The dog slithered from beneath the blanket and took off into the trees.

Aiden rose and held out a hand to help her up. Together they folded the blankets and waited for Mutt to make his return.

When he came to her side, she snapped on his vest and attached the harness to his collar.

Aiden walked her to her car. "I may see you at a couple of those stops. Let's at least have dinner one night."

"Dinner with my hero. That sounds really good." She kissed his cheek. "See you around."


AIDEN WATCHED HER DRIVE AWAY. He admitted she had a lot of emotional healing to get through before she could make any decisions. And the new gallery would occupy the bulk of his time. Still he planned to be a presence now and later in Amarillo. "Moira O'Hara we're not done yet."

**4**

_______

Funks Grove, Illinois

Moira and Mutt left Lexington mid-morning on the following day. They'd taken the time to find a shop that sold Route 66 memorabilia. Tucked in a corner shelf was a stack of blankets depicting the iconic Route 66 logo. She bought three: one for her dad, one for herself and the one she'd promised Mutt.

"See, big guy, your own blanket. Let's spread this out for you. If you get cold, grab an edge and pull it over you." Unfolding the thick flannel throw she draped it across the back of the front seat and the seat itself. She patted the soft throw. "Up, Mutt." The dog made the jump and sniffed the fabric. He settled in his place and allowed Moira to buckle his "seat belt".

"Warm enough for you, Mutt?"

He sighed, grasped a corner of the blanket and pulled it down. Nesting in the mound of fabric, Mutt lay is head on Moira's leg and slept.

The short twenty-nine mile trip passed in peace. Soft doggy

snores kept her from becoming sleepy. Arriving in McLean, she pulled into the parking lot of a major hotel chain. Since she planned to stay in the area for a couple of days, she chose the hotel for the additional conveniences. Yes, it was a short drive to Funks Grove, but the full breakfast, extra large room and king size bed made it worth the commute. She would relax for the remaining daylight hours and begin exploring Funk's Grove in the morning.

She knew when to arrive for tours of the old growth forest and the demonstrations for the making of their famous maple sirip. Her research included the times the store was open, and when to visit the other attractions in Funks Grove. There was plenty to do over the next two days and she looked forward to it.

One thing she especially anticipated was meditating in the chapel in the wood. From the pictures she'd seen, the open air chapel appeared serene and inviting. She needed the peace to forge a connection between the past she was beginning to remember and the future.

FROST COVERED the ground the next morning. When Mutt jumped into the SUV and placed a cold paw on her knee she knew he needed warm paw covers. A set of soft leather shoes was in her bag. They had a light fleece lining that could keep the pads of his feet from getting too cold and possibly cracking. But they were soft enough that they would not hinder his ability to walk and run.

"I know it's cold, big guy, but the sap is running. We want to be there when they tap the trees."

"The making of maple sugar and sirup dates back to the Native Americans who settled the area long before the Funk family arrived. It is said that an Iroquois chief, Woksis, buried his hatchet into the trunk of a Maple tree. The next morning he removed the hatchet and went out to hunt. A bowl was beneath the gash made by the hatchet and the sap dripped into the bowl. Thinking the vessel to be full of water, Woksis's wife poured the liquid into a pot of venison stew. Both the chief and his wife were pleasantly surprised by the taste and the process of making sirup from sap was discovered." The guide paused as he emptied a bucket of sap into a holding tank.

"Hazel Funk became the owner in the 1920's," the man continued his story of the grove. "The land was put into a trust so that it would remain in the family. She also requested the spelling "sirup" be used as it was the most popular spelling in Webster's Dictionary for maple sirup made without adding extra sugar."

Moria recalled the history of the Funks Grove sirup as she and Mutt followed the workers in emptying and replacing the four gallon metal buckets. "The gathering season," the guide explained, "begins in mid to late February and runs through the middle of March. We are entering the end of the season."

"Too bad we won't be able to tap a tree," Moria stated.

"Tapping a tree is an art. The tree must be forty years old and at least fourteen inches in diameter. No more than two taps are put into a tree. And the holes are one and a half inches in depth. The diameter depends on the type of tubing or spout used."

"That is certainly a precise process. I think tapping is best left to the experts," She laughed.

The guide emptied the collected buckets into a holding tank. "We'll boil the sap at two hundred nineteen degrees for about one and a half hours. It will be moved into another holding tank until it can be bottled."

He continued to explain the process as he walked Moria and Mutt back to the Maple Sirup store. She thanked him for his time and went into the building. She dropped Mutt's harness as she knew he would not leave her side. Grabbing several bottles of the darker sirup she placed them in her basket and walked around the shop looking for something special for her father. He'd been her rock all those months she'd been in the hospital and in rehab. He would have made the trip with her, but she'd been insistent on coming alone.

She'd been lost in her thoughts and had not noticed that Mutt no longer walked by her side. She began looking for him and soon heard a growl followed by a whine. She found him in a back corner trying to bat a travel mug off his snout. The lid lay on the shelf and she guessed the last customer hadn't put the cap back on the mug.

Moira laughed at the sight of her companion trying to free himself from the offending mug. She snapped a couple of pictures before setting her basket down and dropping down beside him. "Hey, buddy, you got yourself into a bit of a pickle here. Take it easy, we'll get it off." Wrapping a hand around his nose she gently twisted the mug until it came loose in her hand.

Setting it aside she put her arms around her dog and allowed him to whine his troubles away.

"This will teach you not to wonder off. You've never done that before and it frightened me. I guess I'll just have to keep hold of the harness from now on."

Standing, she reached for the harness. Mutt took one last swipe at his nose before resuming his walk down the aisle. He stopped suddenly. "Come on, boy." Mutt stood his ground staring at a shelf of cloth dolls. He put a paw on one of them. She lifted the doll from the display. "Do you want this?"

He sniffed the toy but did not immediately reach for it. "Here, we'll take it to the cashier." He held the doll in his mouth, but did not clamp down and pierce the fabric. When they got to the register, he dropped the doll on the counter and watched while the clerk rang up the purchase. Instead of putting the doll in a sack, she held the toy over to Mutt and encouraged him to "go ahead and take it".

They loaded the purchases into the SUV and walked over to the Funks Gem and Mineral Museum. Aiden stood at the door as if waiting for them.

"I noticed your car in the lot, but wasn't sure where I'd find you."

Moira smiled. "We've been in the Maple grove learning about

sirup. Then we went shopping. I think Mutt's bored with my company. He found a new friend."

Mutt trotted up to Aiden and allowed him to examine the toy. "Did you take a good look at this doll?"

"Not really. Why?"

"It resembles you. She has your hair and eye color and her mouth is shaped like yours. Your pal found a miniature version of you."

"Oh, Mutt." A tear trickled down her cheek as she hugged the Shepherd. "I love you too."

"Quit blubbering." Aiden instructed. "We have one of the best gem, mineral and fossil collections around."

He led them through the displays, stopping at the open venues to touch the gems and minerals. "I can't believe the differences in the textures of the crystals and stones. They are truly beautiful," she stated.

"And rare. Some of these pieces are not found in any other open display. What few exist are hidden in vaults never to be seen by men." Aiden placed her hand in the crook of his arm and walked her to the door.

"I'm staying in McLean."

"We are too. What hotel are you in?" she asked.

It turned out they were in the same hotel. "Can we have dinner tonight? There's a good steakhouse nearby."

"What about Mutt?"

"Service dogs are welcome."

"In that case, yes, I would love to have dinner with you."

THEY WALKED three blocks to the steakhouse. Once they were seated, Mutt laid down at Moira's feet.

Aiden ordered a rib eye, medium rare, with a loaded baked potato and a house salad. Moira chose a small filet mignon. Instead of a loaded potato she opted for butter only on her baked potato. She also chose a salad. Aiden chose the wine.

"You know a bit about me, Aiden, but I know nothing about you."

"What do you want to know?"

"Basics. Where were you born? Do you have a family? Have you ever been married? What's your educational background?"

"That's a lot of questions for such a short acquaintance."

"You know those things about me.

He sipped his wine. "I was born in Philadelphia thirty-two years ago. I'm a Leo in case you're interested. I have a brother, Ian. My father was a doctor and my mother is an attorney. Never been married. Never been in love. I have a PHD in art history."

"So you're Doctor Thornton?"

"Yes. The PHD wasn't good enough for my mother. She wanted me to be an MD. On the other hand, Ian is an attorney with a minor in geology. He's also a certified gemologist."

"Who's older, you or Ian."

"Ian."

His answers were short, almost abrupt. But Moira kept digging. "Are you close to your family?"

Aiden focused on the window across the room. "My father and I were close. He died from cancer a couple of years ago. My mother considers me the black sheep of the family because I didn't follow her career choice. I see her when I can, but I can't say the visits are always pleasant.

"Ian and I are friends as well as brothers. Our jobs keep us on the go, but we get together when we can."

Before she could ask another question, Aiden turned the tables. "How about you? Brothers or sisters? Ever been married? How old are you? A guy needs that information so that he can avoid being accused of robbing the cradle."

Moira laughed. Mutt lifted his head at the unusual sound.

"I'm sorry, but I can assure you there's no cradle robbing.

Thank you for the compliment. I'll be thirty the last of June. Never married. Like you, my job left no time for serious or even non-serious relationships. I'm an only child. My mother had a heart attack when I was in high school and died before we could get her to the hospital. So it's just me and Dad."

"I bet you are Daddy's princess."

"My dad has been a rock. He's the CEO of a design firm in Amarillo, but he took a leave of absence to take care of me. I wish he could find a good woman. He's so loving and giving and he deserves to be loved and cherished in return."

Their meals were served but they continued to ask questions and become better acquainted.

"You're Black Irish, aren't you?" Moira asked.

"Irish is Irish, Moira. You have the traditional coloring, but to answer your question, yes my ancestors were Black Irish."

"That explains the dark hair and blue eyes."

The waitress brought the check and a "to go" bag. "It's a treat for your dog. Our owner is a veteran and he always has us give a service dog something special."

"Thank you. Mutt is special. I wouldn't be here now without my dog."

"My boss has a Border Collie. She's pretty special, too."

The weather cooperated and the walk back to the hotel was comfortable. Aiden insisted on seeing her to her door.

"Thank you, Moira. I've hoped we could have a friendly dinner since Afghanistan. It was worth the wait." He placed a gentle kiss on her forehead. "See you tomorrow."

"Good night, Aiden," she whispered.

THE NEXT MORNING Moira woke with a sense of excitement. She and Aiden along with Mutt were planning to explore the nature preserve close to Funks Grove. She couldn't wait to get on the trails and finally see the chapel.

"What do you think of Aiden, Mutt? He likes you."

"*Woof.*" The Shepherd picked up his doll from his bed and met her at the door. They were meeting Aiden in the lobby and going to the preserve in his vehicle.

They spent the day roaming the old forest enjoying the beauty of the trees and grasses. They walked to the chapel in the trees. Aiden stepped away to allow her alone time to relax and commune in the quiet forest. All went well for the first ten minutes. Aiden moved forward when Mutt dropped his doll and went to Moira. He placed his paws on her knees and nudged her chin with his snout.

She stared straight ahead, eyes dark and unseeing.

"Please, God," she muttered, "Please no more."

Aiden placed his hands on Moira's shoulders. "Moira, come back."

Mutt's sharp bark broke the spell. Moira shivered and looked into her dog's eyes. "Mutt, are you okay?"

He flicked her nose with his tongue and settled close to her side.

"What happened, Moira? You went away for a few minutes."

"I don't know. I feel as if someone or something stepped on my grave. It's like something terrible is going to happen and I'm powerless to stop it."

She looked across the chapel. A figure appeared at the edge of the forest. She saw the gaunt man that had parked near her SUV at the park in Joliet. She gasped. Who was this man and why was he following her?

**5**

---

Meramec Caverns
Stanton, Missouri

Aiden met Moira and Mutt for breakfast before beginning the drive to Stanton, Missouri and Meramec Caverns, a four point six mile cavern system in the Meramec Valley. The limestone cave complex stretched upwards past the height of a seven-story building.

Moira had studied the geology of the caverns as well as the history. During the Civil War, the caves were called the Saltpeter Mines. Saltpeter was mined to make gun powder. Rusted artifacts were discovered and "traced" to Jessie James. According to popular lore, the caves were a hideout for the notorious outlaw.

The nearby Jessie James Wax Museum in Stanton contained more information regarding the history and exploits of the outlaw.

Not only was a famous outlaw associated with the cave, it is rumored to be the second to last stop on the Underground Railroad before one exited to freedom. The use of the cave to assist slaves in gaining freedom coincided with the use of the system for the manufacturing of gunpowder.

"You know, the Civil War connection makes sense for the Underground Railroad, but the logistics seem off."

"What do you mean, Moiri?"

"I guess I always pictured the route to be more northward from the Deep South, but this connection could work too. There were battles in Missouri, Kansas, and into parts of Texas. I guess I never really considered how far west the overall battle map covered."

"So do you really think Jessie James roamed the Meramec Valley?"

Moira shrugged. "Why not? It makes for good publicity. Everyone loves an outlaw."

Aiden took her arm as they walked the path toward the Caverns. "Do you like the bad boys?"

"Never been attracted to them. In fact, I can't recall ever lusting after a man. Attracted, yes, but I was too busy building my career to be distracted by romance."

"Why are the caverns so important to you?"

"They're underground and dark. The two things I'm not sure I can conquer, but I have to try."

"Mutt and I are here with you and for you."

She scratched behind Mutt's ears as they approached the ticket office. "Stay with me, big guy. I'm scared."

"Ready?" Aiden asked.

Her smile didn't reach her eyes. "Ready as I'll ever be. I have to do this, but I'm anxious. My hands itch and my stomach is doing flip flops."

The next tour would start in twenty minutes. The attendant suggested they take care of "business" before they entered the cave. The cavern did not have rest rooms.

Moira handed Mutt's harness to Aiden. "I'll be right back. Just a warning my buddy likes kids and they like him. Please don't let the children distract him. When he's wearing his vest he's working."

"Kill Joy," Aiden teased as she walked away.

Stepping out of the ladies restroom, she bumped into a tall man. "Excuse me, sir."

She looked up. The man who had been standing at the edge of the forest at the Chapel in the Trees grinned. "No problem, Miss," he said as he walked past her.

Rushing to the spot where Mutt and Aiden waited, she began shaking.

*Is that man following me or was he just another tourist? Why did he make me feel so skittish?*

"You okay, Mori?"

"No, Aiden. I'm terrified I keep seeing that man." She pointed at the retreating figure. "He makes me nervous."

"I've seen him myself, but I bet he's just another tourist. The caverns and the grove are popular stops on the road."

"Maybe, but I still don't like him." Taking Mutt's harness she walked him to an open area So that he could do his thing.

Moira shivered as Aiden joined them near the entrance. "You're pale. Are you sure about this?"

"No, but it's necessary."

"You have your camera? I hear the cavern is spectacular. I'd be disappointed if you missed a photo op."

"I may be terrified, but, Mr. Thornton, I'm a professional. I always have a camera."

He grinned. "Of course you do, Miss O'Hara. I like the bit of color in your cheeks. A couple of minutes ago you were a bit ghostly."

He took her hand and they entered the cool limestone chamber. Her breath hitched. It was dim but not dark. The low light only enhanced the stalactite and stalagmite formations growing in the chambers. She lifted her camera and began snapping pictures of the columns noting the varied colors of the stones. She knew enough geology to know the streaks of color came from the minerals in the water that flowed through the caves.

As they moved from chamber to chamber she became aware of the magnificence of the stalactite growth. Curtains of creamy limestone fell from ceiling to floor; their elegance reflected in the water below the limestone shelf.

The light show began. Pinks, blues, greens, and finally the Stars and Stripes lit up the walls and brightened the chamber. She continued to snap photographs using a 35 mm camera instead of a digital one. She switched to a wide angle lens to get a better shot of the curtains.

They moved to a room with a river running through it. Figures of Jessie James and a member of his gang stood in the water. While some said the outlaw hid out in the caves, others remained skeptical.

*Believe what you will, Moira thought, but it's good fun and quite theatrical.* She took her pictures and grinned. She hadn't been this happy in months.

And then the lights went out.

Women squealed and some giggled. Someone bumped into Moira.

She gasped and began taking short, rapid breaths. Aiden's hand clasped her shoulder.

"Steady." He pulled her closer as Mutt wrapped his body around her legs.

The guide droned on about the depth of the caves not permitting the outside light to enter the rooms. He explained the measures taken to bring electricity to the cavern. Then the lights came back on.

She sagged against Aiden. "Did I scream?"

"No, you did just fine."

The guide conducted their group of about fifteen to the exit. One hour and twenty minutes had passed and Moira was drained.

"I need food and water. You and Mutt must be starving after your guard duty."

They found the restaurant, ordered burgers and fries, and ate in silence. She requested meat patties to go so that Mutt had a treat. Table food was not recommended for dogs, but she considered Mutt to be more human than dog. He understood her and cared for her. He was her friend.

"Aiden, did you notice the silica mines as we drove through Pacific?"

"Yes. Why?"

"Silica is used in making glass. I got to thinking that glass has no say in its design. It's molded or blown into being by a master."

"True, but glass is inanimate. Only humans can make choices. Although Mutt seems to have chosen you, he was trained for a job."

"But he could have rebelled. Even an animal makes a choice. What if Mutt was averse to being trained? He could have flunked out of training classes and gone back to being a pet."

He pushed his chair back and stood up. Offering her a hand, he stated "We need to take this outside."

He tucked her hand into the crook of his arm and walked with her to their vehicles.

"Mutt is a working dog because he was trainable."

"And so was I. I'm beginning to realize I went along with what others chose for me. Don't you see, Aiden, I failed to control my own life. I fell into a mold and permitted others to determine my future. I'm like the silica in the glass; molded into someone's vision of me."

"Again, Moira, you under estimate yourself. You had spunk and drive when I saw you in Afghanistan. It's only since your injuries that you question yourself. There's nothing weak about you. If you were not strong willed, you would not have made it to Germany, much less to standing on your own feet. Quit questioning yourself and your past. Make changes for the future, but always remember you made choices and no one forced you."

"Aiden, you… "

"I do understand. I've been where you are. That's why I'm changing my life and moving to Texas. I know what I want and what will make me happier. I may be the black sheep but I have talents and drive. I'll never please my mother. That's okay. I'll be happy any way."

"Don't you want more? Have you ever thought about finding a wife and having a family?"

"Have you ever considered marriage, Miss O'Hara? You said you have never lusted after a man. Why not? No man ever measured up to daddy?"

The darkening of her green eyes and set of her mouth should have been a warning, but Aiden ignored the signs.

"Maybe I do measure the men I meet by my father. Why wouldn't I? I have no other yard stick. My father is gentle and generous. He picks his battles and sees things through to the end. He's loyal and demands loyalty in return. What's wrong with that?"

"It doesn't leave room for us mortals. We fail before we even had a chance. Is that fair? My lord, Moira, does any man have even the slightest chance with you?"

They reached her SUV and he stood back while she buckled Mutt into his space.

"Do you want to go to the Jesse James Wax Museum or should we find a place to stay the night and get an early start tomorrow?"

"I think the museum might be an idea. At least wax figures won't dismiss what I feel."

"Damn it, Moira O'Hara," he spat.

He grabbed her shoulders and pulled her against him. He cupped her face with his hands and kissed her.

. . .

Her hands clutched his shirt and she hung on as if she feared falling.

Their kiss deepened. Abruptly she broke her mouth from his and shoved out of his hold. Wide-eyed she stared at him. Her breath came in short bursts. "Why?" she asked.

"I wanted you to know how I feel. And if you didn't get it, I'll just say it. Lady, I wanted that kiss back before you got hurt. I knew there was passion under the cold professional front of yours. I don't dismiss what you feel, but don't you ever put yourself down again. You're too good for that."

He left her standing by her SUV. He climbed into his Jeep and waited for her to start her car and lead the way. They did not visit the Jesse James Wax Museum.

**6**
———————

Trail of Tears Monument

Moira wrapped a blanket around her shoulders and keyed the speed dial code into her phone. It was early morning and Mutt was still sleeping. His soft snores broke the silence.

"Hello," a sleepy voice answered on the second ring.

"Daddy, I'm sorry it's early, but I…"

"Moira, honey is something wrong?"

"I'm in over my head, Dad. I never told you about a man I'd met in Afghanistan. His name was Aiden Thornton. I don't really know why he was there. He wasn't a soldier or a reporter. And he stayed in the background. He always sat in a corner at Officer's Club and watched people or read a newspaper. I was attracted to him, but I never approached him and he never said anything to me except an occasional 'Good evening, Miss O'Hara'."

"Times have changed Moiri. It's okay for a woman to approach a man."

"I couldn't do that. I was one of maybe ten females in officers' quarters. Some of the men didn't hold to the 'officer and a gentle-man' tag and looked on the women as fair game. If I'd spoken to Aiden first, it would have been a signal to others that I was open to things."

"Were you?"

"No. I'm not experienced, Dad. The idea of becoming involved with a man, well, it terrified me. It still does."

"Thank, God."

His voice was muffled, and Moira guessed he'd put his phone on the kitchen island and he was pouring a cup of coffee. When-ever something bothered him, he'd put his phone on speaker and get coffee. Maybe discussing her sex life or lack thereof was not a comfortable subject for conversation.

"So you met this guy and nothing happened. Why bring it up now?"

"Aiden was the man that found me in that broken school house. He shielded my eyes from the sun. While the rescuers were digging me out, he kept a hand on my shoulder and talked to me. He stayed until the evac took off. His was the first voice I'd heard in three days.

"I never heard from him again. And when he showed up at the Rialto Theater tour, I didn't recognize him or remember him."

"How did he react to seeing you?"

"Surprised and delighted. He said no one would tell him what happened to me. He thought I died."

"So I take it you two joined up and are caravanning across Route 66?"

"Until last night. We had a fight because I didn't think he really heard what I was saying about my life choices. He all but told me to grow up. I left before I said too much, but now I think I was wrong."

"Can I get in some 'Dad' Questions?" There was a pause. "Moira, has this guy tried anything?"

"What?"

"You know, physically?"

"Of course he hasn't. Aside from a single kiss, he acts more like a big brother than a potential lover. We're barely friends. But…" She fumbled for the words. "Daddy, I think, I want more from the relationship than he does. I'm confused and so afraid I messed things up yesterday. I haven't heard from him. I didn't go down to dinner last night because I was angry. And I want to go down to breakfast, but I don't want to. What's wrong with me, Daddy?"

Collin chuckled. "Honey, it sounds like you are more interested than you are comfortable with."

She gasped. "No. I'm not. I like him and most of the time I enjoy his company."

"If you say so, Moiri. In my day, enjoying someone's company meant more than casual meetings and innocent talk. Your mother and I talked about everything and when there was silence, it was comfortable. She'd reach across the table and hold my hand. I miss enjoying her company."

"I know, Dad. She was special and I envy what you had together. I sometimes wonder if a guy will ever look at me the way you and Mom looked at each other. Sometimes I wanted to suggest you get a room. The passion in your glances was amazing and at the same time comforting."

"I hope you find that kind of love, Moiri. And if this Aiden guy is the one I'll pretend to love him even if I hate him. As long as he makes you happy, I'll be happy."

"I love you, Daddy. See you Saturday."

"I'll have my housekeeper dust and vacuum your house and get you some basic groceries. Call me when you get in."

She disconnected the call and turned to Mutt who was watching her from his bed. He got up and trotted across the room. He laid his head on her knee. "Do you want to go to breakfast or just leave?"

Mutt went to his bed and picked up his doll. Her dog had

gotten into the habit of taking the toy with him whenever they met Aiden for a meal. Moira rolled her eyes. "I should have known you'd side with him. But I want something besides the breakfast in the hotel. I saw a diner down the road. How about steak and eggs?"

AIDEN LOOKED for Moira and Mutt in the hotel dining room, but she never arrived for breakfast. He scanned the parking lot for her SUV, but it was not there. She had left early.

He reviewed their lunch conversation yesterday. He should have realized he'd angered her when she refused to join him for dinner. His sharp words from yesterday's visit to Meramec Caverns had done their damage. In his defense it bothered him that the vibrant woman he's known in Afghanistan now questioned herself and felt she lacked something. He wanted her to see herself as he saw her. She had drive and grit, but she just didn't see herself as a whole woman.

Maybe he had been wrong, What if she saw him as just a friend and not someone that she might love. And if being kissed had upset her, well too bad. He had no intention of apologizing. He'd wanted to kiss her since Afghanistan."

And just where the hell was she? Had he been such a bastard that she wouldn't give him the courtesy of a phone call?

He remembered Moria saying something about the Trail of Tears Monument near Jerome, Missouri.

He tossed his bag into the back of his Jeep and headed west on the Mother Road. He hoped to catch Moira and Mutt before they left the monument, but if he missed them, he'd just keep following the Road until they met up.

THE TRAIL of Tears Monument was around fifty miles from the hotel where she and Aiden had stopped last night. American history had been one of her favorite subjects in both high school and college. Of particular interest was the greedy land grabbing of the white men and the disruption of the lives of the Cherokee, Creek, Seminole, Chickasaw, and Choctaw tribes from the Southeastern United State.

She recalled the orders to move the tribes west to Oklahoma and the reservation land. The Indians were held in camps during the summer months and then moved during the winter. The people were not prepared for the cold. Suffering from exposure, disease, and starvation, thousands died and their bodies were buried along the trail. About one-fourth of the Cherokee nation did not survive the journey.

Larry Baggett built his home on the Trail of Tears as a shrine to the tribes who had made the westward trek. He built his home directly over the Trail according to an old Cherokee.

"Do you believe it, Mutt? Baggett built his home and a stone wall adjacent to the house and blocked the spirits from crossing the path. Baggett told visitors about the spirits knocking at his door. He'd open the door but no one was there."

Moira took pictures of the wall and the wrought iron sign over the gate. Mutt sat facing the stone wall watching. "They aren't around anymore, Big Guy, The Indians left the trail a long time ago."

She continued snapping photos of the deterioration of the property. The Monument sold after Baggett's death in 2003, and the house had stood empty since the sale. Even Baggett's head was missing from his "self-portrait" sculpture.

Stairs lead to the top of the wall. "You can stand down, Mutt. The spirit of the Cherokee Chief won't bother us. He's the one that told Mr. Baggett to build stairs so that the spirits could cross over to continue their journey on the trail. Larry said once the stairs were built, the midnight knocks on his door stopped."

A "No Trespassing" sign was posted on the gate, so Moira was not able to explore the grounds. She could see the structure's faded glory. According to recent reports, the monument had sold and there were plans to reopen the place.

Mutt growled. "What's wrong, Big Guy?"

A figure dressed in traditional tribal garb appeared out of nowhere. "Greetings, Granddaughter. You've endured a long journey."

"Really nice, Grandfather. The renovations on this place have barely started and you are auditioning for the part of the Cherokee spirit who visited Baggart. Let me take a picture for your portfolio. You can brag about having a Moira O'Hara portrait."

She took several shots of the old man…head-on, right and left profiles, and full length.

"Your practical mind will not allow you to believe in the spirits. We do exist, but only those with open minds and hearts will see us."

"Why me, Grandfather?" Do I appear to be that gullible?"

"My child, you have experienced much sorrow and pain for one so young. Your spirit is strong, but you struggle. You seek your way, but like our path along the trail you've encountered obstacles. You love the man, but fear your feelings."

"I don't love him. I enjoy his company." Hadn't she said the same thing to her father just a few hours ago? "We have many differences, Grandfather."

"He follows you."

"There is no future for us. I will make my way to happiness. I don't need or want your wise counsel."

The spirit approached her. "Granddaughter, two men will come into your life. They are the same and yet different. You will love both, but choose one as your life partner. And one you love deeply you will lose. Your heart will mend when you accept a gift of love."

"I don't know what you are talking about, Grandfather. Besides you don't know me. How can you tell my future?"

"Listen to your heart. You will find the answer."

Mutt barked and pawed her leg. "What's wrong, big guy."

He whined and pulled at the leash. He practically dragged her back to her car. "Slow down, Mutt," she commanded, but he ignored her command. He stopped at the passenger door of her car. A sharp bark indicated he wanted to get in.

Moira opened the door. Mutt settled in the seat but when she tried to buckle him in he growled. "What's wrong? Why are you're acting like this?"

Mutt's reaction to the mists around the wall concerned her. "It's nothing, brave boy. I dreamed it. No one was there. I know I upset you, but my mind seems to do crazy things lately. Remember I kissed Aiden last night."

She climbed into the passenger seat with her dog and cradled him in her arms. A passerby might think it strange to see her babying a big dog. But Moira knew her furry friend was upset by what he felt. If she were honest, she'd admit to being a bit spooked herself. But it was so real. Two men the same but different and losing one she loved. She'd swear she had actually spoken with the old chief from Baggett's tales.

A Jeep pulled up next to her SUV. She glanced over her shoulder and watched as Aiden got out and came around to the passenger side. "Is everything alright?"

"I had a vision of aged Indians and scared the spunk out of my dog."

"That would have scared the spit of out of me too, Moira."Aiden scratched behind Mutt's ears. "Are you okay?"

"I'm still shaking. I don't believe in ghosts. Let me show you what I saw." She took out her camera and began scrolling through the recent pictures. Nothing. No images of Cherokee chiefs appeared.

"I don't get it. I took several pictures of the chief, but there's not one shot of him. I think I'm losing my mind."

"I called my father this morning and told him I'm on my way back to Amarillo. I'm ready to be home, Aiden. I'm going to make a few short stops to take pictures, but I plan to be home Saturday. I've been away too long."

"I get that. I'm looking forward to sleeping in my own bed. Maybe we can make Kansas today. Then Oklahoma City tomorrow and Amarillo on Saturday. When we stop tonight, we can plan the stops you want to make."

"That sounds wonderful."

"One more question, Moira. What did the Chief tell you?"

A breeze stirred the bare branches. She stroked Mutt's fur. "He said I'd meet two men who were the same and also different. That I would love both. And I would lose one I love."

He leaned in and kissed her cheek. "Spooky." Scratching behind Mutt's ears he commented. "I think your canine companion is ready to get settled. "Mutt, are you tired of traveling and motel rooms?"

"Woof."

Just outside Baxter Springs, Kansas, they saw a sign for a bed and breakfast. They pulled into the small lot in front of the neat white house with federal blue shutters. A tiny white-haired lady answered their knock. "I have one room available. It had two double beds and a bath."

"You take the room, Moria. I'll sleep in my car."

"Nonsense, Aiden. There's not enough room for you to stretch out and get comfortable. I' can make more room in the back of my SUV. I can sleep in my vehicle."

"That's not going to happen. No way will I let a woman sleep in a car when there are two perfectly good beds in the room."

"My point exactly. And we do have a chaperone. You remember Mutt?"

They took the room and hauled in the luggage and Mutts paraphernalia. Aiden chose the bed closest to the door.

Moira filled Mutt's bowl with food and sat a bowl of fresh water on the floor. While her dog chowed down, she set up his bed in the corner. Aiden came out of the bathroom dressed in sweat pants and a tee shirt. He took a paperback book from a pocket in his duffle bag and crawled into his bed.

"Shower's yours. There's plenty of hot water."

"Thanks. As soon as I finish getting Mutt settled I'll take a quick shower."

He pretended to read when Moira exited the bathroom. She looked too good in her purple yoga pants and matching long sleeved top. She'd brushed the tangles out of her hair and had pulled it back into a pony tail. Even though the beds were separated by a wide night stand, they were too close. Aiden wished there had been two rooms. Moira was just too tempting.

Moira turned out the light on her side of the night table and snuggled under the covers. Aiden was about to follow suit, when he noticed Mutt dragging his bed into the space between the two beds. "I think someone is jealous or protective." She giggled at the sight of her dog going back to the corner to get his doll.

"Mutt gets the girl and I have an empty side in my bed." Aiden turned out his light. "I hope I don't sleep walk tonight. I might step on Mutt. Or trip over him and fall on you."

"Maybe I should move to the far side of my bed and save my fragile bones."

He laughed. And then sobered. "Moira, I'm sorry about yesterday."

"Me too. Kissing you, well I've never been kissed like that."

"Then there are some very stupid men out there." He was silent for a moment. "Moira, if I reached across the space between us and held your hand, would Mutt bite my arm off?"

"Only if I commanded him to."

**7**

———

Oklahoma


Moira woke to a shadowed, silent room. She checked her cell phone to see the time. Eight o'clock. She hadn't slept this late since…she couldn't remember the last time she'd been asleep after six thirty.

She glanced at the mussed bed across from hers. It hadn't been so bad sharing the room with Aiden. He had a wicked sense of humor and had kept her laughing until Mutt gave a sharp bark as if telling them to settle down and sleep.

"Mutt!"

She looked around for her dog only to find his bed had been moved back across the room. His water bowl had fresh water and his food bowl had kibble in it.

She jumped out of the bed. "Mutt." "Aiden."

No response.

She grabbed her jacket from the chair in the corner and headed to the door. Maybe Mutt needed to go out, and Aiden took him for a walk. Perhaps he wanted her to sleep instead of caring for her furry friend.

The door opened as she was looking for her shoes. They seemed to have disappeared.

"Lose something?"

She jumped. "Aiden, where have you been? I woke up and you and Mutt were gone. I was afraid…"

Mutt trotted to her side and rubbed his head against her leg. She began rubbing his head. "You scared me silly, dog. I thought I'd lost you."

"I'm sorry, Moira. My brother called and I didn't want to wake you, so I took the phone and your dog outside."

She looked up from playing with her dog. "Your older brother, the crown prince?"

"He's in the area and wants to get together."

"What does he do?"

"He's been accused of being an international jewel thief."

She laughed. "You're kidding, aren't you?"

"I said accused not that he was."

Moira opened her suitcase and began rummaging for clean clothes. "So what does he do?"

"Nice try, but I can't tell you any more than I did the other night. His work is covert. Most of the time I have no idea where he is."

"That's sad."

"He's going to meet up with us on Saturday at the U Drop Inn in Shamrock. I hope you don't mind that I made that arrangement without talking to you first."

She pulled a pair of gray leggings and a black tunic from the suitcase and headed toward the bathroom. "I don't mind at all."

Aiden folded his sweats and packed them into his duffle bag. "I appreciate you letting Ian join us. Between my work in Afghanistan and his 0n his covert op, we've not seen each other in two years. Even phone calls have been limited."

"You're lucky. You have a brother. I'm an only child. I've often wondered what it would be like to have a sister. Someone I could talk to, share secrets with. Talk about the boys we'd like to ask us out. You know basic girl stuff."

He laughed. "How about arguing over who'd asked Cindy Stewart out first and who got the first kiss?"

"Sounds like heaven."

They finished their packing and loaded the bags into the cars. Aiden locked the hatch and stated. "There's still time to get breakfast. Why don't we eat and then hit the road?"

"I think that's a good idea. For once I'm not excited about what's out there. I just want to be going home."

"We are headed home. Today's Friday. I promised you'd be home Saturday night. We'll make that work."

They finalized their plans as they ate breakfast. They'd stay the night outside Oklahoma City and be in Shamrock around 10 or 10:30 on Saturday. That would put them about two hours from Amarillo.


MOIRA LED the way as they crossed the state line between Kansas and Oklahoma. They entered Vinita and stopped at the former "Largest McDonalds in the world." The 30,000 square foot building housed the restaurant and gift shop.

They stopped to buy Mutt his first McDonald's hamburger. It had been years since Moira had eaten a Big Mac and she looked forward to the burger.

"I'm getting a fish sandwich. That used to be my favorite Mickey D's item."

Over lunch they told tales about growing up when fast food was a special event for birthdays or good report cards. They took a short tour of the gift shop before getting back on the road.

She took pictures of the Old Prior Bridge. The steel truss bridge blended with the bare tree branches. Soon the trees would bud and bloom and the bridge would be bathed in green glory. When September arrived the leaves would change color and the bridge and surrounding woodland would take on a new beauty.

In Tulsa, they stopped at the Route 66 Harley Davidson dealership. They checked out the two-wheeled vehicles displayed in the showroom. But Moira knew she would never dare to get on one of the motorcycles and ride off into the sunset. Mutt looked up at her with a paw on her knee. He cocked his head as if asking "Where do I sit?"

"I've never been to a drive in movie," She confessed while photographing the Admiral Twin Drive-In Theater. Built in 1951 the theater was one of the few remaining twin-drive-in-theaters. "Hey, Aiden, did you know the first movie shown here was Gene Autrey, in *Oh, Susanna!*?"

Moira began singing the song in a slightly off-key soprano. Mutt howled while Aiden laughed.

"No, but I do have an idea. If there's a drive-in theater in Amarillo, let's go see a movie there. I'll buy popcorn and cokes and try to hold your hand in the dark."

"What if Mutt doesn't want you to hold my hand?"

"Not a problem. There will be no chaperones on our date."

"Mutt will object to that. He doesn't like me to be too far from his sight."

She began to relax. There was no pressure. No hurry to get things done. They were just having fun. Moira realized how little fun she'd had since she signed on with the news network.

They made a final stop in Arcadia to photograph the Round Barn. Forty-three feet high and sixty feet in diameter, the barn was built of burr oak timbers. It housed large Route 66 gift shop and a historical display of round barns. The second floor was rented out for special events.

They made an early night of it after stopping for fried chicken dinners and iced tea. Like the previous night they shared a double room. But this time they settled on one bed and talked.

"Why did you leave your job with the recovery team?"

Aiden winced. "I wasn't given many choices."

"They fired you?"

"No, they couldn't do that. The contract wouldn't allow them to dismiss an authenticator. So they let me know they would not be renewing my contract."

"Why?"

"Don't go there, Moiri."

"Aiden Thornton, I'm not allowing you an easy out. What happened?"

"You happened."

"Forgive me if I don't understand."

"We were on a deadline. Our contract expired at the end of the month. If we hadn't recovered the antiquities, we would be paid a flat salary and nothing else. The foreman stated the jewels and icons were top priority and nothing would come between us and our goals. And then I found you in that pile of rocks. The foreman said to leave you. If you weren't dead you would be soon. And we didn't have time to waste on a corpse."

"Bastard!"

"That and more." He paused. "I couldn't leave anyone to die while I looked for gold. What he didn't know was that I had found the treasure. I'd been on my way to tell him when I heard moans from the rocks."

"You lost your job because you saved a life. I can't believe any human would be that cruel."

"It didn't bother me that much, Moiri. I'd already accepted Sutton's job and as I found the treasures, I got the largest share of the bonus money. But I hated that man for what he wanted us to do."

Laying her head on Aiden's shoulder, Moira snuggled close to his side. "Some men have no honor. But there are those who can't be bought or bullied. I'm lucky that the honorable man found me."

"I'm glad I found you, Moira O'Hara. You are the real treasure."

They were silent for a moment. "I'm too tired to move. Can I sleep right here, Aiden? I don't take up much room."

He kissed the top of her head. "I'm very good at sharing."

THERE WERE two vehicles in the parking lot when Moira pulled into the lot on the back side of the Tower Station and U Drop Inn. They'd been on the road since about eight. After Mutt woke them whining and needing to go outside they were unable to go back to sleep. They had packed up and stopped at an all-night diner for breakfast.

Aiden had stopped in Clinton, Oklahoma for gas and to have a tire checked. He told her to go on ahead and he'd catch up. He thought she might like some private time to take pictures before they met up with Ian.

She immediately began taking pictures of the markers and service station. Mutt stretched out on a Route 66 emblem and eyed Moira. His eyes begged her to take his picture.

They entered the U Drop Inn from the travel center. Moira and Mutt circled the large room taking in the various displays of memorabilia and gift items. A tall man stepped into the travel center from the restaurant.

"Aiden, I didn't see you come in."

"I'm sorry you didn't see me and doubly sorry I'm not Aiden." He held out his hand. "I'm Ian Thornton, Aiden's twin brother."

# 8

U-Drop Inn
Shamrock, Texas

Moira shook Ian's hand. "Aiden told me he had a brother, but he didn't say anything about an identical twin."

Ian tilted his head and grinned. "He probably hoped he'd arrive first and handle the introductions. And you must be…"

"I'm sorry, I'm Moira O'Hara. And this handsome gentleman," she scratched Mutt's ears, "is Mutt."

"Hello, Mutt." Ian held out his hand so that the Shepherd could get his scent. Mutt moved to stand between Ian and Moira.

"So you are the legendary Moira. Aiden sings your praises. He told me about you during one of our infrequent conversations. He described you as fearless and mentioned the incident with an over-ardent lieutenant."

"Which one? I had to defend my honor more than once."

Ian led her to a booth in the cafe. "If I remember correctly it had something to do with big guns and derringers."

Moira felt the heat rise from her neck to her face. She buried her face in her hands. "The one night I tried to sound sophisticated and I'll never live it down."

The bell tinkled as the door to the gift shop opened. Aiden came through the door and joined them in the café. The brothers exchanged a quick hug, stepped back to search faces for signs of stress or illness. "You doing okay?" they asked in unison. Moira smiled as the brothers got reacquainted, but Mutt kept looking from one man to another as if he was trying to decide why there were two Aidens.

"It's a zoo out there," Aiden stated. "The town is giving the basketball team a hero's welcome. We're going to be stuck here for about 45 minutes or so."

An attendant from the historical society stood in the doorway. "Coffee's free. Ya'll just have a seat and relax. Just be glad you're here this Saturday instead of next week. The St. Patrick's Day celebration is really busy."

Aiden and Moira slid into the booth that Elvis had once occupied. Ian played waiter and poured the coffee. Mutt stretched out on the floor next to Moira. The trio exchanged stories and laughed while the celebration proceeded down Route 66.

"So, Ian, your brother tells me you have been accused of being an international jewel thief? Would you care to explain?"

He placed a badge and ID folder on the table. "I was undercover for the FBI on a major jewel theft. I infiltrated the suspected ring posing as a fence. I'm a certified gemologist so I was the perfect undercover agent. For a while I taught recruits on theft rings and how to work the suspects. More recently, I've been working on the theft of priceless Columbian emeralds from the Worthington estate."

"The Edward Worthington estate? I thought there were rubies and diamonds stolen. Didn't he own the twenty-five carat Burmese ruby that once belonged to Burma's royal family?"

"He does own the ruby, Moira, but the ruby and seventeen

million in diamonds were left in the vault. Only the emeralds were taken."

"So…"

A FLASH of yellow and black caught Moira's attention. She gasped. Mutt alerted and Aiden reached for her hand. "Moiri, what's wrong?"

"The Mustang that followed us just pulled into the lot."

The bell over the gift shop door announced a new comer. "May I help you, Sir?" the attendant asked.

"Get out," he growled. The bell tinkled as the door opened. A moment later, the sound of the lock snapping into place echoed through the empty room. Footsteps slapped the concrete floor and stopped in the doorway separating the visitor's center and the U Drop Inn café.

Moira gasped. The pale, gaunt man from the road trip stood in the entrance.

He looked at the two men. Pulling a Berretta from the waistband of his baggy jeans, he pointed the pistol first at Ian then at Aiden. "You lied, Warren Grey. I know you have the emeralds."

Ian stood. "You're early, Ralston. Our meeting isn't until ten this evening. And we were meeting in Amarillo, not Shamrock."

"The meeting starts now."

Mutt growled when the thug grabbed Moira's arm and pulled her from the booth. "Get into the gift shop" he commanded. "And control that dog."

"Mutt, heel."

The Shepherd trotted to Moira's side. She laid a hand on top of his head. "Guard." She whispered.

"You two get in there with her." Waving his weapon, Ralston threatened Ian. "Give me the emeralds right now or I start killing witnesses beginning with your look-alike."

"If I had the emeralds, I'd give them to you. I sent them ahead to Amarillo."

"Too bad."

The gunman's aim centered on Aiden's chest. Moira dropped Mutt's leash and pushed Aiden to the ground.

"Bitch!"

Ralston's aim switched to Moira. Mutt leaped at the gunman. Ian drew his weapon, but before he could get off a shot, Ralston fired.

Mutt dropped to the floor. Blood flowed from the wound in his chest.

"Mutt!" Moira screamed. She pulled her sweater over her head and used it to put pressure on her dog's wound. "Call a vet."

Mutt whined. Nudged her leg with his nose. He drew a breath and stilled.

"No. Mutt, don't leave me." she begged.

"He's gone, Moiri. You have to let him go. Come on, honey, stand up." Aiden held out his hand to help her.

Moira reverently laid Mutt's head on the concrete floor. Rising she faced the killer who was now weaponless and cuffed.

"Murderer!" She launched herself at the man. "You killed my dog, my protector, my friend." She beat her fists against Ralston's chest."

"Should have been him." The thug angled his head toward Aiden.

She raked the killer's face with her burgundy polished finger nails. The man screamed as her nails dug deeply into his skin. "It should have been you." She pounded on his chest and ribs until Ian and Aiden pulled her back. Aiden ripped off his jacket and covered her shirtless body.

"Enough, Moiri." He held her while she sobbed. Her tears soaked his shirt.

Outside the celebration continued

. . .

Local police officers lead the cuffed suspect to the city jail. He'd be housed there until Agent Thornton could arrange for his transfer to a federal facility.

The chief of police allowed Aiden to get clothing from Moira's suitcase. Her blood-soaked sweater and jeans would be taken as evidence. Scrapings from beneath her fingernails were also taken for DNA testing to verify the perp's identity. A suspect could refuse to provide a DNA sample. The scrapings would be the Feds' back up.

Moira noticed nothing. She alternated between bouts of eerie silence and gut-wrenching sobs. Aiden stayed close at her side holding her when she cried and just being within reach while she stared into space.

The county sheriff approached Ian. "I'd like to speak with you and your brother." They huddled in a corner of the gift shop. "We need to get Miss O'Hara out of here. I want her gone when our vet takes the dog away. Does she know we have to do a necropsy?"

"I haven't said anything. I'm afraid she won't handle it well," Aiden said.

"We can take Ms. O'Hara to the clinic."

"Sheriff, I'd really like to take her home to Amarillo. She can't give you a statement right now, so I'll make arrangements to bring her back for an interview later."

"We'll give her a couple of days. And we will go to her. I'm sure Shamrock's the last place she'll want to see for a while." He turned to Ian. "Do you have an objection to your brother taking Miss O'Hara home? I can have one of my deputies follow them and bring Mr. Thornton back for his vehicle."

"No, Sir. No objections." Turning to Aiden, Ian placed his hands on his brother's shoulders. "Had I known Ralston would pull this stunt, I wouldn't have called you. I'm so sorry."

Mutt's remains were released to Ian at the end of the week. He and Aiden placed the body in an oak coffin, covered him with his Route 66 blanket and placed his doll close to his heart. Together they brought Baron "Mutt" home to Moira.

According to Colin O'Hara, Moira had not eaten much, nor had she slept. She'd closed herself in her room. She'd cry herself to sleep and wake up to start the cycle again.

"She knows we're bringing Mutt home today?"

"Colin told her. She showed him where she wanted to bury him and the grave has been opened." Aiden answered.

"Have you talked to her?"

"Not really. She did say the sheriff came by and took her statement. I hope today will start the healing process." Aiden stared out the window as they passed the giant cross. "When things settle down a bit, I want to come back to Groom and walk the stages of the cross. I hear the sculptures are fantastic."

Neither of them could think of anything to say. The drive passed in silence until Ian pulled into the driveway of Moira's house.

Colin met them at the door. "She's sitting in the gazebo next to the open grave. My daughter is not talking today." The older man's eyes glistened with unshed tears. "I thought it was bad when I brought her to Chicago, but my baby is dying again."

Ian placed a hand on Colin's shoulder. "Let's hope laying Mutt to rest will allow Moira to begin healing."

"Amen," Aiden stated.

9

_______

Amarillo, Texas
September



Moira stood at the window. The calendar said fall, but the weather felt more like summer. Six months had passed since she'd been forced to leave Mutt on the floor at the U Drop Inn.

Fall was upon the city and leaves dropped from the branches of the tall oak that shaded Mutt's grave.

She had spent the spring grieving for her companion. Then one day she sat beside the grave and realized it was time.

She had plucked a rose and placed it on Mutt's grave. "I've been selfish long enough, Barron Mutt. It's time to let you go. You were my best friend and I loved you so much. You're free now. Go. Run and play in your doggy heaven. Just know that I'll never forget you."

She never looked back. Oh, she would stop by occasionally and put flowers on the grass-covered mound. But she no longer mourned.

Life goes on. While Aiden worked on Ryan Sutton's Route 66 Art Gallery, she had reinvented her career. She received a request from a local magazine to photograph a series of weddings for a garden article. She had freedom to write the copy and select the photographs. The article had been successful and now she had so much work that she could pick and choose her assignments.

She was content with her life.

The doorbell rang. "I'm okay, dad," she muttered as she headed to the door. She peered through the peep-hole. Recognizing the visitor she threw open the door and greeted him.

"Ian, when did you get back?" Moira held the door open so that he could enter. His arms were loaded with flowers, a large package, and a leather loop encircled his wrist.

"Bearing gifts or moving in?"

"Are you offering me a room?"

His grin got her every time. She started laughing. "I have three guest rooms. I guess you could call one of them home when you're in town."

He followed her into the living room. "I wouldn't do that to Aiden. My brother loves you, Moira. He's just stepping back to give you the space to find yourself."

"I know. We started some kind of relationship while we were traveling. But he's reinventing himself just like I am. Maybe someday soon we can work out our relationship."

Ian placed the flowers and the box on the coffee table. He dropped into the oversized chair flanking the sofa. "The flowers are for you. They are a celebration of sorts."

She took the bouquet. "They are beautiful. I love fall blossoms. Their colors are so rich. Thank you, Ian." Moira picked up the cut crystal Fostoria vase from the end table. "I'm going to put the flowers in water. Can I get you something to drink? Have you had lunch?"

"Yes and yes. Ice tea if you have some ready."

"Coming up."

From the kitchen, Moira heard mutterings. She assumed he was talking on his cell phone. Her heart nearly stopped when she reentered the living room carrying two glasses of tea. Sitting next to Ian's chair was the cutest German Shepherd puppy.

"He looks like Mutt."

Ian ruffled the dog's fur. "He should. He's half Mutt."

"What?"

"Mutt's owners were working with a breeding program. They had straws of Mutt stuff from his pre-service dog days. This guy's litter is from the last of the straws."

"And this unnamed pup is the runt and too silly to train."

Moira dropped to the floor. She reached out to the puppy. "You're not a runt. You're compact. That's okay, you'll grow out of it."

Mutt's son took tentative step toward her. And another. He stopped and eyed her. She held out her hand and Muttpup moved forward. He placed his paws on her knees and licked her neck.

Moira laughed.

Ian watched her eyes sparkle as she played with the dog. Aiden should be here. If he could see her right now he'd know without a doubt that she had healed and held no grudges. Her face told a beautiful story of being whole and happy.

"I'll fight you for him, Ian. I want this puppy. I hope you're not attached to him, because he's mine."

"That's what Aiden said when he saw the pup. He's yours. Aiden bought him for you. You need to name the little guy."

The pup was in her lap his bright brown eyes bored into hers. "Your name is Jeff."

Ian roared. "Leave it to you to remember that old cartoon strip about a tall, skinny guy, named Mutt, and a short, compact guy called Jeff."

"This is great. Aiden knew I'd fall for this little guy. Thanks for bringing him home to me. Jeff and I will go shopping later for puppy food, a bed, toys and a blanket. Do you want to join us?"

"I'd love to, but I'm moving into my new place."

"You're moving to Amarillo? That's wonderful. I bet Aiden's happy to have you closer."

"He is. And I've left the bureau. I passed the Texas bar and have joined the Bauer Law Firm here in town. And on behalf of the firm, I'm pleased to announce that you are now free from your old network."

He opened the box on the coffee table. "First, I discovered they were holding on to some of your personal cameras. As that violated your contract, we petitioned the court to assess a fine for the infringement. Your contract stipulated that rights to footage and images not used within eighteen months reverted to you. It's all in the box. One of our attorneys specializes in discrimination actions. He heard about the "ugly" comments and "unsuitable for camera work" remarks and filed suit against the network. The judge ruled in your favor and imposed a damage award. Plus the network bought out the remainder of your contract and added a bonus for the ratings your work netted them. In all," he pulled a check from his jacket pocket, "the network wrote a check for the sum of eighteen and a half million dollars."

She froze as the figure rolled off his tongue. "You made them pay for the abuse and neglect. Thanks, Ian. The money is not a big issue. But having the Network pay-out hurts them and their bottom line. That's validation."

"And your retirement money. Get that check to your bank and visit your accountant."

Ian packed up his paperwork. "Are you going to Aiden's gallery opening Friday?"

"Of course. Ryan asked me to take pictures of the event. Besides I want to be there to support Aiden. He's..."

She was silent for a moment. "He's special to me."

Ian grinned. *"He's waiting for her to make the first move and she's hoping he'll knock on her door."*

"Can you be there about half an hour before the opening? Aiden would like to give you a tour."

"I'll be there."

**10**

———————

Friday Night

Aiden waited in the opening of the main gallery. He hadn't seen Moira since June. Both of them had been so tied up with work they'd settled for phone calls and texts. He was ready to see her.

He remembered some of her texts. She loved the puppy and was having so much fun with him. She and Jeff had gone shopping for a bed and a carrier. He had new toys and his own bowls for food and water. Her career was another topic of conversation. The free-lance work kept coming in and the requests allowed her to test her creativity. It was exciting and she loved being the boss.

He heard the main door open and stepped out to greet Moira.

She was breath taking. Her chestnut hair fell in heavy waves down her back. Even though she would be working, Moira had dressed for the occasion. Her long-sleeved peacock blue gown fitted her torso like a glove. Crystal stars sparkled from a spray that trailed from her right shoulder to her waist. The full skirt brushed the tops of her matching pumps. Diamond earrings sparkled in the light.

Aiden was speechless. This was the woman he remembered from Afghanistan.

"Hello, Mr. Thornton. I'm Moira O'Hara and I'm here to photograph your gallery opening."

"Good evening, Miss O'Hara. Welcome to Sutton's Route 66 Gallery. Allow me to show you around."

They walked through the various rooms named for historic figures and famous artists. The house had been restored to its former glory. The exhibit rooms were painted to accent the style of paintings hanging in the room. The oak floors gleamed.

"You've done a beautiful job, Aiden. I'm so happy for you."

She glanced around the small room off the main hallway.

"Where are your paintings displayed?"

"In one of the back rooms. The room is for new artists."

"Ian said you'd been painting for years. Why aren't you in one the rooms for more experienced painters?"

"Because," Aiden answered, "I've never exhibited my work. I'm a new artist."

"Okay, but once I have my pictures, I'm finding that room. I'm not even going to guess your style. I think I'll know your work when I see it."

They walked toward the front of the building. "Moiri, there's an exhibit I have to show you. It's special and I really want your opinion."

"Okay. Which way?"

He took her arm leading her along the polished hard wood path to a closed door just to the left of the entry.

"Moira O'Hara, I confess to conspiring with your father in obtaining the priceless works displayed here. I hope it meets your approval."

Aiden opened the door and flipped the switch. Soft light fell on the pale grey walls, and folksy music set an atmosphere of the sixties and seventies.

Moira gasped. Tears welled in her eyes. "How did you do this without letting me know?"

"Your father still had your power of attorney. He gave me some of your SIM cards hoping I'd find some photos worthy of being displayed. And I did. I had a hard time choosing pictures for the exhibit."

He moved to the center of the room staying just in her line of vision.

Ian heard her gasp as when she realized the photographs really were hers.

"I can't believe you did this. How long did it take to put it together?"

"It was my project after the crew had shut down for the day. I wanted this to showcase the woman I met and fell in love with."

He watched her as she moved from one photo to the next. His shoulders tensed when she recognized the subject of the pictures on the last wall.

"Mutt," she whispered.

"He was a special friend to you, Moira. He saved my life. He deserves the recognition."

"Do you have a favorite, Aiden?"

"I'm kind of partial to Mutt and Betty Boop at the Polk-a-Dot Drive In. But seeing him with a doll that looked so much like you touched me. Mutt loved you and he respected me. He took the bullet meant for me."

"Can I have a hug, Aiden?"

Strong arms circled her waist from behind. "You can have anything you want from me."

"A hug will do for now, but when the furor from tonight calms I want us to talk. Really talk."

"It's a date."

"You're kind of slow on the uptake, brother. Kiss the girl. And then get to the front door. You've got a line of people waiting to get in."

"You can bet I'm going to kiss the girl, but not with an audience present."

"Moiri, do we open this exhibit?"

She looked around. "Open it."

"Okay. I'll meet up with you when we close."

Ian stepped aside allowing his brother to exit the room and open the outer doors. He walked around the room viewing the photographs "You okay, Moira?"

"Better than okay. I have a brother, a pet, my man, and a job I love.

"Get to work, Sis. He pointed to a picture of Mutt romping in the snow. "I'm buying that one." Ian winked as he left the room.

Moira paused in the doorway. She looked back at the photograph of the staircase to the top of the wall at the Trail of Tears monument. The old Cherokee chief sat on the top step. A smile stretched across his weathered features. She remembered his words.

"You will meet two men, the same but different. You will love them both, but you will choose one to be your life partner. And one you love dearly you will lose."

"I still don't believe in ghosts, but you're a darn good prophet. Yes, I lost, but I've won more than I lost. Thanks for helping me to see that."

"Be happy, Granddaughter." The words reached her ears as she touched the doorknob. She looked back.

The chief was gone.

"I am, Grandfather," she whispered.

# PART V

## FEAR OF HEIGHTS

NANDY EKLE

# FEAR OF HEIGHTS

RAYLENE WAS IN A HURRY to get in the house. She thought she had seen her ex-husband's truck in the neighborhood when she left for work that morning and she didn't want to take a chance on him spotting her.

She dropped her purse and keys in the chair by the door. Her six-and-a-half-year-old daughter, Pearl, and her just-turned-five-year-old son, Jam, came bounding up the steps into the mobile home behind her trying to tear each other apart.

"No, I get the first snack," Pearl yelled.

"No, I do," Jam yelled back.

"Ow! You pulled my hair! I'm telling. Mom, Jam pulled my hair and it really hurt!" She rubbed the offended part of her scalp, then she stomped on his foot.

Jam let out an amazing shriek. "Mom! Pearl stepped on my foot!"

Raylene took a deep breath and shut the door. "Stop it right now! Both of you. No snacks for anyone. Both of you get to your rooms while I figure out supper. Now."

"But, Mom," they both whined in unison.

"Get!" She pointed toward the hallway and twitched her head

in the same direction. Sister and brother looked at each other with unabashed hatred in their eyes, then plodded off to their rooms.

"I'm the only one who gets a snack." Raylene said quietly to herself as she took the tequila from the cabinet and the margarita mixer from the fridge. Thursday, April 20, 2025 had been a sad day at the Mother Road Nursing Home where Raylene worked. As a certified nurse's aide, she assisted the patients with very intimate care: bathing, dressing, toileting, etc. But Raylene enjoyed her job. The patients in the home were the forgotten elderly of Shamrock, Texas. Some of them were still pretty active mentally and physically, but they needed a little extra help with managing things. Some of them needed help moving around. And some of them needed constant care, like a baby. But she loved them all. They were definitely easier to be around than her own two children.

But that day, Connie Fisher had passed away. She was one of the patients still with mental clarity, but had very limited ability to move. She had had a stroke around noon and by one o'clock, she was gone. Raylene and some of the nurses had gathered in the break room talking about Connie and comforting each other. The four grown Fisher kids were there quick as lightning just as the funeral home showed up. The charting had been done, the bed stripped, and the room cleaned. In a week there would be a new occupant.

So, what's for dinner, she wondered as she sipped her drink and stood with the refrigerator door open, just staring inside. She had not set anything out to thaw, and the only things in the fridge were a half gallon of milk, part of a loaf of bread, an egg carton (she knew there were only two eggs left), and an uncovered plate bearing three gray limp-looking hamburger patties. Not very appetizing.

She picked up the phone intending to call Sherry, her best friend and next door neighbor. Maybe she, Sherry and the kids could go out to the U Drop Inn Cafe for burgers. If she had enough to drink the fear of Shane showing up would disappear. However, now that his name and face were back in her mind, she decided against a sit down place; she just wanted to get something fast and come back home. Running into him right now in her state of despair would be disastrous.

"Kids, you can come out now." She heard both bedroom doors open and the pitter patter of little feet running down the hall. She remembered when she was pregnant with Pearl how she giggled at the thought of that phrase. Now she just groaned.

"Ow! You bumped into me."

"No, you bumped into me."

"I'm telling!"

"No, I'm telling."

Then Pearl and Jam yelled in unison, "Mom!"

Raylene was about to completely give up and make them both go to bed for the night. But she felt a little hungry herself, so she stored her drink in the fridge, loaded the kids into her rickety old Saturn Ion, and drove to the little drive through taco place six blocks from the trailer park. She ordered six tacos, two cherry colas, and three apple burritos, then returned to the house thinking how well the tacos would go with the margarita that waited for her.

---

Sherry watched him step out of the shower and walk across the room, water dripping from him to the floor. He sure was a hunk. Yeah, he drank a lot of beer, and yeah, he was her best friend's ex-husband—well, soon to be ex-husband—and yeah, that was because he was a little mean when he was drunk. But he sure was fine. She and Raylene had been best friends since grade school, but she had crushed on Shane nearly that long, too. She knew Shane had slapped Raylene around a few times, but Raylene really could be a sniveling little weakling, and Shane said sometimes he just needed to get her attention.

"Hey, Sherry, Baby." He called her that all the time and she loved hearing it. It was like that old song her grandma had listened to and it made her feel famous. "Do you know what Raylene's lawyer is trying to do to me?"

Shane seemed to have only two things he ever thought about: sex, and Raylene and her lawyer. She looked at him dripping on her carpet. "Oh, baby, do we have to talk about that now?"

"Don't you care? Don't it bother you what she's got her guard dog up to? And how it's gonna 'fect us? 'Cause it will. It will 'fect you as much as me."

"Okay. Tell me. What's he gonna do?"

"Well, my lawyer said that her lawyer is gonna' ask the judge to make me pay ninety per cent of my paychecks for them kids. Ninety percent! That's, like, nearly a hunnerd percent! What does he think I'm gonna live on? He said it's 'punitive', like, a punishment for the way I treated Raylene. But the money ain't for Raylene, it's for Pearl and Jam. Why I got to pay more for them kids because I hit Raylene? That don't make no sense."

Sherry sat up in the bed. "That does sound like a lot. And I agree, if Raylene's the one that got hit, why do they want more money for the kids?"

"I don't know, but I can't let that happen."

"No, I don't blame you."

Shane sat on the bed next to her. He let his eyes droop and his mouth sag in a puppy-doggish way. Sherry was a sucker for that puppy-dog look. "There's just got to be something we can do to make 'em stop."

"What can we do?"

"I'll think about it for a while." Then he covered her mouth with his.

Later that night they lay on the water bed, Shane on his back and Sherry on her side facing him. Her hand rested contentedly on his chest while he continued with his complaining about Raylene's lawyer. Ninety percent of his check was uncalled for, especially when the injured person was Raylene, not the kids. No way he was going to give her one cent more than he already did.

"Ya' know," he continued. "I can't contribute nothing to our relationship if I have to give it all to her."

"Honey, I never asked for nothing. I just wanted you to feel better."

"Well, I can't feel no better if I'm giving ever cent I make to that woman. But I think I know a way to keep from having to do that."

Sherry sighed heavily. She took her hand from his hard chest and rolled to her back. "Now how you gonna do that? Huh? You can't un-hit her."

"No, I can't, even if I wanted to. Hey, did you know a carnival's coming to the big town of Shamrock? They been ordering beers from my store in huge amounts for a couple weeks. It's to celebrate the whole Route 66 thing, and the re-opening of the cafe where you work."

The U Drop Inn Cafe had been re-furbished and opened a year earlier. Sherry worked as a waitress and Shane's announcement was not news to her.

***

Early Friday morning the song, "You're My Best Friend," by Queen blasted from Raylene's phone. Her eyes snapped open and she grabbed it off her bedside table.

"Hey, girl. Aren't you up yet?" Sherry's perky voice screeched through the phone's speaker into her ear.

"Good grief, Sherry. You're so loud. Why'd you bother to use the phone? Sounds like you could just yell from your back door." Sherry's laugh was like fingernails on a blackboard to Raylene this early in the morning. And how early in the morning was it anyway? She could hear a truck racing past her trailer and down the street.

Still cackling Sherry said, "You musta' slept with Jose Cuervo last night. It's 6:00 in the morning and I know you're alarm is about to go off."

"Dang it, Sherry. If you know that, why in the world didn't you wait?"

"I wanted to catch you before you got busy gettin' kids up and ready for school."

Raylene pinched the bridge of her nose. The inside of her head felt like it was full of swirling waters and the room was spinning in the opposite direction at the same time making the tacos from her supper climb the walls of her stomach and threaten to jump out.

"You and me, carnival, tonight," Sherry said.

Raylene took a deep breath, trying to catch some kind of meaning in Sherry's cryptic words. "What are you talking about?" She loved her friend more than she did her own mother, but sometimes she could be so irritating. Especially after Raylene's four margaritas the night before.

"The carnival," Sherry shouted—at least it sounded like a shout in Raylene's head. "You know, the carnival in the field next to the U Drop Inn. I'm going tonight and I want you to go with me."

"I don't know. Shane finally paid his child support, but I gotta get food and gas. And Pearl needs new shoes. Anyway, Shane might be at the carnival, and I don't want to see him."

"You know, you guys have been split up six months and you still use him as your excuse to keep from having any fun. When y'all were together, it was always, 'Shane says I can't go out today,' or 'Shane wants me to clean the house and cook him a meal,' 'Shane told me to stay in' Shane, Shane, Shane. Now you can't have no fun because you might see Shane somewhere. Grow a backbone, Raylene. You sit in that house all the time when you're not emptying bedpans. Just you and them kids. And the kids are making you crazy. You need to get out and have a girls' night—no kids. Take them to your mom's for the night. We'll go to the carnival and eat greasy fair food, drink beers, and ride wild and crazy rides just like we did when we were teenagers."

Raylene felt tears sting her eyes because most of what Sherry said was true. She was afraid to live. Ever since the first time Shane hit her, even her shadow had become a menacing monster. And yes, the kids were driving her crazy. She loved them dearly, had stepped in front of Shane a couple of times to keep them from getting hit. But since Shane had left the house the kids had come out of their shells and were bent on killing each other, and possibly even her. And when was the last time she had been to a carnival? Ridden The Scrambler? Or The Bumper Cars? And oh, that funnel cake! She could almost smell it while sitting here in her bed.

"So?" Sherry chirped.

"Okay." Raylene's answer was so soft she wasn't sure she had even uttered it.

"Was that a yes?"

With her fingers still pinching the bridge of her nose, Raylene nodded her head. "Yes. Carnival. I can do that."

"Good. We'll go about seven tonight. That'll give you time to get the kids to your mom's."

"Funnel Cake!" Raylene giggled.

"Absolutely! Hey, gotta go."

"Yeah, me too. See you tonight." Raylene punched her phone off and scrambled out of bed. She hadn't felt like this in so long she didn't even have a word for how she felt. But the headache. Yeah, she had plenty of words for that headache, nothing she could say in front of the kids, of course.

Both kids were ominously quiet in the car as Raylene drove them to school. She explained to them that she and Sherry were going out that night to do some grown-up stuff and they were going to stay at Meemaw's. In the rear-view mirror Raylene saw Pearl roll her eyes. Whatever. As long as they were quiet back there and didn't get in too much trouble at school. Then Carlene, her mom, could handle them for a while.

She pulled into the "let off" line in front of the school building. Moms wearing work uniforms, jeans and t-shirts, or even business suits were pulling kids out of their cars. Their mouths moving with last minute instructions for a good day and death threats if the day didn't go well. One rusty Buick had a man's hand hanging out the window with a cigarette burning. Raylene could see him raise his thumb and jab toward the car door, motioning the kids in the back-seat to get into the school. Finally her turn came and without a word, Pearl and Jam rolled out of the Ion and meandered their way to the front door. The song, "Rearview Mirror," by the band Pearl Jam played on the oldies' radio station, as her two little warriors trudged up to the door. She sang along quietly with the radio. *"I couldn't breathe, holdin' me down, hand on my face, pushed to the ground."*

Raylene shifted the car into drive and looked in her rear-view mirror. Then she froze. Shane was in the pickup behind her. And he was grimacing like he smelled a dog doodie. She pulled in a deep breath and tried to calm herself. They were in public, he couldn't do anything to her. And she had a copy of the restraining order in her purse. She looked down at her denim handbag for a second and patted it for comfort. When she looked back in the mirror, she realized she was completely wrong. The person behind her didn't look a thing like Shane.

"Woo, Raylene," she said to herself. "You really need to let go. Tonight, will be all about getting Shane completely out of your system. Now get yourself to work."

---

Sherry wiped down the counter at the U Drop Inn Cafe. Shane had left that morning while she was talking to Raylene. Not cool. Raylene could have looked out the window and seen him leave her house—luckily, her friend sounded like she had had her own little party. But one of the kids could have seen him. She'll have to tell him to start parking at Rita's house further down in the trailer park. Everyone knew Rita made her living by servicing every stray "dawg" that came along and had a twenty dollar bill. And Raylene would certainly believe Shane was staying at Rita's.

And how 'bout the plan he came up with last night? She wasn't sure she could do it. She loved Shane—well, she felt sorry for him, and she had lusted after him for a long time. But she loved Raylene too. Raylene was like a weak little puppy that needed a big girl to take care of her. And Sherry was exactly that.

She took the plates from the kitchen window, inspected them to make sure the burgers were exactly what her customers had requested, and headed to the table. The young couple stopped talking as she placed the dishes in front of them.

"A cheeseburger, hold the onions, and another cheeseburger with extra pickles. Here's some ketchup for your fries. Can I get you anything else?"

The man and woman looked at their burgers and smiled.

"Nope. This looks fantastic. Thanks." The man winked at her before she turned to leave.

As she was wiping down the corner table and pocketing the tip that had been left, she noticed a man standing outside the door. He wore a dirty peach colored t-shirt, and it looked as if the neckband was ripping off the body of the shirt. His hair, what little he had, was blond, but so greasy it looked clumped together in a couple of chunks. Beard stubble covered the lower half of his face, and his eyes squinted like he was either trying to see a long way off, or was in so much pain he could barely stay conscious. He seemed to be watching the couple she had just served enjoy their lunch.

She walked to the door. "Can I help you?" she asked the man.

"Oh, no. I ain't got no money. But them burgers sure look good."

"You ain't got money? Did you eat breakfast?"

"No, I was on the train 'til noon. Then I had to leave before they found me."

"Where you headed?"

"Oh, I'm going west, my family's in California. But my car broke down and I been hiding out and riding the box cars, just like in the old, old days."

"Where did your car break down?" Sherry's radar was beginning to ping in her heart.

"In Oklahoma, around El Reno."

"Are you alone?"

"Yeah. My wife and kids are in California. I was out looking for work, but didn't find any. So I started back home."

"What's your name?"

"Merl Carlson."

"Well, Merl. You come on in and sit down. You look like you need a rest and a bite to eat."

"I ain't got no money, but if you got some scraps, I would sure be thankful."

"I think I can help you. Come on in and have a seat. I'll see what we got." She held the door open for him. She thought he seemed nervous, but he stepped in and sat at the counter. She patted her tips pocket as she headed to the kitchen and told Grayson, the cook, she wanted a burger and fries.

She had a soft spot for people who had needs, whatever the needs were. She loved working at the cafe because feeding people made her feel like she was helping them, even if she had to charge them for their food, and, of course, she never turned down a tip. But she was also able to help people like Merl Carlson. And here, on Route 66 in downtown Shamrock, Texas, she saw her share of hungry people passing through.

Her need to help people was also one of the reasons she gave Shane the bed he needed when Raylene had kicked him out the door, and especially now since that lawyer was going to soak him of all his cash.

And she wanted to help Raylene too. Raylene and her fear of heights, her fear of Shane, fear of getting old. She would help

Raylene get rid of some of her irrational fears tonight at the carnival. Then everyone will be helped and Sherry would feel satisfied with her life.

A carnival in Shamrock, Texas. A rare event, and Raylene wouldn't miss it for the world. The only thing that would hold her back was the thought of running into Shane. That was exactly the kind of thing he would love. Shane was a party kinda' guy, and a carnival was the biggest kind of party, especially since this was the first one Raylene could remember being in Shamrock, right downtown, right where the newly re-opened U Drop Inn was on the old Route 66. As she drove to the nursing home, she gritted her teeth. She would not let Shane destroy this for her.

"Come on, kids. Time to go to Meemaw's house for the night. Let's get a move on." Raylene watched the two kids trudge out to the living room carrying overnight bags. Their faces were turned to the floor and their mouths were both in an upside-down "u" shape. She thought they looked more like they were going to a funeral rather than to their grandmother's house. "What's wrong with you two? Hello? Meemaw's house?"

Pearl kept her head down in a pout, but Jam looked up. "Why can't we stay with Daddy?" he asked.

"Well, for one thing, I don't know where Daddy's staying right now."

"I seen Daddy." Pearl piped up. "I seen him at Sherry's house."

"Oh, Pearlie, that's silly. Why would he be over there?"

"I dunno, but I saw him there."

"Yeah. Me too." Jam threw his two cents in.

Raylene looked at both her kids wondering where this fantasy had come from. She had never gotten the idea that they missed their dad all that much. Now all of a sudden they want to spend the night with him? "Well, I don't know what you saw, but tonight you're going to Meemaw's. Now, just get happy about it. Her feelings will get hurt if you act like you don't want to be there." They just stood there with their heads bowed. "Come on. Get happy. Most kids in the world love to stay at their Meemaws'."

Pearl sniffed, then Jam sniffed. Pearl hiccuped a cry and Jam hiccuped a cry. Next thing Raylene knew, both kids had fallen into full on hysterics. Maybe she needed to stay home with them. She knew split ups were hard on kids, especially if they had seen their daddy hit their mama. She knelt down and pulled them both into her arms.

"Look. Daddy loves you both. But I couldn't let him keep staying here. He didn't like living here. You'll get to see him again when this is done. You'll spend time with Daddy, then spend time with me. We both still love you guys a lot. We just can't live together anymore. And right now, Meemaw really wants to see you. She said she's got some marshmallows you can roast over the fire on her stove. Dry it up, now." She kissed them both on the cheeks, wiped the tears from their little faces, and stood up. "And if you're really good kids for Meemaw, I'll take you to the carnival tomorrow.

Two quick intakes of breath. Two simultaneous "Yay!" She had them back. Lord knew where the money would come from, especially after her going out tonight. But she would find the money. And the world would be good again.

———

Raylene got out of Sherry's 'Stang and they walked through the field up to the traveling amusement park. The event was sponsored by the Old Route 66 Association of Texas to celebrate the history of the Mother Road and the re-opening of the cafe. But the two women didn't care about that. They were there for a night on the town. Fun, food, frolic, and even a few thrills. Sherry had promised to buy the drinks and food if Raylene could pay for the rides. Raylene said she could.

Colored lights flashed all around them and music pumped loudly through the air. Raylene felt the deep percussion and deafening guitar riffs deep in her chest as if the band was using her ribs and heart as instruments. Above the noise of the machinery and the music was the screaming of people being hurled around on the rides.

It had been so long since Raylene had been in this type of environment. Smells of fried food invaded her nostrils and she began salivating. But she also caught the scent of diesel and axle grease burning as the rides operated.

She leaned her head toward Sherry. "Oh. My. Goodness." She yelled.

"I know, right!" Sherry screamed back. "See what you been missing locked away in your house with them kids?"

"You're right! So, remind me what to do first."

Sherry grabbed her hand and pulled her toward a hut shaped like a wooden barrel. "Always best to start with a drink, get you loosened up a bit."

Raylene looked at the menu. Pricey. She watched Sherry put her hand in her pocket and pull out some bills. She deserved this, didn't she. What would it hurt if they spent money tonight. Her lawyer had said they would get as much out of that rat-fink soon-to-be ex-husband as could be gotten. So one night wouldn't hurt. And Pearlie's shoes would last two more weeks, then she would get her some new ones with sparkly lights out of her next pay check.

"We want two beers," Sherry told the guy in the kiosk. He opened the cans and handed them to her.

Raylene and Sherry clinked their cans together in a toast, each took a deep gulp, then turned to look at the rest of the park.

"Corn dog, then funnel cake," she said to Sherry. "Can't be a true carnival without that." So that was next on their list.

Raylene licked the powdered sugar from her fingers and looked around at the flashing lights on the rides. "We got to do The Fun House, Scrambler, and The Tilt-A-Whirl," she said.

"And The Swings, the Hyper Loop, and The Ferris Wheel," Sherry answered. Her eyes gleamed.

"You know I can't do the rides that go off the ground."

"Well, you are tonight. Got to get you over some of these phobias you got," Sherry answered while her eyes twinkled some more.

"No way. Isn't it enough I'm here knowing I might see Shane somewhere in this crowd," Raylene asked.

"No. You see Shane everywhere you go. It keeps you from doing anything fun. Tonight, you're shooting the finger at Shane, at heights, at everything that keeps you from enjoying life. And those rides are fun, so you will ride them."

The beer had begun to swish around in Raylene's head. The anxiety that had bloomed at the thought of getting off the ground was turning to a steel bar. She absolutely would do this. Sherry was right again. Time to shoot the finger at all her insecurities, all in one night. Her backbone straightened again. "Okay. I'll do it. But first another beer. Then let's take turns picking a ride."

"Sounds great."

They tossed their second empty beer cans in the trash, then approached the Fun House. Both women had been to Wonderland in Amarillo several times, but the closest thing to a fun house there was the Fantastic Journey. For that ride they just sat in a car on a track and rode through a haunted house.

The Fun House in this carnival was a walk through trailer. They went in the door and immediately the floor began moving. The beers were working on their brains and Raylene fell as the floor heaved upward. Sherry laughed at her and helped her back up. A set of stairs was next on the path and they walked up to the second floor. Here they dodged what looked like punching bags on a conveyor belt, both women laughing hysterically. Then they came to the mirrors. The distorted mirrors made them appear short and fat with long heads, tall and skinny with short fat heads, and one mirror made them both look like their bodies were waving from side to side.

Raylene stared at herself in the short fat mirror. *There you are, you stupid fat slut,* she heard Shane's voice in her head. *You see them gray strands in your hair? And see the extra chins you got? And how 'bout that booty and them droopy boobs?*

Shane's voice was right. She had pulled her brown hair back in a ponytail, the way she wore it every day to keep it out of her way when she worked with the patients at the nursing home. This mirror showed a couple of silver streaks beginning to shine. Her chin was doubled, and the second chin wobbled when she moved her head. No one except she and Shane knew it, but her boobs had become long and droopy like socks with rocks tied in them. And she would never see a size six pair of jeans again, except maybe if she bought them for Pearl when she became a teenager.

She couldn't look away from the mirror, even when tears started running down her face. Even when she started sniffing. Before long she was in total misery.

Sherry put her arm around her. "What? It's just the way the mirror makes you look. See, the waves in it?"

"I know, but it's so close to true. Every morning this is what I see in the bathroom mirror when I'm getting ready for work."

"Aw, honey. It's not true. You look like a grown woman with experience. Most men love women with experience."

"Yeah, I'm experienced at getting slapped around, and stuffing my face with food to feel better. And the crappy part is, I don't feel better after I eat, I feel worse. So I eat more."

"Well, we're eating tonight, then tomorrow you'll start a diet. I'll do it with you." Sherry put her arms around Raylene and patted the back of her head. "Come on. This is boring."

Raylene stuck her tongue out at the image of herself in the mirror. Yes. She would start her diet tomorrow. She would start being a whole new woman tomorrow. She'd get a hair color from the grocery store, paint her nails (Pearl would like hers painted, too), do a little exercise (Jam would do that with her), and go through her closet cleaning out old stupid clothes. When the divorce was final and Shane's child support became regular, she would go to Walmart and get a whole new wardrobe. New, improved, experienced, sexy Raylene.

They walked on through the maze, not much happening. But as they rounded a sharp turn, a wall of what looked like the shoe shelf at the McDonald's playground met them. Each "shoe box" moved up and down, and in the opposite direction of the box next to it. There was no way around it, and there appeared to be another level above it. Raylene and Sherry looked at one another.

"Funky staircase," they said in unison. They had no choice but to climb the funky staircase. Raylene's legs wobbled as one leg was raised and the other was lowered, then vice-a-versa. It was like riding two escalators at one time. She giggled and Sherry giggled, which made Raylene giggle even more, which increased Sherry's giggles. By the time they got to the upper level, they were nearly in hysterics again.

Holding to the handrails, they walked a little farther. Raylene, who was in the lead, stopped suddenly and Sherry bumped into her back, which started the giggling all over again.

Here the floor had been cut out and replaced with metal rollers. So the women could walk across carefully or skate across. Raylene started skating while holding to the hand rail. A huge beer flavored burp escaped her mouth and her feet went out from under her, landing her on her rear end.

Sherry guffawed and held her stomach. "Girl! I know exactly what you need. You need another beer," she yelled loudly at Raylene as she held her hand out to her.

Raylene took Sherry's hand and pulled herself up, laughing just as loudly as Sherry. "You could use another one, too."

A man and two small children walked up behind the women. "Ladies, please. I'd like to get my kids through here," he said. "I got to have 'em home to their moms by ten; one lives on one side of town and the other mom lives on the other side."

"Well, 'scuse us," Sherry said with a little haughtiness to her voice and Raylene snorted and laughed again. The man and kids rolled past the women.

The next obstacle in their path was a huge barrel on its side, spinning. They had to walk through this to the other side of the trailer. Raylene's eyes told her she was spinning like the barrel. Her head joined in, then her stomach also thought she was upside down. Her knuckles turned white as she gripped the hand rail and closed her eyes.

When her feet touched solid ground again, she opened her eyes and saw a dark narrow hallway with what looked like air vents in the floor. Sherry came out of the barrel and pointed to the hallway. Raylene had a lot of phobias, but she could handle dark narrow places. However, she knew Sherry had a streak of claustrophobia. She grabbed Sherry's hand and whispered, "I'll help you."

They took a step and nothing happened. They took another step and still nothing. When their left feet came down for their third step, an air horn blared causing their ears to ring. Simultaneously, a blast of warm air shot through the vent up their legs. Both women jumped a mile in the air and the giggles began again.

At the end of this walkway, the floor disappeared and was joined to the other side by a rickety bridge made of rubber planks. They held the waxy rope hand rails and crossed the bridge where a giant slide waited for them. Sherry looked at the small dark opening and Raylene saw the fear on her face. She grabbed Sherry's hand and said, "Do this and I'll ride the Swings with you. Remember, we are shooting the finger at our fears tonight."

Sherry looked at Raylene. A huge smile spread across her face. "Swings it is," and she jumped feet first in the gaping mouth of the slide. Raylene heard her scream a single word as she sailed through the pipe. "Towanda!" Raylene jumped in when she was sure Sherry was out of the slide and screamed all the way down. She wasn't afraid, but sometimes screaming for screaming's sake was fun.

They walked up to the line for the swing ride. Probably twenty people in front of them, the ride looked like it held more than twenty, so Raylene was sure they would get on pretty quick. She watched as the riders were swinging nearly horizontally off the ground. At least it wasn't as high as the Ferris wheel. She thought she might be able to handle this height, but still felt butterflies in her stomach and sweat on her hands.

"It has to be safe. It has to be safe. They wouldn't run it if it wasn't safe." She chanted under her breath.

Sherry looked at her with a grin. "You okay with this?"

She shook her head. Sherry held up her middle finger and Raylene did the same. "To your fear of heights!" Sherry yelled. Raylene gave a weak chuckle.

The swings returned to their low upright positions as the ride slowed. Two carny men walked around unfastening the restraints and the riders jumped from the seats and went in search of other thrills. The line began to move as the seats were reloaded with new riders.

Raylene saw a guy in a colorful tie-dye shirt moving in a very animated way near one of the game tents. Well, of course she saw animated movement. It was a carnival and that was a game of throwing baseballs at old-fashioned milk bottles. But the way this guy moved had seemed slightly familiar, like someone who might have had a little too much to drink and was raring back to hit someone. And the shirt reminded her of The Whistle Wetter Liquor Store.

Shane's store!

"Sherry, I saw Shane!"

"Oh, who cares." Her eyes seemed to scan the crowd to the side, then came back to Raylene's face. She raised her middle finger again. "Remember?"

"Yeah. Yeah, you're right. Who cares. Right." But she looked back toward the game tent. He was gone. Or maybe he was never there. She had been known to imagine him. And it seemed her kids were beginning to imagine him as well.

The women were ushered to two swings, side by side. The carny man strapped them in and walked away to the next two riders. Raylene looked up to the top of the machine to see how tall it was. Not the highest thing she had ever seen, but enough to make her heart start pumping harder. She yanked on the seatbelt just to make sure it was strong. Sherry was laughing beside her, so she forced a smile.

The seats vibrated, then the top of the machine began to spin. It was slow at first, then sped up. Raylene felt the wind in her hair. *This isn't so bad,* she thought. She used to like the swings on the school playground when she was a girl. She closed her eyes and felt the g-force begin to pull on her. Immediately her heart rate zoomed and she gulped a huge amount of air, too afraid to let it out. When she did open her mouth to exhale, it was accompanied by a scream.

They were spinning so fast their seats were horizontal. Raylene held on to the cable for her life. She opened her eyes and saw the blurred faces of other carnival goers, the blurred ground under her, the blurred clouds in the sky. She snapped her eyes closed again, but the vision she had of the cables snapping free and hurling her from the park forced her to open them again.

"Safe, safe, safe, safe," she moaned over and over. "Oh, dear Lord, help me!" Stealing a glance over at Sherry, she saw her laughing hysterically. Sherry's blond hair, tied back in a ponytail, flew straight out behind her and Raylene was reminded of a witch on a broom flying in the middle of the night.

Her stomach shifted, and she took another gulp of air. How

long would this thing go on? Surely it would wind down in a minute. Really and truly, other than being a little high off the ground, it wasn't that bad. In fact, she could almost think it was boring. Here she sat strapped in a swing, just flying around in a circle. On and on, just one circle. Seeing all the same sights, nothing different, not able to tell one thing from another at this speed. Round and round. Might as well be on a carousel.

All at once, the ride began to slow. Her swing went from being horizontal to being upright again and she could almost touch the grass under them. She looked straight ahead and Shane's face appeared in front of her. She sucked in a breath and blinked. He was gone.

"Did you see him?" she asked Sherry. Sherry's eyes were pointed to the place where Raylene thought she had seen him.

Sherry shook her head. "No." But she didn't say anything else.

They dismounted the swings and walked to the Scrambler, which was between some of the kiddie rides. A merry-go-round of old cars attached to the center machinery by an arm, two kids to a car. The machine drove the kids around in a circle while the lights around the top flashed brightly and the tinny canned music played. When she brought the kids back tomorrow, she knew Jam would beg to ride this. He would want the red fire truck so he could ring the bell.

Pearl would declare herself too big for such a baby ride, and she would beg to ride the Truck Express. This ride was little fiber-glass trucks which ran on a track. But it was different from the car ride because the trucks were only attached to the track instead of being held to the center by an arm. So the kids felt like they were actually driving the trucks.

Before they reached the gate to pay their tickets, Raylene suddenly had to find a bathroom. She hadn't felt this much urgency since before Pearl was born and had bounced around inside her like her bladder was a trampoline.

"Pee break!" she shouted at Sherry and took off toward the

Port-a-Potties, where people were lined up in front of all ten as if they were the biggest attraction in the carnival. Raylene looked at Sherry gritting her teeth and bounced in place to keep herself moving.

Sherry pointed to the cafe just across the field. "Come on. We can use the bathroom there." The girls took off running. They entered the cafe, Raylene running past the diners sitting in the booths and Sherry took a seat at the counter while Raylene ran into the bathroom and slammed the door, locking it just in the nick of time.

While Sherry sat at the counter, a man wearing a brightly-colored tie-dyed t-shirt sporting the words "Whistle Wetter Liquor Store" came in through the door and took a seat next to her.

"So, how's your little girls' night out going? When are you going to do what I told you?"

"We're getting to it. Just hold your water."

"C'mon, Sherry." His voice began to rise. "This is important. It's the only way to get that dad gum lawyer off my back." The noise in the diner suddenly silenced and the customers looked at the man at the counter with Sherry.

"Quiet down," she hissed back at him, covertly glancing at the people who tried to look away as if they hadn't just heard something incriminating. "She'll hear you. We got to take it easy. You know Raylene's scared to death of heights, and it's gonna take another beer or two to get her on the Ferris Wheel."

He grabbed her wrist. He smelled like he had drank a few more beers than she and Raylene had. "The park ain't gonna be open much longer. You ain't got all night." His grip tightened.

Sherry pried his fingers from her arm. "You know, she's seen you all over the park. That's not making things any easier."

"She don't seem to be too worried. You girls look like you're having a blast."

"Well, I have to calm her down every time she sees you. Back off and give us space, or you will have to move in with Rita."

They heard the sound of the air hand dryer in the bathroom. Shane shot Sherry a look that would have melted glass and left the cafe just as Raylene came out.

"I thought I heard Shane out here," she said as she approached Sherry.

"Raylene, Would you give it a rest?" Sherry's annoyance blurted out.

Raylene's face turned red and her eyes grew wet.

"I'm sorry. It's just... I'm just so tired of hearing his name. Let's get back in line for the Scrambler."

Raylene's face turned down toward the floor and both women walked back to the line for the ride. Sherry would never understand what she had been through with him. Sherry had no husband, no kids, no mom who griped and whined at her for not being around enough. Sherry had more money, more men, and all the confidence in the world. How could she ever know what it was like to constantly be told what a mess up she was.

"You know, Sherry, I think I'm done with this night. I'm ready to go home."

"Here, drink this." Sherry shoved a beer in Raylene's hand. "This will make you feel better.

She took the can but didn't drink right away.

"I'm sorry I go on so much about him." Raylene talked while Sherry drank her beer and didn't answer. "It's just that... the hitting wasn't the worst thing he did. He only slapped me a couple of times. Once he grabbed my wrist and twisted it so hard I thought he was going to break it. And a couple of times he acted like he might get rough with the kids, and I made him stop."

"He would never hurt his kids, Raylene," Sherry said. They watched a couple of small children run out of the line toward the carousel. One of the adults yelled at them to slow down and don't talk to strangers.

"Oh, I know he loves 'em. But when he was drinking, he could be pretty mean. And it was only twice he went after the kids. And I stopped him before he could lay a hand on them." Sherry had the beer can back to her mouth. "The worst thing he did to me, he was constantly making fun of me. He told me over and over how fat I am, what a clumsy idiot I am, and how dumb I am. After a while, a person starts to believe it."

"Look, I know Shane was mean to you when he was drinking, but maybe if you had stood up to him a few times, he would've seen you in a different way. Well, whatever. Y'all are getting divorced. You're done with him. But the thing is, you haven't let him go. You just keep being a victim instead of becoming a single woman. I understand about the insecurities you got while y'all were married, but that's over with. You should be trying to build yourself up, not staying down in a hole. And that's what tonight is supposed to help you with."

Raylene took a huge gulp of her drink, then let out a loud burp. Her head was pointed toward the ground, but she turned it sideways and cut her eyes toward her friend. Then she smiled and held up the finger again. Sherry held up her finger and their middle fingers curled around each other.

Raylene held her beer up to the sky. "Here's to a box full of screws to Shane Dickey!"

Sherry held hers up as well. "Screw you, Shane!" She yelled. Everyone in line around them applauded.

"Hey! Look over there." Sherry pointed to a small cabinet in the middle of the field. A heavy power cable led from the back of the cabinet to a metal sidewalk covering about twenty other thick power cables to keep the carnival goers from tripping over them.

"What's that?" Raylene asked.

"Let's go see."

As they got closer to the kiosk, they realized it was an arcade-type machine. Inside was a fortune-telling mannequin dressed in colorful scarves. Four quarters and Madam Zombezi would reveal the secrets of the stars for you. Sherry and Raylene looked at each other, then they giggled and each pulled change from their pockets.

Sherry counted out four quarters before Raylene did, so Sherry went first.

"Don't read it until I get mine," Raylene said. Sherry winked at her and stuck her card in her back pocket.

Raylene took a drink of her beer then handed the can to Sherry. She closed her eyes and raised her face to the dark sky. "Oh, Madam Zombezi," she began in a chanting voice. "Show me the secrets of the stars. Tell me if that no-good soon-to-be ex-husband of mine is going to finally get his in the end." She opened her eyes and fed the quarters into the machine. Sherry was snorting with laughter.

Madam Zombezi's plastic ring-covered hand pushed a small piece of paper, about the size of a business card, through a slot. It immediately fell through to the receptacle and Raylene snatched it. Sherry pulled her card from her back pocket and both women stood looking at each other with the keys to their futures held upside down in front of them. The song, "Rearview Mirror" by the band Pearl Jam cranked up about nine thousand decibels from the speakers and the girls had to shout to hear each other.

"On the count of three," Sherry said. Raylene nodded. "One, two, three."

They turned their cards over and read them.

Sherry's mouth dropped open and she pulled in a deep breath, then snorted and laughed hysterically.

"So, read out loud," Raylene said.

"Ahem," Sherry started, clearing her throat dramatically. "Madam Zombezi says, 'Choose your footsteps carefully lest you fall in a hole and you can't climb out.'"

"Wow. Words of deepest wisdom." Raylene opened her mouth in an imitation of awe.

"Okay. Your turn."

Raylene copied Sherry's dramatic throat clearing. Then she held the card up to her eyes and began reading in a deep throaty voice. "Madam Zombezi says, 'Learn the difference between your friends, your lovers, and your enemies.'" She closed her eyes and raised her head to the sky once again as if in deep meditation. A tear leaked out of Raylene's eye, and Sherry's face had turned a light shade of pink and her lips pursed together like she was holding a mouthful of beer. She would not look at Raylene's face.

"Oh. I think this thing is really alive. It really knows."

"You're drunk, Raylene. It's an electric arcade machine. That was just the next card up."

"No, no. I think Madam Zombezi really knows. I mean, Shane was my lover, but now he's my enemy, right? And I should have known it way back then. But the other thing Madam Zombezi knows is what a good person you are. And you're my friend. You feed people at the diner. You give your clothes to people who need them. You brought me out here to this fun carnival for a fantastic night of thrills to help me get over my fear of Shane and my fear of heights. You've loved me more than my own mother because you've always been here for me. Sherry Higgs, you truly are my B-F-F forever!" She threw herself against the other woman sobbing.

"People are watching, Raylene." She put her hands on Raylene's shoulders and gently pushed her away. "And I'm not that great. I just can't stand to see someone need something they can't have. You need self-confidence, and I want to help you get it."

Raylene's words slurred slightly. "But that's what's so sweet about you. Thank you, dear friend."

Sherry looked at the ground and stuck her hands in her back pockets. "You need to do some walking. C'mon," Sherry said, trying to catch her breath. "Your turn to pick. What are we riding."

Raylene looked around at the colorful lights against the dark sky. She didn't know what time it was, but then remembered it didn't matter. The kids were spending the night at her mom's house, so she didn't have to go home all night if she didn't want to. The Scrambler was one of her favorite rides. The line seemed a little long but who cared. She had all night.

"Scrambler," she said and drained the last of her drink.

"Long line, but it'll be worth it. We better get in it." They both turned and bowed to Madam Zombezi, then headed back toward the line.

They waited for what seemed like forever, but was actually only about fifteen minutes. Just as they approached the gate, Raylene heard a loud whistle and thought she saw the tie-dyed shirt again. She looked at Sherry who didn't say anything. Sherry wasn't looking at her, she was looking in the same place Raylene thought she had seen him.

"Um, hold on a minute. I need to… wait, I think I dropped some of my money over by the fortune teller. Hold my place in line." Sherry walked off leaving Raylene to hold her spot.

---

Shane stood behind the tree watching while the women laughed, cried, and hugged like a couple a gal pals. He had paid for this whole night—the child support he had paid to Raylene, and the hundred bucks he had handed Sherry to get Raylene here.

Raylene had to be the dumbest woman on the earth. What made her think he would just hand over the house, the car, the kids, AND his paycheck to that fat, lazy milk toast? Who did she think she was? The kids they had together, he had to practically force himself on her to get them—not that he wanted the kids to start with. But seeing as that's what happened after sex… And now, knowing her the way he did, he wouldn't be surprised if she had let him have it knowing that she was not protected. Entrapment. Yeah, that's what happened. It was a trap to get his money. Have them babies, claim "spousal abuse," and soak him for ever cent he ever made.

Now he hated her even more.

Well. She never knew her "B-F-F" had had such a crush on him back in high school. And now they's next-door neighbors? Both of 'em were dumb as rocks. Raylene more so 'cause she didn't have a clue he was living there, right under her nose.

Shane smiled. Yep, he was pullin' that one over her eyes, all right.

He thought about the plan he had talked Sherry into. Easy-peasy. She would get that brainless chickenhead up in the Ferris wheel seat, high up above the City of Shamrock, then he would do the rest. That's all. He had told her the only thing he wanted was to scare Raylene into calling off the excessive child support to pay for hitting her. If he had told her what he really had in mind, he knew she would never go through with it.

Genius. Sometimes he amazed himself with his own brilliance.

Sherry headed toward the fortune-telling machine they had just come from. Sure enough, Shane Dickey stood there with anger burning in his face. She set her own face to match his.

"Why you keep stalking us, Shane?" She threw as sharp of a barb as she could work up without yelling at him.

"Why you keep not doing what I told you to do, Sherry? You chickening out? You said you would do whatever you could to help me."

"I'm doing what I can, Shane," she hissed.

"Looks to me like you're just having fun at my expense. Like you got no intention of gettin' her up there."

"What do you want me to do?" She held her pointer finger up and stabbed at the air in front of his face. "You want me to take her by the hand and drag 'er? You want me to say, 'C'mon. We got to get on the Ferris Wheel so Shane can scare you to death and make you tell that lawyer to drop the punitive damages.' You think that will get her up there any faster? C'mon, Shane. You can't be that dumb of a redneck. Get back in the bushes and stay out of the way.

She's nervous enough as it is. I'm having to work through that. Just give us some space."

He grabbed her elbow which stopped her stabbing the air. His fingers dug deep in her flesh. "I'm losing my patience. Get her up there, or I'll take care of her myself. Then I'll take care of you." He squeezed her arm harder and she yelped.

She hissed dangerously, "I'm done with you. Go get your crap out of my trailer." She stomped her heel on his foot, then her knee ground into his crotch. As he crumpled to the ground, she yanked her arm back. Purple spots had already begun to appear. As Shane hit the ground she stomped off.

It had been raining that night six months ago. Sherry sat on her couch watching TV and the wind plowed into the side of her trailer house. She had been with Raylene all day. They both took off work because Raylene had kicked that sorry crap dog of a husband out that week and she was crying and eating all the ice cream in town. She helped Raylene get rid of the rest of his stuff, and she kept tissues, ice cream, and margaritas handy. And then Raylene had passed out.

So, back in her own house, sitting on the couch with the television playing and muddy rain smacking the side of the house like a power washer, there was a knock on her door.

"Oh, Raylene. Go to bed." She yelled.

The banging from outside repeated.

She pointed the remote at the TV and went to the door.

"Is that you, Raylene?"

A low voice sounded on the other side. The voice sounded familiar, but whinier than she remembered. "Shane?"

"Please, Sherry. It's raining and the wind makes the rain feel like needles. Please, Sherry, let me in."

She opened the door and saw her b-f-f's husband standing in

the horizontal rain like a whipped puppy. "Get in here. Are you crazy being out in this weather?" She grabbed his arm and pulled him up the steps into her living room.

He shivered, then sneezed.

"What are you doing out here?"

"Well, I didn't have no place to go. Raylene won't let me in the door, and I didn't have the money for a hotel. So I been sleepin' in my store."

"Oh, Shane. I don't think she meant for you to be out in the rain. Just tell her you need enough out of the bank to get a hotel room."

"No, she ain't lettin' me say a thing. Let me stay here, Sher. Just for a week. Then I'll be out. I promise."

And there it had been. That so sad, so pathetic puppy-dog face. The very face she could not say no to. The memory of fifteen-year-old Shane, staring at fifteen-year-old Raylene and licking his lips, while fifteen-year-old Sherry swallowed her gum and her heart started beating against her ribs. She had known at that moment he would never leave her soul.

Until he had grabbed her arm and promised to "take care of her" with that hateful fire in his eyes. Now it could rain needles and blow baseball sized hailstones and she wouldn't give him so much as a crumb from her table ever again.

---

Raylene was getting tired. She'd had way too many beers, and suddenly the thought of being hurled in circles around and around made her want to hurl the beers, corn dogs, and funnel cake. She thought maybe she could live a while longer without riding the Scrambler. When Sherry came back she would tell her she wasn't a teenager anymore and maybe she was done for the night.

The carny guy at the gate reached his hand out to take her tickets so she could get on the ride, but she didn't put them in his hand. She couldn't see where Sherry had gone, and Raylene wasn't going to do anything until she got back. She motioned for the people behind her to go ahead. So about twenty people did. The gate closed, the assistant walked around checking the seatbelts and safety bars, then he went back to the control board. Sherry still had not come back.

Raylene watched as the center column turned its three arms in one direction while the four cars on each arm spun independently in opposite directions, like an egg beater. The machine sped up, the riders screamed and laughed. The ride sped up even more and the screams got louder. After a couple of minutes the ride began to slow down. The screams also began ebbing.

"Hey, I'm back." Sherry said in Raylene's ear. Her face seemed flushed, and she held two more beers in her hand. Her mouth was puckered and she wouldn't look Raylene in the eyes.

"Is everything okay?"

"Oh. Yeah. Just a… a guy needed… um, there was this guy who was really… he was starving. I, um, bought him a burger and a Coke."

"Now, see, that's just what I was talking about. How much you care about people."

Sherry rolled her eyes at Raylene's comment, then she turned to look toward the direction she had come from.

A moment later, Raylene said, "Well, I've decided I don't think I can ride this tonight. Too much beer. You pick a ride."

Sherry closed her eyes. "Are you sure?"

"Yeah. I've had too much to eat and drink to go in circles that fast."

"Okay. How about the swings again?"

"No, I don't think so. You know, you've been talking to me all night about getting over my fears. I think I'm ready. The Ferris wheel."

Sherry choked on her beer. If they got on the wheel, Shane

would hurt them both. "No, I don't want to traumatize you. We'll do something else. How about a game? Skee Ball?"

Raylene looked determined. "But you've worked so hard to help me. One more time, Sherry. Cure me of my fear of heights."

Sherry closed her eyes. No way out. She had played her part too well. Okay. She had disabled Shane for a while; maybe she had hurt him enough he'd leave them alone the rest of the night. She looked Raylene in the eyes for the first time since kicking Shane. Raylene held up her middle finger with a smile that seemed lined with steel.

So Sherry held up her middle finger.

---

Nick Stanglin had been operating Ferris wheels for most of the past ten years. He had gotten so good at it he was hardly ever asked to work any of the other rides. Three times a day, every day, and sometimes one more time during the night, he would check the wires and cables, making sure everything was intact and running the way it should. He checked the grease levels on all the mechanical parts, kept his eye on the seat belts to watch for fraying, and double-checked the locking mechanisms and the safety bars for each car. And he hovered over the control board like it was his baby. He was as concerned for the safety of the patrons as the carnival owners were.

He watched the big wheel spin at a comfortable level. The ride was supposed to be relaxing; the biggest thrill was being so high off the ground, and spinning slow enough to see the ground from so far up. Most of the people riding the Ferris wheel were there to see all the lights under them, and all the stars in front of them.

He was proud of the work he did, and he was happy to make so many people happy.

---

As they walked toward the Ferris wheel, Raylene noticed that Sherry kept looking behind her. She kept rubbing her arm and she had chugged that beer pretty fast. She knew something had upset her friend.

Standing at the fence, they watched as the operator at the control board ran the wheel a little at a time. When one car reached the ground, the assistant raised the safety bar, unbuckled the belt and assisted the passenger out. This went on for a while until all the seats were empty. Then the process started over refilling the seats with new passengers.

Raylene and Sherry handed their tickets over and were led to the car. She felt the same old butterflies in her stomach and sweat spring out on the palms of her hands.

"Are you sure this is safe?" She asked the woman buckling her in.

"Oh, yeah," the woman answered. "Nick has been running this thing for a long time. He's very careful with his passengers. He checks the machinery and stuff over and over."

"So it's working okay? We're not going to be stranded in this seat?" Raylene felt Sherry roll her eyes. "I mean, well, I'm a little scared of heights and I don't want to be stuck at the top."

"Oh, no, ma'am. You'll do just fine." The woman smiled, waved at Nick standing at the control center, and backed away. "You'll be fine." Nick touched a dial on the board and their seat went backward and raised off the ground, then stopped so the next car could be filled with passengers.

Raylene took some deep breaths. She closed her eyes and gripped the safety bar for dear life. After a minute she heard Sherry muttering under her breath.

"What was I thinking… dumb redneck… and those puppy dog eyes… … don't know why I put up with… don't know who he thinks he is… what a crock…"

Without opening her eyes, Raylene asked, "Are you okay, Sherry?"

"It's nothing. I don't want to talk about it. Sorry. It'll go away. Don't worry 'bout anything. Just keep your eyes closed and this will be over soon, and you'll be cured of your fear of heights. I just wish I could solve your other phobias for you."

The seat raised up another degree and the last car was filled. Raylene couldn't help herself. Sherry sounded so cryptic and weird. Not like herself at all. Her eyes popped open and she looked at her friend. A tear was running down her face. Sherry was always so eager to help everyone. And now she was the one needing help.

"You're crying. What happened?"

"Don't worry about it, Raylene. The guy… the guy I bought a burger for, he was a little drunk and he said some things that bothered me, that's all. That's what happens when you try so hard to help people. They turn on you and treat you like crap. They grab your arm and bruise it, then threaten to… whatever. But, don't worry about it. It's not the first time it's happened, and it won't be the last. I just have to put my big girl panties on and get over it."

"He bruised your arm?"

"I'll heal. No big deal."

"Sherry, that's assault. You should have called the police."

"No. He was drunk. He didn't know what he was doing. Not like he really hurt me. I'll get over it."

Raylene didn't know what to say. This whole thing felt so unlike Sherry. She was so caring and kind-hearted, but she was also plenty able to take care of herself. In fact, Sherry would never allow anyone to manhandle her.

The wheel was moving constantly now, at a slow pace. Raylene tried not to look at the ground. She told herself she should watch straight ahead instead of looking down. But her grip on the safety bar did not loosen. As they rose above the trees, she tried to think of something that would cheer Sherry up, make her laugh, so she thought of the most ridiculous thing she could.

"Do you know what Pearl and Jam told me this morning?" Sherry loved stories about her kids when they acted cute.

Sherry didn't answer. She wiped the tear from her eye and shook her head "no."

"Well, for some reason they didn't want to go to my mom's house. I don't know why, they didn't say. But they both started crying at the same time and said they saw their daddy come out of your house early this morning. Isn't that the funniest thing you've ever heard? Bless their little hearts! I never knew they missed their dad at all. I always thought they only wanted to kill each other—and me while they were at it."

The air between the two women froze. Sherry sucked in a breath and then sobbed quietly, but Raylene heard it.

"What?" She asked. "Sherry? What?"

"Noth… nothing. Why'd they tell you that?"

"I don't know. Maybe since I imagine I see him everywhere they're starting to, too. I told them they had to be mistaken."

Sherry leaned over the rail at looked at the ground, which caused the car to rock slightly. Raylene's head spun so she quickly closed her eyes again. She thought she heard the crowd below them gasp. Her eyes opened again and as the car rocked forward, she saw the tie-dyed t-shirt guy run across the field to the control board.

She heard Sherry suck snot in her nose and sob again.

"Hey. Tell me. What can I do to help you? You should've at least put some ice on your arm."

"Raylene. Just stop. You can't do anything. I'll be fine."

"I know there's something much more than just some drunk bum here at the carnival. You help so many people. Let me help you."

"Please stop with the 'good-girl Sherry' routine. I'm not a good friend."

Raylene was stunned. What could Sherry ever have done that would make her not a good friend? She had taken off work to help her clean out Shane's crap from her trailer. She fed people; she fed dogs on the road; she was helping her get over her worst fears.

"Sher— "

"Raylene, stop. What if I told you… um, what if I told you that… well…" She seemed to be gulping air. "I'm really a terrible friend."

Raylene reached her hand out and touched Sherry's shoulder.

"They did see him leave my house this morning."

The air between them turned even colder. Raylene had no words. Suddenly the lights around them were still and they didn't hear the loud music blaring through the night.

"So, yes, I'm a terrible friend. I've been having an affair with Shane since he moved out of your house. But it's definitely over. I hate that redneck. You were right all along, Raylene. He's a big, dumb bully, and I never want to see him again."

Still, Raylene could not say a word.

"Ever'thing you ever said about him is true. I know that now. I'm on your side, Raylene. I'm on your side. I will help you get him put in jail because he is pure trash."

Finally Raylene spoke. "I don't understand."

Sherry took one more huge gulp of air. "Okay." She started. "I'll tell you everything. I don't want anymore secrets between us." She paused and faced the front, not looking at Raylene, who was not looking at her. "I been crushing on Shane Dickey since were all three in fifth grade. But he liked you more than me. And since we were B-F-Fs, I didn't want to hurt your feelings by trying to take him from you, so I stayed outta' the way."

Raylene felt tears stinging her eyes.

"Then you got pregnant with Pearl, and then y'all got married. And I thought, 'Well, that's that.' But y'all argued all the time and he hit you a few times. Next thing I know, he's outta' your house, and you got lawyers and the divorce is happenin'."

"Did y'all ever sleep together before we started gettin' divorced?" Raylene whispered.

"No. You and me always been better than sisters. I could never have done that to you."

"You know, there were several times he didn't come home all night."

"I swear, he wasn't with me until after you filed for divorce. I swear on my grandma's grave, Raylene. Not until you filed for divorce. Then, two nights after he moved out, he was at my door in tears, in the rain. He was crying his heart out, Raylene. Really, his heart was broke. And you know how I hate to see people sad and broke down. So there was that, and then the old crush feelings came back, and… well… I let him in my house."

"So he's been at your house for, what, six months? And you never even told me?"

"Well how could I? What could I do? He said he was sleepin' in the back room of his store, on the concrete floor. He said he didn't take no bedding from your house because you and the kids needed it. He said he was showering at the truck stop out on I-40. He said he missed you and the kids and he was so sorry for what had happened."

Raylene came to life. "And you believed him? After watching him drink his beer and then yell and scream at us, and even hit me? You believed him? I thought you were smarter than that!"

"I'm sorry. I'm so sorry. I know it was all an act. Now I see what a jerk he is."

"He's a very good actor, as long as he gets what he wants. If he doesn't, he's mean. I'm not sure I trust you anymore, Sherry."

"There's more. I want to open up and be perfectly, completely, totally honest. I'm tired of living two lives."

"More? You mean having an affair with my soon-to-be ex-husband, like, the next day after he moves out, is not enough?"

"There's more and I want you to know about it because… Shane's dangerous. He's scary dangerous and I want to help you."

"Shane's dangerous. Boy, that's a surprise." Raylene's voice began to rise, almost to a shriek. "You took your time to figure that out, Sherry."

"Listen to me. You've been right all night. He's been following us all over the carnival.

Again Raylene lost her ability to talk.

"He's been following us around because he had this plan. He wanted me to get you on the Ferris wheel to scare you into having your lawyer drop the petition for the punitive damage fees in the divorce. He thought if you were scared enough you would agree to anything, anything it took to get down from up here. He's mad and he may try to hurt you, hurt us both." Sherry waved her arm at the glittering stars around them.

Again, Raylene realized how high in the air they were. She looked down and their car rocked forward again. Her head spun and blackness crept into the sides of her vision. She looked straight ahead to keep from fainting. The stars sparkled and made her think of a crowd of people laughing at her for being scared so high up off the ground. Her heart tried to beat its way out of her chest. Her hands gripped the safety bar again and her head froze to the back of the seat.

"Sherry. Sherry, I want down. Make them bring me down, Sherry. I got to get down." Her voice was beginning to rise again and she knew a hysterical scream was on its way up. She couldn't get any air to her lungs.

Suddenly, there was a loud clamor on the ground. Sherry leaned over the bar and watched. Raylene closed her eyes, but the racket was so loud she couldn't control her head leaning away from the back of the seat to look below them. Even though the world under the car where she and Sherry sat was small and seemed to be spinning, she saw a man in a bright colored t-shirt fighting with the carny guy, she thought she remembered his name was Nick. He was pushing the bright t-shirt guy away from the control board, but the t-shirt guy punched Nick in the gut. As Nick fell to the ground his hand touched the board and the wheel cranked into high speed. The wind stung Raylene's eyes and black dots danced in front of her. He heart felt like a boxer punching through her ribs. She couldn't move or scream. The wheel made an entire revolution in less than thirty seconds before the t-shirt guy slammed a fist on the control board.

This time the scream did blast from Raylene's mouth and lungs as she realized the t-shirt guy was Shane. The Ferris wheel screeched to a stop as the car the women were in reached the middle of the night sky. The seat rocked back and forth, and Raylene watched as the stars, dark shapes of trees, carnival lights, and the grass traded places over and over again. She continued screaming.

Sherry put her hands on Raylene's two cheeks and turned her face toward her. "Listen. Raylene. Listen to me. You got to stop screaming. I don't know what Shane's going to do. He bruised my arm, so I told him to pack his stuff and get out of my house. I stomped on his foot and kicked him in the crotch. You got to calm down so we can stop him." They both looked back over the edge and saw flashing red and blue lights as the police drove up to the control booth where Nick ran the wheel. Then they saw Shane jump the gate and begin climbing the wheel toward them. "Are you listening to me, Raylene?"

Eyes wide as the wheel was big, Raylene nodded her head. She couldn't speak, but she nodded.

"He's climbing up here. We can't let him unbuckle us, okay. We got to fight him together. We can do it together, okay?"

Raylene nodded again, her mouth closed tightly.

"Okay. Raylene, he was so wrong about you. You are not fat, you are not dumb. You just need a boost of confidence. If ever in your life you had any self-confidence at all, pull it out now. We can fight him, Raylene. You can do it."

They watched as Shane got closer to their car.

"We'll kick him with our feet and we'll punch him with our fists, and then we'll poke him in the eyes with our fingers. You got that, Raylene? You can do it. We can do it."

"Kick. Punch. Poke. But we're so high up, Sherry. We're so high in the air! What if we fall out?"

"We won't fall out, Raylene." She grabbed Raylene's face again. "Look at me. Listen. Towanda. Remember?" She held up her middle finger. "A sack full of screws to him. And this is going to be that sack full of screws. But you got to be in it with me. That's how we'll beat him, Raylene. We'll do it together. And afterward, he won't bother you and the kids no more. You got it? You can do it, right?"

"I can do it," Raylene breathed so quietly it was nearly a whisper. She pulled in another deep breath, and fought to keep it from turning to another scream.

Then Shane grabbed her foot. "Hello, wife," he said.

Raylene screamed and shook her foot as if she had dog doodie stuck to it. She used her other foot to try to push him off, but Shane grabbed it, too. Sherry scooted her butt over closer to Raylene and began kicking at him with her feet.

"Go away, Shane!" she yelled. "Leave us alone!"

He was pulling himself up, using Raylene's feet as handles. She felt the painful pressure behind her knees as he pulled on her feet with all his weight. Sherry leaned over and slapped his ear.

"Now you don't want to do that, Sherry," he said, and she slapped him again. He pulled himself up enough to grab the seat of the car where the women sat. Hand over hand, he maneuvered himself to the side of the car with his feet dangling in the open air. His mouth was frozen in a deranged toothy grin. Hand over hand, he moved around to the back so that he was holding the back of the seat between the two girls. He raised himself up and planted his feet on the bench of the car. Then he began rocking the seat like a rocking chair. Higher to the front, higher to the back. Again and again and again. The fourth time, the seat did a complete revolution around and Raylene thought her heart would fall out and plummet to the ground. She would never forgive Shane for this. She wasn't sure she could forgive Sherry for her part in the whole drama. She would fall out and die and then what would happen to Pearl and Jam?

At this thought Raylene opened her eyes. She couldn't let that happen. Pearl and Jam were a typical brother and sister, and brothers and sisters had fights. That's just the way it was. But she loved them desperately. Little Pearl with her big brown eyes and naturally curly hair, chasing her brother and laughing hysterically. And little Jam with his sweet infectious laugh, running his cars on Pearl's arms. What mother wouldn't love two such perfect little kids. She did not intend to die. No way!

Raylene looked and her hands clamped to the safety bar, knuckles white like marble. She pried her own hands off the safety bar, took a deep breath, and reached up behind her. Shane laughed like a demented crazy man and swiped her hands away.

"No!" She screamed. Sherry caught on to Raylene's actions and her arms also went up toward him.

"Get away, Shane! Go suck a dog's nose!" She balled her fist up trying to clock him in the face, but he blocked her swinging fists.

"Raylene, you want to spin some more?" And he rocked the car until it made another circle around. Raylene grabbed the safety bar again. Sherry kept jabbing at Shane behind her, but she kept missing him.

"Pearl and Jam. Pearl and Jam," she chanted over and over to herself. The memory of her two darling kids standing at the front door with their overnight bags, both crying. They had been trying to tell her their daddy was up to no good and she had been so caught up in her own problems, she hadn't paid attention. Well, when she got down from here, she would be much better at listening to them from now on.

Strength flooded her arms and her hands flew from the safety bar. Her fists balled up and as her arms flew toward Shane, she shrieked the war cry she and Sherry had used. "Towanda!" Her fist connected with some part of Shane's face.

Sherry screamed with joy at the blow her friend had landed. She was also able to land a couple of punches and blood flew from Shane's nose onto the women's shirts.

They reached overhead together at the same time and grabbed Shane's neck, pulling his head down. They pulled with every ounce of strength they could find and flipped him over the seat and launched him into the air. They watched as he fell into the net spread out under them by the police. He was grabbed, cuffed, and shoved into the back of the patrol car. The crowd of on-lookers applauded and the music started back up again.

They looked over at the control booth and Nick was back at the board. The Ferris wheel began to spin slowly back down. When their car reached the ground level, the carny woman came and unlatched the safety bar, unbuckled the seatbelt, hugged them tightly, and ushered the two women to the nearby EMTs

Sitting on the bumper of the ambulance, Sherry put her arms around Raylene.

"You did it, Raylene. We did it together. Way to go!"

Raylene shook out of Sherry's embrace. "I can't believe you were going to go along with his plan. How can I trust you, Sherry? Your goal of the night was to get me up there so he could terrorize us. What's up with that? Did he turn you against me?"

"No. No, Raylene. It wasn't like that. You know how he can be. And I was… I was confused. I wanted to help him, and I told him I didn't want you hurt. He said didn't want to hurt you, just to scare you so you'd have your lawyer let up on the puni—"

"Yeah, I know what he's like. But, Sherry, I would never, never have let him talk me into doing anything like that to you."

Sherry was openly crying. "I know that, Raylene. I know that. I know I was an idiot. I know I'm a bad friend. Please forgive me, Raylene."

"I think two nights a month, you'll be babysitting for me so I can take a break from those adorable kids of mine. And I think you will start going to the gym with me. And one day this summer, we will take my precious Pearl and Jam to Amarillo to Wonderland. I want them to ride the Ferris wheel there 'cause I think they'll like it as much as I do."

She looked at the patrol car with Shane in the backseat and quietly sang, *"Saw things so much clearer, once you, once you..., rearview mirror!"*

# ABOUT THE AUTHORS

www.wordsmithsix.com

# NATALIE BRIGHT

AUTHOR, SPEAKER, BLOGGER

*Natalie Cline Bright is an author, blogger, speaker, and cattle ranch owner. Her stories and articles have appeared in numerous publications. She holds a BBA from WTSU, enjoys talking to all ages about writing, and is a fan of museums, friendly people, and the Texas sky. She is the author of a middle grade mystery series, a picture book series about rescue animals, and a young adult adventure series set in the Texas frontier. She blogs every Monday about story craft at WordsmithSix.com and posts articles every Friday about the genuine people, places, and fascinating history of the Texas Panhandle.*

# CAIT COLLINS
AUTHOR, BLOGGER

From early childhood, books have been a part of **Cait Collin's** life. Her parents introduced their six girls to books and reading when they were toddlers. That love increased over the years to include writing. A thirty-year veteran of the broadcast industry, Cait lists three documentaries, an award-winning thirteen-week local television series, commercial copy and news copy on her writing resume. She has also written Bible application stories, puppet plays, and two fifteen minute plays for her church youth group. "Brian the Bully won a silver medal for the performers at an annual Bible Bowl competition. In recent years, her focus has changed to fiction. Cait served on the Board of Directors for a local writers' organization as Publicity Chair, President-Elect, three terms as President, and as the Past President. She has been active in youth writing contests and annual writers' conferences. She has presented programs to youth groups and enjoys teaching young people the excitement of written communication.

# NANDY EKLE

AUTHOR, BLOGGER

*Nandy Ekle* writes short stories of horror, thriller, and suspense. She has been writing since before she was a teenager many, many years ago. Nandy is a voracious reader and has, at times, had to challenge herself not to read. Reading all genres of books and stories is where Nandy learned story-crafting skills. She tells people that Stephen King, J.K. Rowling, and Neil Gaiman taught her to write. Nandy's first anthology, **One Murderous Week,** was released in 2018 and is available in ebook or print at amazon.com, barnesandnoble.com, carpediempublishers.com, or can be ordered at any bookstore. You can also order an autographed copy by contacting Nandy Ekle on her facebook author page. Nandy also blogs every Freaky Friday on WordsmithSix.com and welcomes all comments.

# RORY C. KEEL

AUTHOR, SPEAKER, BLOGGER

***Rory C. Keel** is a multi-award winning author of Christian Fiction, Historical and Inspirational writing. His writing has been featured in* The Secret Place *devotional magazine by Judson Press and* Chicken Soup for the Soul: Inspiration for Writers. *He has served the Panhandle Professional Writers (now Texas High Plains Writers) serving as Frontiers In Writing Contest Chair - 2009, President-Elect- 2008-2009, President - 2009-2010, and on the board of Directors as Past-President -2010-2011 and Youth writing contest Judge. Speaking topics include -* Social Media for Writers, Preparing for a Writing Conference and Publishing. *He owns and manages Carpe Diem Publishers Carpediempublishers.com. You can read his blogs every week at WordsmithSix.com and on his website Roryckeel.com.*

# JOE. R. NICHOLS
AUTHOR, BLOGGER

*"Trails End in Texas."*

*Joe Nichols* *and his wife Dianne live south of Canyon Texas where they own and operate a cattle business. He is a gold card holder in the Professional Rodeo Cowboys Association.*

*As an author, "Brutus' New Job" became a feature article in the Western Horseman magazine. He has completed his first novel,*

# ROUTE 66 FUN FACTS

1. In February 1927, Cyrus Avery from Tulsa, created the US66 Highway Association and in an extensive marketing campaign the Route was tagged, "Main Street of America."

2. A goal of the newly formed US66 Highway Association was to make Route 66 the first fully paved highway in the new U.S. highway system.

3. The First Annual International-Trans-Continental Foot Race was held to promote Route 66. Beginning in Los Angeles on March 4, 1928, runners followed the 2,500 mile route to Chicago, and then continued on to New York.

4. The winner of the grueling First Annual International-Trans-Continental Foot Race was 19-year-old Andy Payne, a Cherokee from Foyil, Oklahoma. The 2,500 mile race began March 4, 1928, with Payne crossing the finish line May 26, 1928 and claiming the grand prize of $25,000.

5. By Fall of 1926, new businesses offering diners, lodging and garages could be found all along Route 66.

6. Lodging choices along Route 66 included luxury hotels with golf courses and live entertainment, to the more rustic options like

the Amarillo Cottage Camp, billed as "A modern, quiet, restful cottage camp".

7. The 1929 stock market crash and the ten year recession that followed caused auto courts and luxury hotels to suffer. Route 66 motorists preferred sleeping under the stars and cooking their own food. Communities along the route took advantage of this by advertising free campgrounds, free public showers, and open kitchens for public use.

8. Billboards began appearing on the roadsides of Route 66 by the 1930s, establishing a recognizable brand for some businesses.

9. In 1939 John Steinbeck portrayed Route 66 as an escape for desperate people, a road of tragedy and sorrow, in his book THE GRAPES OF WRATH, and coined the phrase "mother road."

10. Billboards, colorful magazine advertisements, newspaper articles, travel brochures, and picture postcards promoting businesses and landscapes urged people to vacation on America's Main Street during the 1940s. The notion of traveling on the highway Route 66 became an adventure and quest.

11. While on a road trip from St. Louis to Los Angeles, Bobby Troup and his wife, Cynthia, talked about an idea for a song. Troup wrote, GET YOUR KICKS ON ROUTE 66 while in Los Angeles. Nat King Cole recorded the song in 1946.

12. The first Phillips 66 Station in Texas opened in McClean and has been refurbished complete with vintage pumps.

13. W. S. Stuckey Sr. began selling pecan logs at a stand in Eastman, Georgia in 1936. By the 1950s, Stuckey's locations numbered in the hundreds.

14. The 1950s is regarded as the most wonderful of times and the beginning of the end with new construction of an interstate highway system.

15. "The Friendly City" stated a directory with a smiling cowboy to promote the Route 66 corridor through Amarillo, Texas, one of the many directories and guidebooks printed for traveling families in the 1950s.

16. The 1950s saw the rise of franchises taking advantage of advertising and locations along the Route: "Holiday Inn: Your Host from Coast to Coast"

17. The Mother Road did not appeal to everyone. British journalist, Arther Holliwell wrote, "For today Route 66 is America's sucker's highway – as commercialized as Broadway, as vulgar as Miami Beach, and as phony as Sunset Boulevard." London newspaper, August 1955.

18. Stirling Siliphant created a television show, ROUTE 66, which debuted in October 1960.

19. The Bureau of Public Roads filed to remove 839,000 billboards on Federal Highways, which included Route 66.

20. Collectors treasure original materials and specialty items promoting The Mother Road and the businesses that once thrived along the Route.

21. Americans have been joined by travelers from all over the world, who continue to hold an affection and fascination for Route 66.